A DARK MAFIA CHRISTMAS

A SURPRISE PREGNANCY BILLIONAIRE ROMANCE

VIVY SKYS

Copyright © 2024 by VIVY SKYS

All rights reserved.

No part of this book may be reproduced in any form or by any electronic or mechanical means, including information storage and retrieval systems, without written permission from the author, except for the use of brief quotations in a book review.

A DARK MAFIA CHRISTMAS

Mary and Emmett's Story

An Irish Mafia Christmas

1

EMMETT

"Enough."

I unwrap Bonnie's arms from around my neck, dodging her glossy pout at the same time. I grip her wrists tightly in front of her. It's meant to sober her up a little, but instead, it seems to have the opposite effect, and a smile that's trying too hard to be sexy curves her lips upwards.

"Want to play rough, Emmett, huh?" She tries to bat my nose with her fingertip and realizes a beat too late, that her arms are being restrained. The pout is back.

"I want you to come with me and get some water." I lead her towards the bar like a disobedient puppy.

She rises to the role, dragging her six-inch heels and twisting her ankle, catapulting herself into my arms. I can smell the alcohol on her breath, see the runny mascara under her eyes, and the lipstick that almost managed to stick inside the outline of her lips.

"Why don't we go—" she hiccups on cue "—somewhere quiet?"

I stand back, keeping her at arm's length, and order a large glass of water from the bartender. "This is my party," I remind her. "The boss can't be the first to leave."

Bonnie peers all around, swaying on those fuck-me heels, the room full of people slowly coming into focus. "No one will even notice you've gone," she whines like a child who has just been told it's too late to go to the park.

Thanks for that.

The bartender slides the glass of water towards me, and I prop her upright with one arm while I raise the drink to her lips. "Drink this, wouldja. Slowly now!" I have visions of the cocktails she has been downing all evening ending up on my shoes.

Her large brown eyes hold mine while she slurps water and swallows. Her expression crumples into a grimace of disgust. "What are you trying to do to me?"

"Sober you up before you do something you regret."

The comment is missed as the sloppy smile reappears and she cocks a finger at me, clutching the bar for support. "Don't answer that. Yet. Save it for when we're alone."

I glance around for my driver, Dave, who is standing strategically by the door in his customary black suit. I don't even have to signal—the domino effect happens all on its own.

"I've been waiting for you to call me, Em." Bonnie is still talking, her voice rising a notch. I hate being called Em. "You said you would call me…"

A security guard appears from nowhere. He grips Bonnie's

arm, and she glares at him, trying to wriggle free. "Come on, ma'am. A car is waiting outside to take you home."

"Home?"

She looks at him as though he just suggested she strip naked and perform a pole dance on the bar. Although Bonnie would probably enjoy that.

"Emmett? Em? Tell him…"

"Go home, Bonnie." I turn back to the bartender who slides a champagne flute my way.

The guard leads her towards the exit, but she somehow manages to wrench her arm free and stumbles back towards me. "Tell him that we hooked up, Emmett. Tell him." Her eyes grow large with tears.

The thing is, sober-Bonnie is one of the sexiest women in the building. Blond, curves in all the right places, clothes that leave little to the imagination, and a J-Lo butt to complete the picture, but drunk-Bonnie…

I don't need this tonight.

"Yeah, that's right. *We. Hooked. Up.*" She drawls the words to anyone who will listen as the guard herds her towards the exit and the elevator down to the lobby.

I keep my eyes on the champagne glass and sip ice-cold soda. The office is closed for the holidays, and I'm flying home to Ireland tomorrow. I haven't seen my mom in a year. I need to be clear-headed to avoid the when-are-you-going-to-meet-a-nice-girl-and-settle-down discussions that will inevitably dominate the entire visit.

And there's still the little matter of one final job that needs to be settled tonight.

"Emmett O'Hara, you don't get rid of me this easily!" Bonnie shrieks from outside the room.

I don't look around. I know that everyone will be staring at my back, storing up the drama to be recounted via text messages and WhatsApp chats tomorrow when they've shrugged off their Christmas party hangovers. But what's new? Bonnie wasn't the first, and she certainly won't be the last.

I turn around and catch several pairs of eyes widening before the owners pretend to be deep in conversation.

We hold the Christmas party on the top floor of O'Hara Developers every year. It's a huge open-plan space. With the bar taking up the length of one wall, tables laden with canapés on the opposite side of the room, and a DJ set up in one corner, lights flashing along in time with the bass beat, there's ample space to accommodate the staff. No partners invited. We do this as a company, or we don't do it at all.

I'll be forced to sit through a bunch of cheesy Christmas movies by my mom, cousins, and aunties when I get home, without having to watch my employees getting all fake-merry because, hey, it's the most wonderful time of the year, dontcha know?

Don't get me wrong. I'm no Grinch. I just don't understand why people can't be jolly all year round instead of saving it for when the advertising companies say they should be happy spending all their hard-earned money on shit no one wants.

Who am I kidding?

I organize a Christmas party because it's what's expected of me, and not because I want to get steaming drunk and sing along badly to Mariah Carey's 'All I Want for Christmas Is You', with someone's sweaty arm hanging off my shoulders.

Besides, Sonia, my PA, would never forgive me if she didn't get the chance to wear a sparkly dress and reindeer antlers, and dispel the boss's snooty gatekeeper image at least once a year.

On cue, I catch her eye as she makes her way over to the DJ with a cheesy request, and I raise my soda to toast her. She blows me a kiss from across the room. I don't even pretend to catch it.

Then I spot *her*. Or rather, I spot the hair. It's red—not Karen Gillan red with orange tones—but dark, glossy, cherry red. Not from a bottle either. I don't know how I know this, but no one who isn't born with it can achieve that kind of red without spending a shit load of money at the salon. And if I'm correct, this woman, I don't know her name, works in the IT department, she isn't fucking Rockefeller.

Her hair is scraped back into a ponytail, but stray curls have worked loose, framing her face like she planned it that way. I scrutinize her closely—she's a beautiful woman, and I'm a red-blooded male—and I might be wrong, but she's so fresh-faced, she can't be wearing any makeup. Now that I think of it, she's wearing plain black pants and a white shirt, the kind of clothes she would wear to the office, and not the Christmas party.

Didn't she get the memo?

I look around, comparing her to the other women on the dance floor—it's a tough habit to crack—their makeup starting to sheen with the body heat and the lights and the exertion of jumping around to 'Jingle Bell Rock'. Everyone else is trying to rock smoky eyes and ruby-red lips. While she hasn't even borrowed a pot of lip gloss from one of her co-workers.

Another Grinch?

No one forced her to come.

The glass in her hand is empty. I watch her push herself off the wall and wander around the edge of the room. A colleague catches her eye, gestures for her to join the group on the dance floor. But she shakes her head, a half-smile, averts her eyes, and keeps moving.

She's people-watching. She's standing back and watching everyone else getting louder and drunker and sillier, like she's taking notes to report back to the boss in the New Year. The boss. AKA me.

I'm still staring when she looks up. Our eyes meet. I wait for her to turn away, her cheeks growing hot with embarrassment when she realizes that I've caught her out, but instead, she continues drifting around the room as if that never even happened.

"Are you having fun?" Sonia has snuck up on me.

Her cheeks are rosy, and I can smell her perfume wafting from her in waves as she keeps dancing on the spot. She snatches my glass and takes a sip, her eyes narrowing when she doesn't get the taste she expected.

"What are you drinking?"

I'm still following red hair with my eyes. "I'm flying to Ireland in the morning."

"Emmett." She hands the glass back, forcing me to look at her. "It's Christmas."

"So I hear."

"So, live a little. Let your hair down." Her eyes roam to my head and she twists her mouth to one side. "Or whatever the O'Hara version of letting your hair down is."

Her face grows even rosier. No one in New York knows me better than Sonia, even if she doesn't approve of my bachelor lifestyle, and even she doesn't know everything.

"I'll consider myself told."

Angela from finance comes over then, grabs Sonia's hand, and drags her away. "There you are. You're supposed to be dancing."

Sonia smiles at me from over her shoulder before being pulled into a circle made up of most of the finance department and a woman from HR and starts singing along to 'Last Christmas' at the top of her lungs.

Before I can resume my study of red-haired girl, a raised voice catches my attention. This is the trouble with Christmas parties: people get too inebriated too quickly because they're like excited kids waiting to open their presents, and they forget that they're surrounded by work colleagues whom they'll have to face when the office reopens in the New Year.

"Don't lie to me!"

I recognize the voice. It belongs to Hazel, my marketing director, a petite, dark-haired woman with sleek bangs and a penchant for practical flat shoes. She's talking to her fiancé, Max, who works in accounting.

"What?" Max shakes his head and takes a step closer. "What did I do?"

"Stay away from me!" Hazel's face is growing pinker by the second. "I can't believe you would do this to me. It's Christmas…" The tears spill at the mention of the most wonderful time of the year, like she could forgive him if it was January already.

Max, a tall lanky guy who's all knees and elbows, peers all around like someone might rescue him before it's too late. "I don't even know what I've done."

"You fucking kissed her, you asshole!"

Hazel struggles to tug her engagement ring off her sweaty finger, and when it finally comes free, she tosses it at her fiancé and storms off. A group of women follow her, calling out for her to come back and talk about it.

Max watches, frozen, for a few beats. Then he too turns around and walks off in the opposite direction. He doesn't even stop to pick up the ring.

Everyone else seems to gravitate into their own little groups, voicing their opinions on what just happened. No one seems to care that Hazel has thrown away a ring that will break her heart tomorrow when she realizes that it's gone.

But I saw it land. Well, I saw it hit the floor and roll away, surprisingly close to the toes of my shiny black shoes. I bend down and retrieve it from underneath a bar stool and slide it into my pocket. I'll email Sonia later and let her know that I've got it—she'll know what to do.

Drama over, I scan the room for red-haired girl, my stomach twisting with disappointment when I realize that she must've left while I was distracted.

I down my soda in one, and order another.

2

MARY

There's a spill-out bar and seating area on the roof of the building for anyone who wants some fresh air. Well, as fresh as it gets in New York City. The space is strung with fairy lights, and there are warm blankets heaped up in baskets for anyone who wants to stay up here a while and get cozy on the plump sofas.

It's how these people live. They take all this stuff for granted. *Champagne? No problem, here's a bottle of Moet, vintage don't you know.*

I find a quiet corner and peer over the railings around the edge of the wall at the city skyline. The Empire State Building. Rockefeller Plaza where the people who are ice skating look like ants from up here. The Chrysler building.

I smile to myself. I took my surname from the Chrysler building when I first arrived in New York. Before that, I was plain old Mary Scanlan. Mary Chrysler sounded way more exciting, and it meant that no one would be able to find me, not that anyone was looking.

From the party downstairs, I can hear Bruce Springsteen belting out 'Santa Claus is Coming to Town'. It's one of my favorites. Who doesn't love a Christmas tune, especially the old bangers; they just don't make them like that anymore.

I haven't really thought much about Christmas. I mean, you can't avoid it with the tree in the Plaza, and the stores all wrapped up in tinsel and fairy lights and giant red ribbons, but I mean, I haven't thought about *my* Christmas. I'll spend it alone in my crappy little apartment, watching cheesy movies —God I hope there's a new Lindsay Lohan Christmas movie this year—drinking cheap wine, and snacking on even cheesier crisps.

Potato chips. Eight years in the States, and I still can't get used to calling them potato chips.

Favorite Christmas movie? *Home Alone. Miracle on 34th Street. The Santa Clause.* There are too many to choose just one, but I always start the holidays binge-watching every Christmas movie featuring Melissa Joan Hart. I mean, *Holiday in Handcuffs* is an absolute classic, and I defy anyone to tell me otherwise.

I have a stack of romance novels to read, too. Merry Christmas to me.

Someone yells. A guy. My hackles are up—this isn't the kind of yell that belongs at a Christmas party.

I glance sideways along the roof as a beefy man in a black suit rugby-tackles another guy, thick arms wrapping around his legs, and hurls him over the edge.

What the actual fuck?

That didn't just happen. I blink. My blood is pumping around my veins and making me hot despite the sub-zero temperatures and the frost clinging to the walls.

What the actual fuck?

Someone just went over the side of the roof, and no one has moved, no one has screamed, no one has called the fucking police, which is what should be happening right about now.

Move, Mary. Fucking move, would you?

But my body isn't cooperating with my brain, which is screaming at me to take a breath, look over the side, yell at someone to stop the crazy fucking psycho who just killed a man.

I open my mouth to let out the scream that's building up inside me, when a hand clamps over my face, and I'm dragged backwards behind a potted palm tree all lit up for Christmas in its twinkling fairy lights.

"*Help!*" That's what I try to scream. I don't want to die on Christmas, and I sure as shit don't want to die by being thrown off a roof. But my lips stick to the hand covering my mouth, scraping away from my gums, the cry for help swallowed by someone else's sweaty palm.

"Shut up," my captor hisses in my ear. "Keep still."

But I'm not sticking around to prove to a thug wearing a black suit that I can't fly. I swallow. Stretch my lips into what is probably not my most attractive smile and bite his hand.

He yelps.

Now's my chance to escape and alert every fucker in the building that there's a bunch of psychos loose on the roof.

I try to scream a second time, but he's in front of me and his mouth is smothering mine. I squirm as his tongue fills my mouth. My upper arms are being squeezed in a vice-like grip, and the back of my skull bounces off the wall as I try to get away from him.

His tongue stops wriggling around inside my mouth like a fat slug long enough for him to whisper, "Kiss me."

"Like fucking fuck." It comes out as "Ngg, nung, ngg," because it's impossible to talk when someone's tongue is attacking yours.

I finally remember to open my eyes and see what I'm dealing with, and recognize the gelled back coppery hair, the cool blue eyes, and ultra-expensive cologne of the boss of O'Hara Developers. Emmett O'Hara. The man himself.

I feel myself going slack. It's instinct kicking in. Avoid the boss at all costs because no one ever fired a nobody.

I've never been this close to him before. I mean, it would be pretty unbelievable to kiss the boss at a crime scene on the roof of the building he owns. Twice. I've seen him in the lobby, and the elevator, and from a distance climbing out of his chauffeur-driven Bentley, but I make a habit of walking in the opposite direction and keeping my head down. It suits me just fine being known as the girl from IT.

"Everything okay here, Mr. O'Hara?"

Fuck! It's the beef cake in the black suit. All the fight drains out of me and melts into a puddle on the floor. He's going to throw us both off the roof. I'm going to die in the arms of one of New York's most eligible bachelors, and everyone will say, "*Mary who?*"

Emmett O'Hara's eyes widen. A warning. He wants me to remain silent, and much as I hate being told what to do by someone who stuck his tongue down my throat without my permission, I recognize a lifeline when I see one. They seem to know each other. Maybe I only thought I saw him toss a guy off the roof like he was an empty panini wrapper.

"Everything was fine 'till you interrupted." Emmett pulls his lips away from mine, leaning over me protectively with one hand against the wall for support. He hangs his head, glances at me from beneath lowered brows like he's building up to a rant.

I don't move. I still have no idea what's going on here.

The thug's been confused into silence too.

"You spoilt the moment." Emmett only half straightens, swaying precariously towards me like he's had a few too many glasses of Moet. He produces something gold and shiny from his pocket and holds it up to catch the light from the tiny twinkling bulbs decorating the potted palm tree. "You see this?"

I don't think he requires a response, but the wide-necked thug nods anyway.

"I was about to pop the question. She won't accept now, ye fecker, will she?"

He gestures towards me with his head. He doesn't even make eye contact, and I stop myself from blurting out that the least he could've done was propose when he was sober. But he just cussed at psycho dude, and Emmett O'Hara's balls have probably just sealed our fate. Why couldn't he have hidden me inside the plant pot or, I don't know, told me to lie down and thrown a blanket over me or something?

The suit eyes me up, and I can see it in his eyes. He's thinking: *seriously? This is who you're proposing to?*

Yeah, I don't believe it either. In any other circumstances, I'd have yelled at him to keep his sexist fucking eyerolls to himself. But if it means I get to walk out of this building with my limbs still attached to my body, I can rein my temper in. Temporarily anyway.

"Apologies, Mr. O'Hara." He's apologizing for ruining our special moment when he just killed a man. Could this evening get any more bizarre if it tried? "I'll leave you to it."

"Aye, you do that." Emmett takes the words right out of my mouth.

And the guy walks away.

Just like that.

He walks back to the edge of the roof, lights a cigarette, and peers out over the city like he's just enjoying some quiet time alone with his murderous fucking thoughts.

I'm so busy watching the smoke from the guy's cigarette curling up and away and merging with the snowy clouds overhead, that I don't even realize that Emmett has gone down on one knee, until he says, "Will you marry me?"

He's holding the ring with both hands like he's scared he'll drop it and ruin our special moment a second time, peering up at me with those cool blue eyes. Jesus, I never noticed those eyes before.

But I need to get a grip. This isn't real. A man just got killed, and there are sirens wailing through the city, spoiling the Christmas tunes going on downstairs, and this isn't real.

I try to back away, but he has me cornered between the palm tree and the wall. "Game over. You can put the ring away."

His eyes flicker sideways, and I can tell that he's stone cold sober when he turns them back to me. "Be nice. They're still watching." He keeps his voice low.

"And you just happen to carry an engagement ring around in your pocket for special occasions?" I'm done reining it in already.

"Do you want to see Christmas or not?" Wow, he can flash those blue babies when he wants to.

"I... But I..."

I thought it was over. I thought when the suit walked away that I could go back inside, grab my coat from the office, and head home to *Christmas with the Kranks* and a glass of wine. In my head I was already in my pajamas eating a slice of leftover pizza and pretending this was all just a wild hallucination.

"What's your name?" he hisses.

"Mary. Mary Chrysler."

He blinks several times like he thinks I'm messing around. "Mary, will you marry me?" He shoves the engagement ring closer, daring me to reject him.

The diamond catches the glow of the fairy lights, and I find myself reaching out for it, like I'm having an out-of-body experience. This whole scenario is so surreal, it can't be happening to me.

Emmett takes over, compensating for my lack of enthusiasm. He's on his feet. His lips are on mine, and I'm staring into his eyes, while he slides the ring onto my finger. Keeping his back to the suit, he murmurs, "You're going to walk back downstairs to the party with me and you're going to make this look real. Got it?"

I nod.

"Oh my God, I can't believe we're getting married!" I squeal like I'm a sixteen-year-old who just got asked on a date by her first crush. I hold the ring in front of my face, turning it this way and that, forcing myself to smile. "I love you, Emmett O'Hara."

Getting into character, I throw my arms around his neck, wrap my legs around his waist, and kiss him hard on the lips. No tongue. I mean, I don't even know the guy.

"Nice," he says. "Bit OTT, but it'll do."

3

EMMETT

Of all the people in the entire fucking building, it had to be red-haired girl who was in the wrong place at the wrong time. I should've known when I first set eyes on her that she was trouble. I should've walked away, gone home, and forgotten that she even existed.

Testosterone. It has a lot to answer for.

Now that I'm invested, I can't walk away and leave her to dig herself a hole she won't be able to climb out of. They know what she saw. Without me, they'd have shut her up using their own methods, and I can't have that on my conscience.

The best thing I can do for her is to take her home, transfer enough money into her bank account for her to start over somewhere new, and wish her a merry Christmas. Job done.

I set her down on the ground gently, the smell of her perfume clinging to my skin. I don't recognize it. Probably some cheap brand I've never even heard of.

"Right, here's what's going to happen. You're going to keep that smile on your face and walk back inside with me. We're going straight to the elevator, and then I'm going to take you home, and we'll say no more about it, okay? I'll personally see to it that you're compensated for your inconvenience."

"My inconvenience?" Her eyebrows disappear behind the red curls. "A man was fucking killed tonight, and you call it an inconvenience?"

I grip her arm and pull her towards me, trying to ignore her erect nipples pressed up against my chest. I don't understand why she's trying to make this way more difficult than it needs to be. I'm done here. Time for me to go home and prepare for my family Christmas. If only Mary Chrysler had worn her dancing shoes and gotten drunk along with every other fecker at the party.

"Walk. Smile. Act like you're a woman in love." She doesn't move. "Look, I don't want to see your face plastered all over the news tomorrow for all the wrong reasons, okay? I'm trying to help you here, so stop treating me like I'm the bad guy."

My words must get through to her because she wrenches her arm free from my grip. "Fine."

"Fine." I smile at her, the smile I normally save for the tabloids when I'm out on a date. She smiles back at me, and her green eyes light up like someone just switched on flood lights above our heads. I swallow.

She takes over. "Come on, Emmett. I want to show everyone my ring."

She takes my hand and leads me back inside, and I wish that it had been anyone else but Mary Chrysler I was dealing with right now. Before I can get her into an elevator, she drags me in the direction of the party, the floor thumping with the footsteps of people dancing along to 'Step into Christmas'.

"Mary, we're leaving." I stand my ground.

"Oh no." She shakes her head. "You don't get to propose to me, Emmett O'Hara, and then whisk me away without celebrating the good news."

"Mary!" I grip her hand tightly as she reaches the open doorway.

"Smile, Emmett. They're still watching, remember?"

She disappears through the doorway, and I have no choice but to follow her. Damage limitation. The fewer people who know about the fake proposal the better—less questions to deal with in the New Year when I announce that I'm single again.

I catch Dave's eye on my way in and give a brief shake of my head. No one else notices. Mary is heading towards the dance floor, and my stomach sinks when I realize that she is going to dance.

I dash after her, wrap my arms around her from behind, and gesture to the DJ to slow it down a bit. A ripple of disappointment follows when Joni Mitchell's voice fills the room. *"It's coming on Christmas, they're cutting down trees..."* I turn Mary around, slide one arm around her waist, and start moving slowly.

I don't dance. Much to my mom's chagrin, I've never had the natural rhythm of the Irish, and this is all Mary's going to get. One slow dance, and then we're leaving.

"Don't you think it will look odd if we leave without telling anyone that we're going to be married?" Mary's hushed voice penetrates my thoughts, jerks me away from the sensation of her body so close to mine.

"I'm a very private person."

"Emmett!" Sonia is on the dance floor too in the arms of the Head of HR. "I thought you'd gone home without saying goodbye." Her gaze slides across to Mary, faint lines appearing between her eyebrows and quickly disappearing, and I pray that Mary will keep her mouth shut.

"We're getting married." Mary flashes the ring in front of Sonia's face.

I obviously didn't pray hard enough.

"Married?" Sonia stops dancing and collides with her partner's chest. She extricates herself from his arms distractedly, her eyes fixated on the ring. "Who to?"

Mary laughs, the kind of laugh that could be infectious when you're not trying to stay alive. "Emmett. He proposed to me on the roof. Isn't it exciting?"

Sonia licks her lips, trying to process the news, probably wishing she hadn't drunk the last cocktail someone offered her. Finally, she gathers her senses enough to say, "Yes. Oh, my goodness. That is exciting. Emmett, you kept this quiet."

"Spur of the moment." I shrug. "When you know, you know."

"Come here." She pulls me into a hug, rubbing my back like she's trying to keep me warm. Then it's Mary's turn. "I don't even know your name."

"Mary."

"Mary." Sonia holds her hand and studies the diamond. The crease lines between her eyebrows are back. She's no doubt already on Mary's side, thinking what a cheapskate her boss has turned out to be. "Congratulations."

"Thank you. I literally had no idea that tonight would be the night." Mary is enjoying her role a little too much for my liking.

"I think champagne is in order." I pull her away from Sonia and I don't let her go until we reach the bar. "What are you doing?"

"I'm keeping up the pretense like you told me to. What are you doing?"

More hair has escaped from her ponytail, and I get a glimpse of how she would look in bed with her hair all messed up. My cock immediately twitches at the mental image, and I take a deep breath.

"Look, I just want to get you home safely, then we say goodbye, go our separate ways, and enjoy the holidays knowing that we're still in one piece. I don't want anyone else involved."

The smile fades and her eyes grow large with tears. "Are you... Are you calling the wedding off, Emmett? We only just got engaged."

The girl can act, I'll give her that. Maybe she missed her calling, working in IT or whichever department it is that she sits in.

"We're leaving."

"I'm not ready to leave. I don't know about you, but I've never been engaged before, and I want to enjoy it while I can."

I inhale deeply, puffing up my cheeks and holding the air in my lungs.

But before I can think of a comeback, we're surrounded by women all cooing over Mary's ring as if they've never seen a diamond before.

I smile in the background, order champagne all round, and break my promise to myself by downing my first glass in one go. When the women finally move on to spread the word around the room like a wildfire, I slide a glass in Mary's direction.

Her face is flushed, lips moist and parted. She clinks her glass against mine and sips the champagne tentatively. "It's going to be a big wedding. I think I accidentally invited everyone here."

I lean closer and graze her lips with mine. "There isn't going to be a fecking wedding, so don't go getting any ideas."

"Am I or am I not wearing your ring?" She waves her hand in front of my face and swallows another mouthful of wine. It's thirsty work scamming the boss.

And just when I think the evening could not slide any further downhill, Hazel appears in the doorway wailing like a banshee, Max close behind.

"Fuck!"

Mary follows my gaze. "Someone else you had to let down gently, huh?"

I don't give her the satisfaction of a response. There's no way Hazel is getting sucked into Mary's little game, not while she's wearing the woman's engagement ring. "Drink up." I tilt the glass towards her mouth, and for once, she complies.

Dave is waiting for us at the elevator. He doesn't say a word on the ride down to the lobby, doesn't even acknowledge the ring on Mary's finger or the way she keeps staring at it. This is what I pay him for: his discretion.

We're greeted by flashing blue lights and a crowd outside the building, which is fortunately locked up for the night. Dave escorts us out via the back exit and into the underground parking lot. Mary doesn't even notice the car with the blacked-out windows idling near the barriers or Declan, the guy from the roof, flicking a cigarette across the ground.

The police presence has kept Mary quiet where I failed. She sits beside me on the back seat, forehead pressed up against the glass, as we emerge into the night, following the revolving blue lights with her eyes until they're out of sight. The adrenaline rush is fading fast.

"Wait." She slides to the edge of the seat. "Where are we going?"

"Home."

"We're going the wrong way. Tell the driver to turn the car around."

"Change of plan, Mary. You're coming home with me."

"Like fuck am I." She unfastens her seatbelt and bangs on the window separating us from Dave. "Stop the car! I want to get out."

"Mary, look out the back window and tell me what you see."

She turns around and does as she's told, her eyes narrowing when she spots the black car following us. "Are-are we being followed?"

"They'll leave us alone when they realize that you're coming home with me."

"You've got to be kidding me, right? I mean, can't they just get me to sign a document swearing me to secrecy?"

"It isn't how they work."

She slumps back on the seat and fastens her seatbelt. "How would you know?"

"Long story."

The glow of the street lamps lights up her face intermittently as we drive, and I can't help noticing the curve of her lips, the shadow of her thick reddish-black eyelashes, the high cheekbones. "I'm not staying the night." She turns to glare at me, a flush spreading across her face when she realizes that I've been staring at her.

I don't answer.

"Here." She slides the ring from her finger and hands it back to me. "Might as well take your ring back."

"Not my ring."

"I-what? Whose ring is it?"

"I found it."

Her mouth opens into a round 'O'. "You gave me someone else's ring?"

I can't help but chuckle. "You witnessed a murder, and you're worried about wearing another woman's ring?"

"Ugh! It's just ... wrong. This diamond was given to a woman by the person in love with her. It's a symbol of ... love. It's... It's someone else's love story, and now I feel like shit for encroaching on it."

"It wasn't your fault. I gave it to you. You can blame me for encroaching on someone else's love story."

She closes her eyes briefly and leans her head back against the seat. "How can you be so blasé about all this?"

"All this?"

She rolls her head across the seat to look at me. "A guy got thrown off a roof. The roof of your building." Pause. "Shit! Won't the police need to question everyone who was there? Won't you need an alibi or something?" Tears well in her eyes. "That man won't be going home for Christmas. Don't you even feel bad for his family?"

"Sure, I do." Jesus, say it like you mean it, asshole. "But the truth is..."

Mary's eyes are closed, lips parted into a perfect Cupid's bow, her breathing shallow.

4

MARY

Something is humming in my ears. I'm half-awake, that strange place between two worlds where I can either drift gently back into whatever comforting dream I was having, or snatch hold of my thoughts and allow them to drag me back to reality. My eyelids are heavy, so heavy, but I've already gone too far.

Goddammit!

I roll over, keep my eyes firmly closed, try to concentrate on the colors dancing around behind my eyelids. Relax. Let my thoughts slip away...

Do these relaxation techniques actually work on anyone?

The humming is back. I slide my hand out from under the comforter and reach for my phone on the nightstand, but it isn't there. I can't hear my alarm. Is it even a workday?

Voices.

My eyes fly open, and I try to sit up, but the world slips away from me, and I bury my head in the pillow, waiting for the room to settle.

"I'll leave you to it." I don't recognize the man's voice. Has someone broken into my apartment?

Deep breath. Try to still my frantic heart. But everything feels off-kilter; this doesn't even smell like my pillow. Then an image pops into my head: a man being thrown off the roof.

Panic builds up inside me like a tidal wave, and I force myself into a sitting position, wincing as my head spins. Jesus, how much did I drink last night? I never drink at office parties. Did someone try to get me drunk... Did someone *spike* my drink?

Emmett fucking O'Hara!

"Here, drink this, it'll make you feel better."

My fingers are pried open, and a glass is placed into my hand. I open my eyes to find Emmett fucking O'Hara looking at me with concern in those clear blue eyes. I take a sip, track the ice-cold water through my body, and then guzzle the rest of it, shuddering as it goes down.

"Did you spike my drink?" My words are slurred like I'm a raging alcoholic with a permanent hangover.

"I wouldn't say spiked exactly." There's a faint hint of amusement in his tone.

"What would you say then?" The water is threatening to come back out, and I can't be sick in Emmett O'Hara's house, not if I want a job to come back to in the New Year. He's sitting too close to me, and I can't think clearly. "Did we...?"

He shakes his head, the kind of smile on his face that would launch a thousand ships, or something like that. "No, we didn't have sex if that's what you're asking."

Thank the fucking lordy lord.

I can go back to work and not worry about him picturing me naked.

Something happens then, and my stomach lurches like I'm on an airplane. And all at once, I take in my surroundings: Emmett is seated on a couch that isn't a couch because it's attached to my bed, which isn't a bed because there are other seats just like it. And there are round windows, and I can see the sky outside, and the humming isn't coming from a refrigerator or a heating system.

It's coming from the engines of a fucking aircraft!

I swing my legs over the side of the bed and try to stand as the aircraft dips to one side, throwing me into the arms of Emmett O'Hara. The man who proposed to me with someone else's diamond ring, drugged me, and then kidnapped me on his private bloody jet.

"Get off me." I bat his hands away and leap back onto my feet.

"*You* fell on *me*." His voice is so calm it winds me up to cranky time.

I look around the plane for something to stab him with. All I can find is a bottle of water, so I pick that up and start hitting him with it, taking some small pleasure from the way he crosses his arms in front of his face like he's trying to fend off a vampire.

"Stop. This. Plane. Right. Fucking. Now," I grind out between slaps that are nowhere near as hard or as painful as I'd like them to be.

"We're already in descent preparing to land." Emmett snatches the bottle from me mid-swipe and hides it under his seat. "You need to sit down and fasten your seatbelt."

But I'm way past doing what this man tells me. Right now, he has shrugged off the role of boss and stepped straight into the mantle of crazy-abductor-with-a-private-jet-in-which-to-hide-his-victims. I spot his briefcase and pick it up, swinging it directly towards his smug good-looking face.

"No, Mary. Not the briefcase!" He jumps up and wrestles it away from me, and I can't believe how weak I am after whatever it was that he drugged me with. "Sit. Fucking. Down."

"Help!" I yell, my eyes darting around the cabin trying to find a way out. "Help me! I'm being kidnapped!"

He takes a deep breath, stows the briefcase in a cabinet above his head and faces me with his arms crossed over his chest.

"You're not being kidnapped, Mary. We're engaged to be married, remember? Do you think anyone is going to believe that the Managing Director of O'Hara Developers kidnapped his own fiancée?"

The Managing Director of O'Hara Developers.

Even the way he says it makes my blood boil. But it slowly dawns on me that I played right into his hands when I impressed everyone at the office party with his marriage proposal. He's right. No one is going to believe that Emmett O'Hara, player extraordinaire, would need to kidnap the woman from IT. If he wants a woman, all he has to do is snap his fingers and there'll be a whole bunch of beautiful women waiting in line to be chosen.

"Where are you taking me?"

I sound exactly how I feel. Defeated. How does anyone stand a chance against someone who can buy his way out of any situation?

"Home."

"Home?" My head is clearing way too slowly. It's like trying to piece together a jigsaw puzzle blindfolded.

"Sit down, Mary. Please?" He gestures to the seat where I've been sleeping for God knows how long.

I do as I'm told. Even I can tell that the plane is making its descent, and there's no point trying to get away from him while we're in the air. My only hope is to make him believe that I'm going along with his plan—whatever it is—and then try to get away from him in the airport.

"Thank you." He sits in the seat next to me.

He's wearing a sky-blue sweater that clings to his chest and makes his eyes appear even brighter, and it would be so much easier to hate him if he wasn't so goddamned hot.

"Where's home?" I don't dare peer out the window because if I don't look, I can pretend to myself for a little longer that we're still on the same continent.

"Ireland. County Wicklow to be precise."

Tears well in my eyes as I try to work out how much it's going to cost me to get back to the States from Ireland without a private jet at my disposal.

"Look, I'm sorry I drugged you, okay? But, well, you weren't exactly keeping quiet, and these things have a habit of going viral online, and I didn't want my family to find out about it before I had a chance to tell them."

"Don't they have cellphones in Ireland?" I sniff loudly, blinking back tears.

"It wasn't that simple."

"Of course it wasn't," I mutter under my breath.

It never is. I mean, you only have to watch a Hallmark Christmas movie to recognize that the path of boy meets girl and lives happily ever after never runs smoothly. But if he thinks I'm accepting that as a valid reason for abducting me, he really doesn't know me at all.

"The guy on the roof," he continues, "he knows my family."

Oh, well that's just what I wanted to hear. If he doesn't kill me for witnessing him at his psychotic best, the O'Hara family will.

"Haven't you guys heard of Christmas spirit? You know, the season of goodwill and all that? I promise, all you need to do is sit me in front of the TV with Macauley Culkin and a twinkling tree, and I won't breathe a word to anyone."

A smile tugs his mouth up at the corners, and my stupid, cheesy-movie-fueled heart does the stupid fluttery thing that is the staple of every rom com ever made in the history of time.

"No one is going to hurt you, Mary. You have my word on that."

"Well, forgive me if your word doesn't exactly inspire me with confidence, Mr. O'Hara. Who drugged me and flew me halfway around the world without my consent?" I press a finger to my lips and pretend to ponder the question.

"Look, I've already apologized for this."

The plane lists to one side again, and he watches me closely with something that might've passed for concern in his eyes if I didn't know that he was a coldhearted self-absorbed kidnapper.

"We just need to get through Christmas. Then, when everything has settled down, we can go back to our own lives."

Can he even hear himself?

"So, let me get this straight because, you know, you changed the rules while I was in a drug-induced coma."

"You were not in a coma, Mary." Is that amusement in his voice?

"You want me to pretend, *in front of your family*, that we're in love and engaged to be married, and then, when the Christmas tree comes down, we walk away like nothing ever happened?"

"Aye, correct."

"Well, that's easy for you to say. They're your family. They know you. God knows how many other women you've brought home to meet them."

"None, Mary." He shakes his head. "You're the first."

I don't believe him.

"But what about me? I'm going to be permanently scarred. I'll probably need therapy for PTSD." Tears sting my eyes. "My first proposal was supposed to be special, and you've taken that away from me."

His eyes flicker as if he's waiting for the punchline, and then he furrows his brow when he realizes that I'm being serious. "You're being melodramatic now. It wasn't a real proposal. It doesn't even count."

Ugh! The man is despicable.

I press my face against the cool glass of the window and plot my escape. Once I'm free, I'll start plotting my revenge. People like Emmett O'Hara think that they can get away with murder —literally—and it's about time someone taught him a lesson.

WHEN WE STEP off the private jet, my stomach sinks through the floor. Where's the airport? Where's the security, the airline staff, the other travelers? There's nothing here but a huge shed-type building, and a 4x4 with the engine running.

"Wh-where are we?"

"Welcome to Ireland." Emmett, wearing a beige cashmere overcoat, takes my hand and leads me down the steps and towards the waiting car. His driver has already gone ahead and is waiting to open the car door for us. "Smile."

I do. Although inside, I'm screaming, "*Let me out of here!*"

The driver refuses to make eye contact. Of course, he does— he was probably in on the whole abduction thing. The thought of him carrying me, unconscious, onto the private jet makes me cringe, but I refuse to let them see it. I am going to get away from Emmett O'Hara and his murderous family if it's the last thing I do.

Inside the 4x4, I lean against the window and watch the world go by. The countryside is green. Not the kind of green you see in Central Park, but vibrant green, a green that's alive and thriving and fertile. There are rolling hills—who'd have thought that hills could actually roll—and craggy mountains, and blue sky that bleeds into the horizon. There are streams and sheep and endless forests, and not another person in sight.

Sitting back, I realize how much I've missed all this color. I like living in New York with its relentless noise, its varied cultures, and its busyness, but I realize with a jolt that even when I'm in my apartment with the door locked and the blinds pulled and a book on my lap, I never truly experience the kind of peace I feel right now.

I lose track of time with the gentle rumble of wheels on tarmac and the heat inside the vehicle. I empty my mind of all the bad things I want to do to Emmett O'Hara when Christmas is over, and instead, concentrate on the moving vista. Like a child on a family day out, I still want to yell, "Sheep!" whenever I spot some, but I don't.

Emmett has made it quite clear that we are only keeping up the pretense in front of his family. We are not in a relationship. We don't even have to like each other because, come January, I'll never have to see him again.

But inside, I feel as if I can never go back to being the Mary Chrysler I was before yesterday. This might be a game to Emmett O'Hara, but he might just have changed my life with his actions, even though I haven't yet figured out how.

We turn off the road and drive through a set of wide, open gates. I sit closer to the window, my breath creating a ghostly white patch on the glass, expecting to see Emmett's family home. But all I can see are more fields, hills, and woods in every direction.

Emmett's arm snakes around me and he points to a spot beyond the trees. "This is our land. Through there is a salmon stream, and this way—" he gestures to the view from his side of the car "—you'll see the house once we're clear of the woods."

Woods? A salmon stream? Is he fucking kidding me right now?

A scoff escapes my lips before I can stop it.

"What?" His eyebrows are so low his eyes look kind of stormy, and I instinctively back away from him. "It's just home to me."

How could this ever be *just home* to anyone?

When the house finally comes into view, I sit back and gape at it, and I don't even care. It's so vast, it's like ten houses have grown together over the years to create this building of many parts. I mean, it's not a stately home or a castle, but rather a house made of gray stone that couldn't make up its mind what shape it wanted to be, and all at once, I'm eager to get inside and explore.

Emmett is smiling when we pull up outside the door that's decorated with the kind of giant wreath I've only ever seen in the movies. His face looks younger, like a boy who can't wait to come home and tell his parents that he scored his first goal in a soccer match, and I remind myself that it's Christmas. Even Emmett O'Hara won't be an asshole during the holidays.

Then he looks at me, and the smile fades. "I know it isn't going to be easy, but I'd appreciate it if you keep this between us."

5

EMMETT

She doesn't wait for Dave to kill the engine and open the passenger door. She's out of the car, her shoes crunching gravel as she walks around it towards the porch.

"Mary, wait!"

Too late. The front door opens, and my mom is standing there wiping her hands on her faded Christmas apron, her face rosy from the heat of the Aga in the kitchen.

"Emmett! Thank God you're here. The twins have been driving us crazy to go and choose the Christmas tree, and I keep telling them that we can't do it until Uncle Emmett is here."

To prove a point, my eight-year-old twin cousins Joseph and Jamie come bounding around the corner of the house and almost knock me over with the force of their embrace.

"Uncle Emmett, can we go and get the Christmas tree?"

"Everyone else has their tree up already."

"I don't know why we had to wait for you to get here. You're always late."

The twins are identical with red hair that refuses to be tamed, a smattering of freckles across their noses, and boundless energy. Their mom, my Aunt Clare, says that if they don't do after school activities every day of the week, and then go sailing with their dad on the weekends, she'll never get them into bed. It's one way to put people off having kids, spending time in the twins' presence.

"Whoa, I'm pleased to see you too." I watch them, trying to figure out which one is Jospeh, and which one is Jamie. "Joseph?" I raise my eyebrows at the one wearing the Spiderman sweater.

"I'm Jamie. He's Joseph." Sometimes I swear they lie to me because they think it's funny.

"You have to wait for me because I have the final say on what tree we bring home."

"That's not fair," one of them says, but they're already running back inside the house, no doubt to inform everyone that I'm here.

"Ach, stop ye teasing." My mom pulls me in for a hug, and I breathe in her familiar smell that still reminds me of when I was a kid.

She pulls away, and that's when she realizes that I'm not alone.

Her eyes flicker back and forth between me and Mary, more questions on the tip of her tongue. "You never said that you were bringing someone home for Christmas." Her smile is there, waiting for me to introduce her, and I know what she's thinking: dear Lord, please let him finally be settling down.

"Mom, this is Mary."

Mary steps forward, her hand outstretched to shake my mom's hand formally. She appears to be shy suddenly, out of her depth, and I pray this means that she'll be so quiet, they won't get to know her at all. It will make it easier for everyone when this is over.

"Mary. What a lovely Irish name. It's Emmett's granny's name too."

Mom smiles at me, and I tell myself that this is a good start. Only ten days to go.

She wipes her hands again like she wants to make a good impression and hugs Mary, kissing her cheek and then holding her at arm's length so that she can get a proper look at her.

"Look at your hair." Mom teases some curls around Mary's face. "I wish Emmett had warned me that you were coming, I'd have saved the big guest room for you. But that's my son, he likes to keep me on my toes. Come in, Mary. Come in, and I'll get the kettle on. You must be exhausted after the journey."

She takes Mary's hand. It's a gesture so natural, so welcoming, that my mom would've thought nothing of it, until her fingers brush the ring on Mary's finger. She freezes. Her eyes catch mine briefly, and then she raises Mary's hand in front of her face, and she's muttering to herself, "Oh my sweet baby Jesus, my son is getting married."

Mary and I exchange glances. I wish I knew what she was thinking, because it occurs to me now that I know nothing about Mary Chrysler other than she's employed by O'Hara Developers and she has a temper. We haven't even discussed our fake relationship, where we met, or how long we've been seeing each other, so fuck knows what she'll tell them if I don't get a chance to speak to her alone first.

"You kept this fecking quiet, Emmett. What are ye trying to do, give me a heart attack?" Mom squeezes Mary close to her chest and then throws her arms around me. "What a celebration this Christmas is going to be. I'll have to send your pa out for more champagne."

"No, Mom, it's fine. You don't have to do that. We want to keep it quiet and simple."

"Nonsense, Emmett! My only son brings a young woman home and tells me he's getting married, and you think we're going to keep this to ourselves? I'll have to call Maureen. I'll have to speak to Father George. Sweet Lord, please tell me that you'll give me time to organize the wedding."

"Mom." I catch Mary's eye, and she smiles at me like her job here is done. I know she hasn't said a word yet, but I can't help feeling that this has played right into her hands. "We haven't even set the date yet."

"But you'll be getting married here on the estate."

It isn't a question. Everyone in the O'Hara family gets married on the estate, in the folly at the back of the house overlooking the stream. I've always known that's where I'd get married eventually, but I don't want my mom to start organizing a wedding that she'll have to cancel in a couple of weeks' time.

"Of course we will." Mary speaks for the first time, and I catch the slight accent that I haven't noticed before, probably because until now she's done nothing but yell at me. "One of the first things Emmett told me was that he wants to get married here. At home."

Mom strokes my face with tears in her eyes. "Wait till Granny Mary hears about this. You'll have Granny Nina knitting a baby shawl before the new year."

Dave is waiting patiently with my luggage for the greetings to be over. "Usual room?" Is that amusement I see glinting in his eyes?

I give him a curt nod and will him to keep moving. For once I'm grateful that my father won't allow me to share a room with a woman out of wedlock. At least I won't have to worry about dividing the bed in half: my side, her side.

"Where's Mary's luggage?"

Mom frowns at Dave who waits for me to respond. He'll get me out of sticky situations when required, but this line of questioning doesn't come under his remit.

Before I can utter a word, Mary chimes in, "I didn't get a chance to go back to my apartment. Emmett surprised me too…"

Her expression is smug. She might've explained the lack of a suitcase, but I know she's toying with me. She might as well wave a banner above her head saying: *Be nice to me Emmett because I can shatter your mom's illusions just like that.*

"Ach, why didn't you give the girl a chance to pack some clothes?" Mom bats me playfully on the arm and links her other arm with Mary. "Fianna will sort you out. She's about your size and she brings enough clothes with her to last a month."

She's already leading Mary inside the house.

I have to act quickly. Once the women get hold of Mary, we won't get a moment to ourselves to get our stories straight, and I don't want them getting suspicious. The O'Hara women might know how to milk a cow and bake the best soda bread in Ireland, but I never met anyone shrewder in a boardroom.

"It's okay, Mom. Stop fussing. I'll show Mary to one of the guest rooms."

"Stop fussing?" She clucks her tongue at me, but really, she's already sharing a moment with her future daughter-in-law. "You might as well tell the Pope to stop attending Mass."

I try again. "Mary might want to shower before she meets everyone."

Mom hesitates just inside the entrance hallway. "Everyone will be so excited to meet you, Mary, but I can bring towels to your room first if you prefer."

"No, it's fine. I can't wait to meet everyone. Emmett talks about you all the time." She flashes a smile at me over her shoulder as she follows my mom towards the kitchen at the rear of the house.

I have no choice but to follow.

Before I even set foot inside the kitchen, I can hear the squeals of excitement. Auntie Clare and Auntie Erin are already checking out the ring while my mom busies herself filling the kettle and setting it on top of the stove to boil.

My dad and his brothers Uncle Sean and Uncle Ciaran are playing cards at the huge pine table while the two grannies are seated at the opposite end, a ball of thick creamy wool on Granny Nina's lap. Fianna is hovering near the women, waiting her turn. I haven't seen her in almost a year, and she seems to have transformed from a teenager to a woman in my absence.

I'm guessing she's around Mary's age, and if Mary is going to bond with anyone, it will be my cousin. Only, I don't know if that will work in my favor or against me. What if Mary confides in her what's really going on? Can Fianna be trusted to keep our secret?

My dad is on his feet and pulling me into a bearhug before I've barely crossed the threshold. "Congratulations, son. I'll need to drive into Laragh later to pick up some more booze. Ye could've given me a heads-up."

"Aye, sorry. It was all last minute. I didn't think."

"Never mind your dad." Uncle Sean claps my back with his meaty hands. "You know he'll stop off at Jake's and celebrate with a few pints of Guiness while he's at it."

Uncle Ciaran shakes my hand warmly. This is how Christmas always looks in our home. Everyone comes to stay until the new year. Everyone is loud, excited, and often drunk, and I usually can't wait to get back to work once it's all over.

"Congratulations, Emmett." The gentle lilting voice belongs to Fianna, standing in front of me, looking up at me with her brother's eyes. "She's perfect."

My gaze instinctively flits towards Mary, who is watching me with bright eyes. I can't tell if she's loving or hating the attention because I'm trying to see her through Fianna's eyes.

My cousin was always the quiet one, but she withdrew into a rigid-backed shell when her brother Oisin died. According to my parents, Fianna went through therapy to help her deal with her grief, but I only ever saw her at Christmas, and it never seemed like the right time to ask her how she was feeling. Then, I realized that I'd missed the boat. Too much time had passed with no communication, and guilt prevented me from reaching out.

"I'll have someone on my side when I want to watch cheesy movies," Fianna says as if reading my mind and diverting the subject.

"No one wants to watch cheesy movies." Her dad, Uncle Sean, resumes his seat and picks up his card hand.

"I saw you scrolling through the Christmas movie channel last night, Sean." Mom fills a teapot with boiling water. "You thought no one was watching."

"Aye, Dad. Don't bother denying it, I caught it on camera." Fianna slides her phone from her pocket and waves it at him.

"Fecking hell." Sean shakes his head, but his grin is wide. "Can no one keep a fecking secret in this house?"

Everyone laughs. I catch Mary's eye, her expression unfathomable, as the twins come barging into the kitchen, yelling, "Jamie caught a toad. Can we keep it as a pet?"

"Not in here, you can't."

Mom is already shooing the boys back towards the door as Granny Mary says, "Fill a bowl with water and let them keep it for a while. They take after their grandpa; he once kept a whole toad family in a bucket when he was a lad."

While the women are distracted, my dad gestures for me to follow him to his study. Inside, he half fills two crystal tumblers with whiskey and sits behind his desk. I sit opposite him and sip the whiskey, feeling it burn as it goes down.

"Congratulations, son." Dad's eyes are moist. "I didn't think that you were ready to take over from me yet, but I'm proud of you. You've had your fun, and now you've found a decent Irish girl to settle down with." Pause. "Does she know?"

This is what I was dreading. I thought I might've bought some time with it being Christmas, but my father must be eager to step down and hand over the reins. He's kept it peaceful between the Irish families for the past twenty years, but it doesn't mean it'll stay that way when they learn there's a new Don at the helm.

Am I ready?

It was inevitable, but I feel like the hole I dug when I proposed to Mary to save her ass is getting tighter, squeezing me into a shape that doesn't quite fit. This is the way it goes: get married, take over the family helm. It's the reason I never get involved. I've been stalling all these years because the thought of introducing the woman I love to a life of bodyguards, blacked-out windows, and one eye over her shoulder isn't exactly how I pictured starting married life.

Sure, my mom and my aunties take it in their stride, but they came from similar backgrounds. It's the life they were born into. I love them for it, but is it what I want for my woman?

My dad watches me closely, sitting back in his seat, one leg crossed over the other.

"No. Mary doesn't know."

"Don't leave it too long, son. The best marriages are built on trust and honesty."

I smile. Mary and I are fucked then.

"I will tell her."

Weariness settles over my shoulders like a mantle. Since Oisin, my cousin, died, I've been finding it increasingly difficult to turn a blind eye to the dark side of the family business. I wouldn't be where I am without it, but I've been thinking about legitimizing the American branch. In time. When I'm ready to settle down.

"I'll tell her soon."

6

MARY

They talk over each other, laughing and joking in their beautiful gentle accents, comfortable with each other because that's what families do. They are all capable of following at least three conversations at once. Emmett's mom Sinead ushers the boys back outside with the unlucky toad, while discussing the best month for a wedding with her sisters-in-law and asking Fianna to loan me some warm clothes for when we go out and collect the Christmas tree.

She fills a huge earthenware mug with tea and plies me with homemade gingerbread biscuits.

"She'll need more than that." Granny Mary, Emmett's paternal grandmother, knocks back a crystal tumbler of liquid that looks remarkably like whiskey. "They've traveled halfway around the world to get here. The least ye can do is feed the poor girl."

"I'm fine." I honestly can't eat with the thump-thump of my beating heart, but no one is listening to me.

"They're feeders." Fianna leans in and whispers in my ear. "Don't even try to fight it. If you don't eat my mom's gingerbread, she'll think you're on a strange Hollywood-style diet, and the next thing you know they'll be serving you extra roast tatties with your dinner to fatten you up."

I like Fianna. There's something serene about her, the way she doesn't get drawn into the banter and the laughter. She's the wallflower observing the loud and vibrant blooms in the center of the flowerbed. We could be friends, I think, in different circumstances.

I bite off the gingerbread man's head—it's soft on the inside and crispy on the outside, with the perfect amount of ginger, not like the brittle biscuits served in the generic cafés during the holidays.

"I knew it!" Emmett's dad, Patrick, high-fives his brothers. "She went for the head first."

They all look at me as laughter fills the massive kitchen.

"They're talking about the biscuit," Fianna says. "They probably had a wager on what part you'd eat first."

Emmett hasn't joined in the card game. He went outside with the twins to release the captured toad back into the wild, and since he came back, he has been leaning against the counter with a huge mug of coffee in his hands.

He's holding back. At first, I assumed that it was because of me—he's worried that I'll say something I shouldn't—but the more I watch him, the more I'm starting to think that it goes way deeper than our fake relationship. This is a scene straight out of a Hallmark movie, but he doesn't know what role he should be playing. Has he spent so much time in New York that he has forgotten where he belongs?

No wonder his mom is so excited to plan our wedding. She wants her baby home. For good.

I wonder how she'll react when she finds out the truth?

I feel a stab of guilt somewhere deep in my chest and try to soothe it away with a surreptitious mouthful of gingerbread. This isn't my fault. *He* proposed to *me* to cover up the murder on the roof when all I was trying to do was mind my own business.

But the guilt goes way deeper too. I've never experienced this kind of Christmas before, but as a connoisseur of cheesy movies, I recognize a close knit family when I see one. It's the kind of Christmas I've always dreamed of. A huge welcoming home, homemade fruitcake, beautifully wrapped gifts around a real tree that smells of pine. All we're missing is snow, but I'm not ruling it out.

The only problem is, I don't belong here.

"Come on." Fianna stands and takes my hand in hers. "I'll find you a warm coat and some boots. This is my favorite part of Christmas."

In the mud room—they have an actual mud room in this house complete with a selection of heavy waterproof coats, wellington boots, and thick fisherman's socks—Fianna chooses a bottle-green coat and matching boots for me.

"How did you meet Emmett?" she asks while I try on the boots for size and add an extra pair of socks.

Here we go. Storytime.

"At a party." It's mostly true.

"Did Uncle Emmett choose the ring?"

Ouch. This one is going to hurt. "Yes. I had no idea that he was going to propose."

Fianna watches me coolly, and I already hate lying to her. "It's just, I thought he would've given you Granny Mary's engagement ring. Everyone knows the ring is going to be handed down to the eldest grandchild."

My pulse is racing a marathon. Once you start lying, you get caught in a whole sticky web of them, and it's only a matter of time before you start forgetting what you said to begin with. Why couldn't he have just pretended I was a quick fuck on the roof instead of his fiancée? Would've saved us both a whole load of hassle.

"I-I said I wanted something simple."

She eyes up the ring like the diamond is flashing the truth at her in Morse Code. "Granny Mary's ring is a bit of an acquired taste. I'm glad I won't have to wear it." She smiles, and it's so genuine, that the guilt adds another stab to my heart for good measure. "I never thought Uncle Emmett would get married, but I'm glad you're here, Mary."

You won't be, I think.

WE ALL PILE into giant-wheeled 4x4 vehicles and form a procession to choose the Christmas tree that will take pride of place in the family living room. Fianna comes with us, riding in the back with me and Emmett while Dave follows Patrick's car to the tree farm.

The engagement ring conversation has left me feeling a little uneasy. Perhaps Emmett hasn't given his family enough credit; I think they understand him way better than he believes they do, and they're not going to be easily fooled. It's Christmas! He's just gotten engaged to be married. We should be screwing like rabbits not eying each other up from opposite sides of the room.

I lean across him and peer out of the window. "Where are we now?" He flinches, and I feel like hissing in his ear, "Act, you fucker. This was your idea."

He points out the tiny village of Laragh as we pass through. "Our closest village. There's still a way to go."

Asshole. He wants me to sit back and leave him alone, but he doesn't get to make all the rules. Who does he think he is?

I rest my head on his shoulder, entwine my fingers with his, and yawn exaggeratedly. It has the desired effect. He can't push me away without Fianna noticing, and he can't go anywhere because he's trapped in the back of the car with us.

Deep breath. He smells so goddamned good.

I check out his profile, the set of his clenched jaw, the lips pressed together, eyes fixated on the window, and anger blooms inside me. I move my lips to his ear, and whisper, "You smell good."

He swallows hard. I can almost hear the debate being carried out inside his head. Ignore me or respond the way a lover would?

Finally, when I think he's going with option one, he turns to me and plants a kiss on the tip of my nose. "So do you."

Is that it? Is that the best he can do?

I nuzzle his neck and this time, when I whisper, I allow my lips to graze his earlobe. "Later, after we've decorated the tree, can you show me around the house?"

He shoots a look at Fianna who is staring out the passenger window on the opposite side of the car. "Later."

I'm going to hold him to that.

Choosing a tree is way more difficult than it looks in the movies. Sinead wants one with full branches; the men want the tallest one they can fit inside the house; while the twins don't care what tree we get because they're too busy trying to wrap themselves up in green webbing.

Finally, they settle on a ten-foot tall Nordman fir, which gets wrapped and strapped onto the roof of Patrick's vehicle. The mood in the car on the way back is different, more electrified, the prospect of the tree's arrival making even Emmett more vocal. He and Fianna talk about Christmases from when they were younger, telling stories of their dads getting drunk on Christmas Eve and eating the sherry trifle, and Ciaran pulling the tree on top of him one year, and smashing half the baubles.

Back at the house, the men carry the tree inside and set it up while the women start unpacking last year's decorations from cardboard boxes. It puts the tiny fake tree in the living room of my apartment to shame. But I'm so absorbed with hanging sparkling snowflakes and icicles and angel's hair from the branches, that I almost forget the reason why I'm here.

Almost.

Until Sinead mentions the food for the party. "Mary, you can stick the angel on the top this year. I need to start preparing the food or our guests will be arriving, and I'll still be in my apron, elbow-deep in flour."

"Can I help?"

"You're our guest of honor. Fianna can show you to your room and sort out something for you to wear."

"I can't believe you still throw a party every year." Emmett hasn't been anywhere near the tree, still maintaining the aloof boss façade, even in front of his own family.

"It's tradition. It wouldn't be the same if we didn't throw a big bash." Sinead winks at me as she hands me the frothy white angel with translucent wings. "Besides, we have something to celebrate tonight."

I stand beside Emmett and kiss him on the lips. "Smile," I whisper so that no one else can hear.

My guest room is next to Fianna's. I've never seen a home with so many guest rooms. My room is larger than my entire apartment in New York, with a bed that would sleep four people comfortably. It's one of those high bouncy beds with an emerald-green comforter, and fairy lights strung around the metal headboard. I can't resist flopping back onto it like Kevin McAllister in *Home Alone*, a goofy grin on my face.

Fianna's room is equally as large as mine with a red comforter, a giant Christmas teddy on the bed, and tinsel woven around the headboard.

"How big is the big guest room?" I muse out loud.

"It's like twice the size of this. My parents use it when they're here." Fianna opens the doors to a tall wooden wardrobe and stands aside, her gaze flitting back and forth between me and the rack of clothes hanging neatly inside. "Do you always wear black?"

"Um..."

I'm not often lost for words—I'm quiet because I choose to be, and not because I have nothing to say—but when it comes to clothes, I'm so used to trying to blend in that I don't even know what suits me anymore.

"I wear black to work."

"What about when you go out?"

"My idea of a night out is grabbing a pretzel and doing some window shopping on Fifth Avenue."

"But you go out with Emmett, right?" Faint lines have appeared between Fianna's eyebrows.

Fuck! It's hard being someone who isn't me. Someone who would attract a man like Emmett O'Hara and then keep him interested enough to propose.

"They're usually dazzling events where everyone is dressed to kill." I shrug nonchalantly, like I'm blasé about the kind of social life a lot of people would kill for. "But yes, I generally choose black."

Her eyes narrow briefly, and I don't know if she bought it or not, but she's obviously too polite to press me further. "This is your night, Mary. You and Emmett. Auntie Sinead and Uncle Patrick will want to show you off, so I think we should give them something to talk about, don't you?"

Do I? I'm not so sure Emmett would agree ... so perhaps I do after all.

"Ye-es?" What the hell! I'm here now, no turning back. He wanted a pretense, and that's what he's going to get.

Fianna rifles through her clothes and turns to me with a mischievous grin. "We have two choices: we either complement your hair with brown or dark green or..." She pauses for effect. "We go all out and make sure everyone notices you."

"I don't know..." I can see her hand fluttering towards a dark red dress. "Red isn't really my color." It's another lie—I've never worn anything red in my life.

Growing up, I had no one to talk to about style or fashion or what does and doesn't work with red hair—it's not a priority for kids in the foster care system—but I do know that red clashes with red. I mean, it's basic dress sense, isn't it?

"This will be, Mary, trust me."

7

EMMETT

She's doing it deliberately. Holing up with Fianna on the pretext of *borrowing some clothes*, when what she's really doing is avoiding me.

That little stunt she pulled in the car, rubbing her breast against my arm, is going to get her nowhere because if she thinks that she can make this relationship real and blackmail me when we get back, she's picked on the wrong person. We're getting through Christmas and then, that's it. I'll never have to set eyes on Mary Chrysler again.

"Don't be nervous, Emmett." Granny Nina pinches my cheek hard; as a child I told myself that she'd stop doing it eventually, but she never has. And it still hurts. "Mary's lovely. Your mom is already besotted with her."

That's what fucking worries me. She'll get everyone on her side, and then I'll be the bad guy when we call off the engagement.

"I know." I keep my smile in place and remind myself that I'm supposed to be besotted too.

With food covering every available surface in the dining room and kitchen, Auntie Erin comes and stands beside me. Even after everything, I've always been her favorite nephew. "It's not like you to be so nervous, Emmett."

What's with everyone thinking I'm nervous?

"It's obvious that you and Mary are made for each other. I bet your mom is already counting down the days till she holds her first grandchild in her arms."

Jesus fucking wept.

"It'll be a while before that happens."

I'm not even convincing myself with the enamored lover act. Get a grip, Emmett. Ten days of this and then you're a free man again.

"Don't keep her waiting too long. Life's too short, you know." Erin swallows, her eyes growing large with tears. "Anyway, I've got a bone to pick with you."

Okay, what have I done now?

"Granny Mary's engagement ring?"

She blinks away the tears and smiles at the room without making eye contact with any of the guests. It's a skill. Auntie Erin would rather be alone in the kitchen with her thoughts than making small talk at a party.

I'd forgotten all about the engagement ring. "Mary chose the ring."

"You forgot about it, didn't you?" Erin knocks my ribs with her elbow. "Good luck explaining that to Granny in the morning when she's sober."

I smile, seeking Granny out with my eyes. She's sitting at the far end of the dining table chatting to her neighbor Mrs. Kelly, a glass of whiskey in front of her. "I'll just have to keep her glass full then."

Just then, a strange kind of hush settles over the room, and Fianna walks in, closely followed by Mary.

My stomach twists, and my pulse instinctively starts racing when I see what she's wearing. A red dress that clings to every curve, cinched in at the waist with a deep, black leather belt, and cut just low enough to reveal the swell of her breasts beneath a chunky black pendant. Her hair is down, long curls tumbling over her shoulders, and she's wearing the kind of smoky makeup that makes her eyes look twice as large.

The dress shouldn't work with that hair, but it does, and by the collective held breath, I'd guess that everyone else has noticed it does too.

Mary loiters in the doorway, her eyes roaming the room as if she's looking for someone to rescue her when Erin's elbow jabs me in the ribs a second time. "Go on then. Go claim your fiancée."

My legs work of their own accord. They carry me across the kitchen until I find myself standing in front of Mary, who's chewing her bottom lip and waiting for me to say something.

"You look..." My mouth is suddenly dry.

"I think stunning is the word you're looking for," Fianna whispers in my ear.

"Stunning," I repeat, my tongue working on autopilot.

Mary's face lights up with a smile. I mean, it literally lights up, changing her whole face, and man if her eyes haven't gotten greener while she's been getting ready. "Thank you." She eyes me up and down, a tentative smile teasing one corner of her mouth. "You don't look so bad yourself."

I'm wearing a Fair Isle sweater and navy pants. I wouldn't be seen dead in these clothes in New York, but somehow, less than twenty-four hours of being home and I'm like a peacock displaying his feathers in his natural habitat.

She leans closer and kisses me on the cheek. I breathe in her perfume—*Fianna's* perfume—and my lips try to follow hers like they're afraid she'll slip away when my back is turned. I hope that she doesn't notice, but I can tell by the way she slants her eyes, that she did.

But before I can explain myself, my mom comes over and drags Mary away. "I want to introduce you to everyone, Mary. God only knows when my son will bring you back again."

I watch them walk away, and man, that ass. Since when did Mary Chrysler from IT have an ass like that, and how the fuck did I never notice it before?

Because Mary Chrysler never wanted to be noticed. I answer my own question. Sonia didn't even recognize her last night, and Sonia knows everyone in the building.

"Are you happy, Emmett?"

The voice catches me by surprise. Fianna is standing beside me wearing a long floaty dress, her blond hair tumbling over her shoulders like a golden halo giving her the appearance of a water sprite or wood fairy. It has always been the thing I love most about my cousin—she knows who she is.

"Why do you ask?"

She furrows her brow at my response. "Because Mary is the only woman you've ever brought home to meet the family." She sucks in her bottom lip.

There's more to come. "And?"

"And ... I want to know everything about your future wife. Where did you meet? Was it love at first sight? Why didn't you warn Auntie Sinead that she was coming?"

I hear the questions, and I know that these are not the answers Fianna is looking for. She's an O'Hara. She senses that something is off kilter even if she hasn't quite figured out what.

"We met at a party." She doesn't take her eyes off Mary like an artist protecting her creation. "Does love at first sight even exist? I didn't even know myself until last night that Mary would come with me."

"Why?" She turns her attention to me, and her eyes remind me so much of Oisin that my chest aches. "Did you scare her off meeting us?"

I laugh then, the relief tentatively sloping back into my shoulders. Relax, Emmett. We haven't been caught out yet. When the party guests leave, I'll find some time alone with Mary, and we can coordinate our stories before the holidays really begin.

"Would I do such a thing?"

"Well, we all know that you're a Grinch who's only here under protest."

"Hey." I raise my hands in mock surrender and realize that I need a drink if I'm going to get through all the inevitable interrogations tonight will bring. "I haven't complained once."

"I'm just so confused that Mary didn't bring anything with her." *Bam!* "Not even a toothbrush."

"She's been having problems with a neighbor in her apartment block. She didn't want to go back for her stuff."

"So, she's been staying with you?"

Fuck, where's the whiskey when I need it? "She hasn't moved in, if that's what you're asking."

"Why not? Are you afraid of what your parents will say?" She smiles. "Don't worry, I won't tell them."

My dad's booming voice greets the latecomers, and a cold knot sinks in my stomach. "What's he doing here?"

Fianna follows my gaze to a guy called Ronan Blackthorn who has just arrived with his parents. Our families have known each other for as long as I've been alive, but their son isn't welcome in our house. He's the bully who made Oisin's life hell when he was at school.

My fists clench, and I'm about to walk over there and personally escort him out of our house when Fianna's hand wraps around my arm. "Leave it, Emmett."

"Why? What's happened?"

"Nothing…" Her face gives her away. "He's changed, is all."

"People like Ronan Blackthorn never change."

"Emmett, be nice." My mom appears from nowhere like she overheard our conversation above the buzz of chatter that's already spilling through the house. "We've all made our peace with him, and we need you to do the same. It's Christmas."

It might be Christmas, but the guy is still a fucking bully.

"Go find your beautiful fiancée and mingle."

Mom wanders off. I've been told, and she'll expect me to follow through.

"I need a drink," I admit to Fianna. "Coming?"

My dad is popping champagne like soda. We grab a glass each and wander through to the dining room where Mary is chatting to more family friends, head tipped back, and her easy laughter reaching us from the doorway. She doesn't smile at me that way, and I don't know why that makes me feel so inadequate.

I'm the asshole who abducted her from the Christmas party for chrissakes.

Fianna grabs my arm and pulls me into the conversation which, I quickly realize, is about me and Mary. Of course it is. Why did I expect anything else?

"I'm surprised your granny hasn't had something to say about the engagement ring." The voice belongs to Maureen who runs a B&B in Avondale.

Mary stands beside me and links her arm through mine. I can feel her breast rubbing against my chest, and I clench my jaw, warning my cock to stay right where it is. "I wanted a simple ring," she says. "Emmett did try to get me to change my mind."

Her face is so close to mine that I can almost taste her lips.

Stop it! Concentrate. The ring is fast becoming a problem, and I need to nip it in the bud now.

"I gave up in the end." I don't even care that it makes me sound fucking weak, because her hair is brushing my shoulder, and all I can think about is how it would feel to have it wrapped around my fingers, pulling her head backwards and exposing her neck…

What am I now, a fucking vampire?

"You must be Mary." I'm so caught up in a vision of Mary arching her spine and pressing her nipples into my mouth, that I don't spot Ronan coming until he has somehow ensconced himself between Mary and Fianna. "I've heard all about you."

He offers his hand for Mary to shake, and when she unfolds her arm from mine, pulls her into an embrace before she can prepare herself.

I can't take my eyes off the meaty arms wrapped around my fiancée. He watches me from over Mary's shoulder, holding onto her a beat too long for my benefit. I meet Fianna's gaze, and she flashes me a warning with her eyes.

Not tonight, Emmett.

"Emmett." He shakes my hand, grinning like he's pleased to see me. This one is for Mary's benefit. "I can't believe you're getting married." He stands so that his arm is touching Mary's.

"You'd better believe it. We'll be getting married here on the estate."

But he isn't even listening. "Mary, let me introduce you to my mom. She'll be wanting to make your wedding cake."

I watch helplessly as he leads Mary away. She doesn't even glance over her shoulder at me as I hear her say, "Your mom makes wedding cakes? We haven't thought that far ahead yet, but I'm sure she can give us some ideas."

I tune out of the rest of the conversation and make my way

back to the kitchen as soon as I can without appearing rude. They're nowhere to be seen.

My heart is hammering now. He's doing this deliberately to wind me up, and if he dares to lay a finger on Mary, I'll fucking kill him, I don't care what my mom has to say about it after.

The twins tear past me on their way inside from the back garden, and I get a waft of perfume that sends my brain cells reeling.

I step outside onto the decking, which is new, and scan the people smoking on the outdoor sofas. They're not there. But then I spot them towards the back of the seating area staring out across our land, the fairy lights twinkling intermittently across their backs.

They don't hear me coming. I watch as Ronan's arm snakes around Mary's shoulders, and she tries to dodge the embrace, sidestepping away from him and pointing at the moon. A distraction. He tilts his head back to peer up at the silver crescent, and it takes all my willpower to not separate it from his neck.

"Can anyone join in or is this a private conversation?" Of all the corny lines, I had to throw that one into the mix...

"We were just admiring the moon." Mary moves closer to me as if she can sense my simmering anger and is trying to diffuse the situation before it arises.

Ronan faces me squarely, biceps popping beneath his sweater. "Your fiancée is gorgeous, Emmett. Lucky bastard."

I clench my fists as Fianna appears between us, standing way too close to Ronan for my liking. "There you are. I've been looking all over for you." She addresses Ronan, whose lips smile all the way to meet hers.

8

MARY

"Fianna?"

I can feel the anger vibrating through Emmett and shaking the ground beneath our feet. I've no idea what history exists between the two men, but it's obvious that Emmett doesn't like Ronan, and is getting all caveman protective over his cousin.

Fianna shakes her head, a gesture so brief, I almost wonder if I imagined it. "Shall we go back inside? It's wrong of you to keep Mary away from everyone who's dying to meet her."

Emmett's eyes harden like bullets. "I'm not going anywhere with—"

"It's fine." Fianna's voice is gentle but firm.

I've spent less than twelve hours with Emmett's family, but I already understand that the women are forces to be reckoned with. Including Fianna. Whatever Emmett was about to say about Ronan has been swallowed while he waits for his cousin to elaborate.

"We've all moved on," she continues. "We can't spend the rest of our lives in the past."

Ronan, eyes fixed firmly on Emmett, slides his arm around Fianna and pulls her closer to his side. There's nothing romantic about the gesture—it's another caveman move, the bravest and strongest guy claiming his prize: the woman. I can already see how the rest of the evening is going to go: Ronan will parade Fianna around, making sure that they are always in plain view of Emmett.

Emmett balls his hands into fists as a tic appears in his temple. "Have you forgotten what he—"

"How could I?" Fianna shakes her head. "I'm disappointed that you even need to ask." I can hear the emotion clogging her voice. If Emmet can't, then he's a fool, but I'm taking no chances.

"Can we go back inside now, Emmett?" I subtly position myself between him and Ronan. "I'm cold. And there are still so many people to meet."

His gaze bounces off me and back to his cousin who is pulling Ronan towards the seating area positioned around a huge chimenea. I'd like nothing more than to sit out here for a while and soak up the peace of the starry night, but his mom is desperate to show off her son's fiancée, and it's the least we can do for her while we're here.

I cling to his arm as we head back inside. Fianna's shoes are killing me, and I can already feel a blister forming on the back of my left heel. I'm waiting for him to shrug me off or remind me not to interfere in family stuff that doesn't concern me, but instead, he doesn't leave my side.

We collect two glasses of champagne from his dad, Patrick, who scrunches up his face when he sees me and plants a sloppy kiss on my cheek. "My future daughter-in-law. You've no idea how happy we are to have you here for Christmas."

"Thank you." Guilt sticks in my throat like an apple core. "I'm happy to be here."

"He's drunk," Emmett murmurs as he drags me into the conservatory where The Pogues are belting out: *The boys of the NYPD choir were singing 'Galway Bay'*. My favorite Christmas song. The one that never fails to bring tears to my eyes. "Take no notice of him."

How can he be so coldhearted? Doesn't he even care that he is going to break his family's heart when he tells them that there isn't going to be a wedding?

"How can I take no notice of them when they're obviously so happy?" I keep smiling, like a marionette with a sinister grin painted on.

Everywhere I look, people are watching us, their faces beaming with excitement not only for Christmas but for the good news the returning son brought home with him.

Upstairs in Fianna's room earlier, I looked at my reflection in the mirror and tried to see myself through the family's eyes. Am I everything they wanted for Emmett? After their warm welcome, I'd allowed myself to believe that perhaps I was the daughter-in-law they'd been hoping for, but now I can see that I was wrong. They're only being nice to me for Emmett's sake, while he's playing them all for fools.

The joy and anticipation I'd felt coming down to the party with Fianna is evaporating rapidly, replaced by the gut-wrenching reminder that none of this is real.

I spend the rest of the evening going through the motions, smiling, nodding, following Emmett's lead when he answers the guests' questions.

"How did you meet?"

"How long have you known each other?"

"How did he propose? Did he go down on one knee in front of an audience, Mary, or did he do it privately at home?"

I try to inject some enthusiasm into my voice, especially when Emmett is being so attentive. But as the seconds tick by, and the evening gets louder, more raucous, more boisterous even than the twins who've crashed out on sofas in the living room where the Christmas tree lights are twinkling, the more I dislike what we're doing.

There must've been an easier way.

Granny Mary calls us over, and Emmett guides me towards her, his hand on the small of my back. She's in the same seat in the kitchen where we found her when we arrived earlier in the day, her cheeks rosy with the heat of all the bodies in the house and the whiskey she's consumed. But her eyes are clear.

"Let me get a proper look at this diamond of yours, Mary love." She pulls a pair of spectacles from her pocket and places them on her nose with one hand, while pulling my ring finger closer. She examines the ring closely like she's a professional jeweler. "I wish you'd spoken to me first, Emmett."

Emmett's expression doesn't falter—the man is a coldhearted asshole. "This was what Mary wanted."

She looks at me, and I smile back at her, praying that she can't see right through me to the uneasiness crawling through my veins.

"But you didn't give her the choice." Granny Mary removes the spectacles and takes a slug of whiskey. "Did he tell you about my ring?" she asks me.

"I..."

I know the story we're running with, but if I say yes, I'm going to offend her—I haven't even seen the ring I've supposedly refused—and if I say no, I'm going to make Emmett look bad.

"Granny, why don't you show Mary the ring tomorrow?" Fianna appears from nowhere and throws her arms around the old woman's neck, planting a sloppy kiss on her papery cheek. "Then she'll see for herself how beautiful it is."

Fianna winks at me and straightens. "Enough talk about these two lovebirds. I want to dance, and you're coming with me."

She pulls me away and doesn't let go until we're in the conservatory where everyone is now dancing the Macarena. Apart from Ronan, who follows us in, and watches Fianna with a bemused expression on his face.

It isn't long before Emmett comes in and stands guard next to Ronan, his spine ramrod straight giving him his full, intimidating height. Not that Ronan appears intimidated. Without warning, he comes over to join us pulling some John Travolta moves that make the older women giggle.

Emmett's eyes narrow. He doesn't want to dance, but he doesn't want me to dance either. What is his problem? Is it all to do with this Ronan guy, or did he not expect me to have fun while I'm here?

I watch him as one cheesy pop song ends, and another begins. I'm not going anywhere. I remove Fianna's shoes, wincing as I tear the skin off the top of the blister on my heel, and dance barefoot.

The music gets louder. The room gets hotter. Patrick fetches us drinks and encourages his son to let his hair down before returning to the kitchen to resume his role as bartender.

Three glasses of champagne later, and the room is spinning a little. It's the most alcohol I've ever consumed in one sitting, and I want to find a quiet spot in a darkened room, lay down, and close my eyes. But Emmett hasn't taken his eyes off me. I don't know what he's thinking, and I don't like trying to preempt his mood when I know so little about him, but I am not going to stop just because it's what he wants.

If he wants me, he can come and get me.

WHEN THE LAST GUESTS LEAVE, I offer to tidy up and tell Sinead and Patrick to go to bed. I've never seen so many dirty glasses. I fill the sink with soapy water and start scrubbing the glasses that are already piled up on the drainer while Fianna gathers more from the other rooms.

"What are you doing?" Emmett comes in and opens the dishwasher. "That's what this is for."

"It's fine, I like washing up." It's true. Water has a soothing effect on my spiraling thoughts whenever they feel a little out of control.

Emmett rolls up his sleeves and starts clearing the table of food. Fianna wanders in and out with more glasses and used paper plates which she tips straight into a black sack. We work in comfortable silence, but I can't stop the thump-thump of my heart. Emmett and I haven't had a moment alone since we got here, and I get the feeling he has something to say.

Sure enough, he escorts me to my room and waits for Fianna to go to her own room after we say goodnight.

When the door clicks behind her, he opens the door to my room and pulls me inside. We both stand by the door, facing each other, his hand warm and heavy on my arm. I wish he wasn't so goddamned hot because I can't see past the blue eyes, the broad shoulders, and the perfect white teeth, but he doesn't get to manhandle me like this.

I wrench my arm free.

He speaks first. "What was that all about?"

"What do you mean?"

"Dancing all night?"

"It was a party. It's what people do at parties."

I don't know what he wants me to say. I mean, he's made it quite clear that this isn't real—I don't need reminding of that again, thank you very much—but he's looking at me like he's angry that I didn't spend more time with him.

"Anyway." I break the silence because it's unnerving me, and my blister is stinging, and I want to sleep. "What's the big deal with Ronan?"

He watches me so intensely I can't look away. "I don't like him."

That much was obvious.

"It's family stuff."

"Okay."

He hasn't moved so why does it feel as if his lips are closer to mine. My breathing grows shallow, and my heart chooses now to skip a beat. *Great!*

"Can you let my granny down gently with the ring tomorrow?"

He pulls away, opens the door, and then he's gone without so much as a backward glance.

The good night's sleep I was so desperately hoping for is screwed. I've known Emmett O'Hara for twenty-four hours, and already it feels as though we've experienced a lifetime of shit that's going to keep me awake at night. It has nothing at all to do with the fact that the asshole is so hot he could melt butter with his smile.

Nothing at all to do with it…

Ugh! I step out of the dress and drape it over the back of the chair in front of the dressing table, knowing that I'll probably never look that sexy again.

And the asshole didn't even notice enough to make a move.

I climb onto the bed—literally—and pull the comforter up to my chin. Now that I'm in bed, my brain is determined to replay everything that Emmett said today. Every smile that I happened to catch when he wasn't watching, every gentle nuance of his voice when he spoke to his mom and grannies, every accidental touch we shared before he clenched his jaw and went all alpha male on me.

I bury my face in the pillow and let out a silent scream. Why couldn't he have been a ninety-year-old with a walking stick and a silver-haired wife at home? He would have beaten the thug with his stick and sent me on his way.

Instead, I got rescued by the handsome prince with a chip on his shoulder.

Just about sums up my luck.

I must doze off at some point because when I wake up, the smell of fried breakfast is wafting into my room through the gap around the door.

I'm ravenous. Yawning, I throw back the covers and wince as I put my foot on the floor and open up the blister on my heel. Fantastic! Now I have to go downstairs and ask my fake future mother-in-law for a Band-aid and remind Emmett that I'm nothing like the women he usually dates.

I pull on a pair of jeans and a sweater loaned to me by Fianna —seriously, what would I do without her—and head downstairs to the kitchen. Everyone is there.

Apart from Emmett.

"Come on in, Mary," Sinead calls out to me from over her shoulder.

She and Erin are cooking breakfast —Sinead flipping rashers of bacon on a griddle while her sister-in-law stirs a huge tureen filled with scrambled eggs. Granny Nina is still knitting. There's a deck of cards on the table between the brothers. The twins are spooning porridge into their mouths, their asses half off their seats in their eagerness to get outside and explore.

No one is nursing a hangover.

I take a seat beside Fianna while Patrick fills a mug with steaming tea from a pot that's wearing a Christmas-pudding tea cozy. "Where's Emmett?" Jeez, when did I start sounding so needy?

"He had some business stuff to attend to. He'll be back soon." Patrick dunks a shortbread biscuit into his own gigantic mug of tea.

On Christmas Eve? So, he's a hot, *workaholic* asshole.

"Fianna, why don't you show Mary around after breakfast?" Sinead sets a plate down in front of me piled high with bacon, sausages, eggs, fried tomatoes, hash browns, and something else that I think might be black pudding. "Toast is coming."

"On it," Erin calls out.

I can't help smiling. I know I'm an outsider, but they've all accepted me as if there was a Mary-shaped hole just waiting to be filled. The only person treating me like an outsider is the person who's supposed to be in love with me.

After breakfast and two more mugs of tea, Fianna gives me a tour of the rest of the house. There's a games room complete with a snooker table, pinball machine, air hockey table, and mini putting green. There's a small cinema room with twelve plush, red velvet seats and a popcorn machine; a sauna room; an indoor pool; a gym; and an art studio.

Fianna smiles at me. "I know it's a lot to take in, but Auntie Sinead and Uncle Patrick are the most down-to-earth people you'll ever meet."

It's on the tip of my tongue to ask if Emmett is the same, but I manage to stop myself in time. I don't know what happened between us last night or how Emmett will be with me when he gets back, and I don't want to make things any more strained than they already are.

"Who uses the art studio?" It's a bright, airy room overlooking the rear garden—*forest*—with several easels set up, and stacks of paintings stored under white sheets.

"Auntie Sinead paints; she says it's therapeutic even if she never lets anyone see her work. Emmett used to paint before... Well, before he moved out permanently."

Emmett used to paint?

"Let me show you something." Fianna removes a sheet from an easel to reveal a portrait of a young man. "My brother, Oisin." Her voice cracks. "Emmett painted this shortly before my brother died."

"Oh my God, I'm so sorry." I can feel my heart ripping open with hers, and I tell myself that it's okay to be heartbroken over someone I never knew. "What happened?"

Before she can reply, the door opens, and Emmett is standing there, staring at the portrait, with an expression I can't read. Then he's gone.

9
EMMETT

"Emmett?"

It's Mary. I don't stop and wait for her. I can't face all the questions or the fake sympathy. Fianna should never have shown her the portrait; she knows how important it is to me, and until today, she was the only other person who has ever seen it.

Why? What was she thinking, showing Mary Oisin's portrait when she knows nothing about her? I can answer my own goddamned question. She was thinking that Mary is part of our lives now, which means that she should know all there is to know about us, including what happened to Oisin.

"Emmett! Wait! Can I talk to you?"

She's still fucking following me. I head through the mud room and out the back of the house, pulling a waxed coat off the hook as I go.

The door bangs open behind me. "Emmett! Can we please talk?"

"Go back inside, Mary!" I glance over my shoulder at her, framed by the mud room doorway, her mane of red hair all wild around her face.

Big mistake. I'm half tempted to turn around, go back, and tell her everything, but what's the point in forming a connection when this will all be over in nine days' time?

I hear the door close behind me. No footsteps. She finally got the hint that I don't want to talk about this.

I head to the stables. I haven't ridden since I was here last year. I just need to get away from the house for a while, alone, rearrange the thoughts inside my head, and make room for the Christmas spirit that's going to take over the family today.

My horse, Jupiter, nudges my hand with her nose, still happy to see me after all this time. There is no love quite like that of an animal. Unconditional, pure, heartwarming.

"Hey, girl." I nuzzle her face, a goofy smile appearing from nowhere. "I've missed you."

I feel the sharp stab of guilt in my chest. I would miss Jupiter if I thought about her, but burying myself in work when I'm in New York is a coping mechanism. If I don't think about her, about my mom and dad, about home, everything else is manageable.

I saddle her up and fasten my helmet as Mary walks into the stables with Fianna. She's wearing one of Mom's coats and Hunter wellies, and for a moment, she looks like this is exactly where she belongs. How has she managed to infiltrate my family home, charm everyone I know, and claim this setting for herself?

I let Jupiter out of her stall, anger blooming inside my chest. I only have myself to blame, but it won't stop me from wallowing in a little self-pity right about now.

"I'll leave you guys to it." Fianna heads outside, leaving Mary behind.

"Emmett. I'm sorry. I didn't know about your cousin."

What does she want me to say? It's okay; I forgive you for snooping into my life.

"Is that it?" It sounds way harsher than I intended, and I see the way she winces, but I don't soften the words.

"I-I'm here if you want to talk about it."

"Aye, well I don't." I keep walking, Jupiter bobbing her head happily at the prospect of a ride across the land.

It feels good to be back in the saddle. It's the only time I ever truly empty my mind, wipe everything clean, ready to start afresh.

Only I haven't gone far when I hear a cry from somewhere behind me. Tugging on the reins, I bring Jupiter to a halt and turn her around to find Mary on the ground, Fianna's horse, Misty, whinnying as she trots around her.

"What the fuck?"

I could keep riding, but I'm not that much of an asshole.

Dismounting when I reach her, I help Mary onto her feet and check that she isn't hurt. "What happened?"

"I don't know." She chews her bottom lip and shies away from the horse as she comes back for her rider.

I stroke Misty's mane and hold onto the reins to keep her still. "She's calm now. Did you even know where you were going?"

Her mouth twists into a half-smile. "I was going to follow you."

"Mary, I—"

"I've never ridden a horse before."

"You what?" It takes my brain a beat to process this information. "You've never ridden a horse before. You could've broken your neck. You could've caused some serious harm to the horse. Do you have any idea how fucking irresponsible this was?"

Her eyes grow large with tears, and my anger ebbs away leaving me with the overwhelming desire to wrap my arms around her and tell her that everything is alright. No harm done. But of course, I don't.

"I didn't ask to see the portrait, Emmett. Fianna showed me, and then, when you showed up, I saw how much it meant to you..."

She's rambling, but I stopped listening after she said my name. The way it sounded on her tongue, like it was meant to be there, made me feel like even more of an asshole for yelling at her.

"You mounted a horse even though you had no idea how to ride her?"

The smile is almost back as she chokes out a sound somewhere between a laugh and a sob. "I know it was stupid. I wasn't thinking. I mean, I always thought it looked easy."

I peer out across the land towards the stream. This isn't quite what I'd planned, but I'm no longer angry with her. What she did was crazy, but I sense that her intentions were good—if she wanted to destroy me for drugging her, forcing her to wear someone else's engagement ring, and abducting her all the way to Ireland, she would be back inside the house doing it right now.

I check that her helmet is fastened securely, avoiding making eye contact, but feeling her green eyes on me the whole time. Then I check the saddle.

"No wonder you fell. You didn't even fasten it here." I show her the buckle that's flapping about beneath the horse's belly. "You had no control over her."

"Control. Right." She chews her bottom lip, and I wonder how it would feel to kiss those lips again. For real this time. Not because we're keeping up appearances.

"Do you want me to show you?"

Man, those eyes... She gazes at me, wide-eyed like I just told her she won the lottery, and I wonder if she has any clue just how goddamned sexy she is when she looks at me that way.

"Would you do that?"

"Here." I gesture for her to put one foot in the stirrup and hold her waist as she climbs up into the saddle, ignoring how good she feels in my hands. "Get comfortable. Make sure both feet are in the stirrups and hold the reins with both hands."

"Do I talk to her?" It's a genuine question, and I can't help smiling.

"So long as you don't expect her to answer you back."

She giggles, and I realize that this is the first time she has laughed because of something I've said. I want to hear it again.

"Now what?"

I show her how to urge Misty into a gentle walk and then I mount Jupiter, falling into step alongside her. We walk in comfortable silence. Mary is concentrating on staying in the saddle, which gives me the opportunity to watch her unnoticed.

She's graceful without even trying. There's no fear behind her eyes, only awe and respect for the horse, and gratitude for the new experience she has been given. Finally, my eyes settle on her profile, the flushed cheeks, the curve of her lips, the strands of unruly hair sneaking out of the helmet. My blood starts pumping around my body. Or more specifically, it starts pumping directly into my pants.

We stop and dismount by the stream. The ground is too cold and damp to sit on, so we tie the horses to a grand old oak tree and throw pebbles into the water. Mary has never skimmed a stone across the water's surface before and acts suitably surprised when I hit four hops.

"Chrysler isn't my real name." She tosses a stone sideways, mimicking my actions, and frowns when it produces a gentle plop. "I adopted it when I moved to New York."

"What's your real name?"

"Scanlan."

She faces me, and it suddenly slots into place: the faint accent, the sense that she belongs here, my mom's comment that Mary is a beautiful Irish name.

"I never felt as if I belonged here." She faces the water, chewing on her lip again. "That's an understatement. I didn't belong here. I spent most of my childhood in the foster care system being moved from foster family to foster family, none of whom understood that the word 'care' was in the system for a reason. So…" She inhales deeply. "As soon as I was old enough to leave, I booked myself a ticket to New York with the money I stole from my foster father's bank account."

She isn't looking for sympathy. She isn't waving her hands in the air and saying, "*Hey, look at me. As if I didn't have enough shit in my life already, you had to come along and abduct me, asshole.*" And I realize that I've never known anyone quite like Mary Chrysler before.

"Why New York?"

She turns to me and smiles. "It's the city that doesn't sleep. I thought I could lose myself in the big city. Blend in, you know. Become invisible."

Most people move away, leave their past behind to find themselves, but Mary wanted the opposite. It occurs to me then what a shameful waste that would be.

"Did it work?"

"Ha! It did until two days ago."

Cue one Emmett O'Hara and his game changing plan to kidnap her and save her life.

"Mary, I…"

What can I say? I'm sorry I dragged you all the way to Ireland and introduced you to a family that will never be yours. Because what kind of asshole would do that to someone who has never had a proper family to call her own?

But before I can say anything in my defense, a glint of silver in the water catches my eye. I put my hands on her shoulders and turn her around to face the stream. "Over there, Mary." I lower my head so that our cheeks are almost touching and point at the salmon that are swimming just beneath the water's surface.

"What am I looking for?" I feel her whisper-breath on my face and force myself to concentrate.

"Salmon. Watch the surface and you'll see them." Man, she smells so good. Her hair tickles my face in the breeze, and I want so badly to entwine my fingers in it and kiss her pale neck…

She gasps, jerking me back to reality. "I see them. They're huge."

I smile over her shoulder. Maybe I should move away from her right about now, put some distance between us before she realizes that I want to bend her over and fuck her from behind right here where anyone riding past would spot us. But I realize that she doesn't want me in that way, and who can blame her?

Then, she's looking right at me, and her eyes are even greener than I imagined, and when she licks her lips, I close the distance between us before I can stop myself.

My kisses are hard and hungry. I push my tongue into her mouth, and she tilts her head back to accommodate me, her hands sliding in my hair and clinging onto me like she doesn't want to let me go. She wants this too. She wants this as much as I do.

I pick her up, wrap her legs around my waist, my tongue still in her mouth. Her eyes are closed. But she doesn't pull away.

I take her to the closest tree, set her down with her back against the gnarled trunk. I fumble with the zip of her coat while our tongues meet inside her mouth. Yanking it open, I lift her sweater and expose her breasts, pulling away just long enough to look at them.

She's so fucking beautiful.

"Emmett..."

I smother her mouth with mine again, sharing my oxygen with her, the blood pumping into my cock and erasing everything else that's going on in my mind.

"I want you so fucking badly, Mary..."

I scrape her hair away from her face, slanting her chin and tilting her head back even further. Her erect nipples are burning holes through my waxed coat, and I unzip it, shrugging it onto the damp grass behind me.

"Emmett, wait..."

My face is above hers, our eyes locked. "Do you want me, Mary? Say you want me."

"I-I want you, Emmett," she whispers.

It's all I need. I dip my head to her nipples, squeezing her breasts together and sucking on them both. I nibble them between my front teeth, tease them with my tongue, squeeze her breasts. My cock throbs when I hear her gentle groans.

I unfasten her jeans and drag them down over her hips, the flesh on her thighs popping with goosebumps. She gasps as the chill meets her exposed skin.

I drop to my knees in front of her, ignoring the damp seeping through my pants. The hair around her sex is so goddamned fair, with glimmers of red, that I take a moment to admire it before I spread her thighs with my hands and insert my tongue.

"Emmett!" She's panting. Her hand is in my hair. Her legs are trembling.

I find the spot and drag my tongue back and forth, peering up at her erect nipples as she arches her back and thrusts them forward. I want to see her face. I want to watch her come while I taste her orgasm on my tongue, but she has a fist stuffed into her mouth, and it's happening too quickly.

I stop, spread her thighs even wider and insert a finger. She's wet. I start fucking her with my finger, ramming it in all the way. Her pussy clenches around me, and she's so fucking tight.

I pull my finger out and stand up. I remove her fist from her mouth, and she looks dazed, ready to come all over me the instant I touch her again. I kiss her with my mouth open wide and fill hers with my tongue. When she responds, I slide my finger between our lips so that we're both tasting her at the same time.

And Mary laps it up. She opens her eyes, watching me, taking it all in.

"That's you, Mary," I murmur. "Do you like tasting yourself?"

"I..." She blinks several times.

"You taste so fucking good." I lick her off my finger, watching her reaction. "Say it, Mary. Say I taste so fucking good."

"I..." She stops and I lick her lips so that she can taste herself on me too. "I taste so good."

"No, Mary. I taste so *fucking* good."

She gasps as I slide my finger back inside her. I pin her against the tree trunk with my body and pull away, waiting for her to repeat it. When she doesn't, I try inserting a second finger, slowly, easing it in while she pants through it.

So fucking tight.

"I can't hear you, Mary."

"I taste so … fucking good."

I ram my fingers inside her and she leans forward on me, her breasts bouncing against my chest. "How does that feel?"

"Good." She gasps as I ram her again. "It hurts… Just a little."

"Shall I kiss it better?" My lips are on hers. "Mary, do you want me to kiss it better?"

"I don't want… Will anyone see us?"

"Don't worry about that, Mary. No one will come this way. It's just me and you."

"Yes, then. I want you to kiss it better."

I smile at her. Good answer.

On my knees again, I grab her thighs and raise her feet off the ground, pinning her between me and the tree. Spreading them wide, I can get my tongue right inside her, and fuck, she tastes good. She closes her eyes, screws them tightly shut, giving in to her orgasm which explodes onto my tongue.

I don't waste a beat.

I lower her feet back onto the ground, flip her around, and bend her over, unzipping my pants and pushing my cock into her from behind. It's like slamming into a wall. She wraps her arms around the tree, panting. Soft groans escape her mouth, and I lean over her, my cock still throbbing inside her, my lips on her ear.

"Is there something you want to tell me, Mary?"

"No."

I stick my tongue in her ear. "Are you sure?"

A shudder passes through her, and I push my cock in a little deeper. Trying to penetrate the wall.

"I'm sure."

"You wouldn't lie to me, Mary, would you?" I tease her with my tongue in her ear. Holding onto her hips with both hands, I push harder, releasing a breath when something gives. "Were you waiting for me all this time?"

My cock throbs with excitement. It's like this is my first time too, like our bodies were waiting for each other to come along, and I know I won't be able to control it for long.

"Yes," she gasps.

"Oh, Mary…"

I support myself against the trunk with one hand, and push her upper body lower with the other, so that I can feel the pressure of her pussy around my erection. Then I pull myself all the way out, slowly, enjoying that tightness.

"Are you ready for me, Mary?"

"Yes."

I take it slowly, all the way in, all the way out, until I can't hold it any longer. Gripping her shoulders tightly, I explode inside her, my pelvis thrusting against her perfect creamy ass.

When my cock has stopped throbbing, she squeezes me out with her pussy, and I zip my pants back up. I help her upright, pull her jeans back up to cover her nakedness, and lower her sweater over her perfect pink nipples. Then I fasten her coat and straighten her hair.

She watches me the whole time, those green eyes trying to see straight through me.

I kiss her on the lips. Gently. Nuzzle her nose.

"You're fucking beautiful, Mary."

"Emmett…"

"We should get back."

I take her hand and help her mount Misty before untying both horses and climbing onto Jupiter. I wasn't lying when I said that she was fucking beautiful. I wouldn't be lying if I said that what just happened was fucking amazing too. But walking the horses slowly back towards the house, the enormity of what I've done hits me all over again.

This isn't real. The ring on her finger doesn't mean a goddamned thing because it wasn't mine to give. We barely know each other even though we work in the same building in New York.

But all this pales when I think about Oisin. He'll never get married. He'll never get to experience what we just did. He'll never see another Christmas or meet the love of his life or hold his baby in his arms.

I don't deserve this. And I definitely don't fucking deserve Mary.

She looks so serene sitting on Misty's back, her cheeks flushed with excitement. I had to go and ruin it by crossing a line when all I had to do was be polite to her, get through Christmas, and send her on her way. Nope. Me and my testosterone just couldn't leave her alone, could we?

When we reach the stables, I help her to dismount, my hands tingling when they touch her.

"Mary, this doesn't change anything. I understand if you hate me, but when we get back to New York, we go our separate ways as planned."

And like the fucking coward I am, I walk away from her without a backward glance.

10

MARY

I'm numb.

Is he fucking kidding me?

From the stables, I watch him walk back into the house via the mud room, unable to move. Misty nudges my hand, and I rub her nose absentmindedly.

He'll come back, won't he? He'll realize what he's just done, turn around, and come back to apologize. That's what I tell myself, but the seconds tick by, and there's still no sign of Emmett.

I think about what happened down by the stream, my face flooding with heat. What is wrong with me? I knew Emmett didn't care about me, so why didn't I climb back onto the horse and ride back to the house instead of letting him fuck me from behind against a tree?

I groan out loud, turning closed eyes towards the heavy sky.

Because Emmett O'Hara knows how to turn on the charm, and when he does, he's fucking irresistible. No. I can't blame it

A Dark Mafia Christmas

all on him. I had the chance to say no, and I didn't, because he's hot, and there's a spark between us that wouldn't have allowed me to walk away when there was a chance it was going to be fanned out of control.

I'm a goddamned floozy, that's what I am.

"Fuck!" All those promises to myself to never let a man get too close, and what did I do? I let him screw me in broad daylight where anyone could've seen us.

My face grows so hot I could fry an egg on it. What do I do now? How can I face him in front of his family knowing what we've done? No wonder they were surprised to hear that we're engaged to be married—they must all know that he's an arrogant, egotistical fucker who fucks around with women's emotions.

I wish they'd warned me. I wish Fianna had taken me aside yesterday and told me to run while I still had the chance. I thought she was on my side, but she's his cousin, of course, she'll see no bad in him.

I stare at the back of the house, at the fairy lights twinkling behind every window, and imagine the family inside preparing the next meal, cracking open a bottle of Bailey's and a tub of chocolates, and arguing over which movie to watch first.

"You dumbass, Mary," I mutter to myself.

I'm good enough to fuck, but not good enough to be a part of the O'Hara family. I fell for the oldest trick in the book. *You're so beautiful, Mary. You taste so good, Mary. I'm so full of fucking shite, Mary, I believe my own lies.*

Confusion gives way to anger. I'm not sticking around for the next nine days, pretending to be his fiancée, even if it puts me in jeopardy. And I don't care if the psycho thug from the roof knows the fucking Pope. Emmett O'Hara doesn't get to treat me like trash and then shake me off like this.

Screw him.

Screw his family too.

Only I don't want to screw his family because they've welcomed me into their home with open arms. They deserve a better son. Although I'm sure they'd never agree with me.

Determined to grab the clothes I arrived in and sneak back out of the house without anyone spotting me, I enter the mud room and almost collide headfirst with Fianna.

"There you are. I wondered where you'd got to when Emmett came back alone." Her smile fades as she watches me remove the waxed coat and replace it on the hook. "What's happened?"

Her tone has changed, becoming concerned rather than excited, and I have to chew my bottom lip to stop myself from telling her what happened by the stream.

"I fell off the horse." I force a smile. "It's fine, I'm not hurt. Emmett helped me up and gave me an impromptu riding lesson."

Her smile is so genuine that guilt swirls about inside my gut all over again. "Did you ride Misty? Isn't she lovely?"

She links arms with me, and we head back inside the house. So much for sneaking out unnoticed. I'll spend some time with them and make an excuse to go up to my room as soon as I get the chance.

She keeps up a steady stream of chatter all the way to the living room. "We're getting the games out. We need you to persuade

Emmett to join in, he's such a killjoy about these things. And a terrible loser. But you must already know that."

Well, I would, if any of this was real.

The whole family is there. *Elf* is playing on the vast, flat-screen TV on the wall. The two grannies are sitting in armchairs, small glasses of sherry on the coffee table between them. Patrick and his brothers are sitting around a cribbage board set up on the long glass coffee table in the middle of the room, while the twins are arguing over a game of Guess Who?

Huge cushions have been scattered around the floor, and Sinead gestures for me to sit next to her. They're about to open Cluedo, a *Nightmare Before Christmas* version.

"Choose a character, Mary. And watch out for Erin—she always cheats."

"I do not." Erin winks at me. "I can't help it if I have a photographic memory."

I've just gotten settled, if a little precariously, on a red velvet cushion, when Emmett comes in behind us.

"Emmett, you can join in too." Sinead waves him over. "We're having no Grinch behavior this year in front of Mary."

He sits down on the carpet, cross-legged, his eyes barely skimming mine, and I feel heat rise in my cheeks again. How could he do the things he did to me and then feel nothing?

Tears sting my eyes. It obviously meant nothing to him. He said it himself: this changes nothing. So, why was I still clinging to the tiny glimmer of hope that it would?

Stupid. Stupid. *Stupid!*

"We need Prosecco." I didn't even notice Fianna leaving the room, but now she comes back with a bottle glistening with condensation and fetches some tall crystal flutes from a cabinet across the room.

Emmett opens the bottle expertly and Clare pours. A team. The family unit that operates like clockwork because they each have a role to fill.

I sip the liquid and feel my gums fizz. Adrenaline is pumping through my veins so quickly the Prosecco doesn't even touch the sides. Maybe I'll stay here and get drunk instead, show Emmett up because his fiancée can't hold her drink. I swallow a mouthful and wait for it to work its magic.

I've never played Cluedo before, and it doesn't help that I can't concentrate with Emmett sitting directly across the board from me. Every time I look up from my little notepad, he averts his eyes like he's afraid I'll think he likes me or something.

Erin wins. Clare accuses her of cheating. Everyone laughs. And Fianna fetches more Prosecco.

I'm close to winning the second game, but Erin wins this round too.

"Maybe we should pair up," Fianna suggests. "I'll play with mom. Someone needs to keep an eye on her."

"I'll team up with Clare," Sinead says, "and Mary, you can play with Emmett, bring him some luck. He doesn't like losing."

Emmett smiles fondly at his mom and stands up. "I'm out. I have to make a few calls."

"Not on Christmas Eve, lad," his dad says from the sofa. "You stay right where you are, unless you're fetching some fecking beers from the fridge."

Emmett's eyes meet mine briefly, and he's the one who looks away. Is that guilt written all over his too-hot-to-be-true face? I hope it is. I wonder what everyone else in this room would think if they knew how the golden boy is treating his fiancée.

"Anyone else want a drink while I'm in the kitchen?" He glances around the room.

"Hold that thought." Granny Mary eases herself forward in her armchair, white knuckles gripping the arms. "I want to show Mary my engagement ring." She slides a hand into the pocket of her baggy cardigan and pulls out the ring that Fianna mentioned before.

I kneel in front of her, and she places the ring into the palm of my hand.

I sense everyone's eyes on me and make a silent prayer to God to make me like the ring. My mouth is dry from the Prosecco, and my lips still feel swollen from Emmett's kisses. How has no one noticed? Didn't they wonder why we were both missing at the same time earlier, or were they all too busy to notice?

I peer at the ring in my hand, my eyes lighting up when I see the delicate star pattern made up of a single sparkling diamond in the center, a circle of emeralds, and an outer layer of tiny sparkling diamonds forming the star shape around the outside. I pick it up and hold it so that it catches the fairy lights from the Christmas tree, casting dancing patterns across the room.

"Whoa, what's that?" The twins turn around to find the

source of the golden light, and immediately resume their game.

I told Fianna that I wanted a simple engagement ring, but in truth, I never really thought about it before. Holding this platinum ring in my hand though, I don't think I've ever seen anything more beautiful.

I glance at Granny Mary, who is watching me expectantly, tears welling in her pale blue eyes. "What do you think?"

"I love it." My shoulders slump.

This kind woman is offering me her own engagement ring because she thinks I'm going to marry her grandson, but I already know that I can't accept it. *This isn't real, Mary. When we get back to New York, we go our separate ways.*

"It truly is beautiful, but I can't wear it." I place it back in her hand and close her fingers around it. Then I give her a hug, squeezing her tightly while I blink away my tears. "Thank you. It's the most generous thing anyone has ever done for me."

"Someone get me a tissue." Sinead sobs from somewhere behind me.

"I don't understand." Granny Mary peers into my eyes when I release her. "It's yours, Mary. It's always been yours. Emeralds for your green eyes."

I'm sure that I can feel Emmett's eyes boring holes in the back of my skull, waiting for me to do the right thing. I wish that he would help me out here, but I know I'm in this alone.

"I..." Deep breath. Come on, Mary, let her down gently.

But before I can finish, Emmett appears behind the armchair, throws his arms around his granny's neck, and plants a kiss on her cheek. "Thank you, Granny. I think Mary is a little over-

A Dark Mafia Christmas

whelmed right now, but she's right. The emeralds will pick out the green in her eyes."

He smiles at me, and my heart does that funny fluttery thing that belongs in all good romance novels. Then my traitorous heart skips a beat when he goes down on one knee in front of me, removes the fake ring, and slides Granny Mary's ring onto my finger.

Everyone claps and cheers, apart from the twins, who are squabbling over their game of Guess Who? Another glass of Prosecco gets thrust into my hand and I clink it against what feels like a million other glasses.

I sip my drink, my eyes seeking out Emmett's, but his expression is unfathomable. Did he only do that because he didn't want to hurt Granny Mary's feelings? My heart doesn't know how to handle all the drama. Wouldn't it have been better to let her down now rather than in the New Year? I wish I could get inside his head and understand what's going on in there, but then I already know that I won't like what I find.

The rest of the day passes in a blur of games, food, more and more alcohol, and preparations for the big day. At bedtime, the twins prepare a tray with a homemade mince pie and a glass of port for Santa, and a carrot for the reindeer which they leave in front of the fireplace. We all go outside to scatter reindeer food across the lawn, oohing and aahing when it glitters in the glow of the lights decorating the outside of the house.

Then, with the boys tucked up in bed, we get cozy in the living room to watch *It's a Wonderful Life*. Emmett sits on the sofa and gestures for me to sit beside him, a fluffy blanket thrown across our legs. Like we're a couple.

If he's doing this for show, he has everyone fooled.

Including me!

It feels like the most natural thing on earth to be sitting so close to him, joining in the banter about the movie, laughing at the men when they get angry at themselves for losing a round of Rummy. At the same time, I'm hyper-aware of his thigh pressed up against mine, of the smell of his cologne with every breath I take, of his grandmother's engagement ring on my finger.

Afraid to pop the cozy Christmas bubble, I don't move until the movie ends, and everyone stands up to say goodnight. I wish I could've stayed in this moment forever, but when Emmett moves away from me to wish his mom goodnight, his absence is a stark reminder that this isn't going to last. It's make-believe. An act. And sadness crashes through me like a tidal wave.

Emmett walks me to the door of my guest room. The closeness of the evening spent in the living room was nothing like the closeness of our moment by the stream, but they're both equally bewildering.

I wish he would open up and tell me how he feels. How he really feels. Then at least I would know, one way or the other, and I could brace myself to deal with the consequences.

"Emmett…" I face him outside my bedroom door, unable to wrench my eyes away from his lips.

"I didn't want to hurt Granny's feelings. We can leave the ring here when we return to New York." He doesn't wait or expect a response. Instead, he kisses my forehead and walks back to his own room as if nothing has changed.

Everything has changed, I want to scream at him.

Everything has changed for me!

I go into the guest room that I'd entered with such eagerness the day before. Now, even with the bedside lamps switched on and the covers turned down, I shiver. I don't belong here.

At least I know where I stand, I guess.

I sit on the edge of the bed. Tomorrow, everyone will wake up excited, happy, smiling faces eager to open gifts and pitch in with preparing Christmas dinner. If I stay, I'll experience the kind of family festivities I've only ever dreamed of. The holidays will never be the same for me again because nothing else will ever live up to this.

Ever.

I take a deep shaky breath. I know what I must do.

When the house is slumbering, waiting for Santa's arrival, I put on the clothes I arrived in, drag my shoes on over a pair of Fianna's thick socks—I'm sure she won't miss a pair of socks —and find my jacket hanging in the wardrobe. It won't provide much warmth, but it wouldn't feel right stealing one of the warm coats from the mud room.

Leaving Granny Mary's ring on the dressing table, I open the door a crack and peer into the shadowy hallway. Silence. Tiptoeing outside, holding my breath, I close the door behind me with a gentle click.

I don't breathe as I hurry past Emmett's room. I can't hear a sound above the thump-thump of my heart, and the blood gushing around my veins, but I keep moving down the stairs and outside through the mud room which is furthest away from the bedrooms.

Outside, I stand on the doorstep taking deep breaths and wait for my pulse to regulate. The ground is covered with a fine film of white frosting. Just bloody perfect! Tomorrow the family will wake up to a white Christmas, and who knows where I'll be.

Because it's only just hit me that there'll be no public transport running on Christmas Day.

No turning back. If I don't leave now, I won't pluck up the courage a second time. Instead, I'll play happy families for the next nine days, getting to know Emmett's family the way his future wife would, and it'll be even harder to go back to New York when the holidays are over.

Deep breath. Come on, Mary, you can do it.

I step out onto the gravel driveway, my shoe crunching on icy frost. A snowflake lands on my nose, and I tilt my face towards the sky. The sky is gray-white, heavy with the snow still to come. I start walking, and it seems that with each step, the snowflakes grow larger, thicker, colder.

Fuck my life.

Head down, I pull the collar of my jacket up around my ears, hunch my shoulders, stuff my hands inside my pockets and keep walking. One foot in front of the other.

My blister is stinging before I reach the end of the driveway. My fingers are numb. Why didn't I pick up a pair of woolen mittens from the mud room before I left? Hypothermia is a thing, especially when someone has no clue where they're going.

Recalling the trip to pick up the Christmas tree the day before, I turn left when I reach the road and follow it back towards the closest village. I have no idea how far away it is or how long it will take me to walk there, but I hope I reach some form of civilization before morning.

I can't feel my toes. It's like walking on two blocks of ice, my shoes skidding occasionally on the fresh layer of snow. I haven't gone far when I start shivering uncontrollably. There are no street lamps along this rural road, and I'm surrounded by silent skeletal trees in both directions.

I shouldn't have drunk so much Prosecco. My eyes keep straying to the darkness lurking behind the thick trunks, imagining pitch-black eyes following me, my ears straining for the snap of a twig.

The shivering is making it hard to walk. This was a mistake, but I can't go back now. No one will be awake to let me into the house, and besides, I don't want to ruin their holidays if I wake up with a fever in the morning.

Especially when *none of this is real*!

My brain feels frozen too, locked onto the mantra: right foot, left foot. Where is the village? I was so absorbed by Emmett's closeness in the car that I can't remember how long it took us to drive there.

I'm so cold, chilled to the bone, that even my blood no longer feels like it's pumping around my body, and I almost cry with relief when I spot a small bus shelter on the side of the road.

My legs are trembling when I reach it. Made of toughened plastic, there's a wide opening, and a narrow wooden bench running along the back of the shelter, barely wide enough for me to lay on. Out of the snow and the wind, the immediate warmth provided by the meager shelter makes my eyelids heavy.

Huddled inside my jacket, my face resting on the cold bench, I close my eyes and drift off to sleep.

11

EMMETT

Christmas morning, everyone gathers in the kitchen for a fried breakfast. We've always done it this way for as long as I can remember, Buck's Fizz, breakfast, then gift opening around the tree in the living room.

The twins come running into the kitchen with the tray left out the night before for Santa. "He ate the mince pie."

"The reindeer only nibbled the carrot."

"Santa drank his juice though."

Mom and Dad exchange glances. It's always been family time, the only time of the year, according to Mom, when everyone switches off to what's going on outside these four walls. She's probably right. I haven't thought about work since I rode Jupiter down to the stream yesterday with Mary.

It was a stupid move. I let my dick control my brain without a thought for the consequences, and I knew as soon as we got back to the house that Mary wanted more. It was a big deal for her. Of course, it was. And even when I realized that it was her first time, did I stop and walk away? Like fuck, did I. I was already in way too deep, and that's what scared me.

"Where's Mary?" Fianna's question interrupts my reverie.

"She'll miss the Buck's Fizz." Mom gestures to the champagne in the ice bucket. "Go and wake her up, Emmett."

"Maybe we should let her sleep."

"She'll be disappointed if she misses anything." Mom isn't letting this go. "She was so excited about today."

Was she?

"Emmett," Dad joins in, "go get your girl. We're only waiting for Mary."

There's no point arguing with them.

Leaving the warm hustle and bustle of the kitchen behind, I head to Mary's guest room and stop outside. The room is silent. She must still be sleeping.

I knock gently, my knuckles barely grazing the door.

Nothing.

Okay. Maybe she had more to drink than I realized yesterday and is still sleeping it off. I rap the door harder three times, like it's a pre-agreed code. Then I listen.

Still nothing.

"Mary?" My fingers wrap around the doorknob. I don't want to barge in and scare the bejesus out of her, but I don't think she's going to hear me. I try one more time. "Mary?" Louder now.

When there's still no sound of movement from behind the door, I open it carefully, the door shushing across the carpet. I peer inside at the darkened room. The curtains are still closed, but the lamps are on, and I wonder if Mary is scared of the dark.

Then I realize that the bed is empty.

It's empty, but it's obvious that it hasn't been slept in because the covers are turned down neatly on one side, the way mom always likes it, and the comforter is still smooth.

Opening the door wide, I step inside, trying to make sense of the empty room. The clothes Mary wore yesterday when we rode down to the stream are folded neatly on top of the old-fashioned chest at the foot of the bed. A fleeting image of Mary bent over in front of me with her jeans around her ankles, pops into my head, and I brush it aside.

Where is she?

Then I spot Granny Mary's engagement ring on the dresser.

My stomach lurches sickeningly. Mary is gone. I don't know how or when or where she has gone, but I know exactly why she left. Me and my fucking big mouth.

"We can leave the ring here when we return to New York."

I couldn't leave it alone, could I? I had to be sure she understood that what happened yesterday changed nothing. Because I won't allow it to. I don't deserve happiness when I let Oisin down so badly. And Mary deserves better than being sucked into a life where no one bats an eyelid at spilt blood.

I cross the room and pick up the ring. Who am I kidding? Yesterday changed fucking everything. The way Mary looked at me... I can't remember the last time anyone looked at me that way. It sounds feeble and pathetic, but it made me feel special, and I don't know when, or if, I'll ever feel that buzz again.

I need to find her.

Sliding the ring into the pocket of my pants, I dash back downstairs to the kitchen. "Mary's gone." I grab my car keys from a hook on the wall. "I'm going to look for her."

"Gone?" Mom furrows her brow while the word sinks in with everyone else. "What do you mean gone?"

A hushed ripple spreads around the room.

"She isn't in her room. Her clothes are gone too." I don't mention the ring that's burning a hole in my pocket.

"Gone where?" Granny Nina sits forward in her seat, lines creasing her forehead.

"I'm coming with you." Fianna is already on her feet.

"When did she leave?" Dad asks. "She can't have gone far in this weather."

"We'll spread out." Uncle Sean takes control. "Ciaran, you take a car too. We'll search the land."

"Silly question," Mom says. "But she isn't somewhere in the house, is she?"

"Her bed hasn't been slept in." I'm already halfway out the door, Fianna close behind me.

We don't speak as we make footprints in the thick snow on our way to the car. It must've been snowing all night for it to be this deep and untouched; any footprints Mary might've made have been long since covered.

In the car, I crank up the heating and wait for the snow on the windshield to melt. I hope to fucking God she took a coat, or she'll die of hypothermia out there. What the hell is she playing at? It's one way to ruin everyone's Christmas.

"Did you have a fight?" Fianna's voice jolts me back to the present.

I slide the car into gear and drive slowly along the driveway. The snow is still falling, not heavily, but enough to make visibility difficult. I think of Mary wandering around in this weather without a decent coat and boots—if she's still alive when we find her, I'll fucking murder her myself for pulling such a dumbass stunt.

"No."

I pull out onto the road and turn left, Ciaran's brake lights visible in the rearview mirror as he heads in the opposite direction. Mary doesn't know the area, so I'm hoping she'll have headed towards Laragh, the closest village.

"Why did she leave then?" Fianna's gaze flits between me and the road ahead, the car's head beams carving arcs of light across the snow. "Something must've happened. Did she find out who you really are? What was it, huh? Did she read an email that mentioned bumping off someone you don't like?"

I've never heard Fianna speak about the family with such distaste, but I can't think about that right now. Mary is missing because I fucked her and then told her it didn't mean anything. And Fianna is right, that's who I am.

My anger dissipates when I think of my role in Mary's hasty departure. If anything happens to her, I'll never forgive myself. One death on my conscience is enough to deal with, but

Mary's presence here is entirely down to me, and there'll be no shaking this one off. Ever.

"I know there's something you're not telling me, Emmett."

Jeez, the O'Hara women know when to stick the knife in and keep twisting.

"Who is Mary really?" She keeps her voice low.

I think I spot movement in the glow of the headlamps and lean closer to the windshield, rubbing the inside of the glass with my sleeve to clear the steam. I slow the car to a crawling pace, but there's nothing there. My imagination playing tricks on me.

"She's Mary Chrysler. She works in IT." It's the truest thing I've said since I arrived.

I can't tell Fianna that our relationship is fake. Not yet. For her sake as well as Mary's. If Fianna knew the truth, she would tell me to be honest, to stand up to the people who tossed a man off the roof of my building, to do the right thing by Mary. Because, despite the dangerous family connections, she still looks for the best in everyone.

"What about you and Ronan?"

That's it, Emmett. Divert the attention onto the only other person in the car.

"What about us?" She turns her face away from me and stares out the passenger window.

"Don't try telling me that he has changed."

"People do change you know. You've changed. Mary has brought out the best in you."

I grip the steering wheel, keep my eyes on the road. I tell myself that she's only saying this because she likes Mary. She's on her side. She thinks this is all my fault.

It is all my fault. I slam the steering wheel with the heel of my hand.

Mary has brought out *something* in me, even I can't deny that. A softer side. A part of me that doesn't hate the festivities as much as I usually do. I mean, I watched *It's a Wonderful Life* all the way through last night without closing my eyes once or making a work-related telephone call.

I drive in silence. My thoughts are filled with images of Mary in that red dress at the party, her red hair tumbling over her shoulders. Mary dancing barefoot in the conservatory, her face flushed with excitement. Mary's breasts in my hands. Mary sitting straight-backed on Fianna's horse, her face so serene.

It isn't real.

She's only here because she witnessed a murder.

What happened yesterday by the stream was in the heat of the moment, fueled by the excited Christmas energy inside the house.

"What's that?" Fianna leans forward in her seat, the belt stretching across her chest, and points at a bus shelter at the side of the road.

A small black car is parked on the other side of it, the exhaust sending clouds of smoke puffing across the snowy verge. But it's the guy emerging from the shelter carrying something in his arms that I'm more worried about. Is that…

As I watch, Mary tries to wriggle free from the man's grip, pummeling his chest with her fists.

I slam on the brakes, the car swerving from side to side as the tires try to find purchase on the slippery road, and eventually stop on the verge before the bus shelter.

I'm out of the car almost before it has fully stopped, leaving the door open behind me. I hear Mary cry out, "Put me down!" and my vision turns red. I sprint the rest of the distance between the car and the shelter, the guy turning to face me, slack jawed. I've caught him red-handed with Mary in his arms.

He's wearing a beanie hat, and a black overcoat, but I barely register anything else about him. I grab Mary from him, her arms flailing until she realizes that it's me, and cradle her against my chest. Her head flops onto my shoulder. She's so cold, I can feel the chill spreading from her and through my clothes, making me shiver.

"What do you think you were doing?" I glare at the man.

Now that I've got Mary away from him, I can see his bloodshot eyes, and the way he's swaying on his feet. He's fucking drunk, and he was going to put Mary into his car and take her fuck knows where.

"I-I saw her in the shelter. She looked cold."

"So, you thought you'd take her somewhere in your car where no one would find her."

"Emmett..." Her voice sounds so weak, and I could kill the fucker for taking advantage of her. "Please don't." It occurs to me with a sharp stab of guilt that I'm the one who's guilty of abducting her, but at least my intentions were good, even if my actions were not. The same can't be said for this guy.

"It-it wasn't like that." He's a big guy, but he doesn't come at me, because he's a coward who picks on vulnerable women.

"Emmett." Fianna is out of the car and standing behind me. "Leave it. Come on, let's get Mary into the car."

"Yeah." The drunk guy punches the air with his fist. "Go on, get back in the car and drive back to wherever you came from." His expression twists into a sneer as he takes a step backwards, and I see red.

"What the fuck did you say?"

Mary, shivering so violently I'm afraid she'll shatter her bones, tugs my sweater to get my attention. Her face is pale, her skin transparent, and her lips tinged blue, her teeth chattering noisily.

"You found me?" Her voice is hoarse, and I wonder how long she's been inside the bus shelter. I need to get her back to the house and warm her up. "Are you going to take me home?"

"Mary? Is that your name?" The guy is still talking. What's it going to take to get rid of him? "Mary, do you want me to take you somewhere?"

What the fuck?

"You need to turn around, get in your car, and drive away while you still can." I keep my voice low, enunciating every word so that he knows I'm being deadly serious. "Now!"

His eyes narrow. The guy has a fucking death wish.

"Or what?"

That's what he's going with?

Fianna sidesteps around me. "Okay, that's enough, guys. It's Christmas Day. Please," she says to the guy in the beanie, "just go home and enjoy your day. We'll take over from here."

The man's eyes hop between Fianna and Mary who is still lying limply in my arms. "I want to hear it from Mary. I'm not the one who lost her, I'm the one who found her."

His words sting, and the red behind my eyes becomes a swirling mass of fire.

I glance at Mary. "Mary, I'm going to put you back inside the shelter, just for a moment. Fianna will stay with you."

"Emmett, don't." Fianna stands between me and drunk guy. A barrier. But it's too late.

I settle Mary on the bench inside the shelter and flash a warning at Fianna to make sure she doesn't move.

Three strides, and I'm back outside shoving the man in the chest. He stumbles backwards, arms flailing, but manages to stay upright. Then he comes at me, his fist narrowly missing my jaw.

I grab his arm and twist it behind his back, sending him sprawling face-first into the snow with one shove. "If I was you, I'd get back into my car now and drive away."

The guy clambers back onto his feet and tries rugby tackling my legs. But he's drunk, and I have the sober edge, dodging him easily. He lands in the snow a second time, his jaw colliding with the frozen ground beneath the layer of white.

I grab the back of his coat and haul him upright. Turning him around, I shove him back against the shelter, my fist circling his throat. His eyes bulge. His fingers claw at my arm. He reminds me of a fly trapped in a spider's web, and I can't bear the thought of him touching Mary.

"Listen to me carefully. If you ever come near me or my

woman again, I will personally see to it that you have no fingers left to touch another soul with. Do you understand?"

A clicking sound emits from his throat, as his fingers scratch my sweater.

"I'll take that as a yes. Now, I'm going to let you go, and you're going to get back in your car and drive off without a glance in your rearview mirror."

He's still struggling to breathe under my grip, his gray stubbly face turning puce.

"You want to make sure we never cross paths again because I never forget a face."

I shove him away from me, and he stumbles through the snow, dry heaving as he sucks in great gulps of cold air. He hesitates by the driver's door of his car, turns back to face me, and yells, "Fucking wanker!"

I don't waste a beat.

I run, and he scrambles inside the car, slamming the door behind him and driving away on squealing tires.

Adrenaline pumps through my body as I go back to the bus shelter, pick Mary up, and carry her back to the 4x4. Her eyelids flicker as I settle her on the backseat.

"Your woman?" she murmurs with a half-smile.

12

MARY

"Can I get you anything else?" Sinead has been fussing over me since Emmett brought me home, and I feel guilty because it's Christmas Day, and she should be opening gifts and checking the turkey in the oven instead of worrying about me.

"I'm fine, thank you."

I'm on the huge squashy sofa in the living room snuggled under a fluffy blanket. I've drunk two mugs of hot chocolate and eaten an entire tub of shortbread biscuits, and although I still can't feel my toes, I've stopped shivering.

"When are we eating breakfast?" one of the twins asks.

"We're skipping breakfast today," Sinead says. "But you can come and help me make pigs in blankets, and I'm sure Uncle Patrick will let you have some chocolate."

The boys follow their auntie to the kitchen leaving me and Emmett alone in the living room with the twinkling fairy lights and the aroma of roast turkey wafting through the doorway.

He sits on the end of the sofa and rests his elbows on his thighs, deliberately avoiding eye contact.

"I feel so bad for ruining everyone's day," I say. "Is it my fault no one ate breakfast?"

He looks at me then, and his expression seems softer somehow, as if I'm viewing him through a rose-tinted lens. "We always eat too much food on Christmas Day. It'll save till tomorrow."

Tears well in my eyes. I screwed up their Christmas, and everyone is still being nice to me. It's so much more than I deserve, and I know that I owe them an explanation.

"How are you feeling now?" Emmett finally looks at me.

"Aside from guilty?" He nods. "Tired. I feel like someone drained my blood and replaced it with some kind of liquid that never heats up." I swallow hard and hide behind my third hot chocolate. "How can I make it up to your family?"

His eyes dart to my fingers. He reaches into his pocket and pulls out Granny Mary's engagement ring. "You can start by putting this back on before anyone notices it's missing."

My tears start flowing. "I can't, Emmett. It isn't right."

"Why don't you let me worry about that, eh?" He kneels on the floor by the sofa, takes my hand, and slides the ring onto my finger.

It's so different to his first proposal, the fake one on the roof of his office building, that I start choking on the sweet creamy liquid. Two proposals, and I'm still not getting married.

He takes the cup from my hand and sets it down on the coffee table. "I'm sorry, Mary."

There goes my heart again...

"Sorry for what?"

"For ... everything."

I want more than this. My heart is going thump-thump inside my chest, waiting for him to take back what he said yesterday, when I already know that he hasn't changed his mind. He gave me back the ring to keep his granny happy, not because he has suddenly decided that he can't live without me.

Get real, Mary, for chrissakes.

"It's fine."

It's a million miles from being fucking fine, but I won't beg him to like me.

"My parents will want to know what happened. I'll tell them that we had a fight, I said some terrible things, and you didn't want to spoil their Christmas."

I blink back tears. He's only sorry that I ran away and made life more difficult for everyone. I should've just stayed here, played the part of the doting fiancée, ate all their food, drank their champagne, and flashed Granny Mary's engagement ring all over the place. Perhaps Emmett would've been happy then.

"Do you think they'll believe you?"

"I'll make sure they do. I'll tell them it was all me, Mary."

I want to say that it *was* all him, but I don't have the energy.

An image of the man at the bus shelter pops into my head. Was he trying to help? I was too frightened to read the situation, but Emmett threatened to chop his fingers off if he touched me again anyway. A shudder travels down my spine. I'm grateful to be safe and warm, but his reaction was a tad extreme.

I sense that Emmett is about to join his family in the kitchen, but there's one more thing I need to say first. "You called me your woman. You said: stay away from me and my woman."

I watch him closely as a lopsided smile appears on his face. "It was a figure of speech, Mary. I was angry." He stands up. "I'm going to see if Mom needs any help, and then I'll be back. Don't move, okay?"

"Okay."

I follow him with my eyes as he crosses the room. He stops in the doorway and turns around to face me, the same smile still playing on his lips. "No one has ever been more my woman than you, Mary Chrysler."

He leaves before I can say a word.

———

"I want to hand out the presents."

"No, it's my job."

"Boys, you can both do it." Clare must be so used to the twins' constant bickering that it no longer fazes her. Perhaps she doesn't even hear it, tuning it out like she can somehow turn down their volume.

Sinead places a warm hand on my arm. "I'm so sorry we didn't get you anything, Mary. Blame my son for not warning us that you were coming."

I smile. "It doesn't matter. Christmas isn't about gifts."

"Yes, it is." Joseph or Jamie—I can't tell them apart—frowns at me like I just grew a second head.

Everyone laughs, and I'm glad the attention isn't on me. I've taken up enough of their time today; I just want to melt into the background and watch them from afar.

Their piles of gifts grow, the boys excitedly dumping presents onto people's laps as they dip back and forth beneath the tree until every gift has found an owner. Then they sit down and tear the paper off two identical gifts. Scooters.

"Whoa!" They both say in unison. "Can we try them out?"

"Not in here." Sinead stops them from jumping up and racing around the room. "You can take them outside when it stops snowing."

They go around the room, taking turns to open a gift so that everyone gets to see what they've got. Sinead unwraps her gift from Emmett: A Ted Baker bathrobe and a spa weekend-for-two at Dromoland Castle.

"Aw, you sweetie." Sinead blows him a kiss from across the room. "Did Sonia choose this?"

I can't believe she said this, but Emmett only hangs his head in mock-shame. "You got me, Mom. I've been busy lately."

"Lucky your mother loves you, Emmett." Patrick shakes his head but doesn't seem surprised by his son's confession. His gift from his son is an antique gold cribbage board. I don't understand the game, but tears well in Patrick's eyes as he holds the board up for everyone to see.

Fianna goes next. Her gift is a trouser suit from Prada on Fifth Avenue. Her eyes light up when she sees the emerald-green suit complete with gold accessories, and she throws her arms around Emmett's neck, squeezing him tightly.

I envy her this natural reaction, this closeness to her cousin, the effortless abandon with which she hugged him. When she looks at Emmett, she sees the cousin she grew up with, the businessman who lives in New York and flies home for special occasions, the guy who tolerates Christmas for his family's sake.

Whereas when I look at him... When I look at him, I see someone who makes my heart skip around like a child who ate too many sweeties, and I don't even know when or how this happened. But so much has changed since we came to Ireland that I can barely even recall how badly I wanted to hurt him for drugging me and bringing me here.

I sit in my bubble on the sofa, part of the festivities but outside of it at the same time. I don't mind. It gives me a chance to watch Emmett unnoticed. He's aloof, detached from the family even though they seem oblivious. Sure, he smiles and laughs in all the right places, he appreciates his gifts, he even helps the twins open a Monster Truck Lego set and starts building with them. But his heart isn't in it.

Yes, that's it. His heart is elsewhere.

Is it another woman? Is that why he keeps reminding me that this isn't real? Every time he claims to be making business calls, is he really speaking to his girlfriend back in New York? The thought makes me feel queasy, and my pulse starts racing.

It would explain his complete three-sixty on the way back from the stream yesterday. I'm such an idiot. Why did I fall for the charm when I already knew about his reputation as a player? I made the classic mistake of thinking I could change the womanizer, and now I realize how stupid that was.

So, why did he say what he said earlier? *"No one has ever been more my woman than you, Mary Chrysler."*

Like, what does this even mean?

I hear my name mentioned and am jolted back to reality. What did I miss?

Everyone is staring at Emmett like they're waiting for him to perform a magic trick or reveal the punchline to a joke.

Fianna, realizing that I'm clueless, says, "I just asked Emmett what he bought you for Christmas, Mary."

Am I imagining it, or does Fianna know more than she should? She always seems to ask the right questions, the kind of questions that put us on the spot.

I think quickly. "We said that we weren't buying gifts for each other. We have a wedding to plan." I smile and shrug, praying that they all buy it as an excuse. I mean, getting married isn't cheap, but then of course, I'm forgetting that Emmett O'Hara is a billionaire playboy businessman.

Fuck!

"Actually, I do have a gift for Mary." Emmett stands, and heat floods my cheeks.

He smiles at me as he navigates his way across the room avoiding unwrapped gifts and the mountain of scrunched up paper in the middle. What is going on here? Is he going to give me the gift he bought for his real girlfriend back in New York? Is this another piece of jewelry that I'll have to hand back before we leave?

I chew my bottom lip and avoid meeting anyone's eyes.

I don't want someone else's gift. I thought Emmett came and found me this morning and brought me back here because he was worried about me, and now he's going to go and ruin everything again by giving me a present that doesn't belong to me.

He comes back into the room, and I hardly dare raise my eyes to see what he's holding. Come on, Mary, pull yourself together and act! Act surprised and pleased like your life depends on it. Which maybe it does.

I was expecting a small jewelry box wrapped up with a neat red bow, but Emmett is holding what looks like a painting in his hands.

"Sorry, I haven't wrapped it, Mary." He shrugs. "I hope it will make up for the stupid things I said to you yesterday."

Okay, is this for real, or is he still covering for my failed runaway attempt in the night?

He turns the painting around, and my heart literally starts trying to hammer its way out of my ribcage. It's me. It's a head-and-shoulders painting of me, wearing the red dress Fianna loaned to me the night we arrived, my hair loose and tumbling over my shoulders.

"I..." I think I'm supposed to say something, but my brain isn't cooperating.

I study the picture. Emmett has somehow made me look beautiful but in a shy, understated way. I'm smiling out of the canvas as if I'm posing in front of a camera, and I have no idea how he captured me so exquisitely when he barely seems to look at me.

"What do you think?" He's watching me, gauging my reaction, waiting for me to speak.

"How...? I mean, when did you paint this?"

"At night, and when you thought that I was in town sorting out some business stuff."

He almost sounds quite humble, and I tear my eyes away from the portrait to look at him. Emmett O'Hara is hot. I mean, it's no surprise that he has a reputation for being a player. But right now, standing there with a painting of me in his hands, he looks like a regular guy trying to impress a girl. He looks almost vulnerable.

On impulse, I jump up from the sofa, run across the room, and throw my arms around his neck, almost bowling him over. "I love it. No one has ever given me a present like this before."

"Aw, she's done it again," Sinead's voice reaches us from her spot on the other sofa.

"Quick, guys," Clare says. "Where are the tissues?"

CHRISTMAS DINNER IS A NOISY, raucous, fun-filled affair. Patrick carves the turkey at the table; Emmett keeps the sparkling wine flowing; and we all wear paper crowns while telling corny jokes pulled from Christmas crackers.

For a while, I forget about how I came to be there. I forget about the murder on the rooftop, Emmett fucking me by the stream, our fake engagement, and the thought of flying back to New York. Granny Mary's ring feels like it belongs on my finger, and I allow myself to revel in being part of this huge welcoming family.

When we're all stuffed with turkey, roasted potatoes, pigs in blankets, and more vegetables than I can count, followed by homemade Christmas pudding and brandy butter, Patrick announces a toast to the future Mr. and Mrs. Emmett O'Hara.

My pulse races. I still don't know how Emmett is going to react, even after seeing the portrait. I mean, he must have spent some time studying me to have captured the likeness the way he did but studying someone and having feelings for them are two entirely separate things, and I don't even know why I'm still clinging to that glimmer of hope that what we did meant something to him.

So, my heart lets me down again when Emmett leans closer and kisses me on the lips while one of the twins holds a sprig of mistletoe above our heads.

Everyone around the table cheers. But I don't hear them. I'm floating outside of my body, watching Emmett kiss me because I might have zero relationship experience to compare this to, but it sure as hell feels like he means it.

We spend the rest of the day in a food coma in front of the TV while the twins open all their toys and scatter them around the living room until it begins to resemble FAO Schwarz.

I must doze off during *White Christmas*. When I wake up, the fairy lights are still sparkling on the tree, but Emmett and I are alone.

I yawn, blink back tears and sit up on the sofa. "How long have I been asleep?"

"A couple of hours." His mouth twists into the hottest smile I've ever seen.

"You should've woken me up. I didn't thank your parents for dinner."

"You don't need to thank them. I think... I think they're enjoying having you here. And my mom would cook that much food if it was only the two of them here for Christmas."

I smile. This is every Christmas I've ever dreamed of, rolled into one sparkling snowy ball. But there's still something niggling away at the back of my brain, and I'll never forgive myself if I don't mention it now while I've got Emmett to myself.

"Emmett, is there..." I wish there was an easy way to come out with this. "Are you seeing someone back in New York?"

He strokes my leg absentmindedly with his thumb through the blanket someone threw over me while I was asleep. Round and around. Making circles on my thigh. And I think I already know the answer.

Finally, he looks me in the eye and says, "No, Mary. There isn't anyone else."

13

EMMETT

We spend the next couple of days playing games, eating food, drinking Prosecco, eating more food, and dragging sleds up the hill. Typical family Christmas. No one believes Mary when she tells us that she has never been on a sled before.

"Emmett, you'll have to ride with her," Mom says. "We don't want her breaking her neck on her first Christmas with the family."

Mary climbs onto a sled, sits down tentatively like she just agreed to a skydive, and I climb on behind her, trapping her between my legs. I can feel her body heat through my jeans, and when I lean forward and brush her ear with my lips, a shiver travels down her spine.

"Hold on tight, Mary."

I grab the rope, adrenaline coursing through my veins. It's been years since I've been sledding, but I've watched the twins go down the hill without falling off, and it must be like sex, right? Something you never forget.

I push us off, and we're flying faster than I remembered, snow spraying out from under us, and Mary is laughing so much that I can feel her breaths juddering through her body. She's pressed up against me. All I can think about is the feel of her ass between my legs and the citrussy scent of her shampoo from beneath her beanie hat.

We hit a bump right at the bottom of the hill, and we both tumble off the sled. I sprawl face-first in the snow like a starfish, the oxygen leaving my lungs momentarily.

I turn my face sideways to find Mary spreadeagled, face buried in the snow. She raises her head to look at me, and I'm about to ask her if she's hurt when she hurls a handful of snow my way, catching me right in the mouth.

I splutter, wiping my face with my gloved hands, buying myself some time. I see the way her smile fades, concerned that I'm not laughing, and before she can apologize, I'm on top of her, smooshing snow in her face and pinning her down so that she can't escape.

"Ugh! Get off me." She tries pushing me off halfheartedly, laughing too hard to put any force behind it. "Stop, I can't breathe."

I pause for a beat, and the little minx twists herself around beneath me, shoves my hat off, and rubs snow in my hair.

"Playing dirty, huh?" I push her backwards like a snow angel and pin her arms above her head easily with one hand. Before I can think about what I'm doing, my tongue fills her mouth, and she closes her eyes, giving into our mingling breaths. I don't even feel cold. Her body is all I need, and this realization is quite liberating.

She kisses me back, chasing my tongue with hers, and it's this raw passion that surprised me so much down by the stream. Mary isn't like other women. She's like a flower blossoming for the first time and my erection is proof that I want to be the one to open her up. Nothing else exists in the moment.

Until Uncle Ciaran slides past us and catches me on the side of the head with a giant snowball.

I straddle her, the tip of her nose pink, her eyes boring into mine. I want her to say something. I want her to tell me how she feels, but instead, a smile stretches her lips, and she says, "Go, get him."

The moment passes.

Whatever it was.

I know she felt it too, and I float back up the hill, my heart thumping in time with my footsteps.

That afternoon, we all drive down to Jake's bar in the village. It's a small, cozy pub with low ceilings and dark wood beams. The bar counter, I inform Mary, is made from a railway sleeper, and the pub has been in Jake's family for generations. Jake is a tall, broad-chested guy with a thick mop of salt-and-pepper hair, permanently rosy cheeks, and a wide smile that reveals a gold tooth on top.

Everyone in the pub knows the O'Hara family, and it takes us a while to reach the table with all the back-clapping and hand-shakes and Merry Christmases being exchanged.

Mary sits next to me on the cushioned bench, her thigh pressed up against mine. Something has changed between us since I gave her the portrait. She is more attentive, more relaxed around me, more natural, as if she has stopped pretending to be my fiancée and this is who she really is.

It's hard to believe that she works for me, and I've never noticed her before.

I like what I see.

My family seems to have noticed the difference too. Mom winks at her conspiratorially whenever Mary catches her eye and she thinks I'm not watching, as if she knew all along that this would happen.

Still buzzing from the sledding, I slide my hand onto her thigh beneath the table, and she sucks her bottom lip to stop herself from smiling. My head fills with an image of me sliding my cock into her mouth, and I shake it away. I won't be able to sit here all day with an erection, without wanting to drag her outside and fuck her up against the back wall. Next time, we're going to do it properly.

Next time.

Mary orders Guinness—we insist that it's good for you because of its iron content—and swallow a mouthful, grimacing at the unusual flavor. Everyone around the table laughs. I cup her face in my hands and, using my thumbs, wipe away the creamy moustache left behind by the drink. She peers at me with those beautiful green eyes, and I see the heat rising in her cheeks.

Having this effect on her just by touching her face makes my cock twitch. I need to fuck Mary Chrysler again. I need to fuck her every way I can think of, and then some.

"Patrick would've let me wander about with froth on my face for the rest of the day." Mom laughs, dragging me away from thoughts of Mary naked, her ass in the air while I fuck her from behind. "I always knew my Emmett was a keeper."

"Just a shame it took him so long, eh, Sinead?" Auntie Erin joins in.

"You can't hurry perfection." I don't even know where it comes from, but Mary almost chokes on her Guiness, and I hide my smile behind my drink.

A hush settles over the table though when the Blackthorns enter the pub and make a beeline for us. My spine immediately tenses. I remove my hand from her thigh, and ball it into a fist. I don't know what game Fianna is playing with him, but nothing will ever persuade me to like the guy.

"What's he doing here?"

"Emmett." Fianna flashes a warning look my way before turning around and smiling up at him.

The guy bends down and kisses Fianna's cheek, and I can't prevent the growl rumbling deep inside me like a dog sensing danger.

"Merry Christmas, all." Ronan's gaze drifts around the table and settles on Mary. The bastard does it deliberately. "How are you enjoying your first Irish Christmas?"

"It's been the best." Mary smiles with genuine affection at my parents. "I'm still waiting for someone to pinch me."

Unprompted, Ronan leans across the table and pinches the flesh on the back of her hand, and I want to punch him right here, right now. "Aye. You're still here."

Erin and Sean exchange glances, and I get the feeling that they don't like the thought of this guy with their daughter either. Who can blame them after what he did to Oisin? What does she even see in him? All I see is a bully with pumped-up biceps and an ego to match, but I understand my dad's need to keep the peace.

He asks if anyone wants a drink, goes to the bar, and comes back carrying a tray of glasses, which he sets down on the table before squeezing next to Fianna on the end of the bench opposite Mary and me. It's as if a rain cloud is hovering above our heads. The easy banter between family members has been replaced by stilted conversation and periods of silence, something that hasn't occurred since we arrived.

But what unsettles me the most is that whenever I look at Ronan, I catch him staring at Mary.

Later, Mary goes to the restroom, and I watch her pass the group of men standing at the bar drinking stout with whiskey chasers. They're loud, their voices booming around the pub and drowning out the music playing from the jukebox and the growing hum of conversation.

Keep on walking, Mary, I think to myself.

But she must catch a glimpse of a thick neck in a black turtleneck sweater and hear a voice that sounds familiar because she freezes.

Declan.

Then, right on cue, he turns his head, raising a glass to his lips, and I see it in her face that she knows where she has seen him before. She watched him throw a man over the edge of the roof during the office party. She witnessed a murder and then got dragged into a situation that was entirely out of her control, it's unlikely she will ever forget his face.

Fortunately for Mary, she doesn't know the guys he's drinking with. The other dons.

They're the reason I brought her here. No one would've believed the fake proposal if I spent my first Christmas as an engaged man without my fiancée. But I never thought we'd come face-to-face with them.

But the question is: what will Mary do about Declan?

Perhaps I should've warned her. I've had ample opportunities to tell her that he would be nearby while we're out and about, and that it would work in our favor if the families saw us together. But the situation is precarious enough without lighting a flame beneath her anxiety with a flippant comment like, "Hey, you know the thug on the roof? Yeah, we'll probably see him down at the local pub."

After what feels like hours, she keeps walking, and I release a breath I didn't realize that I was holding.

Declan's gaze roams the seating area. His eyes settle on me, and he raises his pint in a toast. All good. He settled my business on the roof. Which means that we have the green light to fake an argument and go our separate ways once we're back in New York.

Only, I'm not entirely certain that's what I want.

Mary might not know it, but I've spent every waking moment since I came home with her face center stage in my mind. Capturing her on canvas was nowhere near as difficult as I'd expected it to be because I was able to study her while she slept on the flight here. She'd probably freak out if she knew that, but man she's easy on the eye.

Ronan's cell phone rings and he stands, murmuring at the table in general that he'll take the call outside. I watch him leave, Fianna's eyes on me.

Something is making me feel uneasy. I can't even follow the conversation at the table while Mary is out of sight.

Fianna nudges my knee with hers. "I never thought I'd see you so lost without a woman by your side." She gives me a sly smile and sips her wine.

A comeback is on the tip of my tongue, but Ronan comes back into the pub with a whoosh of cold air from outside. Instead of coming back to the table, he heads towards the restrooms.

I wait. Maybe I'm being paranoid because I don't trust the guy, but Mary isn't back yet, and he has gone out of his way to antagonize me since the party.

Thirty seconds pass by, and I can't believe Mary has turned me into the kind of guy who hangs on every moment that his woman is away from him, but I know that my gut's right when I see Declan, the guy from the roof, set his pint down and head towards the restrooms. They're not throwing a private party out there, so it can only mean one thing: he senses trouble brewing too.

I stand abruptly, knocking the table with my thighs and spilling drinks over the sides of glasses.

"Emmett?" Fianna's eyes are wide. "Where are you going?"

"I'll be back in a moment."

"You won't do anything silly?"

I don't respond. My pulse is racing because Mary still hasn't come back from the restroom, and I don't like this churning feeling in my stomach. If anyone touches her...

When I reach the corridor leading from the bar to the restrooms, Declan is standing back, hands balled into fists, elbows out and muscles pumped, which is his go-to stance. "Everything alright here?" I hear him say.

I follow his gaze and find Mary with her back to the wall, Ronan's arms either side of her head, his body too close, preventing her from moving.

"All good here," Ronan shoots back over his shoulder without glancing round. "Nothing for you to worry about."

"I was speaking to the lady," Declan says.

"Let me pass," Mary says loudly enough for us to hear.

I've seen enough. I push past Declan, who doesn't try to stop me. Grabbing the back of Ronan's sweater, I yank him away from Mary, his beady eyes widening with surprise. I shove him across the hallway, and he crashes against the opposite wall.

Mary gasps when she realizes what's happened.

My eyes roam her up and down, making sure that she's not hurt. I swear if I'd found a hair out of place, I'd kill the bastard, but she gives a barely perceptible shake of her head, as if she knows what's going on inside my head.

But Ronan recovers quickly. Without wasting a beat, he swings a punch at my face, pure hatred in his twisted expression. I dodge it easily, catching him in the gut with a swift blow. The guy doubles over, clutching his abdomen. But I'm not letting him go that easily. He made a play for my fiancée, and no one gets to do that and walk away unscathed.

I grab his shoulders and shove him back against the wall, pinning him down with my lower arm against his throat. "Go near her again, and you won't see next Christmas."

Ronan's lips twist into a sinister smile. "Who rattled your cage? It was just a friendly chat."

"*You* rattled my fucking cage when you got too close to my fiancée." I can't even stand the sight of him, and it scares me how much I want to hurt him in the moment.

"Emmett, it's okay." I hear Mary's voice from somewhere outside my subconscious. It registers, barely, that she wants me to back down, to walk away and let it go.

But the guy is obviously not prepared to go down without a fight. Maybe a fight was what he wanted all along. His body seems to go limp, and then in one fluid movement, he raises his knee and rams it straight into my groin.

"Emmett!" Mary cries out.

As I double over to contain the pain, Ronan catches my jaw with his fist, and I sprawl backwards. Mary tries to reach me, but Declan grabs her arm and holds her back.

I don't want her to see me fighting. I don't want this to be one of the memories she holds on to when we're back in New York, but no one gets to touch Mary while I'm around. *No one*. Especially not this arrogant fucking bully who tried to destroy my cousin Oisin.

I drag myself back onto my feet, testing my jaw with my hand while Ronan watches with that smug smile on his face. Without warning, I lunge at him, my head colliding with his diaphragm. Ronan lands on his back, his skull connecting with the floor, and I drag him upright by his sweater., shoving him against the wall

Winded, he doesn't move apart from the rise and fall of his labored breathing. Then the smile sneaks back across his face. "You should learn to control that temper. It'll get you into trouble one day."

The strange thing is that my temper is no longer red-hot now that he has opened his mouth. A calm has settled over me because I can see him for the slimy cowardly snake that he is. "Apologize to Mary."

"What for?" He shoots a look Mary's way as if searching for validation. "We were just chatting. No law against that."

"She asked you to let her go, and you ignored her."

"Banter." He shrugs. "We've all had a drink. She didn't mean it—"

I aim a punch at his gut, but my arm is grabbed mid-swing by an iron fist. My dad. "Let it go, son. He isn't worth it."

Fianna is with him. Her gaze hops between me and Ronan, and I pray that she doesn't go to him. Instead, she places an arm around Mary's shoulders and we all make our way back to the table, leaving Ronan alone in the corridor.

14

MARY

Emmett is quiet in the car on the way back to the house. I can't tell if he's angry with me because he thinks I encouraged Ronan to flirt, or if he's embarrassed about fighting in a pub like a teenager. We're barely through the door when he grabs my hand and leads me upstairs.

"We'll be back down for dinner," he says over his shoulder to his mom.

His fist is like metal around my hand. My heart is thumping. Part of me—the sensible, level-headed part that has protected me through everything that has ever happened to me—wants to yell at him to let me go. But the other part—the part that was zapped into life when he fucked me down by the stream—is screaming at me to hold on tight and enjoy the ride.

What if he's going to tell me it's all over now though, I argue with myself.

What if he wants me to take off the engagement ring and fly back to New York with Dave, the bodyguard?

What if I never see him again after this?

We stop outside his bedroom door.

"Emmett...?"

His mouth is on mine before I can gauge where this is going, and my tongue responds to his with desperate frantic movements. I hear the gentle groans coming from me, and I can't believe that I'm even capable of them.

He opens the door, our mouths still locked together, and we practically fall through the doorway and into his room. The room is in a shadowy twilight state—it was light when we went out—like falling into a cocoon.

My pulse is racing. I already know that I'll do whatever he wants me to do because I have never wanted anyone the way I want Emmett O'Hara right now.

Without warning, he drops his pants, his cock springing free and resting against my stomach. I instinctively reach for it and get a brief sensation of velvety smooth hardness before he pushes me down onto my knees in front of him.

He rubs his cock around my face leaving a wet trail across my cheeks, my eyelids, my chin. Pressing it against my lips, I keep them shut, afraid that I won't know what to do with it when it's in my mouth. I part my lips just enough to taste him, and a shudder of anticipation travels through me.

"Open your mouth for me, Mary." The voice is disembodied as I stare at his cock, the fair wiry hairs at the base, the faint line of fuzz running up his abdomen towards his belly button.

There is something about being on my knees with his cock in my face that threatens hysteria to gurgle out of me, but then I feel the tingling sensation between my legs, the way my pussy pulses, and I know that it isn't hysteria. It's desire. Emmett O'Hara in an expensive suit with that air of arrogance riding his shoulders is the kind of man I wouldn't look twice at, but here in Ireland, with his pants around his ankles, knowing that he would protect me with his life...

This Emmett O'Hara is irresistible.

I open my mouth, and he slides his cock in. Slowly. My lips clamping around it.

"Suck me, Mary."

I do as I'm told. I don't even know why, when I could easily tell him to fuck off, stand up, and walk away without a second thought. Only, I do know why. If I walk away now, I'll probably never experience again what I felt down by the stream, and if this is all I can take with me back to New York, then I'm going to take everything that he has to offer.

I suck the end of his cock, teasing it with my tongue, tasting the sticky wetness around the head. But then he pushes it further, and I instinctively gag, tears welling in my eyes.

I pull away, gripping the base with one hand, and catch my breath.

"Take it slowly," he says. "I know you can do it, Mary."

I peer up at him, and our eyes meet. Suddenly, I want to do it. I want to make him feel the way he made me feel by the stream.

His cock is already probing my mouth, parting my lips like they were made for this. I close my eyes and open my mouth wider, letting him in. This time, I control how far his erection goes, clamping my teeth around him and nibbling him gently. I grip the base tightly, enjoying the way Emmett groans when my hand slides along it.

Finally, I find my rhythm. Holding him tightly, I suck harder, easing him in and out of my mouth with my hand, synching my movements with his breathing.

A thrill of excitement runs down my spine when I sense that he is getting close to coming. I'm doing this, I tell myself. His pleasure is my pleasure, like I've just discovered a new gift I never knew I had.

I taste his pre-cum, and he pulls out quickly, pulling me back up onto my feet.

"Strip for me, Mary."

I shake my head. "I... I don't—"

"Do it." His tongue is in my ear, his warm breath on my neck, and I unzip my jeans with trembling fingers.

He pulls away and watches me step out of my jeans and pull off my socks. I remove my sweater and toss it onto the floor as I stand in front of him in my bra and panties. Goosebumps pop on my arms and legs, not from the cold but from his intense stare.

"Take them off."

I unclip my bra and shrug it onto the floor. Emmett's cock twitches when he looks at my breasts, but he doesn't touch me. I slide my panties down over my hips and kick them aside too.

Then, taking me by surprise, he pulls his pants back up, covering his erection, and tells me to lie down on the bed.

"Open your legs, Mary."

I spread my legs wide, and Emmett watches me from his position near the doorway. Then he comes and lays down beside me, stroking my breasts with his fingertips and studying me the way an art expert might study a painting by a classic artist.

His fingers travel down, teasing my pubic hair, a faint smile on his face. "You're so fucking beautiful."

Then, he inserts a finger inside me, probing, pushing, feeling his way around.

"How does that feel?"

"Good," I gasp.

"How about this?" He inserts another finger.

I nod, not trusting myself to speak.

"You're so tight, Mary." There's such a look of concentration on his face, as though he's mapping inside me with his fingers, that I want to kiss him all over.

Raising myself onto my elbows, I kiss him hard, forcing my tongue into his mouth before he can take control. I sense the smile in his eyes.

"How do you want me, Mary?"

Huh? How am I supposed to answer this?

"Like this?" He removes his fingers and straddles me, still fully clothed, his pants rubbing against my pussy. "Or did you like it from behind?"

"Yes." I chew my bottom lip. "I liked it that way."

He gives me a lopsided smile. "Brace yourself, Mary, because

I'm going to give it to you every way I can think of. And then some."

He slides over the foot of the bed and drags me towards him so that my sex is in his face. Spreading my legs wide, he starts licking, gently at first, and then getting harder and deeper, his tongue dragging across my clit and sending my brain cells spiraling away from me. My breathing grows ragged. I grip the comforter in both fists and arch my back, pushing myself onto his tongue, my orgasm ripping through me.

Emmett grips my knees and forces my legs backwards, raising my butt in the air. I watch as he fucks me with his finger, sliding it out and licking my taste with his tongue. Then he frees his erection, and he's inside me, filling me up. My knees are around my ears, and I swear that I can feel him ramming my spine with every thrust.

His mouth covers mine. His hand closes around my throat, and he applies pressure, enough to make me gasp as he breathes into my mouth.

My head spins. My kisses grow more demanding. The harder he pumps into me, the more I want him. My sex throbs around him, his length rubbing my clit as he pulls himself out and then in again.

We explode together. I can no longer feel where my body ends, and Emmett's begins, and when he lies on top of me, his erection shrinking inside me, I wrap my arms around him and listen to his heartbeat thumping in synch with mine.

I DON'T KNOW how long we stay like this, my limbs circling Emmett, our bodies pressed together. When I think that he might've fallen asleep on top of me, he pulls away from me and undresses, his eyes devouring my body.

We take it slowly, Emmett kissing me all over and making me come repeatedly with his tongue. He keeps his promise and fucks me in more ways that I can even remember. We skip dinner, the family going about their day without us.

Finally, when the house is silent, we wrap ourselves in bathrobes and wander down to the kitchen where Emmett prepares omelets using leftover turkey and ham while I watch him from a seat at the pine table. We've hardly spoken in his room, unless it was about sex, and I feel almost shy again now that we're back in the family setting, even though my nakedness is covered by the robe.

We have explored every part of each other's bodies.

I can still feel him between my legs, and I know that if he wanted to fuck me on the kitchen floor, I would lay down and open my legs wide right now.

He slides a plate towards me and sits next to me at the table.

The omelet is smothered with cheese and melts in my mouth. "This is delicious. Where did you learn to cook?"

"My mom taught me." He swallows a mouthful of freshly brewed coffee. "She said no son of hers would grow up expecting a wife to cook for him."

It feels surreal sitting here alone late at night, the two of us, knowing how our bodies react to each other. It's like we're tethered by desire. Or is it lust? How am I supposed to know the difference?

I want to ask him what this means for us. It changes everything, doesn't it? He can't deny that he wants me as much as I want him, but I'm still acutely conscious of the fact that the ring on my finger means nothing. We might have spent the last twelve hours having the most incredible, mind-blowing sex, but it doesn't mean that he wants to marry me.

"Don't, Mary." He leans across and kisses me on the lips. "Let's not talk about what happens after the holidays. Let's just enjoy the moment."

And we do. Because what Emmett O'Hara wants, Emmett O'Hara gets, and if he doesn't say the words out loud, I can pretend, just for tonight, that this is real.

THE FOLLOWING MORNING, we sleep in late. Emmett sneaks me back to the guest room while the house hums with sounds from the kitchen and the living room downstairs, kissing me on the lips as we part outside my door.

I want to tell him that everyone will have guessed why we didn't come down for dinner yesterday, but he seems so contented that I can't bring myself to do or say anything that will burst our bubble and send us careening back to reality. I know I'm clinging to false hope, but it's all I have right now, and like a drowning shipwreck survivor, I'm not letting go.

When I finally wander downstairs, Emmett isn't there. I try not to let my disappointment show on my face as I help myself to coffee in the kitchen and sit down carefully with Fianna and Emmet's grandmothers who have started a jigsaw puzzle across the table. My sore pussy chafes against the seam of my jeans and I hide my face behind my coffee.

Granny Nina peers at me from behind the puzzle lid, frown lines creasing her forehead. "Where did you and Emmett get to yesterday? You missed Erin's cottage pie."

"Mom!" Sinead sucks in a deep breath and flashes a warning glance at her mother that goes unnoticed. "I told you they wanted some alone time."

The heat rises in my cheeks.

"Missed breakfast as well." Granny Mary arches an eyebrow and winks at me as she hands the other woman a jigsaw piece. "I think this is the piece you're looking for."

"I saved you some breakfast." Sinead is already slicing a homemade loaf of bread while Erin uncovers a plate of grilled sausages, bacon, and mushrooms. "You must be starving."

I almost choke on a mouthful of coffee.

Next to me, I hear Fianna chuckling softly. "If I can tear you away from my cousin, do you want to drive into town with me? There's something I'd like to show you."

"Is that okay?" I ask Sinead.

"Aye, we don't have any plans, and don't you dare be asking my son for permission to leave the house either."

"That's settled then." Fianna eyes up the doorstop sandwich in front of me. "Eat up."

I'm excited to go into town with Fianna. I'm intrigued about what she wants to show me, but also, every experience I have here helps me to imagine the kind of childhood Emmett must've had. Because now that I've had a taste of him, my appetite will never be satisfied.

We drive into Laragh and out the other side of the village, when Fianna stops the car outside a derelict low-rise building. She kills the engine, and faces me in the passenger seat, an eager smile on her face.

"I want you to keep an open mind, Mary. Try to see beyond the way it looks now and imagine how it could look once it has been renovated."

"Okay." I feel a twist of excitement somewhere deep inside and try to quell it for now.

Fianna lets us in with a key.

The building is even more dilapidated inside than it looks from the outside. Some of the internal walls have blown, plaster collapsing into heaps on the floor. There's a hole in the ceiling of a downstairs room allowing us to see straight through into the room above. The kitchen looks as if it hasn't been cleaned in years and is devoid of any equipment, loose cables hanging from wall sockets, and we quickly close the bathroom door without venturing inside.

"Well, what do you think?"

Fianna faces me in the middle of a large downstairs room, the only redeeming feature of which is a huge ornate fireplace.

Deep breath. "It needs a lot of work."

She smiles. "My dad knows plenty of people who'll carry out the renovations for me." She crosses the room and peers out the window, gesturing for me to join her.

When I look outside, my breath catches in my throat. The land behind the building is vast and green, surrounded by hills, woodland, and a stream, the scene completed by a waterfall tumbling over a rocky promontory in the distance.

"That was my reaction when I first saw it." Fianna points at the waterfall. "This view sealed the deal for me."

"You own this place?"

A Dark Mafia Christmas

Fianna can't be any older than me, and I can't help comparing my tiny New York apartment with a view of tenement buildings and traffic to this. I'll never afford to buy even the tiniest apartment in the city, and here she is with the keys to a property that would house several families. I'm not envious. I'm in awe.

"My parents gave me the deposit." She wrinkles her nose. "I know I'm lucky that my family can help me out, but I want to finish this without any more financial help from them and their acquaintances."

If she means people like the psycho from the pub the day before, I can understand why.

"What are you going to do with it?"

"I want to turn it into a boutique hotel. I have so many ideas, Mary. Each room is going to be themed, unique, and provide an experience rather than just an overnight stay. I want people to remember it after they've spent a night here, you know. I've never forgotten staying in a hotel in Dublin with my parents when I was a little girl. It was like stepping into another world with the huge chandeliers and the four-poster bed." She takes my hands in hers. "I want people to feel that same excitement when they walk in."

Her enthusiasm is infectious. I can already envisage a fairytale-themed room with antique lace curtains around the bed, an old-fashioned wooden stand with a porcelain bowl to wash in, and a woodland scene painted across the walls complete with fairies, sprites, and pixies.

"You don't think I'm crazy, do you?" Fine lines appear between her eyebrows.

I shake my head. "I don't think you're crazy. I think it's a brilliant idea." A thought occurs to me then. "Does Emmett know about this?"

"No. No one else knows apart from my parents. I just had a feeling that you would see it as I do."

My heart skips a little to think that she told me before Emmett. "I wish I could help."

Her smile is wide, like this was the reason she brought me here. "Why don't you? Why don't you stay and help?"

"I..." My thoughts are falling over each other, trying to remind me of all the reasons why I must go back. But one reason stands out more than all the others.

Emmett.

"Mary." Fianna sucks her bottom lip, psyching herself up for what she's about to say. "You and Emmett... You're not really engaged to be married, are you?"

"Y-you know?" My heart performs a somersault, and I think I'm going to be sick. "Did he tell you?"

"No. But he would never have bought you a ring when he was always going to have Granny Mary's, and you would never have met his family without any clothes of your own." She pauses, choosing her words carefully. "I don't know what's going on—you'll tell me in your own time—but if you want to stay and help me, I would love to have you on board."

Tears sting behind my eyes, emotion swirling around my chest. "Why?" I sniff loudly. "I mean, you don't know anything about me."

She shrugs. "I know that you love my cousin."

"Shit. Is it that obvious?"

"Only to anyone who sees you two together."

The words make me feel nauseous as they spill out. "I'm not sure he feels the same way about me."

"Oh, Mary." Fianna chuckles softly. "You really don't know him at all, do you?"

15

EMMETT

The next couple of days pass by in a blur of stolen moments with Mary. We fuck in the stables, the art studio, and the games room. We fuck on every available surface in my bedroom and Mary's guest room, and it seems that the more I have of her, the more I want.

I've never known anyone like Mary Chrysler. Her body responds to mine in a way that's so natural, so passionate, so hungry and demanding, it's like having my eyes focused with new spectacles. I can see now that everything I did before Mary came into my life was just messing around. It had no substance. No heart.

No strings attached meant that I didn't bother holding onto the memories either.

That's how this is different. I will never forget this Christmas with Mary.

It's as if she has replaced everything that family meant to me until now with a memory that will make my cock twitch every time I think of it.

A Dark Mafia Christmas

She hasn't asked me what will happen when we go back to New York, but I see it in her eyes whenever we are alone together. There's more. She has been spending a lot of time with Fianna, heads together, wide grins on their faces like they're plotting something behind my back. But whenever I ask them what's going on they tell me I'll know soon enough.

Then, on New Year's Eve, I get the call I've been waiting for. A plot of land in Syracuse is going on the market, and I've been promised first refusal. If I close the deal this year.

"Can't it wait a couple more days?"

I wander past the cinema room, phone pressed to my ear, and spot Mary and Fianna inside watching a Hallmark movie where everything is covered in fake snow and the actors are still walking around in stilettos and lightweight coats.

"The client wants to close today. If it doesn't happen, it'll go on the open market and get snapped up by a developer who'll turn it into a new Vegas."

Shit!

"I know it's New Year's Eve, but hey, you can celebrate in style in Times Square with the rest of us."

I inch back to the doorway of the cinema and peer through the crack between the door and the frame. Both women have their back to me, but Mary's hair tumbles over the back of the seat as she tips her head back and laughs out loud at something Fianna said. There's a huge tub of popcorn on the mini table between them, and I'm struck again by Mary's resemblance to a colorful bird in her natural habitat.

I'm not ready to drag her away from all this. My family has spent the last few days bigging up the New Year celebrations which are always held at their friend's property on a farm overlooking the reservoir at Roundwood. I know she'll be disappointed to miss it.

But this deal is too good to pass up. I've already got the plans drawn up for developing an exclusive hotel complex.

Peering through the doorway, the couple on the screen kiss, and Fianna and Mary both cheer, toasting the movie with cans of soda. New York, the office, this deal, all feels a million miles away suddenly, something that exists in the life of someone other than Emmett O'Hara. If I'm going to do this, I need to get my head into gear.

"I'll be there." I turn away from the cinema and head back to my room to pack.

———

"What about the party?" Mom slumps back in her seat in the kitchen, and Dad stands behind her massaging her shoulders. "You said that you were staying until the New Year."

"I know, I'm sorry. I have to close on a deal today, or it'll be too late."

I can hear the disappointment in my own voice and clear my throat. This deal is important. I've been waiting for months for it to happen.

So why do I feel like it's the last thing I want to think about right now?

"So, that's it?" Mom says, her eyes growing large with tears. "You'll fly back to New York and the holidays will be over. When are we going to see you and Mary again?"

That's what this is all about. She has loved having Mary here and was probably hoping that Mary would encourage me to visit more often.

"It isn't over yet." Granny Nina has been staring at the jigsaw puzzle piece in her hand since I came into the kitchen, and now she squints at me myopically over the top of the spectacles perched on the end of her nose. "There's still the party."

"Emmett's flying back to New York today, Ma." Mom instinctively raises her voice because Granny Nina refuses to wear her hearing aid. "They'll miss the party."

"You're flying back to New York today?"

I didn't hear Mary and Fianna come in and guilt floods my chest. I wanted to tell her in private, to explain why we're traveling back early so that she would understand it has nothing to do with her. Not like this.

She watches me from the doorway, the color draining from her face, and it hits me like a blow to the gut that fucking her was a mistake. I never promised her that it would change anything. I never said that this relationship was more than either of us had bargained for, but she'd nurtured the seed of hope anyway, and here I am throwing it back in her face.

This reaction right here is the reason why I always love 'em and leave 'em.

O'Hara Developers is my life, and there isn't a woman alive who will ever understand that. I'd hoped that Mary might be different, but she isn't. She doesn't want to come second to the family business, and I can't have it any other way.

A spark of anger, disappointment, and resentment erupts inside me. I let her get under my skin, and she thinks that she can control me because she's wearing my grandmother's ring.

"Yes. I'm already packed."

My voice sounds way colder than I intended. It's self-preservation. Mary Chrysler has no say in the matter. I brought her here, and now I'm going to take her back.

"Wh-when were you going to tell me?"

Fuck! How does she always do this, turn those huge green eyes on me and make me feel bad?

"You were watching a movie. I didn't want to interrupt you."

"Well, it's not like Mary has anything to pack, is it?" Fianna chimes in. The accusation in her tone is unmissable.

I keep my eyes on Mary. Has she told Fianna the truth? They've been so close the last couple of days, but Mary knows the score. She understands what's at stake.

"I..." She chews her bottom lip, and I want to carry her upstairs and fuck her till she can't walk. "I'd quite like to stay."

"You can stay, Mary." My mom jumps up, walks around the table, and hugs Mary close to her chest. "You know you're always welcome here." Mom turns to me. "Mary can come back to New York in the New Year as planned. We'll take good care of her."

What the fuck is she playing at? Does she believe that if she stays behind, she can make this all come true? Doesn't she understand that fairytales and Hallmark movies are not real?

"I think Mary should come with me."

"Let her stay, son." Even my dad is falling for it now. "Everyone's dying to meet her tonight."

An image of my family and Mary seeing in the New Year, fireworks casting a golden glow across their cold faces, pops into my head, and I realize that I should never have brought Mary here. We could've gone anywhere in the world, and I had to bring her home because that's what a good Irish son would do. And now they've fallen for her, and it'll be hard for them to let her go.

"No, you don't understand." Mary's eyes are still fixed on me like she's trying to preempt my reaction. "I'm not coming back to New York because I'm staying here. In Ireland."

All eyes in the room flit back and forth between me and Mary like they're watching a tennis match.

"You're staying?" Mom says, her face glowing. "That's wonderful news. Isn't it, Emmett? Maybe you'll come back more often now."

I feel the angry tic starting in my jaw. "When did you decide this, Mary?"

"Just this morning." Fianna answers for her. "She's coming to work with me."

"With you?" I blink at my cousin, confusion stealing my thoughts and turning them upside down. "Mary works in IT."

"Not any more she doesn't." They've been conspiring against me, and Fianna is enjoying my discomfort. "I've been waiting to tell you. I've bought a property. I'm going to open a boutique hotel, and Mary has agreed to help me."

A boutique hotel? What the fuck?

"You don't know anything about running a hotel."

"Emmett." Mom furrows her brow. "You of all people should show some support for your cousin."

"What do you think I studied at college?" Fianna watches me coolly. "Oh, that's right, you don't know what I studied at college because you never bothered asking."

It's a low blow, but I can't blame her for hitting me with it because it's true. After Oisin died, I cut myself off from everyone back home and threw myself into work. It was the only thing that didn't hurt. But I didn't give a thought about how Fianna was feeling.

"You're right. I'm sorry."

Fianna's expression softens and she loses the hard glint in her eyes. "I asked Mary to join me. I thought you would approve. Keep it in the family."

She knows something. I'm not sure how much she knows, but she's trying to provoke me into a reaction.

"I do approve. I just wish Mary had spoken to me about this first."

A flush spreads across Mary's face. "I-I was going to speak to you today. We were not supposed to be traveling back for a couple more days."

She's right, but it doesn't change the fact that she got involved with Fianna's plans without mentioning it to me. What else has she been hiding from me?

"Well, I think it's a great idea." Mom is on her feet, collecting plates and mugs and ferrying them back and forth from the table to the counter. "And we'll love having Mary here."

"We'll move into the hotel while it's being renovated," Fianna says. "We both want to be hands on with the work."

So, they've already discussed living arrangements.

"You can talk to me about it now." I address Mary, and man if I don't sound like the biggest asshole going. I see the way my mom purses her lips like she didn't bring me up to be this controlling.

Mary follows me to the conservatory overlooking the garden which is still patchy white with icy snow. I feel her eyes on me, but I stare out the window while I try to reassemble my thoughts.

It shouldn't matter to me where Mary lives, we're going our separate ways after this anyway, so why am I angry with her for withholding her plans? Is it because she didn't discuss it with me before reaching a decision? Did I believe that bringing her here gave me full control over everything she did? Or is it because she'll ultimately be spending more time with my family than I will?

"I'm sorry, Emmett." Mary breaks the silence first.

It hasn't been this uncomfortable between us since my fight with Ronan at the pub, and I don't like it.

"I needed a few days to think about it. That's why I didn't tell you sooner. I…" I hear the emotion in her voice, and I still don't look at her. "I can't come back to New York with you. I can't see you in the office and … and think about our time together here."

"You won't see me in the office." Because I never noticed Mary until the Christmas party.

She takes her time responding. "There's nothing else for me to go back to if I don't have my job. This is an amazing opportunity, and I really want to make it work."

"You could find a job like this in New York. I'll connect you with some of my contacts. They'll find you work if I put in a good word for you."

I choose this moment to make eye contact, and the hurt in her eyes tears my heart open. Who do I think I am, persuading her to change her mind so that I can palm her off onto a client and forget about her?

"Mary, I didn't mean—"

"Yes, you did, Emmett. It's fine, really it is. I've realized how much I've missed this country. I belong here. My roots have been tugging at me ever since we arrived." She smiles. "Here, take your granny's ring."

She slides the engagement ring off her finger, but I stop her. If she takes it off now, my family will never believe that I'm not angry with her for staying in Ireland, and there's no way I can tell them the truth now that they've all fallen in love with her. My parents will never forgive me.

"Tell them tomorrow. At least let them see in the New Year with their excitement intact."

"Tomorrow? After you've gone?"

Fuck, that came out all wrong.

"I know you think that I'm swerving all the responsibility onto your shoulders, Mary."

"Aren't you?"

There's a hard edge to her voice that I haven't heard since she ran away. Was that when everything changed, when I went looking for her and brought her back?

"I'll call them myself. Tomorrow. I'll tell them that we've decided to take a break while you get settled here, and I have so much going on in New York." She isn't saying anything. "Then you can give Granny Mary her ring back."

She stares at me for what feels like hours, her eyes searching mine, looking for something that she isn't going to find. "Fine."

"Fine."

"Good luck, Emmett." She stands on tiptoes and kisses my cheek. "I hope you find what you're looking for."

Then she walks away, and I'm left staring at the door as it closes behind her.

I DON'T SEE Mary again before I leave. She stays in her room when I say goodbye to my family, and even though I stare inside the house while I hug everyone and wish them Happy New Year on the doorsteps, it's obvious that she isn't coming to wave me off.

"I wish you would stay." Mom hugs me tightly. She holds on to my arms when she pulls away and glances over her shoulder. "Don't worry about Mary. We'll take good care of her."

Jesus, if she only fucking knew. "I know you will, Mom."

She dabs her wet eyes with a tissue. "When will you be back?"

"I don't know." Deep breath. I should make more of an effort to see them. "I won't wait so long this time."

I get in the car before she starts crying. As Dave drives slowly along the driveway, I glance back at the guest room window, hoping for a glimpse of Mary, but she isn't there.

It feels like she's punishing me for not giving her more. For not allowing what we have to become something real. But I never gave her false hope; I told her from the start that it would end after the holidays.

So, why does it feel so wrong to be traveling back without her?

16

MARY

I feel like I'm floating around the New Year's Eve party inside a bubble. I see people. I speak to people. But I can't recall any conversations I've had or remember the names of people I've been introduced to. Sinead, sensing that I'm away with the fairies, tells everyone that Emmett got called back to the States on business so that I don't have to keep repeating myself. I'll thank her tomorrow when I'll hopefully feel a little more normal.

I don't know what I expected Emmett to do, but it wasn't this.

He didn't wish me luck for the new venture with Fianna.

He didn't kiss me goodbye.

He didn't beg me to go with him.

There was just ... nothing. It was as if all the time we'd spent exploring one another's bodies happened to someone else. As if it was just another fuck to him.

And this is what hurts the most.

I would never have treated him this way.

We put on our coats and stand outside to watch the fireworks display. The sky is illuminated by the spectacular bursts of color, but they blur through my tears as we count down to midnight. Being in different countries for the first few moments of a new year is an omen—this is obviously how it's meant to be.

"Happy New Year." I turn around to find Fianna standing next to me holding two glasses of champagne. She hands me a glass and clinks the side of it with her drink. "To us."

"To us." I sip champagne and swallow the sob that's threatening to erupt inside me.

After a while, Fianna says, "Emmett was different with you."

Tears finally spill over my bottom lashes. "Different how?"

"More like the Emmett I used to know." Her face glows silver as a starburst firework explodes above our heads lighting up the sky. "He blamed himself for Oisin's death."

"How did he die?" I ask softly.

"Plane crash. He was on his way to New York to go and work with Emmett."

"But..."

I could say that it wasn't Emmett's fault the plane crashed, but I guess everyone he knows has already said this. It's a lot of baggage to carry around on his shoulders though.

"Oisin wanted to get away from here. He was nothing like Emmett. He was always so reserved, even as a child, and battled low self-esteem once he became a teenager. He always looked up to Emmett. He wanted to be like him."

She takes a deep shaky breath. "He was bullied at school. That's why he wanted to go to America as soon as he could."

"I'm so sorry." I don't know what else to say. But Fianna doesn't even appear to be listening. She's staring at the fireworks, pensive, lost in thoughts of her brother, so I take her hand and squeeze it.

She turns to me and her smile is sad. "It's the reason why Emmett and Ronan will never be friends. Ronan was one of the bullies who made Oisin's life hell."

"Ronan?"

Now it all starts to make sense. The way Emmett's hackles were up the instant Ronan Blackthorn walked into the house. The fight at the pub. His anger at Fianna for being nice to the guy. If Oisin wasn't being bullied, he might never have caught that flight to New York. He might still be alive.

And Emmett might not be scared to come home to Ireland.

But then I think of the way Fianna looked at Ronan at the party, and the disappointment in Emmett's eyes when he saw them together.

"You and Ronan?" I ask.

Another deep breath. "Ronan Blackthorn isn't the kind of guy you want to cross. I thought... I thought that if I could get close to him, I could prevent him from hurting anyone else. But now..." She tears her eyes away from the stars fizzing in the sky and looks at me. "Emmett told me what happened at the pub. I'm sorry, Mary. I promise Ronan Blackthorn will never get close to you again."

The O'Haras are protectors. Fighters. Fiercely loyal people. It's lovely to know that they want to look out for me, but I can take care of myself. I always have done.

"You don't need to worry about me. I'm a big girl now."

Fianna throws her arms around me and hugs me tightly. "For what it's worth, I think my cousin is an idiot for going back to New York without you."

"His loss." Only, I'm not sure if I'm trying to convince her or me.

Fianna and I move into the hotel a week later.

"It'll be an adventure," we tell her family. "We'll sleep on camp beds until the owner's accommodation is ready, and anyway, we'll be too exhausted to care."

It's almost true. At least, the exhausted part is.

Once we start stripping plaster from walls and ripping up floorboards, we realize that the building requires a lot more work than we at first thought. Before we can even start renovating, we have to get the building moisture proofed, rewired, and replumbed, which means that we're practically going to be living on a building site for a while.

Nothing fazes Fianna though. She has her vision, and while the tradesmen are carrying out their work, we start creating mood boards for the themed bedrooms to the backdrop of hammers, drills, and radios blaring out pop music.

Sinead and Erin pop in every day with homemade meals and try convincing us to go home until the place is habitable, but we quickly settle into a routine of waking up early, making coffee over a camping stove, and popping into a nearby café for breakfast. Besides, I've seen the way Fianna bats her eyelashes at one of the electricians, a dark-haired guy called Connor. I think he likes her too because not a lot of work goes on when she's around, and I'm praying that he'll ask her on a date before the work is completed.

One morning, I wake up later than usual feeling queasy, and almost throw up when I smell the coffee brewing in the small metal pot. One hand clamped over my mouth I wander through the building looking for Fianna. She never said that she was going out early, but when I hear voices coming from what will be the reception area when the hotel opens, I assume that she's with Connor.

Then I hear a voice I recognize, and my heart starts thumping frantically.

Emmett?

I was going to leave Fianna to it, but I have to check for myself. Opening the door a crack, I peer around the room that's littered with chunks of plasterboard, tools, lengths of cable, and radiators waiting to be installed, until my eyes settle on Fianna and a man who has his back to me.

My body immediately responds by sending shivers down my spine and a tingling sensation between my legs.

Why is he here?

Why didn't he let me know that he was coming back?

Why didn't Sinead say anything, unless she didn't know either.

I can't move. I don't know how Emmett is going to react to seeing me again, and the longer I stand here overthinking it, the more uncertain I become. Perhaps he came here to tell me that he's never coming back again. Or... My stomach lurches sickeningly, sending another wave of nausea crashing through me when I realize that perhaps he's here to tell me that he's getting married ... to another woman.

I'm about to back away, grab my shoes and coat, and disappear outside until he's gone, when he turns around and looks directly at me.

Oh my God, he's even hotter than I remembered. Clean and hot. And I suddenly feel frumpy in yesterday's clothes and one of Fianna's oversized cardigans. I haven't washed my hair in days, and there's dirt under my fingernails.

But he's walking towards me, and I hear Fianna say, "I'll leave you guys to talk in peace," and my legs are refusing to cooperate.

Emmett opens the door and eyes me up and down, a bemused smile tugging at the corners of his mouth. "I'm quite enjoying your new look. Very ... homely."

"Homely? That's what you're going with?"

Because hearing his voice has transported me straight back to our surreal Christmas, and I want to kiss him and feel him inside me and my body isn't ever going to let me forget it.

"What would you prefer? Comfortable? It suits you. It's kind of ... sexy."

Okay, what's going on here? He flies back to New York early, doesn't even kiss me goodbye, tells his family that we're on a break, and now he's telling me that I look sexy? Whoever said that women are complicated?

"Why are you here, Emmett?" Because if this is how it's going to be for the foreseeable future, I don't think I can handle it.

His mouth twitches like he has a lot to say and doesn't know where to begin. Finally, he says, "I wanted to see you."

"Me?" I blink. Did he just say that? "Why?"

"Because, Mary, you've fucking bewitched me. I haven't stopped thinking about you, and every moment that I've spent away from you has felt like ... well, like a part of me was missing. I knew it when I boarded the aircraft to go back to New York. I knew it when I landed at Newark, and I sure as shit couldn't ignore it when I went back to the office."

I'm trying to soak up his words so that I can replay them in my head when he goes away again, but my pulse is racing, and it's hard to think straight. This is what I wanted. This is everything I wanted him to say to me, and more, but how can I believe him when I keep hearing his voice in my head telling me that this isn't real?

"Say something, Mary."

"I..." I shake my head. "What are you saying, Emmett?"

"I'm saying that I can't live without you. I thought I could. I told myself that none of it was real, that I brought you here against your will, and you would never be able to forgive me for that, but I was lying to myself."

"But..." Did he just say that he can't live without me? "I don't understand."

He smiles. "What part of I can't live without you don't you understand?" Then his expression falters. "Fuck. I just poured my heart out, and you don't feel the same way. Fucking idiot. I knew I shouldn't have left it so long. I was going to fly straight back the next day, but..." He rubs his stubble with both hands. When he speaks again, he lowers his voice like a child admitting he ate the last biscuit. "I didn't want to seem too desperate."

I step closer, so close I can see the gray flecks in his eyes. "I do feel the same way."

"You do?" So close I can feel his breath on my face. "But you didn't want to come back with me."

"I didn't want to go back to New York. It's not the same thing."

"I-I can't stay here though, Mary."

"Why not? The Internet is a wonderful thing, you know."

He laughs out loud. Then he picks me up and spins me around, his lips on mine. When he sets me down, his expression grows serious.

"There's something I must tell you, Mary. I should've told you sooner, but, well..." He swallows hard, and I don't think he has ever looked sexier than he does right now. "I didn't want to frighten you."

Frighten me?

"Emmett, I was frightened the night I met you."

"I know." He scrunches up his nose and blinks several times. "I wasn't entirely honest with you that night."

"You don't say." I smile.

He inclines his head, conceding the point. "I knew what was happening on the roof. You see, my family, we're Irish Mafia. My father—"

"Patrick?"

I nod. "He's kept the peace with the other families, but I'll be expected to take over one day. When I'm married. And, well, I wanted you to be aware of what you're getting into. It can be dangerous. My position comes with its own risks, but I promise I will never allow any harm to come to you. There will always be someone looking out for you."

"You mean, like Dave? And Declan?"

"Yes, but you will always have me looking out for you, Mary. Always. I just ... I just wanted you to know."

It all falls into place now. I'd suspected, of course, when Emmett didn't react to the murder on the rooftop, but it's not something you think about when it isn't staring you in the face. Then, when Declan was there in the pub, keeping an eye on me when Ronan followed me to the restrooms, it started to become clearer.

How do I feel about falling in love with a Mafia Don?

Strangely, I feel safe when I'm with Emmett, and I believe him when he says that he'll never let any harm come to me. The rest I'll have to figure out as we go along.

"I had my suspicions, Emmett." I shrug.

"You did?"

"I didn't put two and two together and come up with the word Mafia, but I guess I might've done it in time."

"And...?" His eyes grow even bluer if that's at all possible.

"And I still love you, Emmett O'Hara."

He grins at me. "Don't move."

My heart is throwing a party inside my rib cage. Emmett O'Hara has the power to flip my life on its axis, and it seems that this is exactly what he is doing. Again.

He goes down on one knee, right there on the dusty rotten floorboards of the hotel hallway, slides his hand into his pocket, and produces Granny Mary's diamond ring. "Mary Chrysler, will you marry me?"

My heart turns the volume up a notch. I'm smiling so hard my cheeks hurt, and I think I say, "Yes," but I can hardly hear my own voice over the blood gushing in my ears.

Emmett slides the ring onto my finger and kisses me, and I know that wherever he is, is going to be home from now on.

EPILOGUE
MARY

September that year, it's the launch of our boutique hotel.

We've called it simply 'Ours' because Fianna and I have put a tiny piece of our heart and soul into every room.

"Ready?" I peer around the reception area that is aglow with warm fairy lights.

It's hard to believe that this is the same building we moved into in January, the building where we slept on camp beds in the dining room, snuggled inside sleeping bags with a portable heater to keep us warm when we were not working. Fianna was able to bring all of our (sometimes) farfetched ideas to life, finding practical solutions to make them work.

The reception has floor-to-ceiling windows allowing the outside in, the interior walls strategically fitted with flush lighting that alters with the seasons. Tonight, the entire space is bathed in a warm orange glow, the tiny fairy lights flickering across the walls and scattering patterns across the floor like falling leaves. It's magical, and magic is exactly what we wanted to bring to the hotel.

The bedrooms are themed. There's a woodland room, an ocean room, a royal room complete with turrets, a velvet-draped four-poster, crowns, and silk robes, a Titanic room (Fianna's first choice), and my particular favorite: the Christmas room. The bed is a sleigh, there are snow globes everywhere, and snow falls outside the window ... even in summer.

Fianna widens her eyes at me and squeals. "The first guests arrive tomorrow. This is it, Mary. No turning back."

For a woman who was born with the O'Hara confidence, she has hardly eaten today, and has wandered from room to room, testing lighting, smoothing comforters across beds, and straightening curtains that are already immaculate.

"Everyone is going to love it." I squeeze her hand.

"What if Liam O'Doherty hates it? What if his review says that we're a couple of women trying to play big-girl games?"

I laugh and shake my head. "You invited Liam O'Doherty as the only journalist here tonight for a reason. When he gives us a glowing review, we'll be fully booked through to 2030."

She smiles and her shoulders relax just a little. "This is what I love about you Mary, your unwavering optimism."

"And my crazy ideas." I wrinkle my nose, thinking of more qualities. "And my culinary skills."

Fianna grimaces. "Your culinary skills are ... unique, but please don't ever apply for a job as a chef."

The door opens, and Emmett comes in looking smart in a silver suit with a black rollneck sweater underneath. He kisses me on the lips and then lowers his head to kiss my swollen belly, a gesture that has become so natural I know

I'm going to miss it when the twins arrive. "How are my babies?"

"I think they're more excited than the rest of us, I swear they're having their own party in there."

"That's my girls." Emmett slides his arm around me and sticks his tongue in my ear, sending shivers down my spine. "You look beautiful."

His breath is warm on my cheek, and the familiar tingle spreads between my legs. I will never not feel sexy in his presence, and there are still days when I pinch myself to be sure that I'm not dreaming.

I push him away from me playfully. "Not tonight. You don't want me to go into labor halfway through the party."

"We've still got another three weeks. How am I supposed to keep my hands off you for that long?"

"You only have to keep your hands off me tonight." I move his hands away from my belly and deliberately place them by his sides.

"Ugh, guys, I'm standing right here." Fianna's voice interrupts us.

This is how it is when we're together; it's as if no one else exists in the world but us, and I can't wait to include our babies in our bubble.

"It's okay, Emmett is keeping his distance." I flash him a mock warning glance and he raises his hands, palms facing outward, in surrender. "Nothing is going to spoil this evening."

"Thank fuck for that." Fianna inhales deeply. "I mean giving birth in one of the rooms would be publicity, but someone will have to clean that mess up."

I laugh, and Emmett grimaces. "On that note," he says, "I'll go check on the food."

For the first few months of the year, Emmett divided his time equally between Ireland and New York much to his mom's joy. Sinead should've had a whole Brady Bunch of kids, but she had a medical condition that brought about early menopause shortly after Emmett was born, so he literally got her undivided love and attention his whole life. She's going to be an amazing granny to our children.

Emmett moved back home to Ireland permanently when we discovered that I was pregnant. I was more shocked than he was—my cycle had never been regular, and it didn't even occur to me that I might be carrying his baby when I was a couple of months late. Even with the nausea in the mornings that destroyed my love of a peaceful early-morning coffee while looking out on the waterfall.

We're staying at the family home for now until our own home is built. Sinead cried when we told her that we'd be moving into our own place when it's ready, until we pointed out that she'll be able to see it from the conservatory window. She has already figured out that our children will be able to run across to granny's house after school for homemade cookies and milk and is planning their first trip to Lapland for Christmas as soon as they're old enough to appreciate it.

They are the family I always dreamed of, and I wake up every morning feeling like the luckiest woman alive.

A 4x4 pulls up outside the hotel and Sinead and Patrick climb out, closely followed by Fianna's parents, Erin and Sean. Clare and Ciaran pull up behind them on the driveway—they arranged babysitters for this evening, afraid that the twins would break something or spill juice on the carpets before the first guests even check in.

Sinead hurries over to me, kisses my cheek, and holds me at arm's length, eyes narrowed. "How are you feeling?"

"Fine." I smile. "No twinges, no pains. I feel … amazing."

"I can vouch for that." Fianna joins us. "I had to force her to sit down earlier. I found her on her hands and knees fitting mousehole decals to the baseboards in the Christmas room."

"I couldn't resist them when I found them in that new shop in Laragh yesterday. They're so cute." I realize that Sinead is still watching me closely. "Don't worry, I haven't been overdoing it."

"You were in the nursery until late last night."

"I found some decals for the babies' room too." I hesitate. "I know they'll sleep in our room for a while, but I just wanted to get it finished."

"Your belly has dropped." Sinead looks around for Clare and Erin who come straight over. "Do you think she has dropped?"

They both eye my belly critically while a blush creeps steadily across my face.

"Aye." Clare places a hand on my belly.

"She's been nesting too," Sinead adds.

"Don't worry, Mary." Erin smiles. "We'll keep an eye on you. We've all had babies, so we know what we're doing."

Patrick walks around the women and places an arm around my waist. "Come with me, Mary. My granddaughters will come out when they're ready."

We wander through to the dining room where the table is covered with canapés and silver champagne buckets. Patrick hands me over to Emmett, the O'Hara men protecting the future generation.

"Everything okay?" Emmett's eyes instinctively drop to my swollen belly too.

"I'm fine. No need to fuss."

Just then, I get a twinge that starts somewhere deep and low inside me and grows, my belly becoming hard as rock. It keeps growing, blocking out my surroundings and forcing me to breathe deeply while I grip the back of a seat.

"Mary?" Emmett's clear blue eyes are filled with concern.

I blink the room back into focus. "It's fine. Braxton Hicks contraction."

He pulls out a seat and eases me into it. Suddenly, the realization that I have to get these babies out sneaks up on me, and my eyes fill with tears.

"What is it? What's wrong?" He kneels in front of me the way he did the day he proposed in the same room although it isn't recognizable now.

"Hormones." I sniff loudly.

He smiles. "I'll get you some water."

"I'd prefer champagne."

He leans closer and kisses me on the lips. "A small one. I don't want my girls getting drunk in there."

I hear the soft pop of a cork, and Emmett returns with a half-filled crystal champagne flute. Before I've taken my first sip, the party guests start arriving, filling the hotel lobby with conversation and laughter.

"That's us." Emmett helps me onto my feet. "We're on."

The evening passes in a blur of conversation and excited murmurs of appreciation as we give friends, family, and neighbors a guided tour of the rooms.

Fianna looks as if she is floating around the rooms, Connor by her side, her face glowing as she opens door after door, and tries to view the rooms from a visitor's perspective. They are breathtakingly beautiful. I know I'm biased, but this is the kind of hotel I would choose to stay in if I was visiting Ireland, and I'm so proud of what we've achieved in just nine months. We've set up a board in the dining room with before-and-after photographs, and the guests' reactions make my heart swell with joy.

I don't have any more practice contractions, and I forget all about it as the party grows louder, music filling the reception area from discreet speakers set up behind the front desk.

"Happy?" Emmett has joined me outside the hotel where I'm trying to cool down in the gentle evening breeze.

I smile at him. I don't need to say the words out loud. Emmett knows what I'm thinking before I do a lot of the time.

He kisses me on the lips as something inside me seems to give and my water breaks, splashing his shiny black shoes, and creating a puddle outside the hotel entrance.

"Emmett..." I grip his hand tightly, panic crashing through me and making it hard to breathe.

He peers down at the damp ground, his brow furrowed. Then

realization rearranges his features into a wide smile. "Hey, it's okay, Mary. I'm here."

"I'm..." I don't want to say the words out loud.

I don't want to admit that I've kept myself busy for nine months so that I didn't have to think about this moment. Because I'm scared. I'm not scared of giving birth. I'm scared that I won't be the mom our daughters deserve, that I'll let them down at some point, and they'll have to grow a tough shell behind which to hide themselves away from the world. The way I had to.

As if reading my mind, Emmett takes my hands in his and lowers his head so that our eyes are level. "You are going to be the best mom ever, Mary. Our daughters are going to be loved more than any other children have ever been loved in the history of time because they have you, and me."

I nod, sniffing back tears. "I love you."

"I love you too, Mary. Come on, let's get ready to meet our daughters."

―――

Thank you for reading Emmett and Mary's love story, I sure hope you enjoyed it as much as I did creating it.

Kindly help me by sharing and leaving your review they help me out a lot as an independent author.

Stay tuned for another drama filled Christmas Novel this time set in Russia- a Bratva Prince and his American Princess or is she?? She's a social work college student who finds herself on a flight to Russia to meet her new husband- the big monster who will save her family if she will give herself to him in marriage.

Are you following me yet? If not click here so you don't miss out on my new releases and deals.

If you enjoyed A Dark Mafia Christmas you will absolutely adore Elio and Caterina in Mafia King's Secret Baby, An Arranged Marriage, Enemies To Lovers Romance. You will love their little daughter Luna, Here is an a little taste...

Mafia King's Secret Baby
Elio Rossi and Caterina De Luca's Story

Chapter 1

Caterina

"It's not a death sentence, Caterina. It's a wedding."

I grit my teeth. My brother Marco, six years older than me and my self-appointed life ruiner, is sitting behind his huge desk with his hands folded like he's some kind of supervillain.

To be fair.

He kind of is.

At least, he is to me right now.

"Marco," I say slowly, my breath hissing through my teeth. "It's not just a wedding. You know full well that the Rossi family murdered our parents. Do you really think that history isn't going to repeat itself, especially given the circumstances?"

The circumstances, of course, are too similar to ignore. It was six years ago that our parents died in a tragic accident on the way back from an engagement party.

My engagement party.

To the same man that Marco is asking me to marry again.

He huffs out a breath and steeples his fingers, and I resist the urge to roll my eyes. "Caterina, this is the only way. I can't keep the business afloat without the contracts that the Rossi's bring in. If we can't keep the business afloat, we can't—"

"Find out what happened to Mom and Dad," I interrupt him. "I know, Marco."

We stare at each other across the desk.

Marco is the oldest of the four of us. Unfortunately, he's not my only brother. There are two more, Dino and Sal, born close enough that anyone who can count would be a little suspicious, and then me.

The baby.

A title that Marco, at least, has taken seriously.

Sal, who is closest to me in age, at least treats me like a human being. I haven't seen him in months; Marco has him on some kind of overseas connection for us since he speaks the best Italian.

Marco is also fluent, of course, and Dino can get by.

A Dark Mafia Christmas

I can order ice cream and ask to see the beach, and that's about it. Mostly I just make vowel sounds and look angry if people are using Italian around me, and it seems to work pretty effectively. Then again, I've never been to Italy, so I could be wrong.

But it hasn't failed me yet.

Marco blinks at me. "Caterina."

"Marco," I respond. It's not fair that he doesn't have a longer name I can make him angry about. He knows that I hate being called Caterina, but he insists that Cat is too American.

As though we haven't been American for at least four generations.

I fold my arms. "Do you really think that *he* is going to honor this stupid contract anyway?"

"He has to." Marco's face grows dark and shadowed as the specter of who we're referring to enters the conversation.

Him. Elio Rossi.

Marco's former childhood friend.

My one-time future husband.

And our current biggest enemy.

"Marriage contracts simply can't be legally binding anymore," I argue. "That has to be a thing that went the way of the dinosaurs in the '60s."

"Dad wouldn't have negotiated it if that were the case," he says with a frown.

Marco frowns a lot these days.

For a split second, my heart aches for my older brother.

He was only twenty-eight when he was suddenly the head of everything. The legal business. The illegal business. Dad was a healthy man, and no one expected him to die.

Then again, I was only twenty-two when I became a mom so…

I guess no one got what they were hoping for.

Life has a way of doing that, I guess. Not in the sunshine and roses 'everything works out in the end' type of way.

No, for people like us, it's mostly the 'die-or-go-to-jail-for-a-long-time' way.

Or, in my case, have a baby when you're still a baby, and spend your life trying to hide her from her father, because if he finds out…

I shiver. That's the other reason that I'm here begging my brother to call it off.

Elio cannot know about his daughter.

Because if he finds out, I think he's probably going to kill us both.

Marco, however, thinks our family's dwindling resources will be enough to keep Elio and his goons at bay until I can figure out the evidence that we need to prove that Elio and the rest of the Rossi family had our parents killed.

I think this is a terrible plan.

He has entirely too much faith in me, our security, our Aunt Rosa, and our ability to pin the murder on Elio and his siblings.

I have faith in nothing anymore. My only hope is to keep my daughter safe. And you can't do that based on faith.

A Dark Mafia Christmas

"Marco. This is a shitty plan."

"Language, Caterina."

I do roll my eyes then. "I'm a grown woman. I've had a literal child. I can cuss if I want to."

"Not if you're going to play the part of a good Italian wife you won't."

I'm pretty sure that Marco's ideas of a 'good Italian wife' are based on mob movies and Grandpa's tales of mob life in the '60s, but I don't point that out.

To my knowledge, which is based on the internet and no other experience, Italian women have moved into the modern world with the rest of us.

Then again, families like ours and the Rossi's go way back in history so...

Maybe old habits die hard.

"Luna will be just fine," he says with a genuine smile.

I don't return it.

He notices and the smile fades. "Caterina, seriously. You think that I would let my favorite niece come to any harm? If Elio finds her, he's a dead man," Marco says with a drop in his voice that makes me shiver.

Sometimes I forget that my brothers, while being my brothers, are also gangsters.

And they can be pretty freaking scary if they need to.

"I don't doubt that. I know how much you love Luna. But Marco..." I squeeze my eyes shut against the tears that prick at the edges of my vision.

"Sorellina, I know. I know what I'm asking of you. I promise you that if I thought you or Luna would be in danger, I wouldn't do it. It's our only course of action, yes. But more than that, it's a plan that will work," he emphasizes the last word softly.

I shut my eyes tighter as the tears flood me. "Please don't make me do this," I whisper.

I really am begging now.

I hate it.

I don't beg. Not to Marco, not my two other brothers. Not to anyone.

But I don't want to see Elio ever again. Let alone marry him.

"Caterina, I swear to you. It's a foolproof plan. We just need—"

"Zietto Marco!" a small voice squeaks.

Instantly I steel myself. Luna can't see me cry.

I won't let her know how hard this is.

To her knowledge, she's just going to stay with Nonna Mia for a while, my grandmother's ancient half-sister. Nonna Mia is a black sheep in many ways, and since her connection to the family is tenuous at best, we figure she would be the best spot to hide Luna while we try and bring down Elio and the Rossis.

Also, she lives on a farm and has goats. Luna will be charmed the entire time.

There's a blur of dark hair and light-up shoes, and my child throws herself in Marco's lap. He laughs, then stands and swings her around. Her delighted shrieks are a balm to my nerves, but only slightly.

A Dark Mafia Christmas

Any guilt that I've had over the years about Luna not having a father is entirely erased when she's around my brothers. The three of them are protective as hell, and they spoil her better than any father could. They're perfect together.

All the more reason that we don't need Elio to be a part of our lives. Now, in the future, or ever again.

"Zietto, did you know that the outside of your door is seven feet and three and one four inches tall?"

I grin while Marco pretends to be surprised and engages with Luna.

Luna has been really into measuring things lately. I would blame her kindergarten teacher, but I love it. Her school does a lot of experiential learning, and a local hardware store gifted them all tape measures.

Luna has always loved to build and construct, so she's been really interested in understanding how things are put together. There's no doubt that she's been outside of the office carefully measuring the doorframe for this entire conversation.

There's also no doubt in my mind that she was blissfully unaware of what we were talking about.

Being five is a blessing, and Luna is an even bigger one.

"We should go," I whisper. It's not safe for Luna and me to be around the main house; there's no doubt that Elio and his spies have eyes all over this place.

Luckily, my grandfather was a wildly paranoid man, and Luna and I could use the tunnel system that he installed to our advantage.

Elio hasn't found out about her yet. He appears to have no

interest in me whatsoever past that night, which is fine with me.

I'm done hating him for his indifference.

Apparently, my brothers and I have moved into a much colder phase of our feelings for Elio.

Revenge.

"One week, sorellina. Then we begin."

I gulp.

One week of waiting. And then it's time to marry my worst enemy.

And the father of my child.

———

The drive back to our townhouse is quick. I live close enough to the main house that I'm easy to get to if needed, and so that the security that Marco pays for can easily zip back and forth if required to.

Hans, my personal bodyguard, is German, unusual for a mafia hire, but he's a great guy and a fantastic bodyguard. I wave at him as we walk in. He waves back; he and his wife are expecting a little girl in a few months, and he's been asking a lot of questions about Luna's birth in order to prepare to be supportive.

I love that. It's exactly the kind of father a kid needs.

After I settle Luna in for bed, I pour a glass of the Prosecco that I'm trying to bring to market and go out to my balcony. I linger, just for a minute, and grab the locket that I never take off.

A Dark Mafia Christmas

Its only contents are a picture of my mom and me.

"I miss you, Mamma," I whisper at the sky.

My mother was a ray of sunshine. She had been against the marriage contract with Elio from the beginning and had only agreed when the last of her uncles was thrown in jail, right before I was born.

I wasn't certain what the exact terms of the contract were. My dad and Elio's dad had come up with them while they were out drinking and carousing in Atlantic City, of all places, and they had ensured that neither one of their families had access to the safe deposit box.

A brilliant plan.

My mother thought so as well. She berated both of them, but at the time, I hadn't been born yet. The deal was to have Giovanni Rossi's first son marry Antonio De Luca's oldest daughter.

Who turned out to be me.

To my knowledge, Marco still hasn't seen the original document, and neither has Elio. The location of the original contract is still a mystery.

But the terms aren't.

The Rossi family runs a shipping empire. They import luxury goods from every corner of the globe, but mostly through Europe.

Those goods come into ports that were, at one time, staffed by De Luca workers. The De Lucas would then take the goods, along with anything else that showed up in those crates, and turn them into cash, which the Rossi's would get a cut of.

A healthy cut of goods that were both legal and illegal.

The Rossi family is Italian. Like, Elio and all of his siblings except one were born in Italy and they only have citizenship in America because of some slick dealings and greased palms.

The De Lucas, via my great-grandfather and great-grandmother, came to the United States around the turn of the century. At first, we did quite well; there's a whole section dedicated to us in The Mob Museum in Las Vegas. I've never been, but Dino says that it's a hoot.

Then, along with the rest of organized crime in America, the feds got smarter than we were, and one by one, De Lucas filled up prisons from sea to shining sea.

With the lack of manpower came a decline in our ability to be the pin in the Rossi flow of goods. We still have a solid presence on the docks in the Port of New York, but it's nowhere near what it used to be.

My dad and Elio's dad must have been drunk on some prime shit, reminiscing about some old times, in order to dream up this ridiculous arrangement.

With the unification of the families, the Rossi's agreed to only use De Luca docks and De Luca distributors to sell. This is a terrible plan because the amount of goods that Rossi Industries brings in would vastly overwhelm our workforce.

I have no idea what Elio gets out of this deal.

Well... I did once. I grimace and sip my Prosecco.

Me.

There was a time when Elio and I would have been good for each other. I was a wide-eyed girl, just starting my junior year of college. He was handsome; he was my brother's age, and they had been friends since grade school.

I can't remember how handsome he is.

Physically, I'm capable of remembering. I see his unusual grey eyes every time I look at my daughter's face. I see the slope of his cheeks, the tilt of his nose. There's no doubt that she has Elio's face.

Thank God it's a pretty face, for both of their sakes.

And thank God even more for the fact that her personality is all mine.

I'm capable of remembering how handsome Elio is for sure.

But I *can't* remember it.

Because if I think about how attractive he is, how he makes my knees feel soft and wobbly when he smiles that dimpled smile, I'm going to do something stupid.

And I can't be stupid.

Not in this.

Not when so much is riding on it.

Elio Rossi made me very, very stupid once.

And I'm never going to be that girl again.

Elio

There's only one week left until I finally get my revenge on Marco De Luca.

It's going to be the longest fucking week of my life.

Since I dislike spending any time stewing in my own dread, I've decided to spend the week at my villa in Tivoli as a way to avoid the impending disaster of the marriage contract.

It's a little treat. Something I'm giving myself before my life totally goes to hell, and I turn into the villain in so many stories.

It's a price I'm willing to pay if it means that our parents will finally be avenged.

I take a deep breath, inhaling the light scent of the orange blossoms from the trees that are scattered through my property.

I love it here. This is the only one of our many familial properties and holdings that is truly and completely mine. I bought it seven years ago, intending for the villa to be a wedding gift for the beautiful and young Caterina De Luca.

She never saw it, so it became a gift to me. It's a haven, of sorts, that I have used many times since that horrible night.

If I had to, however, I'd trade it to have my parents back in a heartbeat.

I'm brought from my reverie by the crisp sound of heels clicking down the marble hallway to my office. "Boss," my twin sister Gia, knocks on the doorframe in a very cursory gesture of respect before entering my space. "New intel."

I grimace.

First, Gia only calls me 'boss' when she's got some really fucking bad news.

Second, if the intel is new, I don't want it.

The plan was perfect as I had it. If there are any adjustments, any pivots...

That perfection is gone.

And I demand nothing but perfection.

Softly I curse in Italian before looking at my sister. "What, Gia?"

She raises her eyebrows, and her hands crack like she's holding back from punching me in the face.

Well.

That makes two of us, I guess.

"Your bride-to-be is suspicious as hell."

I snort. I know that's the truth: for years she was simply beneath my notice, and so I didn't invest any time into finding or keeping her in one place.

Quite honestly, I never wanted to lay eyes on Caterina De Luca ever again.

And yet.

I sigh.

Being a Rossi is a sacrifice. It costs us everything and gives us everything.

I'm sure my father didn't intend for that to include the cost of his life when he said it, but here we are.

Both of our lives, gone.

Given to the family. To the business. Given in service of a deal with the devil that wore the face of a friend.

The De Lucas were close with us once. American, though their ancestors had come from Italy, they were my family's 'in' to the ocean of untapped buyers that the States offered us.

Somehow, every last one of them landed behind bars. Which meant their ability to operate ports and find markets for our particular brand of exports diminished.

Which meant their usefulness to us ended.

It never made sense to me that Father had entered into such a stupid bargain with the De Lucas. We didn't need them.

After their grip on the Port of New York loosened, we found other pathways. The Russians. The Japanese. Hell, even the Irish offered a more promising route to American markets than the De Lucas did.

But after one weekend in Atlantic City, my father came back and declared that he and Antonio De Luca had made an agreement. An arrangement. Binding the two families together.

An oldest son for an oldest daughter.

The irony, of course, is that the oldest daughter was also the youngest daughter. Six years younger than me, Caterina De Luca started out as my friend Marco's little sister.

That's how I thought of her. For years. I had known, of course, that we would be married at some point.

My father made it very clear to me when I entered my teens that any female companionship that I managed to wrangle would have to be non-committal at best, because Caterina De Luca would be my wife someday.

As with all of the men in my family, my father had a healthy appreciation for sex workers and mistresses, and while he did not discourage the use of either, he did encourage me to keep it quiet. I didn't need to be told twice, and it wasn't like I could mess around too much anyway.

After all, for every private party or club I went to, my bride's older brother was right there next to me.

I would miss Marco, I supposed.

If I did not hate him so violently.

"What is the intel, Gia," I say with exactly as much exasperation as I feel.

She slaps down a packet of pictures. "Bodyguard. On her 24/7. Looks like just one though. A condo. I think she nannies for a little girl in the family. Any of the brothers have a good time they forgot to keep under wraps?"

Gia's puns will be the death of me.

Provided, of course, that any of the other multitude of actors slavering for my demise don't work out.

"Marco probably not. I imagine he got the same level of emphasis that I did about accidental... mishaps."

"The others?" she prompts.

I frown. "Dino and..."

"Sal. The hot one," she clarifies.

"Gia. He is three years younger than you."

She arches an eyebrow. "Hotness doesn't have an age."

Ugh. She sounds so *American*. "He is the son of the man who killed our parents."

"Yeah, yeah. He's still hot. Anyway. Either one of them have a surprise baby?"

I sigh. "We should look into it. That type of leverage could be useful."

"More useful than being married to their precious baby angel younger sister?"

Her tone is sharp. I know she doesn't approve of this plan.

It is, however, the best option.

"We will have a backup. If the child proves useful, we will make use of it. If Caterina is the most useful, we will make use of her. Find out who is the father, and we will go from there."

Gia gathers the pictures and taps them sharply, collecting them back into one pile. "You know," she says with a pause. "You don't have to do this."

I close my eyes. "Not this again, Gia."

"Listen. We can send Enzo. He can work his way up in the organization..."

"Enzo, who is nearly identical to Father at that age?"

Gia shakes her head. "They don't know. It's not like there's a picture of him lying around the De Luca estate or anything."

"Marco will know. He spent plenty of time with Father and I."

"I know, but if we can just find the contract..."

I slam my fist down on my desk. "Enough, Gia!"

The hurt in her eyes cuts me, but I hold her gaze. Gia and I are fraternal twins, but our looks are so similar that when we were both tiny and sported terrible bowl cuts, people would mistake us for each other.

She is my sister. My best friend. My closest confidante.

And even to her, I am a monster.

Sacrifice. "We are not looking for the contract, Gia. There's no point. The only way for us to get Marco and the De Lucas to admit that they killed our parents is to use their greatest weakness against them.

"Caterina is young. She's naïve. She's been sheltered by three older brothers who would do anything for her, and she's the person who will hurt them the most when we take her."

Gia's expression morphs into something hard. Her lips draw tight, and the corners of her eyes look pinched.

"I understand, boss."

With that, she leaves.

I sit back in my chair. My head is pounding now, and I lean forward to pinch the bridge of my nose between my fingers. The orange blossom-scented air reaches out to me again, and I inhale deeply, letting it soothe me as I try to think around the pulsing in my mind.

Everything that I said about Caterina is true.

She is the youngest of the De Lucas. She's been painfully sheltered by her three older brothers to the point where her innocence is so obvious on her face that it's almost palpable.

After Marco and I graduated from business school, I moved back to Italy. An American education through young adulthood was plenty for my family, but the promise of a business degree had been mine.

The last time I saw Caterina prior to our engagement party, she was fourteen. She was all legs and glasses and frizzy, wild curls. Remembering Gia at that age, I had been polite but indifferent. I had kept a wide berth from her, because she was a child.

When I saw her again at our engagement party, I had been expecting that child.

But instead, a woman had shown up.

I think Marco may have pinched me a little too hard when his sister, on the arms of Sal, the brother closest to her in age, walked into the room.

I breathe in the citrus blossoms again. Dio santo, I remember everything about that night.

Her dress. A lilac color that made her look like some kind of fairy tale princess.

The way her skin glowed in the candlelight.

The way her lips had rounded on my name, shaping it into syllables that I knew, but hearing them from her made me feel reborn.

The way her eyes glittered when we danced.

My jaw works as I try to stop myself from remembering more.

Because there is so much more to remember.

The sweet surprise of her lips as I parted them with my tongue. The little noises she made when I pushed the gown off of her shoulders, releasing her pert breasts to the cool night air.

The way she gasped my name, first as she came around my fingers, next as she came...

Read Mafia King's Secret Baby FREE With Kindle Unlimited and available on Paperback.

ABOUT THE AUTHOR

VIVY SKYS the author of Steamy Contemporary Romance novels, featuring smart, strong, sassy and witty female characters that command the attention of strong protective alpha males, from Off limits, Age Gap, Bossy Billionaires, Single dads next door, Royalty, Dark Mafia and beyond Vivy's pen will deliver.

Follow Vivy Skys on Amazon to be the first to know when her next book becomes available.

Fashion diary

패션 다이어리

권순수 지음

미호

Prologue

**오랜 친구와 나누는 속 깊은 수다,
거창하지 않아도 숨통이 탁 트이는 소소한 대화,
나는 당신에게 그런 의미가 되고 싶다**

〈프로젝트 런웨이 코리아〉가 끝난 이후, 패션 디자이너가 되고 싶은 학생들에게 많은 메일을 받았다. 대부분 이제 패션을 시작하려고 하거나, 이미 경험을 했지만 풀리지 않는 고민들로 도움을 요청하는 내용이었다. 처음 메일을 받았을 때는 수많은 성공한 디자이너를 두고 나에게 이런 것들을 물어보나 아리송했다. 하지만 하나하나 질문에 대답해주면서 그 의문이 저절로 풀렸다. 그 친구들은 성공한 디자이너의 무용담이 아닌, 현재 우리가 살고 있는 세계에서 마주하게 되는 고민에 대해 나눌 진솔한 대화 상대가 필요했던 것이다.

난 아직 세상적으로 무엇을 크게 이룬 사람도 아니고, 그들의 고민에 일일이 멋진 정답을 줄 수 있는 위

치는 더더욱 아니다. 오히려 그렇기 때문에 지금의 내 생각과 모습을 이 책에 솔직하게 담으려 했다. '이렇게 해야지 멋진 디자이너가 된다'라고 말하는 대신 '나는 지금 이렇게 패션 디자이너가 되어가고 있어. 너는 어떠니?' 하고 물으며 대화하고 싶었다.

　이 책은 처음 내가 디자이너가 되기로 결심한 순간부터 지금까지 있었던 소소한 일상을 기록한 일기장이다. 〈프런코〉를 통해서 어쩌면 조금 더 멋지게 포장되었을지 모를 내 모습이 아닌, 낡은 티셔츠 차림으로 나만 보는 일기장에 쓸 이야기들을 담았다. 런던에서, 아직은 너무나 부족하지만, 패션 디자인을 가슴 뛰게 사랑하는 한 사람으로서.

　글을 쓰면서 혼자 울기도, 웃기도 많이 했다. 내 삶을 돌아볼 수 있는 계기가 되어 감사했고, 지금의 나를 보며 미래를 기대할 수 있었기에 많이 뿌듯했다. 무엇보다도 글을 쓰는 내내 즐거웠고, 기뻤다. 이제 출판을 코앞에 두고 있는 상황에서 이 책을 읽게 될 사람들을 생각하면 가슴이 설렌다. 이 책을 집고, 열어준 누군가에게 감사하다는 말을 건네본다.

　한 가지 바람이 있다면, 나에게 메일을 보냈던 학생들과 상황이 그다지 다르지 않은 혹은 몇 년 전의 나와 비슷한 일들로 고민하는 친구들이 이 책을 펼쳤을 때, 내 사소한 생각들이 그들에게 조금이라도 도움이 되면 좋겠다는 것이다. 또한 이름도, 얼굴도 모르지만 이 책을 펼치고 있을 누군가에게 좋은 친구 같은 책이 되었으면 좋겠다. 런던에서 패션을 공부하는 말 많은 친구가 조잘조잘 이야기하는 느낌이 충분히 전해지길. 함께 같은 길을 걷고 있다는 것만으로도 기분이 좋아지는 하나 더 생긴 느낌이 들기를.

런던에서 순수가

Contents

Prologue 004

.1 순수의
프로젝트 런웨이 코리아

014 나의 샌드위치 이어, 프로젝트 런웨이 코리아

022 천천히 걸어가는 나만의 템포, 나만의 시계

030 경쟁에서 살아남는다는 것

036 국내파도, 해외파도 없다! 좋은 디자이너만 있을 뿐

042 내겐 과분한 기회 〈프런코〉와 그 이후의 이야기

2 나는 멋진 디자이너가 되고 싶다

- **050** 너는 정말 옷 만드는 걸 좋아하는구나
- **060** 아트와 패션, 그 작고도 큰 차이
- **072** 이브 생 로랑 블라우스와의 조우
- **078** 사랑할 수밖에 없는 드레스 반 노튼
- **086** 나에게 집중하는 시간, 요지 야마모토 전시
- **092** 나는 빈티지가 좋다
- **100** 사막에서 오아시스를 만나다! 인스피레이션
- **110** 세인트 마틴에서의 마지막 프로젝트

Book 패션을 공부한다면 꼭 읽어보세요 **116**

3 런던 다이어리

- 122 여유와 느림이 있는 곳! 내 사랑, 런던
- 128 때때로 외로워진다면, 로열 페스티벌 홀
- 134 마약 대신 로트렉을 만나다
- 142 오늘 왠지 예뻐 보인다면, 매니큐어 때문일 거야
- 148 벼룩시장에서 쇼핑하기
- 156 자연의 색이 내 모든 감각을 깨우고
- 164 초등학교 3학년, 내 꿈이 시작된 날
- 168 내가 런던에 있는 것은 기적이다
- 174 자유로운 사고를 가진 세인트 마틴 친구들
- 180 즐거움과 욕심은 종이 한 장 차이
- 188 머리를 자르고 자유를 얻었다

Habit 패션을 공부하는 학생에게 필요한 세 가지 습관 194

Epilogue 202

순수의
프로젝트 런웨이
코리아

1
**나의 샌드위치 이어,
프로젝트 런웨이 코리아**

작년 한 해는 세인트 마틴에서 마지막 학년^{final year}을 남겨두고 가진 샌드위치 이어^{sandwich year}였다. 샌드위치 이어란, 학교를 떠나 1년 동안 회사나 다른 곳에서 일하면서 더 많은 경험과 실력을 쌓는 학년이다. 나 또한 졸업을 앞두고 샌드위치 이어를 가지기로 했다. 2년 동안 패션을 공부하면서 가장 갈급했던 건 아이러니하게도 옷을 만드는 것이었다.

세인트 마틴은 4주 혹은 2주짜리 프로젝트 방식으로 수업이 진행된다. 한 프로젝트당 옷을 하나에서 한 벌까지 만들기도 한다. 예를 들어, 4주짜리 프로젝트는 리서치와 아이디어를 발전시키는 데 2주 정도 쓰고, 1주는 디자인과 가봉을 하고, 나머지 1주는 실제로 옷을 만든다. 한 학기에 4개에서 5개의 프로젝트가 있으니 결국 한 학기에 옷을 4벌에서 5벌 정도 만든다는 얘기다.

나는 생각과 리서치에 많은 시간을 투자하는 세인트 마틴의 수업방식이 정말 마음에 든다. 옷을 만들기 전에 충분한 생각과 아이디어의 발전을 통해 자신의 생각을 옷에 담을 수 있는 디자이너가 될 수 있게 도와주는 바람직한 수업방식이다. 단지 한정된 시간이 아쉬웠다. 할 수 있는 프로젝트는 정해져 있고, 만들어보고 싶은 디자인의 옷은 한정이 없으니 말이다. 패션을 공부한 지 2년밖에 안된 나로서는 4주에 한 번씩 옷을 만드는 수업만으로 옷에 대한 궁금증과 열정을 풀기에는 부족했다.

머릿속에 이미지로만 존재하는 평면의 드로잉을 실제 사람이 옷을 입었을 때 아름다운 입체로 만드는 과정은 몇몇 기술을 아는 것만으로는 끝나지 않는다. 수도 없이 디자인을 바꿔가며 시도해야만 머릿속의 모양이 실제 입체로 나타난다. 옷을 많이 만들어보지 않았던 나로서는 이미지를 눈에 보이는 입체로 만들어가는 과정이 즐거웠다. 진정으로 인체와 옷의 관계를 이해하고, 공부하는 데는 입체로 원단을 다루는 작업이 반드시 필요하다고 생각했다. 선생님들의 말에 의하면, 존 갈리아노가 세인트 마틴에 다닐 때 그는 매일 늦게까지 학교에 남아 입체 작업과 이런저런 색다른 시도를 했다고 했다.

난 평소에는 학교에서 프로젝트를 진행하며 공부하고, 집에 돌아와서는 내가 시도해보고 싶은 입체 작업에 도전해봤다. 하지만 항상 충분하지 못한 시간이 답답했다. 프로젝트가 없는 방학에는 한 달 내내 집에 틀어박혀 온 종일 옷만 만들기도 했다. 그래서 작년에 계획한 것은, 샌드위치 이어에는 나의 갈급함을 충분히 해소할 수 있을 만큼 옷을 많이 만들어보는 것이었다. 물론 좋은 디자이너 회사에서 인턴을 하고 싶다는 생각도 있었다. 하지만 그것보다 내가 궁금해하고 만들어보고 싶었던 옷을 충분히 완성해보고 싶었다.

〈프로젝트 런웨이 코리아〉^{이하 〈프런코〉}는 이런 나의 갈증을 해소시켜주었다. 더구나 재미있는 방법으로 즐겁게 작업을 할 수 있는 기회이기도 했다. 옷을 신나게 많이 만들어보는 것, 머릿속에 있는 이미지를 패스트푸드같이 빠르게 입체로 만들어내는 것은 학교를 다니는 동안 너무나 하고 싶었던 일이었다.

반쯤 완성된 파이널 컬렉션의 옷. 처음 가져본 나만의 작업실에서 행복한 시간을 보냈다.

작업에 열중하고 있는 내 모습. 파이널 컬렉션을 향해 달려가고 있다.

예상대로 〈프런코〉에서의 작업은 즐거웠다. 매회 미션을 받을 때마다 즉흥적으로 머릿속에 떠오르는 생각과 이미지를 그림으로 그리고, 어떤 작품이 나올지 모르는 상태에서 그것들을 입체로 옮겨 갔다. 어처구니 없을 정도로 전혀 예상치 못한 작품도 있었고, 어떤 것은 머릿속의 생각과 딱 맞아떨어지는 것도 있었다.

제레미 스캇이 심사를 맡았던 미션, 가수 씨엘의 무대의상을 만들라는 미션을 받자마자 하트 모양의 옷을 만들고 싶다는 생각이 떠올랐다. 한번도 만들어본 적 없고, 어떻게 만들어야 할지도 모르겠지만 그저 재미있을 것 같았다. 그렇게 '사랑에 빠진 드래곤'을 주제로 오버사이즈 재킷을 디자인했다. 다소 강한 느낌을 주지만 하트를 모티브로 했기에 유머러스한 분위기 또한 놓치지 않았다.

이게 진짜 하트 모양이 되기는 할까? 옷을 만들고 있는 나조차도 어떻게 될지 감이 안 잡혔다. 먼저 철사를 구부려 하트 모양을 만들고 마네킹에 붙여서 드레이핑을 했다. 가봉이 끝나고 스티로폼이 들어간 원단으로 재봉을 마치고 두근거리는 마음으로 옷을 뒤집었는데 뽕! 하고 하트 모양의 어깨가 나왔다. 순간 온몸에서 전율이 일었다. 이렇게 열 가지 미션을 수행하는 동안 다양한 방법으로 옷을 만들며 즐거운 시간을 보냈다. 몸은 힘들었지만 신나게 옷만 만들면 되는 매일매일이 즐거웠다.

하지만 정말 즐거웠던 시간은 열 가지 미션이 끝나고 시작됐다. 마지막 미션까지 살아남고, 마지막 세 명 안에 들게 되면서 컬렉션을 준비할 기회가 온 것이다. 그것도 많은 사람들 앞에 선보이게 될 컬렉션이라니 정말 신났다. 4개월 동안 내가 원하는 주제로 내 생각을 온전히 담아서 하루 종일 옷만 만든다고 생각하니 말할 수 없이 행복했다. 처음 한 달간 여행을 하고, 리서치를 하고, 아이디어를 발전시키고, 내 생각을 옷으로 표현하기 위한 준비에 들어갔다.

아직은 공부하는 학생이기에 이번 컬렉션을 통해 한국의 다양한 기술과 환경을 활용해보자고 다짐했다. 런던에서는 환경이 주어지지 않아 해보지 못했던 작업들이 많았기 때문이다. 손 염색, 프린트, 레이저 커팅, 뜨개질, 실리콘 작업, 플라스틱 작업, 본뜨기, 조소 작업, 후로킹, 신발 만들기 등 실제 컬렉션에 적용되지 않는 많은 작업을 한 달 동안 맘껏 해봤다. 그중 몇 가지는 쇼가 있기 며칠 전 작업 과정 중 실수가 생겨 엄청 난감하기도 했지만, 그러한 시도까지도 소중한 경험이었다.

또한 디자인을 입체로 만들기 위해 끊임없이 가봉을 했다. 그 당시 두 달간 사용했던 패턴지가 200장 정도였고, 광목이 150미터였으니 원 없이 작업했다고 할 수 있겠다. 하루하루 보내면서 조금씩 옷에 대한 이해가 늘고 있다는 생각이 들었고, 완벽하지는 않지만 주어진 시간 안에 컬렉션을 준비할 수 있었다. 어떠한 방해도 없이 내 생각에 집중하고, 나의 생각을 옷으로 만들었던 네 달이라는 시간은 다시는 오지 않을 소중한 기회였다.

프로그램이 끝날 즈음, 일등에 대한 욕심이 없었던 것은 아니었다. 태어나서 처음으로 컬렉션을 준비했기에 나의 작업을 사람들한테 인정받고 싶었다. 하지만 내가 갈급했던 옷에 대한 궁금증과 작업에 대한 열정을 후회없이 쏟아냈기 때문에 다시 돌아봐도 감사하고 즐거운 시간이었다. 컬렉션을 준비하면서 내 자신을 발전시켜 나가고 부족했던 부분을 많이 채울 수 있었다. 마지막 촬영 날, 일등을 발표하고 나서 했던 마지막 인터뷰가 생각난다.

"우리는 계획을 세우지만 그 계획이 현실로 실현되는 것은 정말 어렵다. 나 역시 샌드위치 이어를 통해 옷에 대한 갈급을 풀 수 있을 거라 기대했지만, 이렇게 완벽하게 실현될 줄은 몰랐다. 더구나 내가 계획했던 것보다 더 멋진 방법으로 말이다."

프로그램이 시작될 때 내가 원했던 것보다 더 많은 것을 얻었다. 내가 집에 가지고 가기에는 너무나 소중한 경험이었고, 그냥 받았다고 하기에는 가슴 벅찰 만큼 감사한 선물이었다. 처음으로 나도 모르게 카메라 앞에서 눈물이 났다. 다시 런던으로 돌아온 지금, 샌드위치 이어가 끝나가고 있으며, 파이널 이어가 나를 기다리고 있다. 나는 다시 옷을 사랑하는 학생으로 돌아왔다.

2 천천히 걸어가는
나만의 템포, 나만의 시계

난 느린 것을 좋아한다. 순수한 시골 냄새 나는 부모님의 영향인지, 타고난 천성인지는 잘 모르겠다. 어쨌든 나는 빠르게 움직이는 도시보다는 시골이 좋고, 놀이동산에서 노는 것보다는 잔디밭에 아무것도 안 하고 누워 있는 것이 좋다.

운이 좋은 것은 내 친구들도 나의 이런 성격과 많이 닮았다는 것이다. 한국에 있는 친구들은 1년에 한 번, 여름방학 두 달밖에 볼 수 없다. 하지만 한국에 가면 수도 없이 함께 여행을 간다. 친구의 말을 빌리자면, 우리에겐 소위 '역마살'이 있어서 한군데 오래 있는 것을 못 견뎌하는 거란다. 한국의 많은 곳을 다녔지만, 재미있는 사실은 캐리비안 배이나 놀이동산처럼 젊은 여자들이 좋아할 만한 곳은 한 번도 가지 않았다는 것이다. 우리가 하는 여행은 2박3일간 친구 할머니네 집에 가기, 버스 타고 전라도와 경상도를 넘나드는 화개장터나 청학동 가기 등 어떻게 보면 참 재미없는 코스다. 하지만 우리만의 템포로 천천히 내 자신을 세상에 풀어놓는 이런 여행이 나는 훨씬 즐겁다.

패션에 있어서도 나만의 시계가 있다. 째깍째깍 한 걸음, 한 걸음 천천히 걸어가는 나만의 시계. 이것이 남보다 느린지, 빠른지는 모르겠다. 어쩌면 남들과 똑같을 수도 있다. 하지만 확실한 것은 주위의 속도와 상관없이 나만의 템포가 있다는 것이다. 처음 붓을 잡기 시작했을 때부터 지금까지, 좋은 패션 디자이너가 되기 위해 하나하나 차근차근 배우며 즐겁게 작업하려고 노력하고 있다.

하지만 나도 처음에는 욕심을 부렸고, 급한 성격으로 조급해했다. 패션을 심도 있게 이해하기 위해 예술고등학교에서 서양화를 전공했던 나는 누구보다 패션을 빨리 시작하고 싶었다. 하지만 패션을 시작하고 마음처럼 멋지게 작업이 진행되지 않아 답답한 시간을 겪기도 했다. 책에서 봤던 천재 디자이너들처럼 마음만 먹으면 마네킹 위에 천을 대고 가위를 휘날리며 열정적으로 옷을 만들 수 있을 줄 알았는데, 실력이 따라주지 않았다. 옷의 구조를 제대로 알지 못하고, 입체에 대한 이해 없이는 아무리 천재라도 그렇게 옷을 만들지는 못한다. 엄청난 능력을 지닌 천재라면 가능할지 모르겠지만. 나는 그런 천재도 아니었고, 모자라는 실력에 마음이 급해졌다. 내가 공부해야 할 것이 산더미 같았고, 그렇게 조급해한다고 한번에 모든 것을 배울 수 있는 것도 아니었다.

바로 앞에 있는 것을 잡으려면 전력을 다해 뛰어야 한다. 하지만 나는 이제 막 달리기를 시작한 아주 멀리 뛰어야 할 사람이었다. 더구나 어릴 적부터 순수미술을 하시는 아버지를 보며 예술의 세계는 끝이 없다는 것 또한 알고 있었다. 끝이 없는 길을 어떻게 뛰어간단 말인가. 또한 뛰어가면 반드시 빨리 지치는 법. 그때부터 나는 모든 걸 배우고 알고 싶은 급한 마음을 진정시키고, 천천히 내 템포대로 걸어가야겠다고 생각했다.

하지만 이렇게 째깍째깍 돌아가던 나의 시계가 갑자기 가속도가 붙은 적이 있었다. 바로 〈프런코〉였다. 이 프로그램이 시즌 1을 시작했을 때 난 런던에 있었기에 한국에서 젊은이들 사이에 얼마나 인기 있는 프로그램인지 잘 몰랐다. 내가 프로그램에 출연하고, 방송에 나가면서 느낀 것은 생각보다 많은 사람이 〈프런코〉를 본다는 것이다. 한창 방송이 나가던 시기에 난 홍대 앞에 있는 작업실에서 컬렉션을 준비하고 있었다. 그리고 경희대 앞에 있는 언니 집에 살면서 매일 경희대와 홍대를 오갔다. 대학 주변이라 젊은이들이 많았고, 나를 알아보는 사람도 정말 많았다. 어떤 사람은 같이 사진을 찍자고 했고, 사인을 해달라는 사람도 많았다. 어디를 가든 적어도 몇 명은 나를 알아봤다. 싫지 않은 묘한 기분이었다.

〈프런코〉에 출연하고 컬렉션을 준비하면서 나의 실력이 많이 나아진 것은 사실이다. 컬렉션을 준비하는 3개월 동안 수도 없이 많은 가봉을 했으니 실력이 안 늘 수가 없었다. 하지만 난 패션을 시작한 지 얼마 되지 않은, 가야 할 길이 먼 학생이다. 아직 패션을 공부하고 있는, 긴장되고 떨리는 마지막 학년을 남겨두고 있는 학생이다.

그런데 〈프런코〉에 출연하면서 갑자기 사람들이 나를 학생이 아닌 패션 디자이너로 부르기 시작했다. 마치 로또를 맞아 평민에서 벼락부자가 된 사람처럼 말이다. 한순간에 신분이 바뀌어버린 나에게는 아주 이상한 일이었다.

처음에는 누가 디자이너라고만 불러도 쑥스럽고 이상했는데 시간이 흐르면서 많은 사람이 나를 그렇게 부르자 자신도 모르게 내가 진짜 디자이너가 된 것 같았다. 물론 내 이름으로 '서울 패션 위크'에서 컬렉션도 갖게 되었고, 많은 사람에게 내 옷을 선보이긴 했지만 아직 내 신분은 학생인데 말이다. 물론 대학을 졸업한다고 디자이너가 되는 것은 아니며, 학생 신분으로도 디자이너가 될 수는 있다. 하지만 나는 아직은 더 배워야 하는 사람이다. 그래서 지금은 나를 학생이라는, 조금은 더 가능성이 많은 신분으로 묶어놓고 싶다.

내가 〈프런코〉 이전보다 실력이 나아졌다고 해도 그건 내가 조금 발전한 것뿐이다. 난 지금 내가 어디에 있는지 누구보다 잘 안다. 어디로 가고 있는지, 내가 지금 얼만큼 왔는지도 잘 알고 있다. 〈프런코〉는 인생에서 한번 올까 말까 한 너무나 값진 기회이고 경험이었지만 내가 가는 이 길에서는 하나의 이벤트일 뿐이었다. 내가 〈프런코〉에서 뭔가를 이뤄야 하고, 내 길의 끝이라고 생각했다면 일등에 대한 욕심이 더욱 컸을 것이다. 하지만 〈프런코〉는 어디까지나 좋은 신진 디자이너를 배출하는 텔레비전 프로그램일 뿐, 거기서 일등을 했다고 성공한 디자이너가 되는 것도 아니고 꼴등을 했다고 디자이너가 될 수 없는 것도 아니다. 그저 내가 패션 디자이너로 가는 길에 있었던 행복하고 감사한 경험이었다.

컬렉션도 끝나고 모든 방송이 끝났다. 그리고 짧은 기간에 생각지도 못했던 많은 것을 경험했다. 컬렉션을 준비하면서 내 실력이 나아진 것은 물론이거니와 이제는 옷을 제대로 이해한다는 자신감 또한 생겼다. 그리고 많은 사람이 나를 알게 되었고, 너무나 감사하게도 나의 옷을 좋아해줬다. 마치 비밀스런 지름길을 찾은 것처럼 내가 수고해서 걸어가야 했던 길을 몇 단계 뛰어넘은 기분이었다. 운이 좋아서 힘든 과정을 즐겁게 달려오기는 했지만 내가 가야 할 길 위에 있는 것은 여전했다. 모든 것이 끝나고 하루라도 빨리 나의 작업 공간이 있고, 학교가 있는 런던으로 돌아가고 싶었다.

방송이 나간 직후 많은 곳에서 연락이 왔었다. 개학을 앞둔 9월 말, 아직은 시간이 남아 있었고 〈프런코〉를 통해 받은 관심으로 다양한 일을 할 수도 있었다. 지금 생각해보면 할걸 그랬나, 하는 좋은 제안도 있었지만 나는 학교로 돌아가기로 했다. 내가 가야 할 길 위에서 흔들리고 싶지 않았다. 〈프런코〉 출연 이후 사람들이 나를 디자이너라고 부르자 나도 모르게 학생의 모습을 잊어버리고, 이대로 빨리 '패션 디자이너'가 되고 싶은 욕심이 생겼다.

내가 차근차근 배워야 할 것들이 건너뛰어도 될 것같이 사소하게 느껴졌다. 이미 사람들이 디자이너라고 불러주는데 이 정도면 되는 거 아닌가, 하는 생각마저 들었다. 〈프런코〉는 내가 좋은 디자이너가 되는 데 큰 도움이 되겠지만 이 프로그램을 통해 얻은 사람들의 관심과 빨리 몇 단계 건너뛰고 싶은 욕심은 차근차근 먼 길을 걸어가야 하는 나를 방해하는 위험한 유혹이기도 했다.

빨리 런던으로 돌아가서 예전의 나로 돌아가고 싶었다. 그런 달콤한 유혹이 잠시라는 것을 잘 알고 있었기 때문이다. 사람들이 나를 디자이너로 부르든 말든, 나는 아직 학생이다. 하지만 빨리, 쉽게 뛰어가고 싶은 욕심이 나를 자꾸 부추겼다. 그래서 나는 빨리 런던으로 돌아가고 싶었다.

패션에는 지름길이 없다. 지름길처럼 보이지만 그것은 단지 조금 더 빨리 갈 수 있는 길일 뿐, 결국 똑같다. 같은 지점을 목표로 할 때, 지름길로 온 사람은 천천히 걸어온 사람이 볼 수 있는 많은 것을 놓칠 수도 있다. 빨리 목적지에 도착한 만큼 고민하고 성숙할 수 있는 시간 또한 부족했을 것이다.

　패션은 남보다 몇 골을 더 넣으면 이기는 게임이 아니고, 결승점을 지나면 끝나는 경기도 아니다. 죽을 때까지 발전해 나가야 하며, 조금씩 넓은 시각과 마음으로 더 좋은 패션을 해야 할 것이다. 나는 그런 패션 디자이너의 길을 걸어가고 싶다. 빨리 뛰어가서 목표지점에 도달하는 것이 중요한 게 아니라, 천천히 걸어가며 내가 보는 아름다운 세상을 사람들에게 전하는 좋은 디자이너가 되고 싶다.

　런던으로 돌아온 나는 다행히도 그 어느 때보다 행복한 시간을 보내고 있다. 〈프런코〉 때문에 조금은 빨리 먼 곳까지 걸어오게 된 것에 감사하며, 다시 내가 가야 할 이 길 위에 섰다. 책을 읽고, 옷을 만들고, 친구와 커피숍에서 몇 시간이고 수다를 떨고, 아이들을 가르치는 아르바이트도 하고 있다. 〈프런코〉가 시작되기 전의 모습으로 하루하루 내가 가야 하는 이 길을 다시 걸어가는 것이 행복하다. 가끔씩 나를 알아보는 한국 사람을 런던 거리에서 마주치기도 한다. 그럴 때마다 오래 전에 꾸었던 행복한 꿈이 생각나는 것 같다. 나에게 실제로 일어나지는 않았지만, 생각만 해도 기분 좋아지는 그런 꿈 말이다.

오랜만에 런던의 햇살을 만끽하다. 파릇파릇한 공원에 누워 체조 중.

3 경쟁에서 살아남는다는 것

〈프런코〉는 경쟁이 핵심인 프로그램이것. 열다섯 명의 패션 디자이너들이 모여 매회마다 미션을 받고, 미션에 맞는 옷을 만들고, 심사를 통해 등수를 가린다. 가장 점수가 낮은 사람은 탈락되고, 가장 점수가 높은 사람은 우승자가 된다. 경쟁을 하지 않을 수 없는, 다른 디자이너보다 더 뛰어나야 살아남는 프로그램이다. 아이러니하게도 나는 경쟁이라는 프로그램에 출연하긴 했지만 경쟁이라는 단어와는 어울리지 않는 사람이다. 어쩌면 경쟁을 즐기는 사람이 되고 싶어하지 않는다는 게 맞는 표현이겠다.

프로그램에 출연하면서 난 한번도 일등을 하고 싶다는 말을 한 적이 없다. 그렇다고 내가 일등을 하고 싶지 않은 것은 아니었다. 당연히 나도 누구보다 잘하고 싶었고, 최고가 되고 싶었다. 하지만 그런 마음이 내 자신을 뿌리째 흔들 수 있다는 것을 알고 있었다. 그래서 그런 마음을 갖지 않으려고 더 많이 노력했다.

나는 어려서부터 미술을 좋아하는 아이였다. 그림 그리기, 만들기처럼 손으로 하는 모든 것이 재밌고 신났다. 대회를 나가면 상장을 받아오고, 미술시간에는 선생님께 칭찬도 많이 들었다. 다른 건 몰라도 미술에 있어서는 내가 항상 최고인 것 같았다. 그런 환상이 깨진 것은 고등학교 때였다. 중학교 때까지 지방에서 살았던 나는 예술고등학교에 진학하기 위해 혼자 서울로 올라왔다. 작은 우물에서 내가 최고라고 생각하며 살던 개구리가 드디어 우물 밖에 있는 큰 세상을 보게 된 것이었다.

예술고등학교 친구들은 정말 뛰어났다. 입시미술을 오래 했던 몇몇 친구들은 기능적으로 엄청난 수준에 도달해 있었다. 나 자신의 재능에 대한 자부심이 대단했던 나는 항상 그랬듯이 언젠가는 이 학교에서도 최고가 될 수 있을 거라 생각했다. 그런데 어떻게 된 것이, 실기시험만 보면 꼴찌였다. 1학년, 2학년이 지나면서 나아지겠지 기대했던 성적은 전혀 나아지지 않았다. 나도 모르게 점점 주눅이 들었다. 나도 모르게 좋은 성적을 받는 친구들의 그림과 내 그림을 비교해보았다. 오랫동안 실기시험에서 좋은 성적을 받기 위해 그림을 연습해온 친구들과 내 그림은 애초에 비교가 되지 않았다.

　　공식처럼 정해진 틀 안에서 무한 연습을 통해 얻어진 테크닉과 안정감 있는 그림이 예전에는 전혀 부럽지 않았지만, 조금씩 마음이 흔들렸다. 뭔가 부족해 보이고 촌스러운 내 그림이 싫어졌다. 나도 모르게 좋은 점수를 받는 친구들의 테크닉을 따라 하기 시작했다. 시간이 지나면서 내 그림은 이런저런 테크닉으로 뒤범벅이 되어갔다. 더 이상 그림을 그리는 것이 즐겁지 않았다. 정신을 차리고 보니 어릴 적 그림을 그리며 행복했던 나는 온데간데없고, 온갖 기교로 친구들을 따라잡으려고 발버둥치는 내가 있었다.

　　대학 입시를 앞두고 결단을 내려야 했다. 지금까지 익혀왔던 테크닉을 모두 버리기로 했다. 다시 내가 좋아했던 그림을 그려야겠다고 생각했다. 성적이 안 나와도 내가 즐거워했던 그림을 다시 그리고 싶었다. 나는 작은 화실을 다니며 차근차근 자신에게 질문해가며 입시를 준비했다. 내가 어떤 그림을 그릴 때 기분이 좋은지, 어떤 생각으로 사물을 바라보는지 내 자신이 주체가 되어 그림을 그리기 시작했다. 누구보다 더 잘 그리려고 하지 않았다. 좋은 점수를 받는 테크닉도 버렸다. 어릴 적 그림으로 말했던 그 시절처럼 내 마음에 귀를 기울이며 그림을 그렸다. 놀랍게도 그림 실력이 하루가 다르게 늘어갔다. 결과는 이화여대 차석 입학이었다.

누군가와 비교해 더 나아지기 위해서, 더 높은 곳으로 올라가기 위해서 예술을 할 수는 없다. 예술은 일등, 이등을 가릴 수 없는 것이기 때문이다. 순위를 매기는 것은 예술의 목적 자체를 잊어버리는 일이기도 하다. 자신을 표현하는 수단인 예술이 누군가와 비교된다는 것이 말이 안되는 것이다.

하지만 예술에서도 최고는 존재한다. 세상에는 엄청난 돈을 버는 디자이너도 있고, 어떤 부분에서는 비교 자체가 불가능한 최고의 아티스트도 있다. 중요한 것은 그들이 누군가와 비교해서 최고가 아니라 스스로 최고라는 사실이다. 루이 비통이 샤넬보다 잘해서, 더 많이 옷을 팔아서 최고가 아니라 루이 비통이나 샤넬은 그 자체가 스스로 최고이다.

예술은 최고에 대한 절대적인 기준 또한 없다. 누군가는 샤넬을 최고라고 하고, 어떤 사람은 동네에 있는 작은 양복점이 최고라고 말한다. 세상에서 엄청난 존재감을 발산하든, 몇몇 사람만이 가치를 알아주든 모두가 최고인 것이다. 그 최고가 되기 위해 가장 중요한 것은, 절대적인 기준에서 남보다 더 높은 곳에 있어야 하는 것은 아니다. 결국 예술을 하는 주체가 자신만의 멋진 목소리를 가지고 있어야 한다.

 며칠 전 런던의 로열 페스티벌 홀에서 열린 오케스트라의 공연을 관람했다. 그로부터 며칠 후에는 첼시에 있는 작은 재즈바에 다녀왔다. 몇백 명이 관람하는 유명 오케스트라와 동네에서 할머니, 할아버지들을 앞에 두고 공연하는 밴드는 비교가 불가능할 만큼 스케일이 달랐지만 나는 두 공연에서 똑같이 감동을 느꼈다. 그 큰 공간을 압도하는 웅장한 오케스트라의 연주는 공연장을 뒤흔들 만큼 감동적이었다. 하지만 첼시의 재즈바에서 공연한 밴드 멤버들의 얼굴 또한 내 기억 속에 선명하게 남아 있다. 서로 눈빛이 오가며 피아노와 바이올린, 드럼을 연주하는 그들은 입가에 미소가 떠나지 않았다. 그들의 흥겨워하는 모습은 내 가슴을 가득 채울 만큼 행복한 모습이었다. 만약 그들이 자신들의 연주를 웅장한 규모의 오케스트라와 비교했다면 과연 행복할 수 있었을까. 그 어떤 것도 비교 자체가 무의미할 만큼 자신들에게는 최고의 공연이었다.

 〈프런코〉에서 좋은 성적을 거둘 수 있었던 것은 자신의 목소리에 집중하려고 노력했기 때문이라고 생각한다. 나와 다른 출연자들의 능력을 비교해서 경쟁하기보다 나만이 가진 것에 집중했고, 내가 진정 원하는 것을 바라보기 위해 노력했다. 프로그램 성격상 탈락자와 우승자가 생길 수밖에 없었지만 나는 열다섯 명 중에서 누구보다 잘했다거나 누구보다 부족하다고 생각하고 싶지 않다. 누구에게나 장점과 단점이 있고 비교될 수 없는 자신만의 목소리가 있다. 난 누군가와 경쟁하고 이겨서 최고가 되는 것이 아니라 최고라서 최고인 최고가 되고 싶다.

작은 동네의 밴드 공연이든, 멋진 오케스트라든 자신들만의 목소리를 온 열정을 다해 뿜어내는 진정 멋있는 최고 말이다.

4

국내파도, 해외파도 없다!
좋은 디자이너만 있을 뿐

국내파와 해외파, 생소한 단어들이다. 〈프런코〉에서 쓰지 않았다면 한번도 들어보지 않았을 것 같다. 개인적으로 어떤 기준으로 그룹을 나누는 것이 싫지만, 어쩔 수 없이 나눠지는 것이 이해가 안 되는 건 아니다.

나도 한국에서 대학에 입학하고, 한 학기를 다녔다. 한국에서 패션을 전공하고 일하는 친구들도 알고 있다. 그렇지만 국내에서 공부하는 학생들이 어떤 교육을 받고, 어떻게 디자이너의 꿈을 키워가는지 잘 알지 못한다. 비록 한 학기지만 그 짧은 시간에 내가 느낀 한국의 예술 교육은 너무나 실망스러웠다. 성적을 위해 과제물을 제출하고, 학생 개개인의 발전보다는 일정하게 굴러가는 커리큘럼에 맞춰진 수업이 안타까웠다. 내가 생각하는 대학 교육이란, 자유로운 사고와 자신이 주체가 되어 전문성을 발전시키는 곳이었지만 현실은 그렇지 못했다.

물론 이해는 된다. 성적을 내기 위해서 공부하고 점수를 잘 받기 위해 공부하는 교육을 10년 넘게 받았으니 그것이 대학이라고 해서 한순간에 바뀔 수 있을까. 하지만 이해가 된다고 해서 용납이 되지는 않는다. 언젠가는 바뀌어야 한다. 꿈을 꾸는 학생들을 위해서도 바뀌어야 하고, 한국 패션 시장의 힘을 키워 나가기 위해서도 그래야 한다. 자신이 주체가 되어 생각할 수 있게 하고, 그럴 만한 시간을 주고, 진정으로 자기를 계발시킬 수 있는 커리큘럼을 학생들에게 제공해야 한다. 채점의 기준이 일러스트 100장 이상이면 A, 더 많이 그리면 A+인 과제는 없어져야 한다. 그 대신 자기 성찰과 고민이 평가의 기준이 되는 과제여야 한다. 자신의 작업에 대해 목소리를 높여 이야기할 수 있는 시간을 주고, 학생 각자가 목소리를 가질 수 있게 격려하는 것이 대학의 몫이다.

  세인트 마틴이 그렇다. 4주마다 진행되는 프로젝트는 자신이 주체가 되어 작업을 진행한다. 주어지는 것은 주제와 가이드라인뿐이다. 주제에 대해 고민하고, 조사하고, 내가 이것을 통해 하고 싶은 작업이 무엇인지 생각하게 한다. 중간 중간 선생님과 그동안의 작업을 상의하며 도움을 받기도 한다. 하지만 선생님들은 나의 개인적인 사고를 절대 바꾸려 하지 않는다. 도움이 되는 방법을 일러주거나 내가 찾아보면 좋을 자료들을 소개는 해주지만 내가 하는 작업을 그만두게 하는 경우는 없다. 과연 어떤 기준으로 나의 생각이 틀렸다고 말할 수 있을까. 디자인 혹은 예술의 세계에서 틀린 것은 없다. 단지 조금 모자랄 수는 있고, 다를 수는 있지만 말이다. 나의 디자인을 바꾸는 것 또한 있을 수 없다. 좋은 디자인을 선택해주고, 레이아웃을 바꾸는 데 도움을 주기는 하지만 디자인 자체는 내 것이다. 모든 선생님이 그런 것은 아니지만 여러 프로젝트를 하는 동안 나를 지도해주신 선생님들이 모두 그랬다.

  하지만 이런 좋은 교육환경이 반드시 좋은 디자이너를 만드는 것은 아니다. 소위 해외파라 하더라도 선생님의 눈치를 보며 자신이 주체가 되는 작업을 하지 못하는 사람도 있다. 점수를 잘 받기 위해 눈치를 보며 겉모습만 반지르르한 작업을 하는 친구들을 보면 답답하다. 좋은 점수를 받을 수는 있겠지만 학교를 떠나 모든 것의 주체가 자신이 되어야 할 때, 이끌어주는 사람이 없을 때는 길을 잃고 만다. 자신이 가진 깊이가 없는 사람은 텅텅 빈 속이 금세 드러나게 되어 있다.

그 반대로 한국에서 공부했지만 멋진 디자이너가 되는 사람도 많다. 교육은 주체적인 사고를 방해할 수는 있지만, 그 사람이 가진 진정한 꿈과 목소리를 막지는 못한다. 말하고 싶은 내면의 목소리가 있다면 환경은 중요하지 않다. 더 좋은 패션 시장이 있고, 자유로운 사고를 격려하는 교육은 단지 외부에 있을 뿐이다. 그러니 국내냐, 해외냐 하는 것이 중요한 게 아니라 내 자신의 목소리에 주체가 될 수 있는지, 없는지가 중요하다.

해외에서 공부한다는 것이 이미 형성된 좋은 예술적 환경과 혜택이라는 사실을 부정할 수는 없다. 바로 옆에 박물관도 있으며, 아트책들로 가득한 도서관도 있다. 무엇보다 자신이 주체가 될 수 있도록 도와주는, 디자이너로서의 목소리를 가질 수 있게 격려하는 학교가 있다. 하지만 그것이 패션 디자이너가 되기 위한 필수 조건은 아니다. 있으면 좋겠지만 그것이 없다고 좋은 디자이너가 될 수 없는 것은 아니라는 얘기다.

그보다 더욱 중요한 것은 자기 자신이다. 학교는 어디까지나 학교일 뿐, 학생을 대신하는 것은 아니다. 성공한 디자이너가 하나같이 우리가 생각하는 좋은 학교를 졸업하지도 않았다. 스스로 자신의 길을 개척하고, 모든 가능성에서 처음인 사람들이었다. 정말 중요한 것은 자신이 지닌 내면의 가치를 알고 그 가치를 소중하게 생각할 수 있어야 한다는 것이다.

그러기 위해서는 환경에 휘둘리지 않고, 주변 목소리에도 흔들리지 않아야 한다. 하지만 그것이 어렵다는 것 또한 잘 알고 있다. 나도 환경 때문에 패션을 포기했던 순간이 있었다. 갓 스무 살이었던 어린 나이에, 제한적인 시각을 가진 나로서는 환경에 휘둘릴 수밖에 없었다. 지금도 예전의 나처럼 패션 디자이너가 되고 싶지만 환경이 여의치 못해서 꿈을 접어야 하는 사람도 있을 거라 생각된다. 하지만 환경은 환경일 뿐, 어떤 것도 중요하지 않다. 국내든지, 해외든지, 학교를 다니지 않았더라도 상관없다. 자신의 목소리에 귀 기울일 수만 있다면, 패션을 사랑한다면 된다.

우리는 모두 자신만의 재능이 있다. 그것이 작든 크든, 그 재능을 키워가는 곳이 국내든 해외든 어떤 것도 상관없다. 자신의 재능을 감사하게 생각하고, 그것의 가치를 아는 것이 중요하다. 나는 사람들이 이렇게 자신을 소중하게 생각했으면 좋겠다. 환경에 휘둘리고 자신이 갖지 못한 것에 연연해하며 자신을 힘들게 하지 않았으면 한다. 내가 그러했고, 그러한 포기로 인해 깜깜했던 그 시절의 어려움을 알기 때문이다. 어떤 상황에 놓이든 자신에게 주어진 것에 감사하며 살아갔으면 좋겠다. 그렇다면 반드시 그 재능이 언젠가는 빛이 날 거라고 확신한다.

〈프런코〉에서는 디자이너들을 국내파와 해외파로 나눴지만 난 조금 다른 기준으로 나누고 싶다. 혹시나 패션 디자이너를 꿈꾸는 어린 친구들이 이 프로그램을 보면서 이런 이분법적인 사고로 패션에 접근하지는 않을지 적이 걱정스럽다. 혹시나 유학을 갈 수 없는 환경의 친구들이 그 꿈을 포기하거나, 국내에서는 좋은 디자이너가 될 수 없다고 은연중에 생각하거나 무조건 유학만 가면 좋은 디자이너가 될 거라는 말도 안되는 생각을 하지는 않을까 염려된다.

그래서 나는 예비 디자이너들을 주어진 환경에 의한 구분이 아니라 환경을 이기는 사람과 환경에 휘둘리는 사람 또는 자기의 내면에 귀 기울이는 사람과 세상의 말을 듣기만 하는 사람, 자신의 가치를 귀하게 여기는 사람과 그렇지 못한 사람으로 나누고 싶다.

5 〈프런코〉와 그 이후의 이야기

〈프런코〉 시즌3이 끝나고 벌써 1년이라는 시간이 흘렀다. 매번 느끼는 거지만 시간이 얼마나 빠른지 놀라울 따름이다. 최근 인터넷 기사를 통해 〈프런코〉 시즌4에 학교에서 얼굴을 보곤 했던 세인트 마틴 졸업생이 출연한 것을 보게 되었다. 오랜만에 보는 간호섭 교수님과 김석원 디자이너님, 전미경 편집장님 그리고 이소라 언니의 얼굴도 반가웠다. 출연자들이 모여서 단체로 찍은 사진을 보니 나도 그 당시로 돌아간 듯했다. 뭐가 뭔지도 모르는 채 방송을 찍고 첫 회가 방영되던 날, 텔레비전에서 내 모습을 보고 얼마나 신기했는지 모른다. 그때 한창 컬렉션을 준비하고 있었기에 매회 챙겨 보지는 못했지만, 최소한 11시에 맞춰 '본방 사수'를 하려고 뛰곤 했던 기억이 새롭다.

첫 회 방송에서는 내 모습이 몇 번 나가지 않았다. 처음 작업실에 들어오는 모습, 작업 공간에서 기도하는 모습, 내가 누구라고 소개하는 정도였다. 많이 기대했는데 몇 분 나오지 않아 나도, 부모님도, 친구들도 모두 허탈해했다. 3회 때 김태희 씨 미션을 할 때에는 일등을 해서 처음으로 내 얼굴이 화면에 많이 나와 기분이 좋았다. 지금 생각해도 그때, 드레스를 만들면서 재미있었다.

〈프런코〉에 나가기 전에 내가 다짐했던 것은, 일등을 하기 위해서 내가 잘하는 것을 하는 것이 아니라, 한번도 해보지 않은 것들을 작업함으로써 나의 경험 밖에 있는 가능성을 최대로 끌어내자는 것이었다. 실제로 1회부터 10회까지 단 한 번, 9회를 제외하고는 그 동안 한번도 해보지 않은 방법으로 작업을 했다. 원단 선정에서부터 만드는 방법까지 모든 것을 도전하고 실험해보고자 했다. 어떤 결과가 나올지 모르는 상황이었지만 그만큼 신나고 즐거웠다. 그때 그 드레스도 지금까지 한번도 쓰지 않은 보닝^{boning}을 이용해 만들었고, 작업 결과가 생각보다 좋아 그 이후에도 자주 보닝을 가지고 작업하게 됐다.

또 생각나는 에피소드는 리바이스 청바지를 가지고 작업했던 팀 미션이다. 나는 워낙 눈물이 많은 사람이다. 툭하면 울고, 슬퍼도 울고, 즐거워도 울어서 〈프런코〉에 나가서는 울지 않기로 마음먹었었다. 감정에 이리저리 흔들리며 휩쓸리고 싶지 않았기 때문이다. 억지로 가식적인 모습을 보이는 것이 싫었기 때문에 억지로 기쁜 것도 슬픈 것도 싫었다. 카메라가 비치지 않는 곳에서야 수도 없이 울었지만 몇 번은 카메라 바로 앞에서 눈물을 흘렸다. 첫 번째가 리바이스 팀 미션이었고, 또 한 번은 방송을 끝내고 나서 했던 마지막 인터뷰에서였다.

팀 미션 때는 내가 팀장을 맡았기 때문에 우리 팀의 성적을 내가 책임져야 한다고 생각했다. 옷을 다 만들고, '어쩌면 내가 탈락해서 집에 갈 수도 있겠구나' 하는 생각이 머릿속에 스쳐갔지만 설마 했었다. 그런데 생각보다 혹독한 평가를 듣고 나서는 확신이 들었다. '여기까지구나. 오늘 짐 싸서 집에 가겠구나. 그래도 잘했어.'

탈락자를 뽑기 전, 결과를 기다리는 동안 난 이미 마음의 정리를 끝낸 상태였다. 은근 고집이 센 내가 이끈 팀이 이 모양이 되었으니 내가 집에 가는 건 당연했고, 내 실력보다 훨씬 잘했으니 그것으로 충분했다. 그렇게 웃으면서, 감사해하며 떠나기로 결심하고 무대 위로 올라갔는데 내가 아니라 같은 팀원 언니가 탈락했다고 했다. 너무 놀라서 그 결과를 받아들이기에는 뭔가 잘못됐다는 것을 머리보다 몸이 더 잘 알고 있었다. 무대 위에서 이러지도 저러지도 못하고 문을 바라보면서 꼼짝 못하고 서 있었다. 내가 탈락한 게 아니라고 하니, 한편으로는 너무 기뻤지만 이건 아니라는 생각이 들었다. 나 때문이라는, 나 때문에 누군가 탈락해야 한다는 사실이 감당 안될 만큼 슬펐다.

그 미션 이후부터는 〈프런코〉에서 작업하는 것이, 이번 기회가 더더욱 내 것이 아니라는 생각이 컸다. 내가 있어야 되는 자리가 아니기 때문에, 집으로 돌아갔어야 하는 사람이 남아 있다는 생각으로 언제든지 탈락해도, 이미 충분히 얻었다고 생각했다. 여기까지 온 것만으로도 감사하고, 그 이후부터는 잘해서 일등을 하기보다는 '덤'으로 받은 미션들을 즐겁게 해보기로 결심하자 원래 내 것이 아니라는 부담 없는 마음으로 작업할 수 있었다. 그다음 씨엘 미션에서는 일등을 했고, 가장 부담이 컸던 마지막 회에서는 오히려 담백하게 작업해서 일등으로, 최종 세 명에 들 수 있었다.

컬렉션을 준비하는 내내 덤으로 주어진 기회에 감사해하며 즐거운 마음으로 더 배우고 더 성장하기 위해 작업했다. 그리고 꿈같이 즐거웠던 3개월의 준비 기간이 끝나고 컬렉션 날이 되었다. 방송에서는 내가 워낙 감정의 동요가 없어서 좀 더 '신나는 척'하거나 감정을 더 드러내길 원했지만, 그날도 심장이 터질 듯한 그런 설렘은 없었다. '내가 준비한 것을 드디어 보여주는 날이구나' 하는 기대감은 있었지만 오늘 죽어도 좋다! 뭐 이런 기분은 아니었다.

이 글을 읽는 분들이 '아니, 그렇게 대수롭지 않게 생각했단 말이야? 그렇다면 그런 기회가 더 절실한 사람한테 주어졌어야 하는 것 아니야?' 하는 생각을 할 수도 있겠다. 하지만 분명한 건, 나에게도 평생 동안 단 한 번밖에 없는 중요하고 소중한 기회였다. 다만 이것이 나의 '끝'이 아니라 내 길의 '작은 시작'일 뿐이라는 것은 알고 있었기에, 이것이 뭔가를 이루기 위한 것이 아니라 덤으로 받은 선물이라고 생각했다. 내가 '대단한 것을 이루었다!'는 가슴 터질 듯한 기분은 아니었다는 말이다.

그렇게 울지도, 별로 절박해 보이지도 않게 이등으로 모든 것은 끝났다. 마지막으로 인터뷰하는 동안 지금까지 내가 받은 것이 얼마나 크고 생각하지도 못했던 큰 기회였음을 알 수 있었다. 졸업하기 전에 컬렉션을 준비하는 기회를 통해 많은 사람을 만났고, 꿈처럼 지나간 반 년의 시간에 대한 기억이 가슴 가득 차올랐다. 선물이라고 하기에는 과하게 넘치도록 받은 이 모든 것에 마지막 인터뷰에서는 참았던 눈물이 쏟아졌다. 참으려고 했는데, 정말 마음 뜨겁게 감사해서 참을 수가 없었다. 사람 마음이 참 그렇다. 방송을 끝내고 며칠 동안은 '그때 일등을 했을 수도 있었는데!' 하는 조금은 서운한 마음이 들기도 했다.

하지만 그 누구도 선물로 받은 덤을 가지고 좋다, 나쁘다, 더 좋은 것을 달라고 할 수는 없다. 난 과분한 선물을 덤으로 받았고, 좋은 결과를 냈다. 이제 1년이 지난 지금 난 새로운 컬렉션을, 졸업 쇼를 준비하고 있다. 그때 그 마음으로, 감사함으로 또다시 세인트 마틴이라는 덤을 내 인생에서 선물로 받았으니, 즐겁게 졸업 준비를 해야겠다. 마음이 벌써부터 벅차 오른다.

2
나는
멋진 디자이너가
되고 싶다

1 너는 정말 옷 만드는 걸 좋아하는구나

어릴 적 패션 디자이너는 수많은 친구들이 꿈꾸는 인기 직업 중 하나였다. 옷을 좋아하고 자신을 꾸미는 데 관심이 많으면 누구나 패션 디자이너가 되고 싶어했다. 나 또한 매달 패션 잡지가 나오는 날을 기다리며 뉴욕, 파리, 런던, 밀라노에서 펼쳐지는 패션쇼를 보며 멋진 패션 디자이너가 되겠노라는 꿈을 키웠다.

재미있는 건, 그 당시 패션 디자이너가 되고 싶어했던 수많은 친구 중 '패션 디자이너'가 아닌 '패션'을 하고 싶어하는 친구는 없었다는 것이다. 옷이 좋고, 옷과 함께 일하고 싶다면 당연하게 패션 디자이너가 되어야 하는 줄 알았다. 사실 옷을 만드는 패션 디자이너는 패션이라는 영역에 있는 많은 직업 중 하나일 뿐인데 말이다.

이렇게 패션 디자이너는 패션을 하고 싶어하는 친구들의 한 가지 옵션이었다. 옷을 좋아해서 옷을 디자인하고, 옷 만드는 것을 공부하고, 패션 디자이너가 되는 길을 걸어가는 친구들을 많이 봤다. 하지만 옷에 대한 관심으로 시작한 패션 디자이너가 자신과 맞지 않아 몇 년간의 공부를 뒤로하고 진로를 바꾸는 친구들 또한 많이 봤다. 옷이 좋아 시작했지만 옷 만드는 것은 즐겁지 않은 것이다.

며칠 전 이런 과정을 거쳐온 언니를 만났다. 한국에서 패션 디자인 공부를 하고, 런던으로 와서 디자인 공부를 더 하다가 그만둔 언니였다. 이렇게 공부한 결과, 자신은 디자인보다는 마케팅에 더 관심이 있는 걸 깨달아서 작은 신진 디자이너 회사의 매니저로 일하는데 규모는 작지만 디자이너의 스타일이 마음에 든다고 했다. 자신이 원하는 일을 하는 그녀는 행복하고 당당해 보였다. 언니는 나에게 요즘 방학인데 뭘 하면서 지내냐고 물었다. 나만의 시간도 많은 요즘, 책도 읽고 런던에 와서 작업실을 새로 꾸며 옷을 만들고 있다고 했다. 언니는 웃으며 나에게 한마디 했다.

"너는 정말 옷 만드는 걸 좋아하는구나."

언니는 많은 사람이 패션 디자인을 공부하지만 진짜 옷 만드는 것을 순수하게 좋아하는 사람은 별로 없다는 것을 아는 듯했다.

내가 패션 디자이너가 되고 싶었던 이유는 단순히 옷에 관심이 많아서, 옷이 좋아서가 아니었다. 어려서부터 순수미술을 하시는 아빠의 영향을 많이 받아 자연스럽게 내 생각을 표현하는 미술이 정말 좋았다. 그리고 어느 날 우연처럼 찾아온 기회로 옷을 만들면서 평면의 패브릭이 입체가 되어 사람의 몸에 감기는, 그 희열을 알게 되었다. 내 생각을 캔버스가 아닌 사람이 입는 옷을 통해 펼치는 패션 디자이너가 되겠다고 결심했던 것이다.

패션을 전공하면서 느끼는 것은, 옷 만드는 일은 하면 할수록 즐겁다는 것이다. 옷 만드는 기술뿐만 아니라 그 모든 것이 좋다. 순수미술처럼 내 생각을 마음껏 펼칠 수 있다는 것도 좋고, 그것이 옷으로 표현되는 것은 더욱 좋다. 시간이 지나고 학년이 올라갈수록 '이것이 내가 평생 해야 할 일이구나' 하는 확신을 갖게 되었다.

난 이렇게 어릴 적부터 하고 싶었던 일이 확실했고, 나이가 들고 제대로 공부하면서 더욱 확실해진다는 것에 감사한다. 또한 참 운이 좋았다고도 생각한다. 적어도 내가 관심이 없고 결국은 하지 않을 일에 시간을 쏟지 않았기 때문이다. 물론 그렇게 그만두더라도 그 모든 경험이 가치가 없는 것은 아니다. 하지만 젊음의 시간은 한정되어 있고, 그 시간에 자신이 진정 원하는 것을 집중해서 할 수 있다면 더 좋지 않을까.

이렇게 패션 디자인을 공부하다가 흥미를 잃고, 중간에 그만두거나 다른 일을 하는 친구들을 보면 대개 한 가지 공통점이 있다. 패션 디자인을 시작하게 된 계기가 '옷이 좋아서'라는 것이다. 다른 것보다 옷에 관심이 많고, 패션에 흥미를 느껴서다. 하지만 옷이 좋다고 해서 모두 옷 만드는 것을 좋아하는 것은 아니다. 옷을 좋아하게 된 이유가 쇼핑이 좋아서인 사람도 있고, 스타일링에 관심이 있어서인 경우도 있다. 아주 많은 이유로 옷을 좋아하지만 아쉬운 건 어릴 적 그 '옷이 좋다'는 이유로 선택할 수 있었던 직업이 패션 디자이너 하나밖에 없었다는 것이다.

패션 디자이너는 패션에 속한 수많은 직업 중 하나이다. 패션 필드에는 스타일리스트, 바이어, 머천다이저, 비주얼 머천다이저, 패션 에디터, 저널리스트 등 옷을 만들지 않고 디자인을 하지 않아도 패션을 할 수 있는 직업이 얼마든지 있다. 실제로 옷을 만들고, 디자인하는 세계에서도 직업은 더욱 세분화된다. 패션 디자이너는 그것을 대표하는 하나일 뿐, 디자이너로 일하는 것 외에도 다양한 직업이 있다. 옷의 이미지에 아주 큰 요소로 작용하는 패션 프린트fashion print, 다양한 소재를 연구, 개발하는 텍스타일textile, 옷을 실제로 꿰매고 만드는 심시트리스seamstress(여자 재봉사), 니트웨어knitwear만을 전문으로 만드는 사람, 옷의 패턴만을 전문으로 만드는 모델리스트 등 수도 없이 많다. 평생 단추가 좋아 단추만 만드는 사람도 있을 수 있다.

옷을 좋아해서 가질 수 있는 직업이 셀 수 없이 많음에도 어릴 적 옷을 좋아하는 친구들이 가질 수 있는 하나의 옵션은 패션 디자이너뿐이었다. 지금도 패션 디자이너가 되고 싶어하는 옷을 사랑하는 수많은 어린 친구들을 본다. 그들의 가장 큰 걱정은 패션 디자이너가 되고 싶은데 재능이 있는지 없는지 확실하지 않다는 것이다. 옷을 좋아하지만 정말 패션 디자이너가 될 수 있을지 확신이 서지 않는 친구들의 고민이다.

분명한 것은 패션 디자이너는 재능이 있어야 할 수 있다. 겉으로는 화려해 보이지만 힘든 직업이고, 그 힘든 과정을 재능 없이 견디는 것 또한 힘들다. 하지만 그 재능은 어떤 능력을 평균해서 남보다 잘하는 것은 아니다. 남보다 그림을 잘 그리고 옷을 잘 입는 것이 패션에서 재능을 의미하는 것은 아니다.

난 재능이란 흥미와 같은 말이라고 생각한다. 자신이 가장 흥미를 느끼는 것이 그 사람이 가진 재능이다. 그 일을 할 때 너무나 즐겁다면 그 일을 잘할 수밖에 없다. 내가 흥미를 느끼고, 가장 즐거워하는 일이라면 그것이 그 사람의 재능이다. 나는 내 생각을 옷으로 시각화하고, 그 디자인을 옷으로 만드는 것이 세상에서 가장 재미있다. 남과 비교해서 누가 잘하는지는 중요하지 않다. 내 기준에서 얼마나 즐거운가, 그것이 가장 중요한 요소이고 그것이 바로 패션을 하는 데 필요한 재능이다.

그 재능을 아는 것은 중요하다. 옷이 좋아도 어떤 방식으로 옷이 좋은지 알아야 한다. 옷이 좋다고 옷 만드는 것이 좋으란 법도 없다. 옷과 함께 일할 수 있는 수많은 직업과 분야 중에서 어떤 것이 자신에게 맞고, 좋은지 알아야만 한다. 옷이 좋아서 무작정 선택한 '패션 디자인'이라는 전공을 졸업하고 후회하지 않으려면 말이다.

나는 운이 좋아서 어릴 적 우연한 기회로 시도한 일이 나와 딱 맞는다는 것을 알게 되었다. 옷이 좋고, 옷을 만들고 싶다면 무엇보다 시도하는 것이 중요하다. 막연하게 옷이 좋다, 옷을 만들고 싶다가 아니라 직접 부딪쳐보는 것이다. 최대한 많은 기회에 자신을 노출시키고 기회를 주면 좀 더 일찍 자신이 흥미를 느끼는 것을 찾을 수 있다.

예전에 친구들과 함께 취미 찾기 프로젝트를 감행했었다. 우리의 모토는 '무조건 해보자'였다. 재미있고 한번 해보고 싶었던 것을 무작정 시도해보는 것이었다. 그렇게 하면 정말 좋아하는 것을 찾을 수 있을까 싶었다. 신발에 관심이 있으면 한번 만들어보고, 탭댄스가 추고 싶으면 한번 춰보자는 것이 우리의 목표였다.

내가 처음 시도했던 일은 '사진 찍기'였다. 한창 필름카메라가 유행했기에 누구나 취미로 '사진촬영'을 들먹였고, 나 또한 관심이 있었다. 많은 사람처럼 나도 당연히 사진촬영에 흥미가 있는 줄 알았다. 게다가 난 시각적인 것을 좋아하고, 예술을 하니 사진 찍는 일을 좋아할 수밖에 없다고 생각했다.

2박3일의 사진촬영 여행. 친구와 함께 큰마음을 먹고, 필름카메라를 들고 여행길에 올랐다. 이곳저곳 돌아다니며 사진을 찍었다.

산에 올라가서도 찍고, 벌레도 찍고, 눈에 보이는 감동을 모두 카메라에 담았다. 2박3일의 사진 여행 끝에서 발견한 것은, 난 사진 찍는 것을 별로 좋아하지 않는다는 것이었다. 내가 좋아한다고 생각했던 일이 실제로 해보니, 그다지 재미가 없었다. 더구나 나는 사진보다 내 눈으로 보고, 마음으로 기억하는 것을 더 좋아했다. 내 생각과 달리 그렇게 반대일 수가 없었다.

　누구도 해보지 않고서는 알 수 없다. 옷을 좋아하니까 옷 만드는 것도 좋아할 것이라는 어림짐작이 틀릴 수도 있다. 내가 예술을 한다고 해서 사진을 좋아하는 것이 아닌 것처럼 말이다. 옷에 관심이 있고, 패션을 하고 싶다면 '패션 디자이너'라는 결정을 내리기 전에 패션의 많은 것을 시도해보기를 권한다. 쇼핑이 좋다면 쇼핑을 끝도 없이 해보고, 옷 만드는 것이 좋다면 실제로 옷을 만들어본다. 머릿속의 생각을 벗어나 행동으로 옮기는 것, 그렇게 자신이 가진 진정한 재능을 찾아야 한다.

　또한, 패션 디자이너는 겉으로 보이는 것처럼 속이 화려한 직업이 아니다. 세계 곳곳을 여행하며 영감을 얻고, 생각나는 대로 쓱쓱 디자인을 하고, 멋있게 드레스 한 벌을 완성시켜 아름다운 모델에게 입히는 것이 패션 디자이너가 아니라는 것이다. 물론 화려해 보이는 직업이기는 하지만 그런 디자이너가 되기 위해, 옷 한 벌을 완성하기까지는 피나는 노력과 노동이 필요하다.

　패션에는 1 더하기 1은 2라는 공식처럼 딱 맞아떨어지는 정답이 있는 것도 아니고, 어디까지 달려가면 골인하는 끝이 있는 것도 아니다. 대학 졸업장이 있고 특정 자격증을 딴다고 해서 패션 디자이너가 되는 것도 아니다. 옷을 잘 만들고 재능이 있어도 시장을 잘 알지 못하면 옷이 팔리지 않아 적자가 날 수도 있다. 시시각각 변하는 패션 시장에서 소위 '살아남기' 위해서는 이 모든 안 좋은 가능성을 안고 가야 한다. 그리고 무엇보다 패션을 하기 위해서는 누가 뭐래도 패션을 좋아해야 한다. 알렉산더 맥퀸에서 인턴십으로 일할 때, 겉으로는 화려해 보이지만 스트레스를 견디지 못해 힘들어하는 사람들을 많이 봤다. 세상일이 다 그렇겠지만 패션에서는 나 하나로는 끝나지 않는 일들, 나 하나로는 정답이 나오지 않는 일이 너무나 많다. 나의 끝내주는 아이디어로 옷 하나 잘 만드는 것이 전부가 아니다.

그렇다고 패션 디자이너가 아주 몹쓸 직업이란 얘기는 아니다. 수많은 부정적인 변수가 있는 만큼 너무나 좋은 가능성 또한 존재한다. 정답이 없는 만큼 나만의 정답을 만들 수도 있다. 반드시 이렇게 해야 이렇게 된다는 공식이 없으니, 내가 생각하는 대로 나만의 길을 개척해갈 수도 있다. 이제까지 세상에서 멋지게 성공한 수많은 디자이너의 길을 따라가지 않더라도 다른 성공의 길의 첫 번째가 될 수 있다. 공식이 없는 만큼 자유롭기 때문이다.

실제로 너무나 매력적인 직업이기도 하다. 패션은 사람의 외모, 아름다움에 지대한 영향을 미친다. 세상에 옷을 안 입고 사는 사람은 없다. 누구나 패션에 관심이 있고, 관심이 없더라도 '옷 참 못 입는다'는 말을 듣고 싶어하는 사람은 아무도 없다. 인간의 아름다워 보이고 싶은 절대 욕구와 떼려야 뗄 수 없는 것이 패션이다.

인간을 아름답게 만들어주는 패션, 얼마나 매력적인가? 그것이 있어도 그만, 없어도 그만인 것이 아니라 반드시 있어야만 하는, 미래에도 없어서는 안 될 중요한 것이니 더더욱 매력적이다. 이런 매력을 알아차린 수많은 사람이 패션을 하고 싶어하고, 심지어 그 세계를 동경한다. 그리고 내가 가는 길과 같은 패션 디자이너가 되기 위한 길을 걸어가고 있다.

내가 패션을 하고 싶어하는 어린 친구들에게 꼭 이야기하고 싶은 것은 '옷에 관심이 있다 = 패션 디자이너가 되고 싶다'는 아니라는 것이다. 어릴 적 친구들이 옷을 좋아하고, 옷과 함께 일하고 싶다면 당연히 패션 디자이너가 되어야 한다는 그 공식은 정답이 아니었다. 몇몇 친구는 그렇게 옷을 좋아해서 대학에서 패션 디자인을 전공했지만 졸업을 하고 나서야 다른 일이 하고 싶다고 했다. 가장 안타까운 것은 그 친구들이 정말 옷은 좋아했지만 옷 만드는 일과는 맞지 않았다는 것이다. 옷을 좋아하는 사람들이 가질 수 있는 많은 직업의 기회를 알지 못하고 무조건 패션 디자인을 해야 한다는 생각에서 비롯된 결과이다.

옷을 좋아한다면, 패션업계의 다양한 직업 중에서 자신이 재능을 발휘할 수 있는 분야를 찾는 것이 중요하다. 나처럼 옷을 사랑하는 사람들이, 어린 시절 사소한 오해가 만들어낸 잘못된 판단으로 그렇게 좋아하는 패션을 아예 그만두는 사람이 없었으면 좋겠다. 패션이라는 범주 안에서 자신의 재능을 찾고, 그것을 즐겁게 해나가는 사람들이 많았으면 좋겠다. 자신이 원하는 곳까지 멀리 돌아가거나 혹은 멀리 갔다가 다시 출발점으로 허탈하게 돌아오는 일 없이 말이다.

2 아트와 패션,
그 작고도 큰 차이

언제부턴가 책이 참 좋다. 틈만 나면 도서관에 간다. 학교 도서관, 서점, 동네 도서관 등 책이 있는 곳이라면 어디든지 좋다. 내 방 발코니에 앉아 따뜻한 햇살과 바람을 맞으며 책을 읽는다. 가끔씩 답답할 때면 좋아하는 책 한 권 들고 스타벅스에 가서 몇 시간이고 보내곤 한다. 한 번에 열 권 이상 빌리지 못하는 학교 도서관에서 나의 체크아웃check-out 리스트는 항상 열 권이다.

조금은 부끄럽지만 내가 스무 살 때까지 교과서 빼고 읽은 책은 딱 두 권이다. 〈몽실언니〉와 〈찰리와 초콜릿 공장의 비밀〉. 어릴 적 동화책이야 수도 없이 읽었지만, 나이 들고 내 손으로 직접 펼쳐서 읽은 책은 고작해야 두 권이다. 그 두 권마저도 며칠 동안 읽은 것이 아니라 도입부가 정말 재미있어서 읽다 보니 하루 만에 끝낸 책들이다. 그럼에도 불구하고 내가 어휘력이 심히 모자라거나 이해력이 떨어지는 것은 아니니 참 다행이다.

지금에 와서 생각해보니 난 기본적으로 '이야기'라는 것에 흥미를 별로 느끼지 못하는 것 같다. 장편소설은 읽기를 시도한 적이 없을뿐더러, 책이 아닌 텔레비전에서 나오는 드라마도 별로 좋아하지 않는다. 어려서부터 예술 공부를 해왔기 때문에 글씨보다는 그림을, 소리보다는 시각적인 자극을 더 좋아했고, 그래서 그동안 나에게 흥미롭게 다가왔던 책이 별로 없었던 것도 사실이다. 집 앞 도서관에 있는 가장 재미있는 미술 코너에 책이 몇 권 되지 않았던 것도 사소하지만 이유라 할 수 있다.

런던에 처음 와서 가장 놀랐던 것은 책이었다. 학교 도서관엔

책이 정말 많았다. 책의 숫자가 많아서라기보다는 재미있는 책이 정말 많았다. 세인트 마틴의 도서관은 아트 서적이 세계에서 손에 꼽힐 만큼 많다고 한다. 내 키보다 훌쩍 큰 책장에 아트 책으로만 빼곡한 도서관이다. 우리 언니는 어릴 적부터 빵을 좋아해서 항상 크면 빵가게를 하고 싶다고 했었다. 마음껏 빵을 먹을 수 있게 말이다. 우리 언니에게 있어 빵집 같은 공간을 나도 드디어 갖게 된 것이다. 눈을 감고 손을 뻗어 수만 권의 아트 책 중에 아무거나 집어내도 너무 재미있는 책들로 둘러싸인 곳 말이다.

게다가 그런 도서관이 한두 곳이 아니었다. 런던에 있는 몇몇 예술 학교는 런던 예술 대학교 University of Arts London 라는 이름으로 운영되고 있어서 어느 학교의 도서관도 마음대로 출입할 수 있었다. 학교마다 각기 파인아트, 패션, 포토그래피, 그래픽 등 특화된 주제가 있었고, 모두가 흥미로웠다. 내가 이사를 가는 동네의 기준이 런던 예술 대학교 University of Arts London 에서 얼마나 가까운지가 될 정도였다. 작년에 살았던 집은 캠버웰 예술 대학 Camberwell Art College 과 걸어서 1분 거리였다. 파인아트 서적은 많지 않았지만 매력적인 곳이었다. 수업이 일주일에 두세 번밖에 없는 주에는 그 학교 학생도 아니면서 시도 때도 없이 가곤 했다.

세인트 마틴도 더 이상의 책이 있을까 싶을 정도로 패션 서적이 다양하고, 패션의 각 분야별로 세분화된 책이 많았다. 패션으로 런던에서 유명한 학교인 런던 컬리지 오브 패션 London College of Fashion

학교에는 책의 종류도 많지만 책마다 카피^{copy}의 수가 많다는 것이 마음에 들었다. 세인트 마틴 도서관은 책은 많았지만 카피가 적어서 원하는 책을 보려면 기다려야 하는 경우가 많았다. 그와 반대로 런던 컬리지 오브 패션학교에는 넉넉한 카피가 있으니 항상 원하는 책을 빌릴 수 있었다.

하지만 그 어떤 도서관과도 비교할 수 없을 만큼 최고가 있으니, 예전 집에서 버스를 타고 15분만 가면 있는 곳으로 아트 책의 천국이라 할 수 있는 런던 컬리지 오브 커뮤니케이션^{London College of Communication}의 도서관이다. 한번 가면 몇 시간이고 빠져나올 수 없는 그런 곳이었다. 패션뿐만 아니라 아트에 관한 모든 책이 있다고 해도 과언이 아니다. 난 패션 서적이 엄청 많은 세인트 마틴 도서관도 좋지만 더 넓은 주제의 아트 책이 두루 갖춰져 있는 런던 컬리지 오브 커뮤니케이션 도서관이 가장 좋았다. 시간이 날 때면 끝도 없는 아트 서적을 종횡무진하며 마음 가는 대로, 느낌 가는 대로 책을 골라 한아름 안고 구석 바닥에 앉아 읽곤 했다. 하루는 내가 좋아하는 에드가르 드가^{Edgar Degas}의 화집을 모두 골라 감상하기도 했고, 그리스 건축에 대한 책을 읽기도 하고, 뜨개질하는 법을 배우기도 하는 등 매일매일이 새롭고 재미있는 놀이터였다. 그렇게 마음껏 책을 읽다 해가 져서 배가 고프면 집으로 돌아오곤 했다.

다양한 책을 읽게 되면서 자연스럽게 생각이 많아지고, 내 생각을 뒷받침하는 자료도 손쉽게 찾을 수 있었다. 당연히 나에게 도움이 되고, 무엇보다 즐거움을 주었지만 한 가지 아쉬운 점이 있다면, 그렇게 일정한 주제 없이 마구잡이로 들어온 지식이 내 머릿속에 정신 없이 흩어져 있다는 것이었다. 어린아이가 그림책을 보듯이 휙휙 넘기며 눈으로만 보는 책들은 깊이 있게 내 안에 남지 않았다. 책의 내용은 어디까지나 내가 아닌 다른 사람의 생각을 거쳐 나온 것들이다. 그것이 시각적으로만 다가온다면 너무나 단편적인, 금방 날아가버릴 수 있는 것들이었다.

처음 강을 만난 물고기처럼 이리저리 휘휘 돌아다니는 게 아니라 이제는 정신 좀 차리고 차분해져야 할 때가 왔음을 느꼈다. 그때부터 나는 다시 읽기 시작했다. 한없이 머릿속에 쏟아붓던 그 모든 것을 나의 생각으로 한번 걸러내면 나오는 내 진짜 관심사에 대해 자세히 알고 싶어졌다.

처음 시작은 역시 패션이었다. 항상 예술과 패션의 그 오묘한 관계에 대해 알고 싶었고, 다른 사람의 생각을 알기 위해 그와 관련된 책들을 읽기 시작했다. 사진을 보고 휙휙 넘기지 않고, 글자를 읽기 시작했다. 눈으로 보는 것에 너무나 익숙했기에 글자를 읽는 것이 쉽지는 않았다. 하지만 예전과 달리 금세 흥미로운 이야기로 책에 빠져들었고 버스를 탈 때도, 누군가를 기다릴 때도 시간이 나면 그 이야기가 궁금해서 책을 펴곤 했다. 그러면서 다른 사람의 생각도 알게 되고, 점점 나의 고민도 깊어졌다. 아트와 패션, 누군가는 아트가 패션이라고 하고, 또 누군가는 패션은 단지 패션일 뿐이라고 한다. 하지만 그 어떤 생각도 진리이고, 정답은 아니다. 내가 생각하는 가치관이 나에게는 정답이고, 그것이 내 세계를 만들어갈 뿐이다.

나는 패션을 아트라고 생각한다. 나의 생각을 표현하는, 그리고 그 생각을 사람들과 대화하는 수단이 되는 아트. 하지만 아트와는 다르다는 생각도 한다. 왜냐하면 이 패션이라는 아트는 사람들에게 입혀졌을 때에만 빛을 발하기 때문이다. 미술관에 전시를 하고, 수많은 사람이 보고 감상하는 것이 패션은 아니다. 살아 있는 사람 위에 입혀져야만 생명력을 갖는 것이 진정한 패션이라고 생각한다.

주변을 보면 신인 디자이너들 중에 나와는 다른 생각으로 패션을 하는 사람들이 있다. 사람들이 입을 수 없지만 굉장한 아이디어로 아름다운 옷들을 만든다. 어떤 사람은 이런 옷을 보고 대단하다며 감탄하기도 하고, 때로는 패션은 이해하기 어려운 것이라고 말한다. 솔직히 나는 왜 그런 사람들이 굳이 패션을 하는지 모르겠다. 차라리 아무 조건이 없는, 표현의 한계가 없는 순수미술을 하는 것이 더 나을 수도 있다. 왜 사람들이 입지도 못하는 옷을 통해 자신들의 아이디어를 표현하는지 모르겠다. 차라리 조각이나 설치미술 쪽이 더 어울릴 것 같은데 말이다. 어차피 사람들이 못 입고, 전시되어야 할 작품이라면 말이다. 물론 이것 또한 나만의 생각일 수도 있고, 편협적인 시각일 수도 있다. 하지만 적어도 내가 하고 싶은 패션은 그런 것이 아니다.

이것은 창의력과는 거리가 있는 문제다. 몇몇 사람은 패션쇼에서 선보이는 옷들을 '웨어러블하다' 혹은 '창의적이다'라는 두 개의 카테고리로 나눈다. 창의적이지는 않지만 예쁘게 입을 수 있는 옷이냐, 아니면 입을 수는 없지만 창의적인 옷이냐는 것이다. 하지만 나는 그렇게 패션을 나누는 것이 싫다. 패션에 있어서 이 두 가지는 절대 떨어질 수 없다.

새로운 생각을 풀어낼 수 있는 창의적인 능력이 패션에서는 반드시 필요하다. 과거와 지금 시대를 알고, 미래를 내다보는 것이 패션에서는 아주 중요하다. 샤넬, 이브 생 로랑 등 창의적이고, 아름다운 옷들을 만들어낸 디자이너들이 있었다. 그들은 그 시대의 사람들이 생각하지 못한 아름다움을 옷을 통해 보여줬다. 전시장이 아니라 실제 사람들의 옷장을 바꾼 디자이너들이었고, 지금의 우리 옷장에까지 영향을 미치고 있다.

지금 시대를 살아가는 디자이너 중 패션의 창의력을 가장 쉽게 설명할 수 있는 디자이너는 후세인 샬라얀Hussein Chalayan일 것이다. 전기로 색깔이 바뀌는 옷, 모양이 변하는 옷 등 감탄을 금치 못하는 멋진 작업을 많이 했다. 비록 기술이 모자라고, 환경이 다르기 때문에 그가 만드는 옷이 오늘날 거리에서 받아들여지기 힘든 부분이 있다. 하지만 그는 입을 수 없는 옷을 만드는 디자이너가 아니다. 반대로 사람을 배려하고 생각하는 디자이너다. 미래를 생각하고, 시대를 앞서 나가 미래의 사람들이 입을 수 있는 옷의 기초를 만드는 디자이너인 것이다. 사람을 염두에 두지 않고 창의적이라는 탈을 쓰고 만들어진 옷과는 엄연히 다르다. 패션의 창의력 뒤에는 이렇게 반드시 사람에 대한 배려가 있어야 한다.

패션에서 가장 중요한 것은 사람이다. 그 옷을 입는 사람이 없는 옷은 생명이 없는 것과 같다. 하지만 요즘 패션을 공부하는 학생들이나 주위를 보면 그 옷을 입는 사람이 없는 패션을 하는 경우가 종종 있다. 사람에 대한 배려가 없는 옷. 디자이너는 자신의 아이디어나 생각을 표현한 조형물을 만들고, 옷이라는 이름으로 사람 위에 강압적으로 올려놓는다. 이런 학생들이 많이 오해하는 것 중 하나가 '입을 수 없는 옷'을 '오트 쿠튀르 haute couture'라고 생각하는 것이다. 오트 쿠튀르를 마치 입을 수 없는 옷을 만드는 것으로 오해하기 때문에, 그런 근거로 자신들의 작품이 입을 수 없더라도 '패션'은 된다고 생각하는 것 같다. 하지만 오트 쿠튀르는 입을 수 없는 옷이 아니다. 물론 지금의 시대에는 입을 수 없는 옷이 될 수도 있다. 오트 쿠튀르는 어디까지나 프레타포르테 prêt-a-porter 이전에 사람들이 입던 옷이었다. 시대가 변하고 그런 옷을 입을 상황이 점점 줄어들게 되면서 마치 입을 수 없는 옷이 되어가고 있지만 말이다.

이렇게 아트와 패션의 관한 나의 생각은 수많은 책을 통해 차근차근 정리되었다. 사실 책에서 본 어떤 것도 나의 가치관에 딱 맞는 정답을 제시하지는 않았다. 책을 통해 많은 정보를 얻고, 다른 사람의 생각을 알아갈 수는 있다. 하지만 가장 중요한 것은 책이 사람을 생각하게 한다는 것이다. 그런 과정을 통해 정리되지 않은 채 뒤섞여 있는 생각이 조금씩 자리를 잡아가고 있음을 느낀다. 지금까지 항상 궁금해하고, 불확실한 주관으로 패션을 해왔다면, 지금은 내가 원하는 것이 무엇인지 알면서 패션을 하고 있다. 내가 무엇을 원하는지 알면서 물건을 만드는 것과 우선 만들고 보자는 생각으로 만드는 것에는 엄청난 차이가 있다.

이런 연유로 부모님들이 자식들에게 책을 많이 읽으라고 귀가 닳도록 이야기하는 것 같다. 책을 읽다 보면 자연스럽게 생각이 깊어지는 것을 느낀다. 책을 보는 것이 아니라 '읽기' 시작하면서 생각이 쌓이게 되고, 나도 모르게 많은 고민을 하게 되었다.

요즘 한창 즐겨 보는 것은 유명 디자이너들에 관한 책이다. 물론 사진만 봐도 누가 디자인한 것인지 짐작할 수 있을 정도로 수많은 작품을 책으로 봐왔다. 도서관에서 가장 손쉽게 부담 없이 볼 수 있는 것이 유명 디자이너의 컬렉션이나 작품을 모아놓은 책이다. 물론 지금까지의 작품을 눈으로 보면서 배우는 것도 많다. 하지만 그것은 어디까지나 다른 사람의 작품일 뿐, 오히려 너무 많은 작품을 보는 것이 안 좋을 수도 있다. 시각적으로 섞여버린 수많은 정보로 인해 내가 주체가 되어 새로운 생각을 하는 데 방해가 될 수 있기 때문이다.

지금까지 시각적으로 디자이너들을 알아왔다면, 요즘은 그 디자이너의 본질을 알아가는 데 흥미를 느끼고 있다. 내가 주로 읽는 책은 자서전이나 누군가가 그 디자이너에 대해 쓴 글들이다. 어떻게 패션을 시작했는지, 그들이 생각하는 패션이 무엇인지, 그것이 어떻게 작품으로 표현됐는지 사진이 아닌 글로 만나고 있다. 매번 어떤 디자이너가 좋다고 이야기하면서 확실한 근거도 없이, 그래서 시도 때도 없이 좋아하는 디자이너가 변하는 친구들도 있다.

나 역시 좋아하는 디자이너가 수시로 변해왔다. 시각적으로 아름다운 작품을 만드는 것은 그 디자이너가 좋아질 이유가 되기에 충분하다. 그러나 그 디자이너의 작품에서 배우는 것보다 더 중요한 것이 그 디자이너의 생각을 배우는 것이다. 작품을 배우는 것은 어디까지나 그 사람의 결과물을 보는 것밖에 안된다. 정말 안 좋은 경우에는 자기 자신의 것은 없고, 어떤 스타일만을 따라가게 되는 최악의 상황에 맞닥뜨릴 수도 있다.

내가 관심 있는 디자이너 한 명, 한 명을 글로 만나고, 작품보다 그들의 배경과 생각을 알아가면서 많은 것을 배우고 있다. 예전에는 단지 작품이 멋져서, 창의적인 작품을 만들어서 좋아했던 디자이너들이 이제는 조금은 다르게 다가온다.

최근에 나의 마음을 사로잡은 디자이너는 이브 생 로랑이다. 물론 그는 작품만으로도 너무나 멋진 디자이너지만, 그의 생각과 시대적 배경을 알게 되면서 더욱 멋진 사람이라는 것을 알게 되었다. 자신의 가치관이 확고하고, 생각하는 것을 시대적 배경과 상관없이 표현할 수 있었던 것. 그리고 미래를 내다보고, 여성을 진정으로 생각했던 그의 삶은 말로 설명할 수 없을 만큼 멋지다. 조금은 외람된 말이지만, 이브 생 로랑과 내가 많은 부분에서, 특히 아트와 패션에 관한 시각이 많이 비슷하다는 것을 알게 되었다. 책을 읽는 내내 이브 생 로랑이 내 생각이 정답이라고 맞장구를 쳐주는 기분이었다. 이렇게 멋진 디자이너가 나의 생각에 동의한다는 것이 내가 확신을 가지고 패션을 할 수 있게 하는 힘이 되었다. 그의 작품을 단지 눈으로 봤을 때는 절대로 알 수 없었던 사실이었다.

이렇게 책을 통해 디자이너의 내면에 있는 세계를 알아가는 것이 요즘 큰 즐거움 중 하나이다. 오늘도 도서관에 가서 이브 생 로랑과 발렌시아가에 대한 책을 빌려왔다. 책을 통해 생각이 확장되고, 가치관이나 관점이 조금씩 정리되는 것이 기쁘다. 다른 디자이너들을 알아감으로써 내가 어떤 디자이너가 될 것인지 내 자신을 알아가는 중이다.

책이 줄 수 있는, 단편적으로 주는 지식이 아닌 나를 찾아가는 진정한 기쁨을 누리는 것. 이제야 새롭게 알게 된 아주 중요한 사실이다. 오늘도 발코니에 앉아 책을 읽어야겠다. 밤늦도록!

최근 나의 마음을 사로잡은 디자이너 이브 생 로랑의 책.
아트와 패션에 관한 시각이 나와 많이 비슷해 책을 읽는 내내 기분이 좋아진다.

3 이브 생 로랑
블라우스와의 조우

런던에는 채러티숍charity shop이 많다. 런던 어디를 가도 동네에 한두 개 있는 채러티숍은 사람들이 더 이상 안 쓰는 물건을 기증 받아 판매함으로써 자선기금을 마련하는 중고가게로 가끔씩 좋은 물건을 싸게 구입할 수도 있다. 저마다 역사와 이야기를 간직하고 있는 빈티지 제품을 좋아하는 나는 동네에 있는 채러티숍에서 독특하고 재미있는 물건을 구입하기도 한다.

새로운 동네로 이사온 지 일주일째 되는 오늘 아침에는 장을 보러 갔다가 집 바로 앞에 있는 채러티숍에 잠깐 들렀다. 사람들의 손때가 묻었지만 그 자체로 따뜻한 물건들, 반짝반짝 빛나는 새것보다 손때가 탄 낡은 물건을 더 좋아하는 내가 오랜만에 기분 좋게 구경하며 돌아서려는 순간, 한쪽 구석에서 조용히 빛나고 있는 것이 눈에 들어왔다. 속이 비치는 블랙 원단에 금색 실로 자수가 놓인 블라우스였다. 원단 자체로도 아름다웠지만, 봉긋하게 솟은 어깨선도 참 예뻤다. 구석구석 꼼꼼히 옷을 살피다 앞부분에 달려 있는 단추를 보고 깜짝 놀랐다. 작은 끈이 돌돌 말려 있는 단추로 책에서나 보던 디테일의 단추였는데, 설마 하는 마음에 라벨을 살펴보니 역시나, 이브 생 로랑 블라우스였다. 그것도 1960년대 처음 이브 생 로랑 레디투웨어ready to wear(기성복) 라인으로 나온 리브 고시Rrive Gauche가 적힌 라벨이었다. 심장이 두근두근거렸다. 재빨리 계산을 하고 집으로 돌아왔다.

집으로 오자마자 조심스레 옷을 입어봤다. 50년 된 옷이라고는 믿기지 않을 정도로 아름다웠다. 어떻게 그 옛날에 만들어진 옷

(위) 3년 전 우연히 들른 크리스티 전시장. 박물관에서나 볼 수 있는 옷들을 가까이서 살펴볼 좋은 기회였다.
(아래) 이브 생 로랑 블라우스. 오래된 라벨이 인상적이다.

이 지금의 미적 기준으로 봐도 이렇게 아름다울 수 있다니 다시 한 번 이브 생 로랑에 대한 존경심이 일었다. 살아 있는 듯 고귀한 자태의 블라우스가 내 옷장에 들어왔다고 생각하니 감동이 몰려왔다.

예전, 지금은 너무도 유명한 하우스들의 초기 옷들은 정말 아름답다. 옷 하나하나가 숨 쉬고 있는 듯, 마치 하나의 생명체 같다는 느낌이 들어 신기하기조차 하다. 옛날 옷에 대한 나의 찬사가 어쩌면 맹목적으로 들릴 수 있겠지만, 같은 레디투웨어라도 장인들이 만든 느린 옷과 매 시즌 쏟아져 나오는 오늘날의 옷은 비교가 되지 않을 만큼 그 깊이가 다르다. 예전 옷들은 느리고 침착하다. 오트 쿠튀르와 반대되는 레디투웨어라고는 하지만 초기 옷들은 하나의 예술 작품과도 같다.

이렇게 내가 옷을 보는 세계관이 달라지게 된 계기는 3년 전 친구와 우연히 들른 전시 때문이다. 세계적으로 유명한 경매회사 크리스티 Christie's 에서 초기의 레디투웨어 의상들을 사람들에게 판매하기 전에 열었던 전시였는데, 대부분 크리스챤 디올과 랑방, 발렌시아가, 이브 생 로랑의 초기 옷들이었다. 박물관에서나 볼 수 있는 옷들을 가까이서 살펴볼 수 있는 운명 같은 기회였다. 일생에 한 번 있을까 말까 한 그런 행운의 날, 나는 그렇게 우연적으로, 아니 어쩌면 필연적으로 역사에 길이 남을 옷들과 마주했던 것이다.

책이나 사진에서만 보던 옷들은 내가 상상하던 것 이상이었다. 오래되어 생명을 잃은 박제된 느낌이 아니라 여전히 강인한 아름다움을 발산하고 있었다. 무엇보다 인상적이었던 것은 옷들이 인체를 억압하는 억지스러움 없이 물 흐르듯 자연스러웠다. 그럼에도 실루엣이나 디테일이 반세기 전의 옷이라고는 믿을 수 없을 만큼 창의적이고 아름다웠다.

여성이 어떤 옷을 입었을 때 진정 아름다운지 디자이너가 깊이 있게 고민한 흔적이 묻어나는 옷들을 보면서 옷을 입는 사람에 대한 디자이너의 배려와 사랑이 그 옷들을 여전히 유효한 생명력으로 빛나게 하는 것은 아닌지 생각해보았다.

그날 나는 패션을 하면서 가장 중요한 것을 잊고 있었다는 것을 깨달았다. 빠르게 변하는 패션 시장에서 새로운 것을 만들어내야 한다는 압박감으로 옷을 입는 사람을 배려하고, 그 마음을 옷에 담아야 한다는 것을 잊고 있었던 것이다. 그것만이 가장 창의적이고 아름다운 옷을 만드는 디자이너의 유일한 길이라는 생각이 들었다.

온전히 내 생각이 주체가 되어 여성을 진심으로 사랑하는 마음으로 옷을 만드는 사람이 되고 싶다. 나만의 생각으로, 나만의 방법으로 만드는 옷들은 창의적일 수밖에 없으며, 여성의 아름다움에 대해 진지하게 고민하고 배려한 옷은 그 자체로도 의미가 있다.

오늘 나는 훌륭한 선배 디자이너들한테 그러한 사실을 배웠다. 우연히 내게 온 이브 생 로랑 블라우스는 다시 한번 내가 가야 할 길에 대해 말해주고 있었다. 우연이 아니고서는 가질 수 없는 이 블라우스는 내가 해야 할 일을 잊지 말라고, 지금 이대로의 마음으로 옷을 만들라고 말하는 듯했다. 블라우스 한 벌이 주는 소중한 깨달음에 마음까지 따뜻해지는 감사한 밤이다.

레디투웨어 의상에는 여성의 아름다움에 대한 디자이너의 진심 어린 배려와 사랑이 고스란히 담겨 있다.

4

**사랑할 수밖에 없는
드리스 반 노튼**

난 드리스 반 노튼Dries Van Noten을 사랑한다. 패션에 대한 그의 미학과 철학뿐만 아니라 그의 옷을 사랑한다. 그의 옷에는 강압적으로 아이디어를 쏟아내지 않는 여유와 느림이 배어 있다. 내 상상을 뛰어넘는 컬러 매치, 프린트의 조화, 옷을 입는 사람에게 강요하지 않는 여유롭고 아름다운 실루엣…. 그의 옷이 미학적으로 아름다운 것은 당연하다.

하지만 드리스 반 노튼의 옷은 쉽게 접할 수가 없다. 옷을 판매하는 곳이 적어 구매하기가 어렵다는 말이 아니다. 세계적으로 400여 곳에서 그의 옷을 판매하고 있는데, 런던만 해도 플래그숍은 아니지만 셀프리지, 리버티 등 유명 백화점에서 그의 아름다운 옷을 만날 수 있다.

그럼에도 불구하고 드리스 반 노튼은 쉽게 접할 수 있는 디자이너가 아니다. 그 이유가 광고를 하지 않기 때문이다. 지금까지 수많은 잡지와 광고 캠페인을 접해왔지만 단 한 번도 드리스 반 노튼의 광고를 보지 못했다. 광고는 빠르게 변화하는 패션 시장에서 브랜드의 이미지를 판매하는 중요한 요소이다. 대부분의 브랜드가 시즌에 맞춰 앞다투어 광고를 내보낸다. 고객들에게 새롭거나 혹은 전통적으로 지켜가고 있는 브랜드 이미지를 매 시즌 어필한다.

그런데 아이러니한 것이 광고를 통해 고객들에게 먼저 다가가지 않음에도 불구하고 그 어떤 브랜드보다 상류의 고급스러운 고객층을 확보하고 있다는 것이다. '나 정말 고급스러운 옷이에요'라고 광고하고 사람들에게 어필하지 않아도 옷 자체가 자신의 가치를 드러내는 브랜드인 것이다. 실제로 그의 옷을 구매하는 고객은 사회적 지위가 있는, 쉽게 말해 상류층이 많다고 한다. 광고를 하지 않고 사람들에게 쉽게 그 가치를 오픈하지 않는다고 해서 그가 고객을 배려하지 않는 것은 아니다. 오히려 그 정반대다. 그는 자신의 고객층을 정확히 파악하고 있으며, 고객들이 자신에게 원하는 아름다운 옷과 그 옷에 대한 자유를 충분히 부여한다.

2년 전 파리를 여행하다 우연히 발견한 드리스 반 노튼의 매장. 백화점에서는 그의 옷을 많이 봤지만 한번도 그의 플래그숍에 가본 적은 없었다. 어떤 브랜드를 제대로 알기 위해서는 반드시 플래그숍에 가봐야 한다. 백화점 한편을 차지하는 매장과 달리 플래그숍은 그 브랜드의 진정한 가치관 내지 미학을 확인할 수 있다. 그의 매장은 다른 하우스 브랜드처럼 규모가 크지도 화려하지도 않았다. 겉모습으로 요란하게 내가 가치 있는 브랜드라고 말하지 않았다. 어떠한 광고를 하지 않는 것처럼 허세와 위화감이 없었다.

런던에서 내가 즐기는 일 중 하나는 백화점과 브랜드 매장을 찾아가 디자이너들의 옷을 구경하는 것이다. 대부분의 옷이 내가 구매하기에는 엄청 비싼 가격이다. 그곳 직원들도 내가 옷을 구매하러 온 것이 아니라는 것을 잘 안다. 두 손 가득 학교 준비물을 들고 컨버스화를 신고 청바지를 입은 내가 명품 매장에서 무엇을 사겠는가. 디자이너들의 옷을 구경함으로써 그 브랜드를 이해하는 공부를 하는 것이다. 사진이 아닌 실제로 옷을 가까이에서 살펴보는 공부는 즐겁지만 가끔씩 매장에서 느껴지는 위압감은 부담스럽다.

파리의 드리스 반 노튼 플래그숍. 오르세 미술관으로 가는 길목에 있다.

드리스 반 노튼의 매장은 패션에 대한 그의 미학과 가치관이 그대로 묻어난다.
또한 그의 옷을 입는 주 고객층의 성품과 삶의 모습이 담겨 있는 듯했다.

브랜드의 가치를 충분히 지급할 수 있는 고급스러운 고객층을 확보하고, 그 고객층에게만 어필하는 것은 당연할 수도 있다. 하지만 과시하듯 일반인을 밀어내는 듯한 도도한 태도의 일부 매장은 내가 추구하는 패션에 대한 미학과 맞지 않는 부분이다. 물론 브랜드의 옷 자체가 지닌 미학과는 전혀 다른 이야기지만 말이다.

파리의 드리스 반 노튼 또한 내가 지갑을 열 수 있는 가격대의 옷은 아니다. 내가 즐겨 찾아가는 숍들처럼 높은 가격대의 옷들이다. 하지만 그의 파리숍은 가정집의 거실을 옮겨온 듯했다. 커다란 테이블과 에스닉한 패브릭 소파가 눈에 들어왔다. 큼직하고 소담스러운 꽃들이 여기저기 흐드러지게 놓여 있었다. 거실의 한편에 걸려 있는 옷들의 유니크하고 대담한 컬러의 프린트가 꽃들과 어우러져 절묘한 분위기를 연출했다.

물론 그의 매장 역시 다른 명품 매장처럼 고급스러웠다. 평범한 거실이 아니라 한번도 가본 적 없는 상류층의 거실이 떠올랐다. 하지만 위화감을 주는 분위기는 아니었다. 몇몇 명품 매장에서 느껴지는 거부감이 아니라 나를 감싸는 여유로움이 느껴졌다. 넓은 마음을 가진, 그 마음을 나눠줄 수 있는 여유를 가진 누군가와 이야기하는 듯한 느낌이랄까. 이리저리 치이며 치열한 삶을 살면서 자신의 뛰어남을 과시하는 것이 아니라 조용한 존재감으로 자신의 가치를 이야기하는 여유가 있었다. 그의 매장은 드리스 반 노튼의 패션에 대한 미학과 가치관이 그대로 묻어났다. 또한 그의 옷을 입는 주 고객층의 성품과 삶의 모습이 담겨 있는 듯했다.

드리스 반 노튼의 옷을 입는 사람들은 자신을 과시하거나 트렌디한 패션 리더로 보이기 위해 그의 옷을 선택하지 않는다. 그들은 그의 옷이 주는 아름다움과 자유로움을 선택한 것이다. 고가의 옷이 사람을 덮어 그 사람을 가치 있게 만드는 것이 아니라, 사람이 주체가 되어 옷을 입고 아름다워지는 것이다. 드리스 반 노튼은 자신의 옷을 입는 사람들에게 강요하는 것을 싫어한다고 한다. 스타일이나 실루엣을 강요하지 않는, 디자이너가 아닌 실제 옷을 입는 사람이 진정 옷의 주인이 될 수 있게 한다. 자신의 아이디어를 옷에 강요하고, 트렌드라는 이름으로 사람들의 옷장을 매 시즌 뒤흔드는 지금의 패션 풍토와는 반대되는 사람이다.

예전 시대의 패션을 향한 나의 사랑은 무한했다. 랑방, 이브 생 로랑 같은 디자이너들의 옷에 담긴 미학을 동경하고 무한정 애정을 보냈지만 오늘날 패션에 대한 애정 또한 크게 다르지 않다. 그런데 시대가 흐르면서 옷에 대한 주체가 변하고 있다는 것에는 불만이다.

레디투웨어의 역사가 깊어지면서 점점 새로운 것에 대한 욕구가 생겨나 그에 대한 디자이너의 부담감 또한 커진 것이 사실이다. 그런데 때로는 새로운 아이디어가 다소 강압적으로 옷에 표현되는 경우가 있다. 그런 옷들이 멋있게 보일 수도 있지만 나에게는 심술이 잔뜩 난 뾰족한 사람처럼 보일 때가 있다. 보는 사람이, 누구보다 입는 사람이 불편하게 느껴지는 옷들 말이다. 트렌드라는 이름으로 사람들에게 어필하는 옷, 몸을 혹사시키면서까지 입어야 하는 옷은 내가 생각하는 옷의 미학과 많이 어긋난다. 매스미디어의 영역이 확대되면서 고객들에게 옷 말고 브랜드를 이야기할 수 있는 통로가 넓어졌다. 그런데 아이러니하게도 그렇게 됨으로써 고객과 브랜드는 가까워지는 것이 아니라 더 거리감이 생기는 것 같다. 옷을 판매하는 브랜드이지만 옷 이전에 말하는 것들이 더 많아졌고, 또 그것을 그 브랜드의 가치로 받아들이게 됐다.

요즘 유행하거나 주목받는 옷들이 아름답지 않다는 것은 아니다. 트렌드가 광고가 사람들에게 어필하는 것이 싫다는 것도 아니다. 하지만 가끔씩 사람이 패션을 입는 것이 아닌, 패션이 사람을 입게 된 것 같은 분위기가 싫다. 난 사람들이 옷에 대해 좀 더 자유로웠으면 좋겠다. 그렇기 때문에 나는 사람들에게 자유를 줄 수 있는 그런 옷을 만들고 싶다. 넓은 마음으로 옷을 입는 사람들을 수용할 수 있는, 그런 여유롭고 아름다운 마음을 가진 옷들을 만들고 싶다.

자기가 잘났다고 허세를 부리는 브랜드들 사이에서 조용히, 하지만 깊은 울림을 전하는 드레스 반 노튼. 넓고 여유로운 마음으로 옷을 입는 사람들을 받아주는 그의 옷을, 그리고 그를 사랑한다.

5

**나에게 집중하는 시간,
요지 야마모토 전시**

혼자 했을 때 더 좋은 일 중에서 반드시 혼자 해야 하는 일이 전시회 가기다. 주변을 신경 쓰지 않고 나만의 템포로 작품을 감상하고, 생각할 시간을 가질 수 있기 때문이다.

오늘은 오래전부터 수첩에 메모해놓은 요지 야마모토의 전시를 보러 빅토리아 앤 알버트 뮤지엄 Victoria and Albert Museum(이하 V&A)에 갔다. 점심 시간 느지막이 출발해 1시경에 도착, 조금 과장을 보태 백 번도 넘게 온 V&A지만 올 때마다 한껏 느껴지는 기분 좋은 두근거림으로 오늘도 설렌다. 아, 좋다. 나도 모르게 크게 숨을 들이쉬며 나오는 말에 웃음이 나왔다. 사랑하는 남자를 만나러 가는 것이 이만큼 설렐까? 남자보다 예술이 좋으니 난 타고난 예술가구나, 하는 쓸데없는 생각을 하며 걷다 보니 요지 야마모토의 전시장 앞이다. 안내책자를 받아 들고 전시장 안으로 들어갔다. 하얀 벽면에 그려진 드로잉들, 오른쪽 벽면을 따라 설치된 영상과 요지 야마모토 특유의 형태가 눈에 띄는 의상들이 마네킹에 입혀져 전시장을 가득 채우고 있었다.

겉치레 없이 솔직한 그의 작품처럼 간결하고, 쉽게 전시되어 있어 딱 요지 야마모토의 전시 같았다. 전시장에서 우연히 만난 가이드로 일하는 친구 말에 의하면 벽면의 드로잉은 요지 야마모토가 직접 전시장에 와서 그린 것이라고 했다. 게다가 친구는 운이 좋아 요지 야마모토가 그림을 그리는 걸 봤다고 했다. 지금, 이 전시장에 살아 있는 요지 야마모토의 존재감이 느껴졌다.

친구와의 대화를 뒤로하고 설레는 마음으로 작품들을 살펴보

(위) V&A 곳곳에 전시되어 있는 요지 야마모토의 의상들.
(가운데) 요지 야마모토 전시장 내부.
(아래) 전시장 밖의 숍에서 판매하는 요지 야마모토의 책.

기 시작했다. 책에서 본 요지 야마모토 특유의 자유로운 디자인과 형태감은 익히 알고 있었지만 실제로 꼼꼼히 살펴보니 더욱 대단하게 느껴졌다. 예상하지 못한 방식으로, 그러나 자연스럽게 흐르는 옷의 형태를 따라 눈길이 가다 보니 한 마네킹을 뺑뺑 돌고 있는 나를 발견했다. 그렇게 나도 모르게 작품에 빠져들어 전시장 안을 뱅글뱅글 돌며 다녔다.

세계적으로 유명한 디자이너의 전시를 많이 봤지만 전시를 볼 때마다 느끼는 건 그 디자이너만이 가지고 있는 정체성이다. 물론 작품들을 가까이서 보며 옷을 구성하는 방법과 기술도 많이 배울 수 있지만 그것은 어디까지나 그 디자이너의 기술을 카피하는 것에 지나지 않는다. 요지 야마모토 또한 작품 하나하나가 대단하지만, 그것보다 더 굉장한 건 요지 야마모토만의 철학과 고집이었다. 자기 자신이 원하는 것이 무엇인지 확실하게 알고, 그것에 집중할 수 있는 고집. 그것이 이 모든 작품을 만들어낸 배경이 된 것이다.

난 디자인 공부를 하면서 가장 어려운 것이 자기 자신에게 솔직한 것이라고 생각한다. 내가 어떤 생각을 하는지, 진심으로 자신이 원하는 것이 무엇인지 아는 것은 어렵다. 세상 사람들이 하는 말과 빠르게 변하는 환경에 흔들려 진정한 자기 자신을 지키기 어렵기 때문이다. 성공에 집착하지 않고, 세상의 기준에 내 자신을 맡기지 않아야 마침내 들을 수 있는 게 자신의 목소리다. 언젠가 미우치아 프라다가 이런 말을 했다. 자기 자신이 누구인지 알고 그것에 집중하는 것이 자신이 성공할 수 있었던 이유라고. 내 생각과 딱 맞아떨어지는 그 말에 동감하며 다시 한번 의지를 다졌던 기억이 난다.

누구처럼 되고 싶고, 누군가 했던 것처럼 멋진 작업을 하고 싶은 것은 당연하다. 오늘도 요지 야마모토 전시를 보며 나도 이렇게 형태감에 뛰어난 사람이었으면 좋겠다고 생각했다. 하지만 다시 한번 나에게 해주고 싶은 말은, 난 요지 야마모토와 다르다는 것. 그렇게 요지 야마모토는 그의 멋진 전시장에 남겨두고 나는 출구로 나왔다. 그 누구도 나 대신 되어줄 수 없는, 나 자신만이 될 수 있는 나에게 미래의 더 멋진 전시장을 기약하며 훈훈한 결말을 지었다.

밖으로 나오자 기분 좋은 빗방울이 떨어져 더욱 나를 들뜨게 했다.

그 누구도 나 대신 되어줄 수 없는, 나 자신만이 될 수 있는 나에게 미래의 더 멋진 전시장을 기약하며.

6 나는
빈티지가 좋다

내 옷장의 80퍼센트 이상은 빈티지다. 몇 년째 입고 있는 옷부터 액세서리, 가방에 이르기까지 거의 모두가 빈티지, 쉽게 말해 중고 물건들이다. 나의 빈티지 사랑은 어릴 적부터 시작됐다. 중학교 시절, 소위 '구제'라고 하는 낡은 옷들이 좋았다. 빤짝빤짝 빛나는 새 옷과는 다른 느낌, 누군가 입어서 빛이 바래고 모양도 조금씩 변한 모습이 좋았다. 쇼핑이 목적은 아니지만 학교를 마치고 친구들이랑 시내에 있는 구제시장에 들르곤 했다. 산더미처럼 쌓아놓은 옷을 파헤치며 예쁘고 싼 것을 발견하는 것이 보물을 찾는 것마냥 재미있었다. 엄마는 왜 누가 입었던 옷을 사냐며 못마땅해하셨지만 말이다.

나이가 들면서 빈티지에 대한 사랑은 더 심해졌다. 청바지나 흰 티셔츠 같은 기본 아이템 말고는 거의 다 빈티지일 정도로. 그렇다고 내가 새 옷을 싫어하는 것은 아니다. 옛날 옷과 마찬가지로 깊이가 있고, 만든 사람의 정성과 입는 사람에 대한 배려가 묻어나는 옷은 새것이라도 좋아한다. 랑방이나 드리스 반 노튼처럼 매장에 가서 손으로 만지기도 황송할 만큼 정교하고 아름다운 옷들은 보는 것만으로도 행복하다. 이런 옷을 매일 입을 수 있다면 얼마나 좋을까 싶지만, 학생 신분인 나의 경제력으로는 어림도 없다.

그런데 내가 지불할 수 있는 범위의 가게들에서 파는 새 옷은 참 재미없다. 재미가 없는 걸 떠나 가볍다. 호떡처럼 쉽게 꾹꾹 찍어서 나온 옷들 같다. 가끔씩 마음에 드는 옷이라도 몇 번 입으면 그 빤짝함을 잃어버리는 인스턴트 같은 느낌도 싫다. 좋은 옷은 입을수록 분위기가 나는데, 어떻게 된 것이 요즘 옷들은 입으면 입을수록 허름해진다. 대량생산에 의해 아무런 감정도 없는 옷들이 세상에 쏟아져 나왔고, 옷이 버려지는 순환도 빨라졌다. 그만큼 더 많이 옷을 만들게 되고, 쉽게 만들면서 옷이 가벼워진 것 같다. 예전에는 옷을 사면 몇 년은 입었는데 요즘은 한 해만 입어도 초라해져서 그 다음 해에는 입기가 민망할 정도다.

내가 구입할 수 있는 범위에 있는 새 옷들은 내 마음에 들지 않고, 마음에 드는 새 옷은 능력이 안되니 내 눈은 자연스레 빈티지로 향하게 되었다. 처음에는 사서 한번도 입지 않은 옷도 많았고, 집에 와서 보면 너무 낡은 옷들도 있었다. 하지만 지금은 옷걸이에 빼곡히 걸린 옷들 중에서 좋은 아이템을 쏙쏙 골라내는 도사가 되었다. 좋은 것을 발견할 수 있는 눈만 가지고 있으면 나에게 어울리고 잘 만들어진 아름다운 빈티지 옷을 쉽게 찾을 수 있다.

빈티지 쇼핑에서 중요한 것은 각각의 아이템이 지닌 가치를 알아보는 것이다. 난 겉으로 보이는 디자인이 예쁘더라도 잘 만들어지지 않은 빈티지 옷은 사지 않는다. 굳이 새 옷보다 더 싸지도 않고, 깨끗하지도 않은데 옛날 옷을 사는 이유는 뭘까? 빈티지를 좋아하는 나는 아이러니하게도 빈티지 스타일을 좋아하지는 않는다. 특정 시대, 예를 들어 1940년대, 70년대 스타일을 좇아서 옷을 입지 않는다는 이야기다. 그럼에도 불구하고 내가 빈티지를 좋아하는 이유는 좋은 옷을 입는 것이 좋아서다. 다시 말해, 옛날 옷이라는 이유로 잘 만들어지고 가치 있는 옷을 저렴하게 살 수 있다. 현재 중국을 비롯한 아시아 지역의 공장에서 찍어내는 옷들과 다른 정성과 배려가 있는 느낌 좋은 옷, 그래서 난 빈티지가 좋다.

　물론 옛날 옷이라고 해서 모두 좋지는 않다. 그 당시에도 감정 없는 옷들을 만들었을 테고, 그런 옷들이 빈티지라는 이름으로 팔리기 때문이다. 하지만 자세히 살펴보면 가치 있는 옷들은 마무리나 버튼 등의 디테일이 다르다. 언뜻 보기에 매력적이라도 급하게 만든 옷들은 그만큼 값어치가 없음이 금방 드러난다. 그런 옷들은 요즘 쉽게 만들어진 옷들과 마찬가지로 쉽게 질리고, 심지어 사람을 허름하게 만든다. 허름해 보이는 스타일을 좋아한다면, 그것도 각자의 취향일 테니 할 말이 없지만 말이다.

　하지만 빈티지 스타일 중 이보다 더 나쁘기도 쉽지 않다. 왜 똑같은 돈으로 말끔해 보일 수 있는데 허름해 보이는 것을 택하겠는가? 정성이 깃든 빈티지 옷은 입었을 때 품위가 느껴지고 성품이 다르다. 그런 옷은 신기하게도 질리지가 않는다. 몇 년이 지나서 다시 꺼내 입어도 좋다. 언니의 낡은 옷을 물려 입는 것은 정말 싫어하면서, 남이 입었던 옛날 옷을 돈 주고 사서 입는 것. 이것이 가치 없는 빈티지와 좋은 빈티지를 구별하는 차이점이다.

　좋은 빈티지를 구별하는 것이 쉬운 일은 아니다. 가장 먼저 꼼꼼하고 정성 들여 만들었는지 디테일을 확인해야 한다. 자극적인 디자인이 마음에 드는 빈티지 옷을 발견했을 때도 라벨을 확인하거나 안감과 봉제 방법을 체크하는 것이 좋다. 또 하나, 내가 좋은 빈티지 아이템을 찾을 때 중요하게 생각하는 것은 그 옷만이 지닌 독특한 텍스타일과 프린트다. 요즘에는 쓰지 않는 독특한 프린트의 옷은 그 가치가 더욱 특별하다. 내가 구입한 빈티지 옷들은 대부분 프린트가 유니크하다. 같은 꽃무늬라고 해도 색깔 조합이 독특하거나 배열이 다르면 눈길이 간다. 최근에는 전혀 프린트되지 않는 주제로 만들어진 옷들도 있어서 더욱 가치 있게 느껴진다. 예쁘면서도 독특한 프린트와 텍스타일을 찾는 안목이 있다면 빈티지 쇼핑에서 실패할 확률은 적어진다. 그런 아이템을 발견하는 게 쉽지 않으니 몇 년이고 입을 때마다 만족스러운 나만의 옷이 된다.

    빈티지 쇼핑에서는 실제 내가 입을 옷이라는 것을 염두에 두어야 한다. 가끔 나는 입지 않을 것을 알면서도 빈티지 옷을 구입한다. 나는 옷을 공부하는 사람으로서 문학을 공부하는 사람들이 책을 읽는 것과 마찬가지로 좋은 옷을 공부하는 차원에서 구입하는 것이다. 그럴 때는 그 옷만의 독특한 점이라든지 지금은 잘 볼 수 없는 그 시대만의 디테일과 디자인이 옷을 구매하는 가장 중요한 요소가 된다.

    하지만 옷을 입기 위해 고를 때는 그 기준이 완전히 달라진다. 각자 체형이 다르고, 어울리는 옷이 다르기 때문이다. 세계 각국에서 수입한 빈티지의 경우에는 우리나라 사람과 체형이 다르기 때문에 모양도 다르다. 일본 빈티지는 대부분 팔이 짧은데, 나는 키가 크고 팔도 길어서 잘 맞지 않는다. 디자인이 마음에 들어 일본 빈티지를 구입하는 것은 평생 입지도, 버리지도 못하는 옷을 옷장에 걸어두기 위해 사는 격이다.

    과도한 오버사이즈 재킷은 빈티지한 느낌은 주지만 어깨가 작은 체형은 반드시 입어보고 어느 정도 수선이 가능한지 살펴보고 구입하는 것이 좋다. 옛날 옷의 특징을 잘 활용하는 것도 좋지만 무엇보다 자신의 체형에 잘 어울리고 아름답게 보이는지 살펴야 한다. 그리고 반드시 얼룩이 없는지도 체크한다. 살 때는 '이 정도야 괜찮겠지' 하고 생각할 수 있지만, 실제로 그 얼룩 때문에 옷을 버릴 수도 있다. 더욱이 흰 옷 같은 경우에는 꼼꼼하게 확인하고, 얼룩이 있으면 되도록 구입하지 않는 것이 좋다.

빈티지 쇼핑에서는 빈티지가 줄 수 있는 장점을 최대한 활용하는 것이 중요하다. 빈티지는 스타일의 영역이 넓다. 쉽게 말해, 트렌디한 요즘의 옷과 달리 다양한 스타일의 옷이 있다. 따라서 정해진 범위 내에서 옷을 고르는 것이 아니라 내가 주체가 되어 스타일을 고를 수 있다. 또한 보다 다양한 스타일을 시도할 수 있다. 빈티지숍에 가서 내가 원했던 아이템을 사는 것은 어렵다. 하지만 내가 한 번도 시도하지 않은 예쁜 아이템을 발견하고, 생각지도 않았는데 너무나 잘 어울릴 때. 그것이 빈티지를 입는 진정한 묘미이다.

이번 봄에 한창 자주 입었던 빛바랜 민트 컬러 트렌치코트가 있다. 트렌치코트를 한번도 입어본 적 없는 나로서는 어울리지 않을 거라고 지레 생각했다. 하지만 색깔이 너무나 예뻐서 결국 구입했고, 의외로 나에게 잘 어울렸다. 내가 입는 옷의 범위가 한층 넓어진 것이다. 새롭게 발견한 사실은, 트렌치코트가 롱 원피스와도 잘 어울리고, 청바지와도 무난하게 어울리는 마술 같은 아이템이라는 것이다. 게다가 핏fit도 넉넉해 편하기까지 했다. 많은 사람이 트렌치코트를 입지만 이렇게 오묘하게 아름다운 색깔과 디자인의 트렌치코트는 내 것밖에 없으니, 이런 희소성의 가치 또한 빈티지의 매력이라 할 수 있겠다.

작년에 〈프런코〉 때문에 한국에 머물면서 젊은이들 사이에 빈티지 옷을 입는 것이 유행이라는 것을 알고 놀랐다. 하지만 나는 그 또한 파워 숄더 재킷처럼 잠시 유행하다 바람처럼 사라져버릴 거란 생각이 든다. 왜냐하면 대부분 오버사이즈 재킷에 닥터마틴 부츠를 신고 있었기 때문이다. 조금씩 디자인은 달랐지만 이렇게 입는 것이 유행에 지나지 않았기 때문이다. 개중에는 '한국에도 이렇게 옷을 입는 사람이 있단 말이야?' 하는 생각이 들 만큼 빈티지를 멋지게 연출하는 사람도 있었다. 빈티지가 어떤 스타일이든, 어떤 시대를 좇아가든, 나처럼 옛날의 정성이 담긴 옷을 좋아하는 것이든 아니든 아무런 상관없다. 중요한 것은 옷을 입는 사람이 주체가 되어 빈티지 아이템을 자기 것으로 만들어야 비로소 제 빛을 발한다는 것이다.

패션을 함에 있어 시대의 흐름에 민감해야 하고, 이 시대가 원하는 것이 무엇인지 알아야 하는 것은 당연하다. 그것이 트렌드라는 이름으로 세상에 나온다면 그것 또한 무시해서도 안된다. 사람들에게 새로운 시선으로 옷을 바라볼 수 있게 하는 권유와 초대 같은 의미를 지니는 시도 말이다. 예를 들어, 이브 생 로랑이 처음 여자들에게 입힌 턱시도 재킷 같은 것이 패션에는 반드시 필요하다. 어쩌면 진정한 디자이너가 사람들에게 제공해야 할 가장 중요한 일이기도 하다.

하지만 강요하듯이 유행이라는 이름으로 옷을 묶어버리는 것은 싫다. 잠시 사람들을 현혹하여 아름답고 새로운 것처럼 보이게 하지만, 언젠가는 거짓이 드러나는 옷을 만들어내는 것은 더더욱 싫다. 그래서인지 빈티지 옷 또한 유행이나 어떤 스타일처럼 번지는 것은 그다지 마음에 안 든다. 너도나도 비슷한 옷을 입고, 금방 지겨워지는 것은 빈티지와는 정반대되기 때문이다.

　나는 빈티지 옷이 나만의 것이기 때문에 좋다. 유행이 아닌 내가 주체가 되어 옷을 고를 수 있고, 일반 매장에서는 찾을 수 없는 독특하고 잘 만들어진 아이템을 살 수 있어서 좋다. 내가 학생이 아니라 돈을 버는 사회인이 되면 랑방에 가서 맘에 드는 옷을 척척 사는 날도 올 것이다. 하지만 그때도 빈티지숍에 가서 멋진 아이템을 발견하며 행복해할 것이다. 요즘은 없는 프린트와 디테일, 디자인의 빈티지 옷들이 여전히 그곳에 있을 것이기 때문이다.

　나이를 먹을수록 그런 옷들이 쌓인다면 아마도 내 옷장은 보물 같은 옷들로 가득 채워질 것이다. 몇 년 만에 입어도 항상 빛을 발하는 가치와 생명력 있는 옷들로 가득한 옷장. 내가 빈티지를 사랑할 수밖에 없는 이유다.

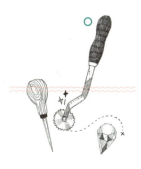

7 사막에서 오아시스를 만나다!
인스피레이션

오늘 아침 교회에 가는 길, 마음이 터질 것처럼 설레서 걸어갈 수가 없었다. 몇 주간 내 주위를 맴돌며 열릴 듯 말 듯 나를 애태우던 영감이 드디어 떠올랐기 때문이다. 마지막 졸업 학년의 컬렉션 주제를 생각하고, 그것을 표현하는 방법에 대해 연구하고 있었지만 뭔가 껄끄럽게 안 풀리는 부분이 있었다. 하고 싶은 주제는 몇 달 전에 정했지만 그 주위를 돌기만 하는 애매한 상황.

아하! 하고 확신이 서는 그런 것이 나오지 않았었다. 이놈 때문에 최근 소파에 앉아 몇 시간을 고민하다 밤을 새우고 새벽에야 잠이 든 적이 하루 이틀이 아니었다. 그러기를 몇 주, 드디어 오늘에서야 이 애매모호 답답했던 마음이 뻥 뚫리는 정답이 나왔다. 그 정답을 찾은 기쁨은 사막에서 오아시스를 만난 기분이랄까. 하늘에 있는 모든 공기를 삼켜버릴 듯한 기쁨, 마음 간질간질하게 설레는 행복하고 감사한 기쁨이다.

작업에 있어 영감을 받아서 이런 기쁨을 느낀다는 것이 우습게 들릴 수도 있겠지만, 디자인을 하는 사람이라면 조금은 공감할 수 있지 않을까. 반대로 영감이 쉽게 떠오르지 않거나 뭔가 나올 듯 말 듯하며 나오지 않을 때의 그 고통 또한 예술을 하는 사람이라면 공감할 것이다.

내 주위에 예술을 공부하는 친구들을 보면 대부분 이렇다. 작업이 잘 진행될 때는 괜찮지만, 그렇지 못할 때의 답답함과 속상함을 어찌 말로 표현할 수 있겠는가. 그 스트레스를 견디지 못해 히스테리를 부리는 사람은 물론이거니와 가끔은 밑도 끝도 없이 수업시간에 우는 친구도 있다. 아이러니한 것은 예술은 자기가 원하는 것을 표현하는 것이란다. 원하는 것을 표현하는 데 뭐가 그렇게 잘 안 된다는 것인가? 그런데도 실상은 작업이 정말 안될 때가 있다. 하긴 해야 하는데 할 수 없고, 24시간을 머릿속을 따라다니며 괴롭히지만 결론은 안 나는 그럴 때가 가장 괴롭다. 작업은 해야 하는데 영감은 떠오르지 않을 때의 답답함은 겪어보지 않은 사람은 모른다.

　이 문제의 시작은 내 마음을 울리는 '영감이 없다'는 것이다. 영감이 없는 것까지는 괜찮다. 그런데 영감이 없는데도 작업은 해야 하는 상황은 괜찮지 않다. 나 같은 학생은 정기적으로 학교에서 해야 하는 프로젝트가 있고, 직장에서도 나름대로 해야 하는 일이 있다. 개인 브랜드를 가지고 작업하더라도 매 시즌 옷을 만들어내야 한다. 해야 할 때마다 반짝반짝 영감을 받아서 작업을 시작하면 더 없이 좋겠지만, 항상 그렇지는 못하다. 가끔은 프로젝트를 받고서야 무엇을 할까, 하는 고민을 시작하기도 하고, 프로젝트 중간에 주제를 바꾸는 일도 생긴다. 확실한 것은 풍성한 영감이 없는 상태에서 억지로 진행한 작업의 결과가 좋을 리 없다는 것이다. 그러면 영감을 받고 시작하면 되지, 뭐가 문제일까 싶지만 문제는 영감은 찾는다고 받아지는 것이 아니다.

　프로젝트를 받으면 학교 도서관에 사람들로 넘쳐나는 것이 우리 학교의 풍경 중 하나이다. 너도나도 산더미처럼 책을 쌓아놓고 복사할 페이지를 찾으며 휙휙 책장을 넘긴다. 거의 대부분의 학생이 프로젝트가 시작됐으니 자료를 찾고, 영감을 받기 위해 도서관을 찾는다. 하지만 나는 절대 가장 먼저 도서관에 가지 않는다. 바로 하고 싶은 것이 떠올랐을 때는 조사를 하러 도서관으로 직행하지만 적어도 하고 싶은 주제가 없는 상태에서는 절대 도서관에 가지 않는다. 쉽게 말해 영감을 받으러 도서관에 가지는 않는다는 것이다. 이것이 나만의 작업 철칙이다.

    세인트 마틴 1학년 때에는 나도 프로젝트를 받자마자 도서관으로 달려갔다. 이 책 저 책 찾아가며 나의 눈에 들어오는 것을 모조리 모았다. 그렇게 모으고 모아서 관심이 가는 것을 중심으로 작업하며 아이디어를 발전시키고, 디자인을 했다. 내가 진정 무엇을 하고 싶은지에 대한 고민이 부족한 상태에서 무한정으로 받아들여지는 책의 정보는 나를 피곤하게 만들었다. 정보는 많지만 작업의 깊이는 얕아지고 혼란스러웠다.

    도서관에 있는 책들의 정보는 지나치게 방대하다. 어디서부터가 정보의 시작이고 끝인지 알 수 없을 정도로 다양하다. 프로젝트를 받고 영감을 얻기 위해 랜덤으로 뽑아 드는 책들의 모든 내용이 나를 현혹시켰다. 이것도 하고 싶고, 저것도 재미있어 보이고, 많은 것이 흥미로워 보였다. 책으로 나온 것들은 거의가 누군가의 손과 생각을 거쳐 나온 작품들이다. 당연히 흥미로울 수밖에 없다. 이렇게 쏟아져 나오는 것을 필터링 없이 모두 받아들이다 보면 내가 진짜 말하고 싶은 것이 무언인지 내 생각을 잃어버리게 된다. 겉모습만 반지르르한 얄팍하고, 속이 빈 작업이 되고 마는 것이다.

    내 생각을 잃어버린 작업은 나를 피곤하게 만들었다. 프로젝트를 받으면 영감을 얻기 위해 도서관에서 몇 시간이고 보냈다. 책에서 영감을 받는 것이 안 좋다는 이야기는 아니다. 나도 가끔은 사진집 또는 유명 작가의 그림 한 장에서 영감을 받기도 한다. 영감을 받기 위해 책에 있는 것을 찾아 다니는 것이 슬픈 일이라는 것을 말하고 싶다. 랜덤으로 책을 뽑아 들어 내 감각을 깨우게 하는 것을 찾아 다니는 것, 영감을 받기 위해 여기저기 뒤지는 것이 얼마나 슬픈 일인지 그때는 몰랐었다.

그것은 무엇보다 피곤한 일이었다. 영감을 받아야 하기에 영감을 찾아 헤매야 했다. 프로젝트를 받으면 촉각이 곤두섰다. 재미있는, 새로운 그런 영감. 나에게 무엇을 하고 싶은지 묻지도 않은 채, 영감을 찾기 위해 온 신경을 곤두세웠다. 책을 뒤지고, 고민하고, 조금이라도 흥미로우면 복사를 했다. 그중에서 하나가 들어맞아 작업을 시작하기도 했고 시각적으로 다가온 것들이 흥미롭기도 했지만, 내 마음을 울리는 그런 영감은 아니었다. 그렇게 작업하다 보니 가장 큰 문제는 작업에 흥미를 잃어간다는 것이었다. 작업의 시작이 나를 흥미롭게 하는 영감이 아님에도 작업을 해야 하기 때문에, 할 것이 없어서 영감을 의무적으로 찾아 다녀야 하니 진행이 재미있을 리 없었다. 즐거워야 할 작업이 부담으로 다가왔다.

하지만 하늘은 나의 편. 다행히도 그런 공허함을 바꿔놓은 일이 있었다. 에세이를 쓰기 위해 읽은 책 한 권에서 나의 생각을 바꿔놓는 글귀를 발견했다.

'모든 것을 듣기 위해 노력한 것이 듣고 싶은 나의 욕구조차 파

괴했다.' – 데이비드 투프의 《Haunted Weather》

나의 상황과 딱 맞아떨어지는 글귀였다. 영감 받기 위해, 흥미롭고 새로운 것을 찾기 위해 노력했던 것이 내가 작업하고 싶은 욕구마저 없애버렸던 것이었다. 작업하는 것만큼 즐거운 것이 없는 나의 흥미조차 뺏어간 '영감을 받아야 한다'는 그 압박감. 영감을 받기 위해서 헤매는 그 행동이 나를 얼마나 피곤하게 만들었는지 그제서야 알게 되었다.

천천히 다시 생각해보기 시작했다. 영감은 찾는 것이 아니라 받는 것이었다. 자연스럽게 나에게 오는 것, 내가 좋아하는 것들, 나의 관심을 끄는 것들은 내가 찾아 나서서 얻는 것이 아니라 내 삶 속에서 받는 선물이라는 것을 깨달았다. 내 마음을 진심으로 울리는 영감으로 작업하고 싶다는 마음이 간절했다. 그것이 내가 패션을 하고, 옷을 만드는 근본적인 이유라는 것도 다시 한번 기억하게 되었다. 옷을 만들어야만 하는 상황에 놓이다 보니 영감이 떠올라서 옷을 만드는 원래의 정상적인 과정을 잊어버렸던 것이다. 당연한 것인데도 이렇게 상황에 속고, 나에게 속아서 잊어버리게 되는 일이 많다는 것에 새삼 놀랐다.

이미 차고 넘치게 많은 영감이 내 안에 있었다. 나에게 솔직하기만 하면, 묻기만 하면 나오는 것이었다. 내 마음을 울리는 것들, 따뜻한 노래 한 곡, 파란 가을 하늘, 할머니의 걸음걸이 그 모든 사소한 것이 모두 내 마음을 움직이는, 내가 작업을 통해 말하고 싶은 영감이었다. 나에게 마음을 열어 마음껏 느낄 수 있도록 허락하니, 내 마음은 영감으로 넘쳤다. 어떨 때는 시각적으로 흥미로운 것도 있었고, 또 어떨 때는 사람의 마음이나 감정이 될 수도 있었다. 그 어떤 것이든지 내 마음을 시작점으로 나온 그 영감은 지금까지의 것과는 달랐다. 내가 시작이고 주체가 되는 영감은 나를 움직이게 했고, 즐겁게 작업하게 했다.

하지만 거기에도 사소한 문제는 있었다. 그런 영감이 반드시 프로젝트를 시작할 때 마법처럼 나타나지 않는다는 것이다. 혹은 영감을 받았더라도 더 이상 아이디어가 진전이 안될 때도 있다. 그럴 때는 앞서 이야기했듯이 더 이상은 작업이 진전되지 않는 답답한 상황에 마주한다. 주제라는 영감은 있는데 그게 어떻게 시각적으로 진전되어야 하는지 애매모호한 그런 상황과도 같다. 그럴 때면 난 다시 내 자신을 좀 더 느낄 수 있도록 허락한다. 노력하는 것이 아니라 허락한다. 아이디어를 쥐어짜려고 방에, 도서관에 틀어박혀 있는 것이 아니다. 영감을 받으려고 노력하는 시간 대신 좋아하는 가수의 노래를 마음껏 듣는다든지, 맛있는 음식을 먹는다든지 그렇게 말이다. 더 느낄 수 있도록 좋아하는 것들을 하면서 내가 진짜 작업하고 싶은 것이 무엇인지 느끼게 허락한다. 조금 더딜 때도 있지만 반드시 정답은 찾아오게 되어 있다. 내가 영감을 찾는 것이 아니라 영감이 나를 찾아오게 만드는 것이다.

그게 바로 오늘 아침이었다. 내 자신에게 솔직할 때 찾아오는 진정한 영감은 나에게 큰 기쁨이다. 그 기쁨은 작업의 즐거움으로 이어진다. 진정으로 하고 싶은 말이 있으니, 표현하고 싶은 것들이 있으니 어떻게 신나게 작업하지 않을 수 있을까. 결과물이 좋은 것은 말할 필요도 없다.

예전 〈프런코〉 때문에 컬렉션을 준비할 때, 3개월을 하루도 쉬지 않고 매일 작업실에 갔다. 물론 일요일에는 교회도 가고 조금 쉬기는 했지만 집에서 뜨개질이라도 했다. 작업에 대한 열정과 즐거움 때문에 쉴 틈이 없었다. 집에서 버스로 한 시간 정도 거리에 작업실이 있었기 때문에 항상 막차가 끝나기 15분 전까지 작업을 했다. 집으로 가는 버스 안에서는 내일 할 작업을 생각하며 들뜨곤 했다.

그 시간이 얼마나 즐거웠는지 모른다. 내가 하고 싶은 주제가 매일 조금씩 발전하고, 내 눈앞에 나타나고, 그것이 마지막으로 옷으로 만들어지는 과정이 정말 즐거웠다. 그것의 시작점은 내가 하고 싶은 주제가 너무나 확실했기 때문이라는 것을 알고 있었다. 티베트에서 느낀 '느리게 사는 삶의 아름다움'은 한 치의 의심도 없이 살아가는 이곳 사람들의 모습을 전하고 싶은 나의 마음이었다.

내가 하는 작업의 시작점은 거의 대부분 사람들에게 이야기하고 싶은 것들이다. 그것이 사람의 감정이든, 삶의 방식이든, 슬픔이든, 기쁨이든, 좋은 노래의 한 소절이든 말이다. 시각적으로 아름다운 옷을 만들기 이전에 더 깊은 이야기가 있는 옷을 만들고 싶다. 내 옷을 입는 사람들이 내가 아름다운 방법으로 표현한 이야기를 들을 수 있었으면 좋겠다. 난 내가 디자이너라기보다는 아티스트에 가까운 사람이라고 생각하기도 한다. 옷에 의미를 주고, 옷을 통해 사람들과 이야기하는 아티스트. 물론 나와 다르게 내용보다는 시각적인 아름다움을 최고로 치는 디자이너도 있고, 조금 더 새로운 것들을 만들어내는 발명가의 마인드를 가진 디자이너도 있다. 그 어떤 것도 디자이너의 정석은 아니다. 하지만 난 옷이라는 매체를 통해 사람들과 이야기하고 싶다. 내 이야기를 하고 싶고, 사람들이 내가 보는 아름다운 세상을 내가 만드는 옷을 통해 내 이야기를 듣고 더 알게 되었으면 좋겠다.

그것이 내 마음 깊숙한 곳에 있는, 나로 하여금 즐겁게 옷을 만들게 하는 영감의 시작이다. 사람들을 사랑하는 마음을 가지고 내가 느끼는 것들을 그대로 느낄 수 있도록 허락해줄 때 들을 수 있는 진짜 '영감' 말이다.

영감은 찾는 것이 아니라 받는 것이다. 자연스럽게 내게로 온 영감들로 가득 채운 작업실 벽면.
이제 즐겁게 옷을 만들 일만 남았다.

8 세인트 마틴에서의
마지막 프로젝트

꿈만 같았던 세인트 마틴에서의 3년이 지나고 이제 마지막 학년이다. 올해 세인트 마틴은 새로운 건물로 이사를 했다. 내가 입학할 당시부터 이사를 운운했지만 올해 드디어 과마다 시내 곳곳에 흩어져 있던 학교들이 킹스 크로스 스테이션 King's Cross Station 에서 걸어서 5분 거리에 있는 커다란 공장 같은 빌딩으로 합쳐졌다. 이번 이사는 세인트 마틴의 새로운 시대를 여는 시작이라고 할 만큼 대단한 이슈였다. 올해 졸업생들은 그런 의미에서 첫 번째 졸업생이 될 것이다. 나 역시 그중 한 명이 될 것이고.

요즘 마지막 학년의 학생들은 졸업 프로젝트 준비가 한창이다. 지금이 1월 중순이니 2월 초에는 디자인을 끝내야 하고, 3월 중순까지는 가봉을 마쳐야 한다. 5월 중순에는 졸업 쇼가 기다리고 있다. 졸업만을 위해 달려온 것은 아니지만 나에게도 졸업 쇼는 큰 의미가 있다. 4년간의 학교 생활, 정확히 파운데이션 과정까지 합하면 장장 5년의 시간을 세인트 마틴에서 보냈고, 이번 졸업 쇼를 끝으로 나의 학업 또한 마무리될 것이다.

패션의 '패'자도 모르고 입학해서 힘들었던 1학년 첫 학기와 겨울 방학. 그 무거운 마음으로 뉴욕에 놀러 가 친구랑 밥을 먹다가 울었던 기억. 비록 44점을 맞았지만 나의 잊어버린 시각을 찾게 해준 터닝포인트가 되었던 1학년 봄학기의 셔츠 프로젝트. 4월 이스터 easter 방학 때 한 달 내내 집에 틀어박혀 옷만 만들었던 기억. 처음 해본 포토슛을 찍던 날, 처음으로 '디자이너'라고 불렸던 날의 설렘. 밤 10시, 아무도 없는 학교 스튜디오에서 작업하며 혼자 신이 나서

춤추며 노래 부르던 일. 작업을 마치고 버스를 타고 나서야 실밥투성이인 내 모습을 발견했던 일. 아침 8시에 가장 먼저 학교에 와 성경책을 읽으며 하루를 시작하고 마음을 다잡던 기억들…. 어느 하나 소중하지 않은 것이 없다.

이제는 정말, 수많은 기억을 뒤로하고 마지막으로 내가 소중하게 간직할 한 가지가 남아 있다. 내가 사랑하는 세인트 마틴에서의 마지막 작업이 될 마지막 프로젝트가 남아 있다. 나의 마음을 가장 움직이는, 내가 가장 말하고 싶은 주제를 정하고, 그것에 대해 생각하고 리서치하며, 누구보다 즐겁고 행복하게 작업하고 있다. 내 마지막 컬렉션의 주제는 '어메이징 그레이스 Amazing Grace'다. 나를 돌이켜볼 때, 현재 이곳에서 이 모습으로 이렇게 서 있을 수 있었던 것은 모두 하나님의 은혜라는 것을 말하고 싶다. 무엇보다 나를 사랑하시는 하나님의 아름다움을 표현하고 싶었다.

이 주제를 정하고 가장 마음에 걸렸던 것은 선생님의 반응이었다. 선생님이 혹시나 반감을 가지지는 않을지, 처음에는 부끄럽기도 하고 겁이 나기도 했지만, 다행히 그런 걱정은 기우에 지나지 않았다. 프로젝트를 진행하면서 내가 얼마나 이 주제에 빠져 있고, 넘치는 아이디어가 있는지 아시게 되면서 오히려 방학 전의 마지막 점검 때는 내가 만든 원단 샘플을 아무에게도 보여주지 말라고 하실 만큼 좋아하시고 이해하셨다.

요즘 학교에서 혹은 페이스북에서 패닉 상태에 빠진 졸업 학년의 친구들을 만나곤 한다. 모두 '마지막'이라는 이 엄한 단어 때문이다. 뭔가를 이뤄야 한다는, 멋지게 마지막을 장식해야 한다는 압박감과 부담감으로 인해 작은 일에도 쉽게 동요되곤 한다. 다들 얼마나 이기적이 되는지, 웬만해서는 귀찮아서 인사도 잘 안 한다. 게다가 한 번은, 친구와 복도 책상 위에 앉아 이야기하는데 수십 명의 학생이 우르르 복도 밖으로 달려나가는 것이었다. 무슨 일인지 깜짝 놀라서 물어보았지만 대답을 해주는 친구가 한 명도 없었다. 다들 뭘 말하려고 하다가도 제 일에 급해서 뛰어갔다. 알고 보니, 새롭게 사물함을 정하는 날이라 자기 사물함을 '찜'하러 달려갔던 것이었다. 사물함, 그게 뭐라고 다들 눈에 불을 켜고 달려 나갔을까. 결국 난 좋은 사물함을 얻지 못하고 구석에 있는 작은 것 하나를 겨우 얻었다.

그렇다고 이 친구들을 탓하는 것은 아니다. 나도 이 '마지막'이라는 압박감에 시달리기까지 하고 있으니 말이다. 평소에는 괜찮지만 가끔씩 '내가 지금 뭘 하고 있지'라는 생각이 들 정도로 작업이 막힐 때면 불안하다. 인정하고 싶지 않고 괜찮다고 하고 싶지만 나도 불안하다. '잘 못하면 안되는데' 하는 걱정이 물밀 듯이 몰려오거나 '일등하고 싶다'는 욕심이 마음 깊숙한 곳에서 일어날 때는 심하게 동요되기도 한다. 마지막이라는 압박감과 그렇기 때문에 뭔가를 이뤄야 한다는 부담감이 동시에 일어나면 나도 많이 힘들다. 친구를 만나는 것이 내 시간을 내주는 것 같아서 힘들고, 모든 것이 계획한 타이밍에 따라 움직여야만 마음이 편하다.

하지만 난 이 '마지막'이라는 단어에 속고 싶지 않다. 우리 엄마가 항상 하시는 말씀이 "자신이 있는 자리에서 최선을 다하고, 결과는 하나님께 맡겨야 한다"는 것이다. 이것을 내가 할 수 있었으면 좋겠다. 졸업하는 친구들이 최선을 다하는 것은 말할 필요도 없는 사실이다. 패닉하고, 절망하고, 과도하게 기뻐하고, 슬퍼하고, 온갖 정신적인 어려움을 겪으면서 최선을 다한다. 하지만 난 그렇게 되지 않았으면 한다. 졸업이라는 것 또한 내가 지나가야 하는 것일 뿐, 마지막은 아니다. 졸업 후에는 이보다 더 큰 스트레스가 기다리고 있고, 회사에 들어가거나 자신의 브랜드를 차려도, 패션이라는 영역 자체가 스트레스로 똘똘 뭉쳐 있기 때문에 힘들 수밖에 없다.

    패션을 하면서 중간에 포기하는 사람을 수도 없이 많이 봐왔고, 너무나 불행한 일평생을 보낸 유명 디자이너들도 봤다. 지금 내가 이것을 내 것이 아니라고 내려놓지 않는다면, 내려놓지 못한다면 앞으로 얼마나 힘들지 상상이 간다. 욕심 없이 감사함으로 즐겁게 내가 좋아하고 사랑하는 패션을 할 수 있었으면 좋겠다. 지금 이 프로젝트가 마지막이 아닌, 화려한 피날레가 아닌 나를 더 좋은 곳으로, 더 나은 디자이너로 이끄는 '길목'이었으면 한다.

    그래도 요즘 학교에 갈 때마다 마음이 뒤숭숭하다. 아직 끝난 것은 아니지만 이 길을 따라 학교에 갈 날이 얼마 남지 않았다는 생각을 하면 벌써부터 섭섭하다. 대망의 마지막이라는 생각이 들기도 하지만, 그건 사랑하는 사람을 떠나 보내는 아쉬움이지 뭔가를 이뤄내겠다는 포부는 아니다. 때로는 내가 열정이 없거나 패션에 별로 미치지 않은 것처럼 보일 수도 있겠다. 그저 나에게 주어진 것이니까 할 뿐, 잘되든 말든 상관없다는 듯이 보일 수도 있다.

요즘 세대는 무조건 앞뒤 보지 않고 달리는 사람만이 인정을 받는 것 같다. 하지만 난 그 반대의 사람이 되고 싶다. 나중에 사람들이 '나도 저 사람처럼 패션을 하고 싶다' 혹은 '저렇게 행복하고 즐겁게 주어진 것에 감사해하며 아름다움을 만들어내고 싶다'고 생각하게 만드는 그런 패션 디자이너가 되고 싶다. 난 패션을 사랑한다. 이것 말고 다른 것을 생각해본 적도 없고 할 수 있는 것도 없다. 지금도 옷을 만들면서 온몸으로 전율하고 내 몸과 생각이 작업과 일치할 때는 내가 옷이 되고, 옷이 내가 되는 느낌이다. 그만큼 사랑하고 미쳐있다. 내 파이널 컬렉션은 내 마음속의 아름다움이, 열정과 감사함으로 흘러나와 작품 속에 녹아들었으면 좋겠다. 그래서 세인트 마틴에서의 '마지막'을 멋지게 장식할 수 있기를 바란다.

Book

패션을 공부한다면
꼭 읽어보세요

패션 공부에 정말 필요하고
반드시 읽어야 할 책 몇 권을 소개하고 싶다.

Helen Joseph Armstrong의
《Patternmaking for Fashion Design》

패턴 메이킹making은 이 한 권이면 족하지 않을까. 물론 더 크리에이 티브한 패턴의 경우에야 새로운 시도와 경험을 통해 얻어야 하지만, 기본 패턴 메이킹에 있어서는 패턴의 모든 것이라고 할 수 있을 정도로 잘 정리되어 있는 책이다. 학과 교수님이 추천해준 책이기도 하다.

Yves Saint Laurent의
《Yves Saint Laurent》

누구나 알다시피, 이브 생 로랑을 빼놓고 현대의 패션을 논할 수 없을 만큼 그는 세계 패션사에 대단한 영향력을 미친 패션 디자이너다. 2009년 파리에서 있었던 이브 생 로랑의 전시와 함께 출간된 책으로 이브 생 로랑의 인터뷰에서부터 영감의 원천, 컬렉션의 배경, 그의 작업들이 일목요연하게 정리되어 있다. 패션을 공부하는 사람이라면 반드시 알아야 하는 디자이너고, 이렇게 많은 정보를 체계적으로 정리해놓은 책도 드물다. 영어로 출간되었지만 패션을 공부한다면 꼭 권하고 싶다. 책을 펼치는 순간, 왜 내가 그 책을 추천했는지 알게 될 것이다.

Funmi Odulate의
《Shopping for Vintage》

감히 이 책을 빈티지 입문서라고 부르고 싶다. 처음 이 책을 접하게 된 것은 우리 동네에 있는 도서관이었다. 빈티지가 무엇인지, 빈티지에 대한 개념이 제대로 정리되어 있고 런던, 뉴욕, 파리 등 세계 유명 도시별로 정리된 빈티지숍에 대한 정보 또한 유용하다. 이제는 한국에서도 익숙해진 빈티지 패션. 빈티지 마니아라면 한번 읽어봐도 좋겠다.

BBC의
《Planet Earth》

난 다큐멘터리를 정말 좋아한다. 지금까지 BBC나 한국에서 나온 다큐멘터리는 거의 챙겨 봤다. 그중에서도 내가 가장 좋아하는 것은 BBC에서 제작한 《Planet Earth》다. 자연의 진짜 아름다움을 넘어선 경이로움을 확인할 수 있기 때문이다. 인간이 쉽게 닿을 수 없는 세계 곳곳의 황홀함을 간직하고 있는, 인간의 생각과 창의력을 뛰어넘는 자연의 아름다움을 감상할 수 있다.

 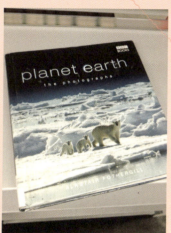

(왼쪽) 세인트 마틴 도서관에서도 발견한 《Shopping for Vintage》.
(오른쪽) 책으로도 나온 《Planet Earth》는 책보다는 다큐멘터리를 추천한다.

3

런던
다이어리

1 여유와 느림이 있는 곳!
내 사랑, 런던

난 내면 깊숙이 시골 사람이다. 겉으로는 그렇게 안 보일 수도 있지만, 몇 시간만 이야기해보면 누구라도 내가 털털하고 소박하다는 것을 알 수 있다. 고등학교 때 서울로 오면서 가장 싫었던 것이 빡빡한 도시에서 생활하는 것이었다. 태어나서 고등학교에 입학하기 전까지 안동이라는 도시+시골에서 자랐기 때문에 빌딩만으로 가득한 환경에서 몇 달을 견딘다는 게 정말 힘들었다. 그때 나는 평생을 살아도 '서울 여자'는 못될 거라 생각하곤 했다. 어른이 되면 서울에서 일은 할지라도 서울 밖에서 살리라 마음먹었었다.

런던은 이런 나의 시골 감성과 잘 맞는 도시다. 물론 대도시이기 때문에 사람들이 늘 바쁘게 생활하고, 출퇴근 시간대의 지하철은 사람들로 빽빽하다. 겨울이나 여름철에는 거리마다 관광객들로 넘쳐나고, 세계 곳곳에서 온 사람들로 뒤섞여 정신이 하나도 없다. 하지만 난 런던이 좋다. 그렇게 북적거리며 정신이 없는 와중에도 할머니는 머리에 스카프를 귀엽게 두르고 천천히 걸어가시고, 카페마다 사람들이 앉아 책을 읽는다. 조금만 외곽으로 나가면 자연을 접할 수 있고, 좀더 멀리 나갈수록 사람들의 삶의 속도 또한 느려진다. 이 재미있는 도시에서 내가 해야 하는 패션 공부와 내 시골 감성이 절묘하게 조화를 이루고 있다.

처음 런던에 와서 가장 좋았던 것은 다름 아닌 날씨였다. 대부분의 사람이 변덕스러운 영국 날씨에 고개를 절레절레 흔들지만 나는 무엇보다 날씨가 좋았다. 런던은 아침에는 해가 쨍쨍 뜨다가도 집 밖을 나설 때면 비가 오기도 한다. 오늘 아침에도 그렇게 눈과 비가 오더니 지금은 푸르른 하늘이 조금 보인다. 내가 한국에서 제일 좋아하는 날씨가 비가 오기 전, 뭔가 우중충한 날씨였다. 하늘에는 먹구름이, 공기는 수분을 가득 머금은 으스스한 그런 날에는 나도 무거운 공기와 함께 땅으로 내려와 차분해지는 그런 기분이 좋았다.

 그런데 런던은 1년의 반 정도가 그런 날씨다. 누군가는 우울하다고 하지만 나는 우울하다기보다 분위기 있는 재즈를 듣는 기분으로 하루를 보낸다. 언젠가 한 달 정도 비가 오고 구름이 가득했을 때는 나도 기분이 처지기도 했지만, 그러다가 햇살이 비치면 반가웠다. 가끔씩 런던의 청명한 햇살이 기분을 전환시켜주니 날씨만큼은 내 마음에 쏙 들었다.

 또 좋은 것은 사람들이다. 도대체 어떻게 이토록 다양한 사람들이 모였는지, 전 세계 사람을 볼 수 있다고 해도 과언이 아니다. 더 재미있는 것은 사람들이 입는 옷이다. 옷 입는 것만 봐도 어디에서 왔고, 어떤 배경을 가지고 있는지 짐작된다. 특별히 좋아하는 것은 영국 할아버지, 할머니 커플이다. 가끔식 지하철을 타면 깔끔하게 차려입은 할머니, 할아버지를 볼 수 있다. 할아버지의 보타이와 할머니의 옛날 구두와 옷도 멋지지만 가장 마음을 감동시키는 것은 그렇게 두 분이 나란히 앉아 계신, 은근히 닮은 모습이다. 나도 늙어서 저렇게 나와 닮은 사람과 함께 있었으면 좋겠다는 생각을 한다.

처음 런던에 와서 가장 좋았던 것은 다름 아닌 날씨였다.
아침에는 해가 쨍쨍 뜨다가도 집 밖을 나설 때면 비가 쏟아지려 해 나도 같이 차분해진다.

사람들이 서로 옷에 신경 쓰지 않는 것도 좋다. 런던 사람들은 자기 마음대로 옷을 입는다. 물론 잘 차려입은 것에 대한 기준이 분명 있지만, 자신이 원하는 것은 무엇이든 입을 수 있다. 옷 또는 패션에 대한 모든 것이 허용되는 곳이다. 그만큼 자유롭고, 그만큼 옷이라는 것이 즐거울 수 있는 곳이기도 하다.

런던을 좋아하는 이유를 쓰라고 하면 끝도 없다. 내가 처음 런던에 왔을 때, 엄마는 내가 물 만난 물고기 같다고 하셨다. 내가 원하는 패션을 마음껏 공부할 수 있으면서도, 내 시골 감성이 그대로 빛을 발하니 숨통이 트이는 것은 당연했다. 벌써 런던에서 5년이라는 시간이 흘렀다. 런던에 처음 왔을 때야 워낙 많은 시간이 남아 있었기에 여기를 떠난다는 생각을 해본 적이 없다. 또한 여기가 내가 있을 곳이라는 생각도 해본 적이 없다. 이제 졸업을 반 년 앞두고 여기를 떠날 수도 있겠구나, 조만간 그게 현실로 일어날 수도 있겠구나 하는 생각이 불현듯 들면 마음이 먹먹해진다.

길지 않은 인생이지만 나는 15년은 안동에서 살았고, 6년은 서울에서, 지금까지 5년을 런던에서 살았다. 물론 나는 한국 사람이고, 한국이 언제나 나의 첫 번째 나라가 될 것이다. 하지만 내가 성인이 되고 나서 많은 시간을 런던에서 보냈고, 내가 알고 있는 소중한 많은 사람이 런던에 살고 있다. 한 명, 한 명 이름을 대기도 어려울 만큼 좋은 사람들을 많이 만났다.

얼마 전 아는 언니가 이런 말을 했다. 시간이 기억되는 것은 그곳에 나와 함께 있었기 때문이라고. 런던은 그 자체로도 내가 사랑하는 곳이다. 나의 시골 사람 같은 감성이 그대로 녹아들어 살 수 있는 도시이다. 하지만 지금 나에게 더 큰 의미로 다가오는 것은, 내가 사랑하는 사람들이 이곳에 있기 때문이다. 그동안 나는 그들과 함께 많은 일을 겪고 소중한 기억을 쌓았다.

한국에도 소중한 친구들이 많으며 무엇보다 나의 가족이 있다. 그들을 생각하면 항상 그립고 보고 싶다. 하지만 나를 더 슬프게 하는 것은 어쩌면 이곳을 떠났을 때 그리워하는 사람들이 더 늘어날 지도 모른다는 예감 때문이다. 세상일이 누군가를 만나면 언젠가는 헤어져야 하지만, 벌써부터 마음이 슬퍼진다. 조금밖에 남지 않은 이 시간을 더 많이 사랑하고, 소중하게 여겨야겠다.

2 때때로 외로워진다면, 로열 페스티벌 홀

런던에서 내가 정말 사랑하는 곳, 엠뱅크먼트 Embankment 역을 지나 런던의 풍경을 한껏 담은 다리를 건너면 만나는 곳이 바로 로열 페스티벌 홀 Royal Festival Hall 이다. 런던에 온 지 5년이라는 시간이 지났다. 많은 곳을 다녔지만 로열 페스티벌 홀은 나에게 특별한 곳이다. 친구와 함께 우연치 않게 처음 찾아갔던 날부터 우리의 스튜디오 넘버2 studio number2 라는 이름을 지어주고 학교생활에 지칠 때면 찾아가곤 했다. 몰래 경비를 뚫고 들어가 보냈던 나의 스물두 살 생일 그리고 마음이 흩어질 때면 찾아가 내 자신을 다독이는 등 나와 함께 보낸 시간이 많은 공간이다.

이곳에서는 날마다 멋진 공연이 열렸으며 운이 좋으면 공짜 공연도 즐길 수 있었다. 하지만 가장 매력적인 부분은 강변을 따라 놓여 있는 테라스의 테이블과 의자, 홀 안쪽으로 군데군데 놓인 의자들이다. 사람들이 부담 없이 편안하게 쉴 수 있기에 항상 사람들로 북적거리는 이곳. 템스 강변을 따라 거닐던 여행객들이 들어와 쉬기도 하고, 퇴근하는 회사원들이 맥주를 마시기도 한다. 혼자 와서 책을 보는 사람도 있고, 자기 집인 양 여기저기 뛰어다니는 아이들도 있다. 참으로 다양한 사람들이 모여 있다.

이곳은 마치 중간 지대 같다. 나이도, 성별도, 직업도, 겉모습이 가진 아무것도 사람들을 가르는 기준이 되지 않는다. 모두가 각자의 사연을 안고 이곳을 찾아왔지만 그들이 어우러져 흥미로운 조화를 이룬다. 제각기 다른 사람들로 채워지는 공간. 매력적이면서도 묘한 곳이다.

로열 페스티벌 홀에서 혼자 책을 보고 있던 아저씨. 빨간 셔츠가 인상적이다.

런던은 마치 중간 지대 같다. 나이도, 성별도, 직업도, 겉모습이 가진 어떤 것도
사람들을 가르는 기준이 되지 않는다.

런던은 외로운 도시다. 친구들을 만나고, 학교를 다니고, 새로운 사람도 만나지만 결국 혼자로 돌아온다. 혼자라는 것에 익숙해져야 하고, 혼자 견디는 법을 배워야 한다. 외로움을 잘 견디지 못해 힘들어하는 친구도 많이 보았고, 마음의 병에 걸리는 사람도 있었다.

고등학교 시절부터 혼자 지내온 나는 다행히도 이런 시간을 잘 견딘다. 누군가와 함께 사는 것보다 이제는 혼자 있는 게 당연하게 느껴지기도 한다. 하지만 가끔씩 마음이 공중에 흩어지는 것 같을 때가 있다. 방 안 가득 내가 흩어져 사라져가는 느낌. 친구를 만나 저녁을 먹고, 수다를 떨고, 쇼핑을 하고, 파티에 가고 모든 것을 다 해봤지만 집에 돌아와서 마주하는 내 자신이 힘들 때가 있다.

그렇다고 사람들에게 항상 의지할 수는 없다. 잠시 나의 빈 마음을 달래줄 수는 있지만 정말 비어 있는 부분을 채워주지는 못한다. 이렇게 가만히 가라앉을 수 없을 때면 가방을 메고 MP3를 귀에 꽂고 집을 나선다. 그리고 로열 페스티벌 홀이 있는 워터루 Waterloo 역으로 향한다.

나는 이곳에 있는 사람들과 전혀 다른 이야기를 가지고 왔지만 이 공간을 그들과 함께 채우고 있다는 것이 좋다. 내가 그들과 전혀 관계없는 사람이라는 것도 좋다. 음악에 맞춰 움직이는 사람들, 이야기 소리, 나와는 상관없는 사람들 속에 섞여 가만 앉아 있으면 이상하게도 흩어진 마음이 가라앉는다.

난 사람들을 좋아한다. 인간적으로 좋아하는 것이 아니라 제각기 다른 사람들의 행동과 말투, 생김새 등 사람 자체가 좋다. 사람이어서 가진 것들을 사랑한다. 가끔은 신기하기도 하고, 재미있기도 하고, 슬프기도 하고 그렇다. 이렇게 혼자 앉아 있는 날에는 몇 시간씩 사람들을 관찰하며 생각에 잠기기도 한다. 사람들을 좋아하기에 좋아하는 일도 사람들을 그리는 것이다. 가만히 앉아 사람들을 바라보며 그림을 그린다. 친구와 즐겁게 이야기하는 사람, 내 앞에 앉아 컴퓨터에 빠져 꼼짝도 안 하는 남자, 저 멀리 창밖만 바라보는 아저씨…. 아무 생각 없이 그림을 그리다 보면 다시 천천히 내가 가라앉는 걸 느낀다.

이곳에서 난 사람에게서 채울 수 없는 공허함을 나와 전혀 관계 없는 사람들로 채운다. 수많은 사람들과 섞여 혼자임을 즐긴다. 마음이 흩어질 때면 찾아가는 곳, 저마다 다른 이야기를 가진 사람들이 모여 하나의 이야기를 만드는 공간이 바로 런던에서 내가 가장 사랑하는 로열 페스티벌 홀이다.

3 마약 대신
로트렉을 만나다

창작, 무언가를 새롭게 만들어내는 것은 즐겁지만 힘든 일이다. 영감이 떠오르고, 작업을 함에 있어 에너지가 충만할 때는 이보다 즐겁고 신나는 일이 없다. 하지만 그렇지 못할 때는 정말 힘들다. 나처럼 학생 신분으로 눈에 보이는 결과물을 보여줘야 한다는 압박감이 있을 경우에는 더하다. 요즘 수없이 듣는 "뭐하고 지내?" 하는 질문에 나는 그냥 싱긋 웃고 만다.

난 요즘 아무것도 안 한다. 수없이 많은 일을 하지만 누가 시키거나 꼭 해야 하는 일이 아니라서 마치 아무것도 안 하고 지내는 것 같다. 하루하루 내가 계획하고 하고 싶어서 하는 일들을 하며 지내고 있다. 런던에 돌아와서 한 달 동안 정신 없이 보냈다. 사람들을 만나고, 이사를 해서 집 정리도 하고, 작업실도 준비하고, 전시도 틈틈이 다녀오고, 하루도 집에서 쉰 적이 없을 만큼 매일 돌아다녔다. 하루라도 집에 있으면 무슨 일이라도 생기는 양 말이다.

오늘은 월요일. 아무 약속도 없고, 해야 할 일도 없는 월요일이다. 최근 들어 이것저것 생각이 많아져서 잠을 설쳤었다. '내일은 늦게까지 푹 자야지' 하고 생각하며 잠자리에 들었지만 새벽 6시, 7시 즈음 몇십 분 간격으로 자꾸 깼다. 아침잠이 많아 일찍 일어나는 게 힘든 나로서는 참 별일이다.

오늘 무엇을 할지 생각했다. 며칠 전 이케아^{Ikea}에서 구입한 프린트 면천으로 쿠션과 베개 커버도 만들었고, 새로 디자인한 화이트 셔츠는 수요일에나 원단을 사러 갈 수 있다. 내일은 저녁 약속이 있고, 그 전에는 커틀트 갤러리^{Courtault Gallery}에서 열리는, 내가 사랑하는 아티스트 중 한 명인 툴루즈 로트렉Toulouse Lautrec의 전시를 보러 갈 것이다. 수요일에는 점심 약속, 저녁에는 교회에 가야 하고, 목요일에는 학원 특강을 위한 인터뷰가 있다. 그런데 오늘은 꼭 해야 할 일이 아무것도 없었다.

도서관에 가야겠다고 생각했다. 하루 종일 아무것도 안 하고 있을 수는 없으니, 뭐라도 해야만 했다. 집에서 걸어서 10분 거리에 윔블던 아트 컬리지Wimbledon Art College가 있지만 아직 한번도 못 가봤다. 웹사이트를 찾아 아침부터 전화를 걸어 오늘 도서관이 열었는지 확인하고, 집을 나섰다. 내일 툴루즈 로트렉의 전시를 보러 가기에 그의 작품을 살펴보고 싶었지만, 하루 종일 뭔가 건설적인 일을 하지 않으면 안될 것 같은 기분이었다. 아트적인 감성을 채워야 할 필요성을 느꼈다. 하지만 오늘은 때가 안 좋았다. 방학 기간이라 일찍 문을 닫는 데다 재정리를 하느라 한쪽 코너는 닫혀 있었다. 몇 시간 앉아서 책을 보려던 계획이 무산되고, 툴루즈 로트렉의 책 한 권만 빌려 왔다.

며칠간 잠을 설쳐서 그런지, 계획대로 일이 잘 풀리지 않아서인지 몸이 많이 피곤했다. 하지만 집으로 돌아올 수는 없었다. 백과사전보다 큰 책을 끼고 카페로 향했다. 집에 가서 쉬는 것보다는 카페에 가서 책을 보는 것이 좋을 것 같았다. 버스를 타기보다 운동도 할 겸 30분을 걸어서 카페에 도착했다. 하지만 그것도 잠시, 몸이 너무 피곤해서 집으로 돌아와야 했다.

많이 피곤했다. 생각해보니 런던으로 돌아온 이후 하루도 제대로 쉰 날이 없는 것 같다. 쉬기는 했지만 내 정신과 마음이 편하게 쉬지 못했다. 오늘처럼 아무것도 할 일이 없는 날조차 피곤한 자신을 가만두지 못하고 도서관으로 데려갔다. 마지막 학년을 남겨두고 있는 지금, 매일매일 뭔가 발전해야 하고, 건설적으로 보내야 한다는 생각이 은연중에 내 자신을 쉬지 못하게 했다. 문제는 못 쉬는 데 있는 게 아니라, 나도 모르는 사이 마음이 많이 불안해져 있다는 것이다.

누구나 자기 자신에 대해서 불안해한다. 엄청난 재능의 소유자라 해도 100퍼센트 자신에 만족하고 확신하지는 않는다. 행여 자신의 작업에 100퍼센트 만족할지라도 삶의 다른 부분에서는 불안해한다. 새로운 것을 창작해야 한다는 부담감과 미래의 불확실함, 인간관계에서 오는 스트레스 등 성공한 디자이너들도 개인적으로는 그다지 행복하고 만족스러운 삶을 살지 못한 경우도 있다. 극단적으로는 자살을 선택하는 사람도 있고, 마약과 술로 그 불안함을 이겨내고자 했던 사람도 있다.

주변에서, 특히 예술을 하는 사람들 가운데 뭔지 모를 불안함으로 힘들어하는 모습을 보곤 한다. 예술이 다른 직업에 비해 확실한 미래가 보장되지 않기 때문에 더욱 그런 것 같다. 한국에서 예술을 하기 위해 온 친구들을 보면, 그 불안함을 이기지 못해 반항적으로 행동하거나 안 좋은 친구들과 어울리기도 한다. 그런 반항적인 삶과 행동이 자신이 원하는 거라면 상관없다. 하지만 그런 불안함을 피하기 위해 마약을 하거나 과하게 행동하는 친구들을 보면 마음이 편하지 않다.

    그런데 오늘 나 역시 그들과 다르지 않다는 것을 처음으로 느꼈다. 내가 불안하다고 해서 마약이라든지 그런 안 좋은 행동을 하는 것은 아니다. 하지만 그런 불안한 마음으로 도서관에 갔던 것이다. 도서관에 가서 시간을 보내는 것이 매일매일 해왔던 일이고, 즐거운 일이기는 하다. 하지만 지금처럼 불안한 마음을 이기기 위해, 아트와 관련된 어떤 일이라도 하기 위해 아직 제대로 알지도 않은 툴루즈 로트렉의 책을 빌려 온 것은 나답지 않다.

    오늘, 나에게 툴루즈 로트렉의 책은 불안함을 이기기 위한 마약이었다. 성공은 했지만 불행한 삶을 살았던 많은 디자이너와 아티스트가 있다. 작품만큼은 천재적이라는 평가를 받았고, 많은 사람의 사랑을 받았을지라도 그 개인의 삶을 봤을 때는 안타깝지 않을 수 없다. 너무나 불행했고, 만족하지 못했으며, 불안한 삶에 힘겨워했다.

    난 작품만으로, 창작활동만으로는 행복한 삶을 살 수 없다고 생각한다. 세계가 인정하는 천재라 해도 그 작품들이 그를 전적으로 행복하게 만들지는 못한다. 나 또한 작업이 즐겁기는 하지만 그것 때문에 불안해하고, 매일매일 불안함을 이기기 위해 노력하는 이상한 상황에 놓이게 되었다. 지금까지는 공부를 하면서 느껴보지 못한 뭔지 모를 감정이었다. 불안한 마음이 내 삶을 컨트롤하는, 결코 기분 좋지 않은 상황이었다.

툴루즈 로트렉의 포스터를 모아놓은 한 권의 책. 노팅 힐에 들렀을 때 10파운드를 주고 구입했다.

불안함의 시작점을 찾아보기로 했다. 졸업을 앞두고 해야 할 일이 많고, 그 일들을 모두 해결해야 한다. 하지만 곰곰이 생각해보니 그것이 불안함의 근본적인 원인은 아니었다. 당연히 더 많이 배워야 하고, 졸업을 한다고 배움이 끝나는 것도 아니다. 끊임없는 발전해야 하며, 더 나은 디자이너가 되기 위해 노력해야 할 것이다. 또한 그런 사실은 이미 알고 있었으며, 차근차근 해나가면 된다. 그런데 목표를 가지고 열심히 뛰어가다 보니 그보다 중요한 것을 잠시 잊고 있었다. 내가 어떤 패션 디자이너가, 그리고 어떤 사람이 되기 위해 열심히 노력하는지 말이다.

내가 되고 싶은 사람과 이루고 싶은 목표는 옷을 뛰어나게 잘 만드는 완벽한 기술의 디자이너도 아니고, 창의력이 우수한 디자이너도 아니다. 단지 좋은 디자이너가 되고 싶다. 누구나 과찬하는 멋진 작품이 아니더라도, 내가 하는 일이 어떤 의미에서라도 세상에 좋게 쓰여지길 바라며, 그런 디자이너가 되기 위해 노력해왔다. 나의 재능이 나만 잘살고 유명해지고, 내 욕심을 채우기 위해 쓰이지 않기를 바란다. 난 하루하루 즐겁게 살면서 주어진 것에 감사하고 노력하면 그런 디자이너가 될 수 있을 거라 믿었다. 유명한 디자이너가 아니라 좋은 디자이너 말이다.

나는 자신만을 위해 살아가는 삶이 행복하지 않다는 것을 누구보다 잘 알고 있다. 재능이 있어서 행복한 것도 아니고, 많은 것을 가진 부자라고 행복한 것도 아니다. 그래서 항상 내가 진정 바라는 것이 무엇인지 생각하며 나 자신을 바로잡으려고 노력했다. 채워질 수 없는 욕심과 확신할 수 없는 미래에 초점이 맞춰지니 불안할 수밖에 없었다. 매일 24시간을 빼곡히 채워서 보내지 않으면 뒤처지는 것 같았다. 점점 마음에 여유가 없어지고 나 자신밖에 보이지 않게 되었다. 이 길로 쭉 가면 불안해하는 나 자신과 불행한 미래밖에 없다는 것을 잘 알면서 말이다.

좋은 디자이너가 되고 세상에 나의 재능을 돌려줄 수 있는 디자이너가 되기 위해서는 열심히 노력해야 한다. 내가 원하는 그런 좋은 디자이너가 되기 위해서는, 내가 어떤 사람이 되고 싶은지 혹은 어떤 디자이너가 되고 싶은지 한시도 잊어서는 안된다. 사람은 너무나 연약해서 금방 잊어버리고, 때로는 아무 일도 없었던 것처럼 까맣게 잊고 만다.

내가 누구인지 기억해야겠다.

그 누구보다도 행복한 나를 위해, 또 내가 원하는 좋은 디자이너가 되기 위해서 말이다.

4

**오늘 왠지 예뻐 보인다면,
매니큐어 때문일 거야**

난 메이크업을 거의 하지 않는다. 자다가 일어난 듯 조금은 부스스하게 헝클어진 머리와 맨얼굴의 조화. 어느 정도 비어 보이는 맨얼굴의 조화가 좋다. 생긴 그대로의 자연스러움을 누구보다 좋아하기 때문이기도 하지만, 바쁘게 학교에 다니고 작업을 하다 보면 매일 아침 예쁘게 메이크업을 할 만한 여유도 없다.

나도 여자로서 남에게 예뻐 보이고 싶은 욕심이야 당연히 있다. 하지만 내 눈에는 빈 곳 없이 빼곡하게 화장한 내 얼굴이 예뻐 보이지 않는다. 완벽함보다 뭔가 묘하게 비어 있는 그 느낌의 내 얼굴이 좋다. 중요한 일이 있을 때는 옷에 어울리게 메이크업을 하기도 한다. 하지만 대부분 맨얼굴의 부스스한 머리로 돌아다닌다.

이렇게 맨얼굴로 사람도 만나고 밖에 나가는 나에게도 중요한 것이 있다. 메이크업보다 더 중요하고, 이것 없이는 집 앞의 슈퍼에도 가기 싫은 것. 내 손끝에서 반짝이는 매니큐어다. 손톱에 색깔이 입혀지지 않은 채 밖에 나가는 건, 마치 옷을 안 입고 나가는 것과 같다. 뭔가 빠뜨린 듯한 느낌이다. 맨얼굴로 밖에 나가는 것은 아무렇지 않은데 매니큐어 없이는 밖에 나갈 수 없는 게 조금은 이상하기도 하다.

가끔씩 매니큐어를 지운 뽀얘진 내 손을 바라볼 때가 있다. 있어야 할 게 없는 것처럼 낯설다. 원래 있어야 할 몸의 일부가 없어진 느낌이다. 손끝에 구멍이 뚫린 느낌이랄까. 매일 메이크업을 하는 사람들은 맨얼굴이 어색하다고 한다. 나는 매니큐어가 입혀지지 않은 손이 인위적인 형광 색깔 매니큐어가 발린 손보다 이상하고 어색하다. 스무 살이 되고 나서부터 내 손끝엔 항상 매니큐어가 발려 있었으니 그럴 만도 하다.

지금까지 쓴 매니큐어를 세자면, 내가 지금까지 쓴 화장품의 숫자보다 많을 것이다. 요즘 자주 쓰는 것은 아홉 개다. 집 안 한 구석을 예쁘게 장식하는 귀여운 녀석들이 저마다 빛을 발하며 쪼로로 줄지어 앉아 있는 것을 보면 나도 모르게 흐뭇해진다.

내가 매니큐어를 좋아하는 이유는 단 하나다. 컬러를 좋아하기 때문이다. 옷과 액세서리 말고 나에게 한 가지 색깔을 추가할 수 있는 것이 좋다. 메이크업은 잘 하지 않지만, 가끔씩 매트하고 진한 체리 핑크나 빨간 립스틱을 바르기도 한다. 이것도 매니큐어를 바르는 것처럼 컬러를 좋아하는 내가 한 가지 추가 컬러를 입을 수 있는 방법이다. 립스틱을 발라서 얼굴이 예뻐 보인다기보다는 나에게 색깔이 입혀지는 것이 재미있다. 뿌연 얼굴에 동동 떠다니는 듯한 인위적인 느낌의 컬러가 내 얼굴에 색종이를 오려 붙인 것 같다.

손끝에서 빛나는 매니큐어는 그런 느낌이다. 하얀 손에, 내 몸에 색깔을 더하는 것이다. 립스틱처럼 내 몸의 일부가 색깔을 입는다. 그 색깔들이 내가 입은 옷, 액세서리의 색깔과 어우러져 재미있는 조화를 만든다. 난 원래 다양한 컬러를 입는 것을 좋아한다. 이렇게 엑스트라로 더해진 손끝의 컬러는 내가 입는 컬러를 더욱 재미있게 만든다.

옷을 입고, 가방을 메고 나갈 준비를 마쳤는데 뭔가 어울리지 않는 네일 컬러를 발견할 때가 있다. 까만 정장에 하얀 양말을 신은 것처럼 굉장히 어색한 느낌이다. 아무도 신경 쓰지 않을 테지만 마음이 불편하다. 그와 반대로 네일 컬러가 옷, 신발, 가방, 액세서리와 절묘하게 맞아떨어질 때는 찌릿하게 스릴이 느껴지기도 한다. 포멀한 티셔츠에 청바지를 입고 카페에 앉아 있는데 우연히 내려다본 손가락 끝의 네일 컬러가 청바지, 신발의 컬러와 예쁘게 매치될 때가 있다. 그럴 때는 왠지 뿌듯하다.

심지어 그날의 네일 컬러에 따라 옷을 갈아입기도 한다. 새로운 컬러의 매니큐어를 구입해서 내 손끝에 새로운 컬러가 입힌 날에는 더욱 그렇다. 손가락 끝에 곱게 발린 새로 산 매니큐어의 색을 지긋이 바라보고 옷장의 옷들을 번갈아 바라보며 색의 조화를 찾는다. 그렇게 매니큐어라는 아주 사소한 것이 옷의 모든 것을 결정할 때도 있다.

매니큐어가 패션에서 중요한 듯 이야기하지만 다른 사람이 느낄 만큼 밖으로 드러나는 것은 아니다. 오늘 많은 사람을 만났어도 누구도 내 매니큐어의 색이 무엇인지 모를 것이다. 하지만 나에게는 매니큐어, 옷, 액세서리의 컬러들이 만나서 신선한 조화를 이루는 그 순간의 짜릿함이 정말 행복하다.

며칠 전 분홍색 꽃무늬와 초록색 잎이 프린트된 셔츠와 청바지를 입었다. 그날 내 눈에 들어온 형광 빛의 연한 초록 네일 컬러와 파란 가죽 샌들, 짙은 오렌지색의 페디큐어 사이의 컬러 매치가 얼마나 기분을 들뜨게 했는지 모른다. 은으로 장식된 가느다란 노랑 스트링 팔찌도 한몫했다. 수많은 컬러를 입었지만 요란하지 않다.

슬쩍 보기에는 많은 컬러도 아니다. 손끝, 발끝, 내 눈에만 들어오는 그 컬러들의 조화는 나만의 것이다.

메이크업을 하는 것처럼 누군가에게 예뻐 보이기 위해 매니큐어를 바르는 것은 아니다. 컬러를 좋아하는 나에게 예뻐 보이기 위해 매니큐어를 바른다. 손끝에서 인위적으로 반짝거리는 그 컬러가 참 좋다. 내 몸의 모든 컬러가 즐거운 조화를 이룰 때면 행복해진다. 몇몇 사람은 그런 내 마음을 알아채기도 한다.

"오늘은 왠지 예뻐 보이는데!"

행복한 마음이 내 얼굴로 드러나는가 보다. 정확하게 내가 매니큐어 때문에 기분이 좋다는 걸 알지는 못하지만 말이다. 오늘은 며칠 전 새로 들여온 연한 오렌지색 매니큐어를 발라야겠다.

내가 매니큐어를 좋아하는 이유는 단 하나다. 컬러를 좋아하기 때문.

5 벼룩시장에서 쇼핑하기

나만의 시간이 많다는 것은 행복한 일이다. 개학하려면 한 달이나 남아 있는 요즘, 내가 원하는 일만 골라 하며 하루하루를 보낸다. 며칠 전까지도 아이들에게 미술 가르치는 일을 했지만, 그것도 끝나고 이제 완전히 자유다. 자기 전에 내일을 생각하면 즐겁고, 아침에 일어나 오늘 나에게 일어날 수많은 일을 상상하면 신이 난다. 일평생, 더구나 이렇게 젊은 나이에 요즘처럼 내가 하고 싶은 것만 하면서 살 수 있는 시간이 얼마나 남아 있을까? 참으로 오랜만에 찾아온 소중한 시간이다.

하루는 공원에 가서 하루 종일 걸어 다니고, 또 하루는 도서관에서 책을 빌려 와 카페에 앉아 몇 시간이고 책을 읽는다. 심심할 때면 라디오를 틀어놓고 몇 시간이고 조물조물 액세서리를 만들며 시간을 보낸다. 자기 전에는 오늘 생각해낸 일과 떠오른 생각을 다이어리에 적기도 한다. 그렇게 소파에 앉아 생각에 빠지면 새벽까지 잠을 못 이루기도 한다. 늦게 일어나도 뭐라고 하는 사람이 없으니 모든 것이 내 자유, 내 마음대로다.

오늘 아침엔 일어나자마자 세수만 하고 서둘러 밖으로 나섰다. 오늘은 토요일로 카부트^{car boot} 세일이 열리는 날이기 때문이다. 카부트 세일은 특정한 날을 정해 주차장이나 큰 공터에 사람들이 물건을 차에 싣고 와서 파는 것을 말한다. 우리말로는 벼룩시장 정도랄까. 사람들이 안 쓰거나 필요 없는 물건을 차에 싣고 와서 트렁크만 열어놓고 테이블에 올려놓고 판다. 모두 자기가 쓰던 물건으로 가게도 아니니 그야말로 각양각색이다.

이런 걸 누가 살까 싶은 어처구니 없는 물건도 많고, 내다 팔기에는 아까울 만큼 예쁜 빈티지 물건도 많다. 돈을 많이 버는 목적으로 판매하는 것이 아니라서 값은 비교적 저렴하다. 좋은 물건을 찾을 수 있는 눈만 가지고 있다면 카부트 세일에서 큰 수확을 거둘 수 있다. 빈티지 액세서리를 너무 좋아하는 나로서는 매주 열리는 카부트 세일이 반가울 수밖에. 게다가 런던에 있는 큰 카부트 세일 중 하나가 내가 살고 있는 윔블던Wimbledon에 있다. 집 앞 버스 정류장에서 10분만 버스를 타고 가면 된다.

대부분의 카부트 세일은 오전 9시쯤 열어 정오 혹은 오후 1시 정도면 사람들이 슬슬 집으로 갈 정리를 시작한다. 윔블던 카부트 세일은 정오면 거의 끝나기 때문에 마음이 급해졌다. 눈을 뜬 것이 벌써 10시를 훌쩍 넘긴 후였다. 어젯밤 여러 가지 생각이 꼬리에 꼬리를 물고 이어져서 새벽 3시가 되어서야 잠이 든 것이 화근이었다. 가끔은 20분 이상 기다려야 하는 날도 있는데 오늘은 정류장에 가자마자 버스가 바로 왔다. 적어도 한 시간은 넉넉하게 구경할 수 있겠다 싶었다. 이제는 제법 가을 같은 하늘과 바람이 기분 좋은 아침이었다.

딱히 무엇을 사기 위해서 카부트 세일에 가는 것은 아니다. 사람들이 이것저것 소소하게 파는 것을 구경하는 것이 재미있다. 하지만 가끔씩 보물 같은 좋은 물건을 발견하기도 한다. 내가 주로 산 것은 빈티지 액세서리다. 그중에서 가장 좋아하는 것은 귀고리. 우리

엄마가 옛날에 했을 것 같은 똑딱이 ^clip-on(이하 똑딱이)^ 귀고리다. 대부분 플라스틱으로 만들어져 조금은 키치^kitsch^한 느낌이다. 요즘은 잘 볼 수 없는 모양과 디테일이 1990년대 패션처럼 묘하게 촌스러운 듯하면서도 재미있다. 매번 갈 때마다 하나, 둘씩 모아온 것이 이제는 제법 많아졌다.

가끔은 흰 티셔츠와 청바지를 입고 오버사이즈의 플라스틱 똑딱이 귀고리만 하기도 한다. 심각하게 멋있지 않은, 한결 재미있는 사람이 된 듯한 느낌이다. 초등학교 시절로 돌아간 것 같은 느낌도 든다. 그러니까 1990년대에는 그런 귀고리를 많이 했었다. 가끔은 학교 앞 문방구에서 뽑기를 해서 소장하게 됐던 싸구려 플라스틱 귀고리. 예뻐서 생각 없이 하고 다녔던, 지금 생각해보면 어이없는 액세서리들이다. 요즘 이런 똑딱이 귀고리를 할 때면, 그때의 재미있는 기억이 떠오른다. 뭐든 좋은 게 좋았고, 싫은 게 싫었던 시절이었다.

어른의 가장 재미없는 부분은 심각하다는 거다. 어른들은 쉽게 마음 가는 대로 살지 않는다. 눈앞에 있는 것이 좋다고 마냥 좋아하며 살 수는 없다. 굴러가는 낙엽에 깔깔거리는 그런 시절이 지나고 저 많은 낙엽을 누가 치울지 걱정하는 사람이 되어간다. 자신도 모르게 현재보다는 미래의 일을 걱정하고, 근심하게 된다. 심각한 것이 나쁘다는 것은 아니다. 나도 점점 깊은 고민을 하고, 세상을 더 넓게 보고, 진지해져 간다는 것은 즐겁다. 그런데 나쁜 점은, 심각한 것을 떠나 좀처럼 쉬운 것이 없어져 간다는 것이다.

나이가 들면서 어린아이처럼 좋은 것이 좋다고 말할 수 없을 때도 있고, 좋아한다고 진짜 좋아할 수 없다는 것도 알게 되었다. 가끔은 싫은 것을 좋다고 하는 일도 있었다. 이렇게 내 마음과 머리가 딱딱해져서 쉽게 뭔가를 좋아하는 것이 어렵게 느껴질 때가 있다. 마음 가는 대로 솔직하게 좋아할 수 있는 그런 마음이면 좋을 텐데 말이다.

좋은 게 좋은 거고, 그래서 좋아하는 것. 아주 쉬운 일이지만 어려운 일이기도 하다. 쉽게 마음이 바로 눈이 되는 그런 사람이 되고 싶다. 머리로 세상을 보는 사람이 되고 싶지는 않다. 내 머릿속의 쓸데없는 걱정 때문에, 선입견 때문에 좋아하는 것을 좋아하지 못하는 것이 싫다. 좋아하는 것을 겁내지 않는 것. 최소한 내가 생각하고 느끼는 것에 있어서 심각하지 않은 쉬운 사람이면 좋겠다. 마음 가는 대로, 좋은 것을 마음껏 좋아하고 싶다.

이것이 내가 패션을 하는 데 얼마나 중요한 요소인지 잘 알고 있다. 언제부턴가 무언가를 진심으로 느끼는 게 어려워졌다. 이제까지 세상의 수많은 패션을 보고, 디자이너를 봐오는 동안 나도 모르게 선입견이나 정답 같은 쓸데없는 것이 내 머리를 딱딱하게 만들고 있는 느낌이다.

뭘 생각하려고 하면 무언가 나를 탁 막는 것이 생겼다. 그게 뭔지는 솔직히 모르겠다. 하지만 그럴 때마다 답답하다. 그들처럼 멋진 패션을 하고 싶은 마음에, 나도 모르게 눈치를 보고 있는 것일까? 성공하기 위해 이리저리 세상의 눈치를 보면서 하는 패션은 정말 싫다. 또한 그렇게 눈치 봐서 성공한 디자이너도 없다. 자기 생각과 좋아하는 것에 솔직한 디자이너만이 성공한다.

조금씩 굳어져가는 내 머리를 풀어주기 위해 요즘은 더더욱 가벼운 마음으로 좋아하는 일들을 하고 있다. 내 마음에게 물어보고, 하고 싶은 일들을 한다. 자유롭게 느끼고 마음껏 좋아하고 있다. 조금씩 머리가 맑아지고, 좋아하는 것을 진정 즐기는 내 모습을 발견하며 행복한 날들을 보내고 있다.

사실 아주 작은 것들이다. 도서관에서 발견한 풀숲에 누워서 웃고 있는 어린아이의 사진 한 장에 마음이 찡하도록 행복하고, 따뜻한 커피 한잔에 황홀하다. 내 가슴 깊숙이 숨어 있는 마음이 모두 살아나는 느낌이다. 더 많이 느낄수록, 옷에 대한 사랑이 커져만 간다. 가볍게, 솔직하게 좋아하기 때문에 진짜 내 마음이 느끼는 것을 사랑할 수 있다.

좋아하는 것을 어린아이의 마음으로 마음껏 좋아할 수 있으며, 내 생각과 마음에 솔직한 멋진 디자이너가 되고 싶다.

(위) 카부트 세일에 날마다 들러 하나, 둘씩 모은 빈티지 귀고리들. 촌스러운 듯하면서도 멋스럽다.
(아래) 매주 토요일에 열리는 카부트 세일. 잡다하고 소소한 물건들은 보는 것만으로도 흥미롭다.

좋은 물건을 찾을 수 있는 눈만 가지고 있다면 카부트 세일에서 큰 수확을 거둘 수 있다.

6 자연의 색이
내 모든 감각을 깨우고

우리 아빠는 화가다. 직접 산천을 다니며 현장의 아름다움을 그 자리에서 바로 화폭에 담아내는 멋진 화가다. 어린 시절 나의 가장 큰 기쁨은 아빠를 따라 사생을 나가는 것이었다. 아빠는 그림을 그리고 나는 산과 강, 계곡을 놀이터 삼아 뛰어다니곤 했다. 시시각각 변하는 하늘의 구름, 제각기 다른 모습으로 흐트러져 피어 있는 들꽃과 벌레들의 경이로운 색깔…. 아버지를 따라다니며 내 마음속을 감동시켰던 그 풍경들은 지금 나의 감성을 만들었다.

지금 생각해봐도 그때의 작은 기억들은 나를 행복하게 한다. 도랑에 가만 앉아서 흐르는 물만 바라보며 한참을 보내기도 했다. 옹기종기 모여 앉은 색색깔의 자갈들 위로 굽이치는 물결이 나를 감동시켰고, 저 바위 밑에 없는 듯 있는 듯 헤엄치는 조그만 물고기들에 넋을 잃곤 했다. 바람의 움직임에 따라 사각사각 스치며 소리 내는 나무들과 그 안에서 멈춰버린 듯한 시간이 좋았다.

아버지를 따라갔던 그곳에서의 기억이 파노라마처럼 내 마음속에 그대로 남아 있다. 내가 천성이 그렇게 타고난 것인지, 아니면 도시의 아이들보다 자연을 많이 접해서 친근한 것인지는 알 수 없지만, 난 자연의 모든 부분이 좋다. 자연을 접할 때면 내 마음을 가득 채우는 뭔지 모를 행복함이 있었다. 숨을 한껏 들이마시는 행복함, 마음이 두근거리며 터질 것 같은 뭔지 모를 기쁨이 밀려온다.

지금도 여름이 되어 한국에 가면 아빠의 사생을 따라나서곤 한다. 옆에 돗자리를 펴고 앉아서 몇 시간이고 자연의 경이로움에 심취하여 시간을 보낸다. 멋진 미술품이 전시장을 가득 채우고 있는 듯한 그런 기분이다. 나의 모든 감각이 깨어나는 기분, 지금까지 내가 배우고, 느낀 모든 감각이 되살아나는 것 같다. 잊어버렸던 세세한 부분까지 내 마음속에서 살아나는 것을 느낀다. 말로는 표현하기조차 힘든 행복한 시간이다.

아티스트는 영감을 받거나 감각이 깨어나는 곳이 제각각 다르다. 내게 있어 자연은 영감의 원천이다. 인간이 만들어낸 것과 반대되는 그 모든 것, 조물주가 창조하여 세상에 존재하는 그 모든 자연이 나의 영감이다. 사람, 나무, 꽃, 바다, 강, 돌, 바람, 햇살, 하늘 그 모든 자연이 나의 가장 깊은 감각을 깨운다. 내가 아름다움을 흠뻑 느낄 수 있고 나에게 진정한 아름다움이 무엇인지 가르쳐준 것은 바로 자연이다.

내가 런던을 사랑하는 이유 중 하나는 자연이 도시 안에 있기 때문이다. 몇 블록만 가면 항상 만나는 공원과 집집마다 피어 있는 다양한 꽃들은 내 감성을 풍요롭게 만든다. 예술가에게 감정이 메마를 때만큼 힘든 시간이 있을까? 바쁘게 돌아가는 세상과 수많은 사람 속에서 딱딱하게 굳어버리고, 색이 빠져버린 것 같은 그런 마음이 들 때가 있다. 그런 마음으로는 작업을 하기가 힘들다. 마음이 굳고, 감각이 죽어 있는 상태에서는 작업이 불가능하기 때문이다. 그럴 때면 난 자연을 만나러 간다. 바다도 좋고, 그것도 여의치 않을 때는 집 옆의 공원도 좋다. 길거리를 지나다가 만나는 꽃들도 좋다. 잠시 마음을 비우고 자연에 나를 맡길 때면 다시 나의 감각이 깨어나는 것을 느낀다.

하늘이 만든 자연의 색깔은 내 컬러 팔레트의 원천이다.
길을 가다가 이런 아름다움을 마주할 때면, 내 눈이 기억하도록
오랫동안 바라보곤 한다.

가만히, 조용히 보고 있자면 감탄하지 않을 수 없다. 어떻게 꽃이라는 같은 이름으로 이렇게 자기만의 다양하고 아름다운 모습일 수 있을까. 꽃잎 한 장에서 오로라처럼 번지는 색깔의 변화, 그것과 잎사귀의 색이 만나 이루어지는 자연스러운 컬러 매치, 난 세상에서 가장 멋진 색깔 팔레트를 꽃이라고 생각한다. 컬러에 대한 책을 찾아보고 공부하지 않아도 된다. 왜냐하면 가장 창의적이고, 아름다운 색의 표본이 자연에 있기 때문이다. 누가 복슬복슬한 크림 같은 연한 핑크색과 형광빛이 나는 연두색의 조화가 아름답다고 가르쳐줄 수 있는가. 핑크도 그냥 핑크가 아니라 복슬복슬한 핑크 혹은 빤딱빤딱한 핑크, 책에서는 볼 수 없는 수많은 컬러의 아름다움을 배울 수 있다.

또한 자연의 모든 것은 독창적이다. 같은 나무의 잎사귀라고 해도 제각기 모양과 색깔이 다르다. 그 모든 것이 저마다의 정체성을 지니고 있다. 누군가의 손에 의해 한번 거쳐지거나 다른 모습으로 변한 것이 아니라 태어났을 때 그대로다. 하나하나가 세상에 존재하기 시작했을 때부터 가진 나름의 주체성이 있다는 것이다. 그렇기 때문에 각자 지니고 있는 깊이가 다르다. 복제품이 없는 자연은 하나하나가 독창적이고, 창의적인 작품이다.

게다가 더욱 놀라운 사실은 제각기 다른 하나하나가 모여서 만들어내는 하모니는 더욱 독창적이라는 것이다. 물고기가 물속에 있을 때의 아름다움, 헤엄칠 때 만들어내는 물결의 아름다움의 조화는 인간이 만들어낼 수 있는 아름다움과는 차원이 다르다. 인간이 만든 가장 아름다운 막대기로 물을 저어도 물고기가 물속에서 헤엄치는 아름다움과는 비교할 수 없다.

그럼에도 가장 경이로운 것은, 자연의 그 모든 색깔, 독창성, 하모니에 어색함이 없다는 것이다. '자연스럽다'라는 말에서 알 수 있듯이, 자연이 만들어내는 조화는 신기할 만큼 전혀 어색하지 않다. 아무리 아름답고 창의적이라고 해도 뭔가 마음에서 느끼는 불편함이 있을 법한데, 그런 것이 전혀 없다. 가끔 머릿속으로 전혀 어울릴 것 같지 않은 컬러의 매치를 자연에서 발견하고, 그 자연스러움에 놀랄 때가 있다.

몇 년 전 친구의 할머니 집으로 놀러 간 적이 있었다. 혼자서 바람을 쐬러 이곳저곳을 돌아다녔다. 비닐하우스도 지나고, 호수도 지나고 마음 가득 자연을 담고 시간을 보냈다. 그러던 중 태어나서 처음으로 식탁에 올려진 가지가 아닌, 대롱대롱 매달려 있는 가지를 보게 되었다. 가지 옆으로 무성하게 난 잎사귀 또한 보았다. 마음이 멎을 정도로 아름다웠다. 검푸른 보랏빛 줄기와 번지듯 일어나는 초록색의 그러데이션. 한 번도 어울릴 거라고 생각해본 적 없는 색깔의 조화는 신선했고 아름다웠다. 그 색깔을 기억하고 아름다움을 간직하기 위해 머릿속으로 사진을 몇 번이나 찍었다.

어릴 적 습관 중의 하나가 이렇게 멋진 자연의 색을 만나면 머릿속으로 사진을 찍는 것이다. 그때의 기쁨을 마음속에 기억하기 위해 몇 분이고 바라보며 색깔 사진을 찍는다. 내가 지금 보고 있는 색깔을 한 단어로 정의해서 기억하면 나중에 그 당시의 정확한 느낌을 잊게 되기 때문이다. 자연의 이런 색깔은 짙은 빨강, 보라처럼 세상에 존재하는 단어로는 정확하게 정의 내릴 수 없다. 처음에는 내 수첩에 '연한 분홍빛이 나는 크림같이 부드러운 색' 이렇게 적어놓기도 했었다. 그러나 지금까지 본 색깔을 모두 적어놓고 항상 볼 수는 없는 법. 꺼내 보려고 해도 어디에 언제 써놨는지 알 수도 없다. 그래서 눈으로 사진을 찍기 시작했다. 너무나 간직하고 싶고, 기억했으면 하는 자연의 색깔을 접하면 내 눈과 마음이 이 색의 아름다움을 기억할 수 있게 몇 분이고 바라보며 사진을 찍는다. 언제 기억하게 될지, 다시 꺼내 쓸 수 있을지 모르지만 내 마음에 우선 담아놓아 내 것을 만든다. 내가 가진 색의 감성이 풍부해질 수 있고 또 이 색의 아름다움이 내가 만드는 작품에 묻어날 수 있게 말이다.

최근에 친구 할머니 댁에서 봤던 가지밭의 아름다움을 상기시키는 일이 있었다. 오랜만에 잡지를 뒤적거리다 지방시의 2011년 가을, 겨울 컬렉션을 보았다. 컬러 팔레트의 대부분을 차지한 짙은 보라와 초록이 만들어내는 고혹적인 아름다운 조화. 여러 가지 텍스처와 프린트로 풀어낸 그 아름다운 조화는 가히 감동적이었다. 그 옷들을 보며 가지밭에 열려 있던 가지가 떠올랐다. 컬렉션의 옷들과 그때 찍었던 머릿속의 가지 사진이 오버랩되었다. 사람이 만들어낼 수 있는 모든 아름다움이 자연에서 시작하지 않았나 하는 생각이 들었다.

우리가 미처 깨닫지 못하지만 우리가 아름다움을 느끼는 색깔의 기준이 이미 자연에 있다고 생각한다. 무의식중에 혹은 태어날 때부터 이미 가지고 있는 기준이나 감성일지도 모른다. 어린아이가 자기도 모르게 아빠의 행동을 따라 하듯 우리의 감성도 자연의 감성을 따라가는 것일 수도 있다. 하지만 모든 사람이 나처럼 생각하지 않는다는 것을 잘 알고 있다. 자연을 너무 사랑하는 사람으로서 자연에게 배우고, 자연과 함께 자라온 나만의 생각일 수도 있겠다.

하지만 적어도 나에게 있어서 자연은 모든 아름다움의 시작이고 끝이다. 자연은 나에게 아름다움이 무엇인지를 가르쳐주었다. 크고 작음, 다르고 같음, 느리고 빠름 이 모든 것을 가르쳐주었고, 그 안에서 나만의 감성을 가지게 해주었다. 자연의 생명 하나하나가 가진 존귀함과 아름다움, 그것들은 지금도 나의 감각을 깨운다. 더욱 풍요롭고 아름답게 말이다.

7 초등학교 3학년, 내 꿈이 시작된 날

지금도 생생히 기억난다. 초등학교 3학년 선생님께서 교육자료로 쓰시기 위해 미술을 잘하는 몇 명을 방과 후에 남겨놓고 한지로 옷 만드는 것을 시키셨다. 원래 손으로 만드는 건 뭐든지 좋아했지만 그때의 느낌은 더욱 특별했다. 거울을 보며 천같이 부드러운 한지를 이리저리 몸에 대보았다. 넓은 평면의 종이가 몸에 휘감기는 느낌에 가슴이 두근거리며 설렜다. 이리저리 오리고 붙이며 시간 가는 줄 모르고 신나게 옷을 만들었다. 옷이 다 완성되고 입어봤을 때 느껴졌던 짜릿한 전율은 지금도 생생하다.

'아, 이거구나! 이게 내가 평생 해야 할 일이구나!'

딱 맞아떨어지는 느낌. 한 치의 의심도 없이 옷 만드는 일이 내가 평생 할 일이라고 믿었다. 그날 이후 내 장래희망은 변함 없이 패션 디자이너였다. 참 재미있는 건 지금도 작업을 끝내고 완성된 옷을 입고 거울 앞에 서면 처음 한지로 옷을 만들었을 때 느꼈던 가슴 두근거리는 짜릿함을 느낀다. 가끔씩 설레는 마음이 주체가 안돼서 혼자 발을 동동 구르기도 한다.

내가 많이 감사하는 일 중 하나는 어릴 적부터 확실한 꿈이 있었다는 것이다. 무엇을 하고 싶은지, 내가 해야 할 일이 무엇인지 확신이 있다는 것. 그리고 그것을 잘할 수 있는 성실함이 있다는 건 정말 감사하다. 그 꿈을 이뤄 나가기 위해 좋은 환경에서 공부할 수 있다는 것도 참 감사하다. 하지만 난 부유한 환경에서 자라지도 않았고, 런던에서 유학을 할 만큼 경제적으로 넉넉하지도 않았다. 처음 런던에 왔을 때는 돈이 없어서 걸어 다니기도 했고, 항상 아르바이트와 학업을 병행해야 했다. 지금은 처음보다는 많이 여유롭지만 여전히 나에게 치장할 돈을 아껴서 원단을 사고, 작업할 때 필요한 것들을 마련하고 있다.

하지만 힘든 시간을 잘 이겨낼 수 있었던 건 내가 받은 큰 선물 때문이다. 어렸을 적부터 한 치의 의심도 없이 내가 해야 할 일을 알고 있었다는 것. 그것이 너무나 즐겁고 신나는 일이라는 것. 내가 받은 이 크나큰 선물이 오늘도 나를 다시 일어서게 한다.

내가 받은 큰 선물. 어릴 적부터 한 치의 의심도 없이 내가 해야 할 일을 알고 있었다는 것.

8 내가 런던에 있는 것은 기적이다

내가 패션 디자이너가 되기로 결심한 건 열 살 때였다. 세인트 마틴에 대해 알게 되고, 런던에서 패션을 공부하고 싶다고 생각한 건 중학교 2학년, 열네 살 때였다. 잡지에서 존 갈리아노와 알렉산더 맥퀸이 매달 빠지지 않고 등장하던 시절, 두 디자이너가 런던에 있는 세인트 마틴 학교 출신이라는 것을 알게 되고 저렇게 멋진 디자이너가 공부했다면 굉장한 학교일 거라고 의심치 않았다. 그때부터 내 꿈을 이뤄 나갈 곳은 세인트 마틴밖에 없었다.

하지만 나도 현실감은 있었다. 언니가 두 명, 남동생까지 있는 우리 집은 영국으로 유학을 갈 수 있을 만큼 넉넉하지 않았다. 처음 부모님께 유학에 대해 말씀 드렸을 때는 귀담아 듣지도 않으셨을 만큼 불가능한 일이었다. 오로지 내 힘으로 영국에 가야 한다는 걸 잘 알고 있었고, 그러기 위해서는 스스로 돈을 모아야 한다는 것도 알고 있었다. 고등학교 시절, 유학 비용을 준비하기 위해 외환은행에서 달러로 저금할 수 있는 통장을 만들었다. 한 달에 몇 달러씩 용돈을 아껴가며 저축했다. 조금이지만 돈이 쌓여가는 것에 뿌듯했고, 이렇게 하다 보면 영국에 공부하러 갈 수 있을 것만 같아서 힘이 났다.

하지만 나이가 들고 현실을 바로 볼수록 영국 유학은 불가능하다는 걸 알게 되었다. 고등학교 3년 동안 모은 달러통장의 돈은 세인트 마틴 1년 학비의 10분의 1도 안되었고, 나머지 비용을 마련하는 것은 머릿속으로 계산기를 아무리 두드려봐도 불가능했다.

'이건 아무리 내가 노력해도 안되는 거구나.'

인생에서 처음으로 내 뜻대로 할 수 없는 일이 있다는 것을 알게 되고, 한국에 있는 의상 디자인과에 가서 공부를 해야겠다고 마음먹었다. 운이 좋아 다행히도 대학입시에 좋은 성적으로 합격했고, 패션을 드디어 제대로 공부하게 되었다는 기대감과 설렘으로 대학생활을 시작했다. 하지만 내가 기대했던 대학생활은 1년 만에 퇴학으로 끝을 맺었다. 교수님들이 학생들에게 바라는 것과 내가 생각하는 디자인 공부는 너무나 달랐다. 나의 1학년 1학기 학점은 0.4였고, 학사경고를 받았다.

학사경고를 받았다는 사실이 괴로운 것은 아니었다. 내가 너무나 하고 싶은 패션 공부를 이 대학에선 마음대로 할 수 없다는 것이 나를 너무 힘들게 했다. 여기에서는 내가 꿈꾸는 일을 할 수 없다는 확신이 생겼다. 아무런 계획도, 준비도 없었지만 더 이상 학교에 나가지 않았다.

그로부터 몇 개월을 어떻게 지냈는지 모르겠다. 아닌 척, 괜찮은 척했지만 세상이 끝난 것 같았다. 어디에서부터 어떻게 시작해야 하는지도 모른 채, 뒤로 돌아갈 수도, 그렇다고 앞으로 나아갈 수도 없는 멈춰버린 상황이었다. 어릴 적부터 확신했던 꿈이 사라져버리는 것 같았다. 내가 가진 것이라고는 패션에 대한 꿈밖에 없었는데, 그게 흐려지니 내 인생이 끝나버린 것 같기도 했다. 일부러 내 자신을 함부로 대하며 처음부터 없었던 꿈처럼, 나는 원래 할 수 없었던 사람이라며 자신을 폄하했다. 그때를 생각하면 지금도 눈물이 날 만큼 괴로웠다. 이것밖에 없다고 생각하며 살았는데 현실에 부딪쳐 포기해야 한다는 사실이 어린 내가 받아들이기에 정말 큰 고통이었다.

모든 것이 없었던 일처럼 무뎌질 즈음, 내가 가진 것이 아무것도 없다며 모든 것을 포기할 즈음 새로운 빛이 찾아왔다. 그다지 하는 일 없어 지내던 중 일산에 사는 큰언니네 집에 몇 달 만에 놀러 갔다. 오랜만에 가본 언니 집에는 옷과 박스가 빈틈없이 쌓여 있었다. 언니가 처음 인터넷 쇼핑몰을 연 2005년 여름이었다. 딱히 하는 일이 없는 나는 그날부터 언니의 인터넷 쇼핑몰 사업을 돕기 시작했다.

사업은 말도 안되게 잘되기 시작했다. 작은 오피스텔에서 시작한 사업은 어느새 직원이 20명이나 되는 회사로 성장했고, 내가 유학을 오기 바로 전에는 100평짜리 사무실을 사용할 정도로 커졌다. 하루가 다르게 사업이 성장하는 것도 좋았지만, 좋아하는 언니와 매일 붙어 지낼 수 있다는 것이 정말 좋았다. 삶의 의미를 잃었던 시절, 언니는 나의 꿈이 소중하다는 것을 알게 해주었고, 내가 사랑받는 존재라는 것을 알게 해주었다.

내 꿈이 전부였던 지난 시절, 꿈이 흐려지니 나조차 사라졌었다. 하지만 난 그 꿈보다 더 소중한 존재라는 것을 깨닫게 되었다. 유명 디자이너가 되어야 내가 가치 있는 사람이 아니라 어떤 일을 해도 나는 그 자체로 소중한 사람이라는 것을 알게 되었다. 언니의 사업을 도와주며 보낸 1년이 조금 넘는 시간 동안 난 조금씩 마음이 회복되고, 환경에 흔들리지 않는 단단한 마음을 갖게 되었다.

착한 언니는 나에게 1년 동안 일한 대가로 4천만 원이라는 큰

(위) 2007년 4월 1일. 런던행 비행기에 몸을 실었다.
(아래) 브리티시 뮤지엄 앞. 잠시 여행 온 친구 승화와 한 컷.

돈을 주었다. 세인트 마틴의 1년치 등록금과 생활비였다. 마치 마법처럼 누군가가 미리 계획한 것처럼 한국에서 세인트 마틴 입학을 위한 포트폴리오 심사가 있었고, 영어시험은 딱 학교에서 요구하는 성적이 나와 한 달 만에 후다닥 런던행 비행기에 오를 수 있었다.

만약 순조롭게 런던에 왔다면 이런 마음이 들었을까. 내가 런던으로 공부하러 갈 수 있다는 것 자체가 감사했고, 나를 있는 그대로 사랑하는 마음을 가질 수 있게 되어 더더욱 감사했다. 가끔씩 버스를 타고 집으로 올 때, 길을 걷다가도 문득 내가 런던에 아무렇지 않게 당연한 듯 있는 게 정말 감사할 때가 있다.

나의 모든 것이 사라져 암담했던 그때, 그 시절에 나의 마음을 밝혀주며 찾아온 한 줄기 빛. 물론 지금도 현실은 힘들다. 하지만 돈이 부족해도, 일이 잘 안 풀려도, 내가 부족하다고 느껴져도 그때 찾아온 그 빛은 오늘도 내 마음속에 꿈이 있음을, 그리고 나의 삶 자체에 다시 한번 감사하게 한다.

9 자유로운 사고를 가진 세인트 마틴 친구들

런던에서 입시를 준비해서 세인트 마틴 패션 디그리^{degree} 과정에 들어갔다. 한국에서는 디그리 시작 전, 파운데이션 과정의 오퍼만 받고 런던으로 갔다. 파운데이션이 끝나고 혼자 포트폴리오를 준비하고, 인터뷰를 하고 세인트 마틴에 합격했다.

당시 한국에서 포트폴리오 학원을 다니며 입시를 했던 친구들의 말로는 한국에서는 지원만 하면 세인트 마틴에 쉽게 합격한다고 해서 별다른 걱정은 하지 않았다. 더구나 파운데이션에서 나름 잘하는 학생 중 한 명이었기 때문에 합격에 대한 부담이 거의 없었다. 어디에서 나오는 자신감인지 모르게 '나야 당연히 되겠지' 하고 생각했었다. 하지만 런던에서 세인트 마틴 패션 디그리 과정에 합격하기란 정말 어려웠다. 매년 전 세계에서 수천 명의 학생들이 지원하지만 150명 정도밖에 뽑지 않는다. 세인트 마틴에서 파운데이션 과정을 이수한 학생들만 지원할 수 있는, 한국에서의 '수시' 같은 개념으로 지원했지만 떨어졌다. 다행히도 일반 지원으로 합격했지만 말이다. 몇백 명의 학생이 포트폴리오 채점이 끝나기를 기다리는데, 열 명 남짓한 합격자를 뽑던 순간의 떨림은 지금도 생생하다.

세인트 마틴은 패션으로 세계적으로 손에 꼽히는 학교다. 그만큼 전 세계에서 재능 있는 수많은 학생들이 지원한다. 신선하고 자유로운 사고로 작업을 해나가는 멋진 친구들 중에는 뛰어난 재능을 가진 친구들이 많다. 가끔씩 학생이 했다고는 믿을 수 없을 만큼 놀라운 작품도 종종 보게 된다. 내 기대와 달리 수시 지원으로 합격하지 못했기 때문에 처음 1학년 학기 초에는 마음이 왠지 찜찜했다.

나의 재능이 저 친구들보다 못한 걸까? 하는 의구심이 마음 한구석에 자리 잡고 있었다. 하지만 그것은 오래가지 못했다. 세인트 마틴에서는 비교라는 것이 불필요하다는 것을 깨달았기 때문이다.

세인트 마틴은 정말 좋은 학교다. 커리큘럼도 좋고 재능 있는 친구들 사이에서 공부할 수 있는 것 또한 좋다. 하지만 가장 좋은 것은 학교에서 학생 한 명, 한 명의 다름을 존중한다는 것이다. 선생님이 학생의 디자인을 고치는 일이 절대 없다. 부족한 점에 대해서는 좋은 방향을 제시해주어 새로운 생각으로 접근할 수 있게 도와준다. 하지만 학생의 생각을 존중하고 나의 디자인 세계를 인정한다. 그런 과정을 통해 얻은 값진 교훈은 친구들과 내가 다르다는 것을 받아들이게 만들었다. 우리는 서로가 가진 장점과 단점이 다르고, 각자의 생각도 다르다. 어떤 면에서는 나보다 뛰어난 친구도 있고, 나보다 못한 친구도 있다. 하지만 중요한 것은 개개인의 패션에 대한 철학과 생각이 존중받을 만하다는 것이다. 서로가 다름을 인정하는 것. 그것은 나를 인정하고 받아들이는 것이다.

학교에서 가장 힘든 것은 내 스스로를 인정하는 것이었다. 그들 또한 나와 같은 고민을 했을 것이다. 나보다 잘하는 친구를 보면 자연스럽게 비교할 수밖에 없다. 세인트 마틴에는 그런 우수한 친구들이 수두룩했기에 더욱 그랬었다. 그렇게 남과 나를 비교하며 내 가치와 재능을 점수 매기게 된다. 내가 어떤 면에서는 그 친구보다 부족할 수 있지만 그렇다고 내가 그 친구보다 못한 디자이너라는 것은 절대 아니다. 나는 다만 그 친구와 다를 뿐이다.

나 스스로 나의 가치를 인정하고 내가 다르다는 것을 받아들이는 것은 아주 중요하다. 이런 서로의 다름을 인정하고, 받아들이는 데는 가장 친한 친구인 헬레나Helena의 도움이 컸다.

헬레나는 패션을 하지만 내가 생각하는 패션을 하지 않았다. 무엇을 하든 남과 비교해서 일등을 해야 하는 것이 당연했던 나와는 달랐다. 헬레나는 자기 자신을 아낄 줄 아는 친구이다. 물론 헬레나가 모든 분야에서 잘하는 친구는 아니다. 자신의 작품을 모두 만족스러워하지도 않고, 자신의 부족함도 잘 알고 있다. 하지만 난 한번도 헬레나가 자신과 다른 사람을 비교하는 것을 들어본 적이 없다. 남과 자신을 비교하며 자신을 힘들게 하지도 않는다. 자신의 다름을 인정하고, 그것을 존중하고, 또 그것에 집중한다. 자신을 받아들이지 못하고 노력하는 것은 기초가 없는 건물을 짓는 것과 같다.

처음 세인트 마틴에 들어가서 다른 친구들을 보며 내가 최고가 아니라는 사실에 견딜 수가 없었다. 은근슬쩍 곁눈질로 친구들과 나를 비교하며 생각하지 않으려고 노력했지만 어쩔 수 없었다. 헬레나는 내가 그런 이야기를 할 때마다 왜 자신과 남을 비교하는지조차 이해하지 못했다. 영국 교육을 받고, 자유로운 사고를 가진 부모님 밑에서 자란 헬레나는 경쟁이 우선되는, 당연히 일등을 하기 위해 노력하는 내가 이해되지 않는 것 같았다.

나의 가치를 알고, 나를 인정하고 받아들이는 것. 그것은 우리가 서로 다름을 인정하는 것에서부터 시작된다. 열등감과 패배의식으로는 훌륭한 작업을 할 수 없다. 난 세상이 볼 때 비록 하찮은 재

세인트 마틴, 내가 좋아하는 일러스트레이션 수업에서.

능일지라도 그것이 자신의 것으로 받아들여질 때, 그것의 가치를 인정해줄 때 비로소 진정한 성장과 발전이 시작된다고 생각한다. 나도 내 자신이 어느만큼 재능을 가지고 있는지 모른다. 또한 그것이 누구보다 더 나은지 혹은 못한지도 모른다. 하지만 난 나의 재능이 가치 있고 소중하게 쓰여질 것이라는 사실을 믿는다.

10 즐거움과 욕심은
종이 한 장 차이

올해는 유난히 졸업을 앞둔 친구들이 많다. 신기하게도 모두 예술을 공부하는 친구들이다. 아트를 공부하는 학창 시절의 마지막 한 획을 긋는 졸업 컬렉션. 그 압박감은 굳이 이야기하지 않아도 친구들의 얼굴만 봐도 알 수 있다. 만나기만 하면 졸업 이야기다. 넌 졸업 쇼 주제가 뭐니? 어떻게 작업할 거니? 누구는 이렇게 했다고 하더라. 이런저런 걱정과 불안, 좋은 작품을 완성할 거라는 조금은 설레는 마음이 섞인 얼굴들이다.

나도 몇 달 동안 졸업만 생각했다. 졸업 쇼 주제에서부터 작업 방법, 시간 계획 등 눈을 뜰 때부터 감을 때까지 졸업 컬렉션 생각으로 가득했다. 지겨워서 다른 생각을 해보려고 해도 어떻게 된 게 쉴 수가 없었다. 뇌가 쉬지를 못해서인지 난생처음으로 밤마다 두통에 시달리게 되었다. 패션을 즐거워하고, 좋아하는 것과 그것이 욕심이 되어 나를 사로잡기 시작하는 것은 한순간이다.

내가 지금까지 패션을 하면서 확실하게 깨달은 것은 전자는 좋은 패션을 하고, 후자는 못난 패션을 한다는 것이다. 어이없게도 그것을 알면서도 가끔은 나도 모르게 욕심으로 패션을 하고 있다. 좋은 작업을 하겠다는 생각이 남보다 잘해야 한다는 욕심으로 번지고, 잘하기 위한 모든 과정이 집착으로 이어지기도 한다.

요 며칠이 피크였다. 몇 달 전부터 시작한 리서치는 욕심 때문에 이미 방향을 잃었고, 그런 생각 속에서 디자인이 나올 리 없었다. 시간이 흐르고 결과물은 안 나오고, 잘하고 싶지만 그렇지 못하다는 패배감이 조금씩 올라오고 있었다. 잘 먹지도 못하고 쉬지도 않아서

몸도 아팠다. 두통에 몸살을 앓고 그 와중에 작업 생각으로 안절부절못하는 모습은 지금 생각해도 그야말로 가관이다.

　　마지막 학년이 힘들 거란 사실은 어느 정도 예상했었다. 이때까지는 감사하게도 별다른 욕심 없이 조금씩 배운다는 생각으로 패션을 했기 때문에 집착이 심하지는 않았었다. 내가 받은 재능을 소중하게 키워 나가는 것. 그것이 나에게 즐거운 일이라는 것에 감사해하며 작업했다. 하지만 그런 나에게도 졸업만큼은 커다란 이슈였나 보다. 욕심이 조금씩 올라오기 시작하는데 그게 눈덩이처럼 커져서 졸업 쇼에서 일등을 하고야 말겠다는 요상한 생각이 되어버렸다.

　　'어떻게 하면 졸업생 가운데 최고로 잘할 수 있을까?'

　　이것이 내 졸업 컬렉션의 주제가 되고 목표가 되었다. 내가 진짜 말하고 싶고, 옷으로 표현하고 싶은 생각은 사소하게 느껴졌다. 그것보다는 눈에 띄고 새롭고 멋진 것을 만들어야만 했다. 제일 잘하는 것이 주제가 되어버린 작업이 잘될 리 없었다. 요란한 테크닉에 집중하게 되고, 쉽게 눈에 띄게 만들고 싶은 인스턴트식 생각에만 사로잡혀 있으니 작업은 점점 더 궁지에 몰렸다.

　　결정적인 것은 학교에 며칠간 나가지 못했던 것이다. 한창 디자인이 나와서 패턴 작업을 해야 하는데 내가 원하는 것에 집중하지 못했기에 디자인이 나오지 않았던 것이다. 아이러니하게도 리서치양과 작업량은 누구보다 많은데 결과물이 없는 상황이었다. 시간이 흐르고 마음이 초조해질수록 작업이 진전되지 않아 답답했다.

　　공중에 떠 있는 느낌이랄까. 땅 위에 차분히 착지를 해야 걸어

갈 수 있는데 공중에 붕 떠서 발만 구르고 있는 기분이었다. 차분하게 나를 다스리려고 해도 욕심과 집착으로 중심을 잃어버린 지 오래였다. 시간이 흐를수록 마음은 점점 더 급해졌지만 결론은 '더 이상은 못하겠다'는 좌절이었다. 그리고 하루가 또 흘렀다.

아침에 일어나서 또 학교에 가지 못했다. 두 손 두 발 다 들어 포기해야 할 때가 온 것이다. 내 욕심으로는 아무것도 할 수 없구나. 그리고 가만히 침대에 앉아 기도했다.

"하나님, 도와주세요. 내 욕심이 내 모든 것을 지배했어요. 다시 감사함으로, 즐거움으로 작업하고 싶어요. 도와주세요."

마음이 차분해지는 것을 느꼈다. 내 욕심으로 할 수 없는 것이구나, 하는 것을 알면서도 잠시 나를 속였던 것을 다시 몸으로 느끼게 되었다. 학교에는 가지 못했지만 오늘을 원래의 나의 중심으로 돌아가는 날로 정하고 집 밖으로 나왔다. 그리고 V&A로 향하는 지하철을 탔다. 이상하게도 평안했다. 더 이상 붕 떠 있는 느낌도 아니었고, 조급한 마음도 들지 않았다. 망했다는 패배감은 더더욱 없었다. 천천히 걸어 다니며 V&A를 구경했다. 원래의 나처럼, 옛날의 나로 돌아간 기분이었다.

'까짓것 일등 못하면 어떠냐. 실수를 할 수도 있다. 못할 수도 있다. 단지 내가 하고 싶은 이야기를 하자. 어차피 욕심을 낸다고 되는 것도 아니니까.'

뭔가 포기하고 나니 보이기 시작했다. 내가 원하는 것들, 원래

혼자서 자주 들르곤 했던 윔블던 힐에 있는 작은 호수. 해 질 무렵의 석양이 무엇보다 아름답다.

졸업 작품 파이널 피팅 날, 내 작품을 입고 대기 중인 모델들. 내가 말하고 싶고 표현하고 싶은 것들은 무엇이었을까.

이야기하고 싶었던 것들, 처음의 그 영감, 나를 감동시켰던 그 영감에 다시 마음이 가기 시작했다. 차분히 집으로 돌아와 맛있게 밥도 먹고, 쉬기도 하고, 지금까지 했던 작업을 다시 돌아봤다. 집착으로 인해 부족한 부분도 있었지만 내가 말하고 싶은 것 또한 가득했다. 처음에 내가 받았던 영감도 소중해 보였다. 다만 일등에 대한 집착이 그 모든 것을 가치 없어 보이게 만들었을 뿐이었다. 이렇게 하면 일등을 하지 못하지 않을까? 하는 두려움에 더 이상 발전시키지 못했을 뿐이다. 욕심을 걷어내니 새롭게 보이기 시작하는 이 아름다운 영감에 다시 집중하기 시작했다.

아트에 있어서 확실한 것은 뛰어나 보이려고 하는 작업은 결과가 좋지 못하다는 것이다. '잘'하기 위해서 하는 작업은 '잘'할 수가 없다. 그 욕심을 걷어내고 진짜 내가 말하고 싶고 표현하고 싶은 것에 가치를 둘 때 진짜 '잘'할 수 있다.

내 것이라고 손에 꽉 쥐고 있으면 그것의 본질을 제대로 볼 수가 없다. 손에 쥔 것을 내려놓아야만 분명하게 보인다. 내가 마지막 학년의 컬렉션을 통해서 하고 싶은 말이 욕심을 걸러내고 나니 담백하고 깔끔하게 보이기 시작했다. 이미 알고 있었는데 이제서야 내가 이것을 말하고 싶었구나, 하고 깨닫게 되면서 다시 한번 그 가치를 인정해주게 된 것이다. 오늘은 고작 몇 시간밖에 작업하지 못했지만 결과물은 만족스럽다. 이렇게 글을 쓸 수 있는 여유까지 생겼다.

다행히도 나는 내일 학교에 간다. 욕심은 없어지고 예전의 그 감사한 마음으로 학교에 간다. 나에게 주어진 재능에 감사해하고,

그 재능을 즐겁게, 소중하게, 가치 있게 여기는 마음을 주신 것에 또다시 감사하다. 내일 아침 일찍 학교에 가서 오늘 나온 디자인으로 작업을 할 것이다. 예전처럼 감사한 마음으로 즐겁게, 즐겁게.

11 머리를 자르고
자유를 얻었다

머리를 잘랐다. 그것도 아주 확 단발로 잘라버렸다. 10년 넘게 항상 똑같았던 나의 머리를 오늘 아침, 짜증나도록 질려버린 이 머리를 잘라버려야겠다는 생각이 들었다. 예뻐 보이는 것과 내가 진짜 원하는 것, 항상 이 두 가지가 문제다. 예뻐 보이기 위해서는 내가 원하는 것을 조금은 양보해야 한다. 그러다 어느샌가 예뻐 보이는 것에 익숙해지면 더 이상 내가 원하는 것을 하지 않게 된다.

10년을 한결같이 고수해온 내 헤어스타일이 그렇다. 지겹게도 10년째 부스스한 긴 파마머리였다. 중학교 때까지는 항상 귀밑 3센티의 아주 짧은 단발이었지만 말이다. 사실 나는 긴 파마머리가 가장 잘 어울리고 예뻐 보인다. 여성스러워 보이고, 왠지 연약해 보이는 이미지. 그래서 10년 넘게 차마 용기를 내서 못생겨질 각오를 하지 못했다. 하지만 오늘 아침에는 지겹다 못해 신경질 나는 이 머리를 기필코 잘라야겠다고 마음먹었다.

거울을 보고 머리가 귀밑까지 오는 상상을 해봤다. 흩날리는 긴 머리에서 느껴지는 여성미가 없어지니, 남자아이 같았다. 못생겨 보일 것이 분명했기에 다시 한번 마음을 단단히 먹어야 했다. 사실 난 이 긴 머리가 항상 싫었다. 예뻐 보이고는 싶지만 여성스러워 보이는 것이 싫었다. 더구나 머리를 묶으면 새색시마냥 참해 보이는 것도 싫었다. '참해 보인다'는 말에 왠지 모르는 거부감이 든다.

사실 난 긴 머리가 항상 싫었다. 예뻐 보이고는 싶지만 여성스러워 보이는 것이 싫었다.
오늘 아침, 짜증나도록 질려버린 이 머리를 잘라버려야겠다는 생각이 들었다.

그럼에도 불구하고 지금까지 이 긴 파마머리를 포기할 수 없었던 것은 예뻐 보이는 것과 남자에게 예뻐 보이고 싶은 마음을 포기할 수 없어서였다. 10년 넘게 나를 괴롭혀온 녀석이다. 어쩌면 사소한 것이고, 여자라면 당연한 것이다. 대부분의 여자들이 그렇겠지만 나 역시 입고 싶고, 해보고 싶은 것들이 참 많다. 패션을 하기 때문에 더더욱 새롭게 시도하고 싶은 것이 많다. 하지만 그 모든 것을 막아온 것이, 남자에게 예뻐 보이고 싶다는 그 마음이었다.

언젠가 잡지에서 남자친구와 데이트할 때와 혼자 있을 때의 여자 연예인 스타일을 비교한 것을 본 적이 있다. 누구보다 옷을 잘 입고, 멋진 스타일의 스타들도 데이트를 할 때는 스커트 또는 원피스를 입어 평범하면서도 여성스러운 이미지를 연출했다. 남자에게 예뻐 보이는 것과 내가 하고 싶은 것은 항상 대립한다. 남자에게 예뻐 보이기 위해서는 내가 원하는 것은 조금 포기해야 한다. 예를 들어, 빈티지 스타일로 많이 쓰는 터번이 그렇다. 보통의 생각과 미의 기준을 가진 남자라면 여자가 터번을 두른 모습을 예쁘다고 하지는 않을 것이다. 그게 아무리 최신 트렌드이고, 고가의 명품 터번이라 할지라도 말이다.

대부분의 남자는 터번을 하고 빈티지 스타일을 스타일리시하게 연출한 여자보다 길게 내려오는 생머리에 화사한 색깔의 카디건과 시폰 스커트를 입은 그녀에게 호감을 표현할 것이다. 물론 모든 남자가 그렇다는 것은 아니다. 예외가 있긴 하겠지만 대부분의 한국 남자, 심지어 패션을 하는 남자들도 여자친구로는 재미없는 시폰 스커트를 입는 여자가 좋다고 했다. 이것이 한국 남자가 가진 보편적인 생각이고, 미학이라면 어쩔 수 없다. 그렇다고 젊은 청춘을 솔로로만 보낼 수는 없지 않은가? 하지만 죽어도 시폰 스커트에 카디건은 못 입겠으니, 내가 가장 예뻐 보이는 긴 머리라도 유지해야 했다. 내가 남자들이 받아들일 수 있는 범주 안에 들기 위해 최소한으로 지켜야 하는 것이 비로 이 긴 머리였다.

런던에 오면 머리를 자르겠다고 다짐했었다. 시폰 스커트만 좋아하는 남자들도 없으니 내가 하고 싶고, 입고 싶은 것을 모두 해야겠다고 생각했다. 드디어 남자들의 눈치를 보지 않고 내 마음대로 그렇게 하고 싶었다. 하지만 런던에서는 또 머리를 자를 수 없는 나름의 이유가 생겼다. 키가 크고, 마르고, 머리가 긴 동양 여자. 한국에서는 아주 예쁜 편은 아니었지만 여기서는 내가 희귀하고 심지어 아름답기까지 한 편이었다. 우선은 키가 크고, 마른 동양 여자라는 것을 신기하게 생각했다. 그리고 가장 부러워하는 것이 내 머리카락이었다. 머릿결이 좋지 않은 외국 사람들은 나의 길고 윤기 있는 머리를 정말 좋아했다.

그래서 또 머리를 자를 수가 없었다. 이렇게 5년이 흘렀고, 한국에서의 5년을 더하면 10년을 같은 헤어스타일을 했던 것이다. 내가 진짜 하고 싶은 것은 마음 깊숙이 묻혀버리고, 사람들의 눈치를 보며 은근슬쩍 10년을 보냈다. 그런데 요즘 며칠간 이 머리가 불편했다. 딱히 머리가 불편했다기보다는 이 머리처럼 이도 저도 아닌, 어찌할 수 없는 마음이 불편했다. 뜨겁지도, 차갑지도 않은 미지근하게 살고 있는 내 자신에게 신경질이 났고 드디어 어정쩡한 내 모습에 폭발했다.

나를 가장 불편하게 만들었던 건 세상과 사람들의 눈치를 보고 있는 모습 때문이었다. 졸업 전에 하고 싶고, 시도해보고 싶은 일이 많았는데 언제부터인가 세상 눈치를 보느라 포기하는 일이 많아졌다. 반대로, 누가 시키지도 않는데 그래야 할 것 같은 묘한 의무감에 억지로 하는 일도 많아졌다. 졸업은 다가오고, 마음은 급해지는데 이러지도 저러지도 못하는 마음에 답답했었다.

중심을 잃은 사람은 넘어지게 되어 있다. 중심을 잃은 나는 아직 넘어지진 않았지만, 흔들흔들 위태로운 모습이었다. 누구의 마음에 들고, 누구에게 예뻐 보이기 위해 사는 것인지 정확히 알지도 못한 채, 그렇게 세상과 내 마음을 왔다 갔다 넘나들고 있었다. 두 길에 한 발씩만 담근 채, 제대로 뛰지도 못하고 절뚝거리고 있었다. 내가 원하는 것을 향해 나가자. 이리저리 세상의 눈치를 보며 미지근하게 살지 말자.

이 케케묵은 머리부터 잘라야 했다. 마음먹은 김에 당장 미용실로 갔다. 미련 없이 머리를 단발로 확 잘라버렸다. 허리 가까이 길게 내려오는 머리카락이 싹둑 잘려 바닥으로 떨어지는데, 말 그대로 10년 묵은 체증이 내려가는 것 같았다. 집으로 가는 쇼윈도에 비친 내 모습은 안타깝게도 머리가 길었을 때보다 덜 예뻐 보였다. 분명 덜 예쁜고 묘하게 얼굴이 커 보이는 것도 같은데 기분은 날아갈 듯이 좋았다. 조금은 못생겨 보이는, 오랜만에 마음에 쏙 드는 내 모습이 그곳에 있었다.

Habit

**패션을 공부하는 학생에게
필요한 세 가지 습관**

어려서부터 예술 공부를 해왔고, 고등학교 때는 입시용 미술을 오랫동안 배웠다. 런던에 오면서 가장 걱정되었던 것은 오랜 입시 준비가 오히려 안 좋은 영향을 미치지는 않을까 하는 것이었다. 얼굴이 깨끗하지 않으면 아무리 화장을 해도 예뻐지지 않는 법. 혹시나 아트에 대한 잘못된 선입견이나 습관이 몸에 배어 있다면 런던에서 공부를 시작하기 전에 새롭게 비워야만 했다. 바로 BA 코스로 진학할 수도 있었지만, 세인트 마틴의 파운데이션 코스부터 듣기로 결정한 것은 아트의 기본을 다시 배우고 싶어서였다. 그동안 아트라는 이름으로 해온 모든 것을 비우고 처음부터 다시 시작하기로 했다.

파운데이션 코스 수업은 정말 즐거웠다. 매일 아침이 기다려졌고 집에 돌아오면 새벽까지 시간 가는 줄 모르고 즐겁게 작업을 하다 잠들었다. 한국에서 입시를 전제로 미술을 할 때는 항상 잘했다, 못했다는 평가가 따라다녔기 때문에 은연중에 '잘해 보이기' 위해 노력했었다. 하지만 그 잘한다는 기준 또한 너무나 한국적인 것이었고, 그것이 아트의 정답은 아니었다. 지금까지 잘해 보이기 위해 해왔던 방법이나 생각은 잊기로 했고, 전혀 새로운 접근으로 작업을 했다. 그리고 망치기 위해 노력했다.

항상 안정된 범위 안에서만 작업하고, 잘해 보이는 방법으로만 작업했던 나로서는 망치는 것이 가장 어려웠다. 안 해본 방법을 시도한다는 것이 두려웠다. 너무 이상해지거나 내 마음에 안 드는 결과물이 나올 수도 있었다. 그럴 때마다 나에게 많은 가르침을 준 것은 친구들이었다. 세인트 마틴 파운데이션 과정에는 세계 각국에서 다양한 배경과 지식을 가진 700명의 학생들이 모여 있다. 그들과 섞여서 아트를 공부할 수 있었던 것은 어쩌면 큰 행운이었다. 정답이 있는 것처럼 그것만 따라 작업하던 나를 새로움에 눈뜨게 했다. 결과에 대한 두려움 없이, 자신의 감정과 생각에 따라 자유롭게 작업하는 친구들. 좋은 결과물을 위해서가 아닌 아티스트 자신이 진정한 주체가 되어 작업하는 과정을 조금씩 배워 나갔다. 그 과정 중 가장 도움이 되었던 세 가지 습관을 소개한다.

스쳐 지나가는 모든 것들의 기록, 메모하기

생각이 많아지고 표현하고 싶은 것들이 늘어나면서 메모하는 습관이 생겼다. 그때그때 받은 영감이나 생각을 잊지 않기 위해 항상 작은 수첩을 가방에 넣고 다니며 메모를 했다. 어떨 때는 일기처럼 나의 감정이나 생각을 적기도 했고, 중요한 일이나 새로 발견한 좋은 디자이너, 봐야 할 패션쇼 등 모든 것을 기록했다. 패션과 관련된 일은 영어로 해야 했기에 되도록이면 영어로 생각하고, 메모하기로 했다.

지금까지 잃어버린 것을 빼고 모아온 수첩이 열 권도 넘는다. 수첩을 살펴보면 지금은 당연한 것들이 그 당시에는 엄청난 발견을 한 것처럼 적혀 있고, 내가 쓴 것이 맞나 싶을 만큼 신선한 생각도 있다. 새롭게 발견한 봉제 방법이나 좋은 단추를 파는 가게, 지나가는 여자의 코트를 보고 느낀 점 등 사소한 것까지 메모했던 게 결과적으로는 스쳐 지나간 모든 순간을 내 것으로 만드는 작업이었다.

(위) 몇 권 잃어버리긴 했지만 지금까지 모아온 낡은 수첩들.
(아래) 2008년에 남긴 기록들. 예전의 내 생각들도 돌아보면 새롭다.

항상 가지고 다니는 작은 스케치북. 이디를 가든 사람들의 얼굴 표정, 움직임 등을 그리곤 했다.

금방 잊혀질 것들을 메모로 남기면 다시 한번 생각하고, 기억하게 된다. 쌓여가는 메모만큼 내 생각이 자라고, 내 안에 보물들이 점점 쌓여 가는 것이다.

사람을 관찰하고 사람을 스케치하기

어릴 적부터의 습관이지만 패션을 공부함에 있어 큰 도움이 되는 것은 스케치다. 사람을 좋아하고, 사람의 얼굴 표정, 움직임 등에 관심이 많은 나는 사람 그리는 일을 좋아한다. 친구를 기다리거나 혼자 버스에 앉아 있을 때면 가방에서 스케치북을 꺼내 사람들을 그리곤 했다. 그래서 나는 항상 스케치북이 들어가는 큰 가방을 가지고 다녔다. 스케치북이 들어가느냐, 안 들어가느냐가 가방을 선택하는 기준이 될 정도로 말이다. 시간이 조금이라도 나거나 흥미로운 것을 발견할 때마다 그림을 그렸다. 가끔씩 혼자 아무 생각 없이 카페에 앉아 몇 시간이고 지나가는 사람들을 그렸다. 그럴 때면 마음이 차분해지고 즐거웠다.

지금도 그 습관은 여전하다. 내가 쓰는 수첩은 줄이 그어진 공책이 아니라 언제라도 그림을 그릴 수 있는 스케치북 같은 형태이다. 수첩 중간 중간에는 사람들이 자주 등장한다. 가끔은 메모보다 그림이 더 좋은 기록이 될 때도 있어 기억할 일들을 그림으로 그린다. 사람 그리기는 어떤 목표를 가지고 한 일이 아니라 온전히 나의 즐거움을 위한 일이었다. 하지만 패션의 중요한 부분 중 하나가 사람, 즉 인체를 이해하는 일이기 때문에 결과적으로는 공부에 큰 도움을 주었다.

무엇보다 손으로 쓱쓱 그림을 그리기 위한 기본을 잘 닦아놓을 수 있는 계기가 되었다. 어느 디자이너나 옷을 만들기 전에 스케치를 하고 디자인을 한다. 스케치 과정 없이 바로 머릿속에 있는 것을 마네킹 위에 만들어내는 경우도 있지만 디자이너에게 있어 일러스트는 빼놓을 수 없는 중요한 요소다. 실제 옷을 만들기 전에 그 느낌과 디자인, 색상, 옷감 등을 일러스트로 표현한다. 패션을 공부하고 디자인을 구상하면서 머릿속에 있는 옷을 보다 쉽게 그림으로 옮길 수 있었던 것은 그동안 그려온 드로잉 덕분이다. 학교에서 선생님들도 드로잉이 익숙하지 않은 친구들에게 사람을 많이 그려볼 것을 권한다.

✏️ 작은 것들에 귀 기울이는 연습하기

습관이라기보다 관심이랄 수 있는 건, 스쳐 지나가는 작은 것들에 귀를 기울이는 연습이다. 이 작은 것들이란 꼭 형태나 크기가 있는 것들이 아니다. 바로 중요하지 않은 것을 이야기하는 것이다. 보통 사람들이 중요하지 않다고 생각하는 것들을 마음으로 보는 것을 의미한다. 우리는 주변의 일상적인 것들도 잘 기억하지 못한다. 창문, 침대, 숟가락 등의 단어로 사물을 기억한다. 그것들이 어떻게 생겼는지, 오늘 아침에 쓴 숟가락은 어떤 모양인지도 모를 때가 허다하다.

파운데이션 과정의 첫 번째 프로젝트를 진행할 때였다. 정확하게 기억은 안 나지만 일상에서 선, 입체, 모양을 발견하고 그것을 작품으로 만드는 것이었다. 카메라와 스케치북을 들고 나가 돌아다니며 눈에 보이는 모든 것을 관찰했다. 내가 아침에 지나갔던 그 길에 있었던 맨홀의 모양이 아름다웠고, 녹이 슬었다는 것이 전부였던 철의 색깔이 아주 예쁜 것을 보았다. 세상이 다르게 보이기 시작했다. 그동안 스쳐 지나갔던 사소하고 작은 것들에 대한 아름다움을 발견했다. 그때가 세상이 다르게 보이기 시작한 터닝 포인트였던 것 같다. 예전이라면 지나쳤을 사소한 것들이 내 발걸음을 멈추게 했다. 마치 어린아이가 처음으로 눈을 떠 이제껏 보지 못한 새로운 세상을 보는 것 같았다. 단어라는 이름으로 묶어왔던 모든 사물이 깨지고, 시각으로 반응하게 된 것이다.

　예전보다 세상을 더욱 넓고 많이 볼 수 있게 되면서 내 마음은 더욱 풍족해졌다. 그것은 내 작업의 영감의 원천이 되었다. 세상에 나를 내던지기만 하면 쏟아져 나오는 영감들. 도서관에 가서 케케묵은 책까지 찾아가며 억지로 찾으려 하지 않아도 나를 둘러싼 모든 것이 내 작업의 시작점이 되었다. 그때부터 세상은 아름답고 흥미로운 작품들로 가득한 살아 있는 박물관 혹은 갤러리가 되었다.

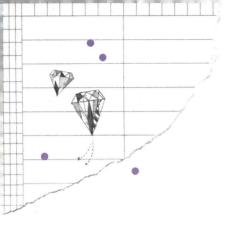

Epilogue

한국과 달리 영국 대학들은 1년에 세 학기가 있다. 가을에 시작해서 크리스마스 전에 끝나는 가을학기, 한 달간의 방학 후 3월 중순까지 봄학기, 또 한 달간의 방학 후 한 해의 마지막인 여름학기. 오늘, 어느덧 마지막 학년의 두 번째 봄방학의 마지막 날을 맞았다.

재미있는 것은, 세인트 마틴의 패션 디자인과 마지막 학년은 1년 동안 하나의 프로젝트만 진행한다는 것이다. 1년 전체를 졸업 패션쇼를 위해 쓴다. 지난 가을학기는 러서치만, 이번 학기는 디자인과 과목으로 6주 동안 가봉을 했다. 다가오는 마지막 여름학기에는 원단으로 컬렉션을 준비하게 된다. 졸업 컬렉션의 중간 과정을 보내면서 이번 학기는 어느 때보다 힘들었고, 반대로 가장 즐겁고 감사한 시간이었다. 아침에 학교에 가서 하루 종일 가봉을 하고, 밤이 되어서야 집으로 돌아오는 똑같은 나날을 6주간 보냈다.

첫 주는 패기가 넘쳤다. 매일 학교 문을 여는 8시 반에 일등으로 학교에 갔다. 디자인 과정에서 좋은 평가를 받았기 때문에 좋은 결과를 얻을 수 있을 거라는 기대감에 힘이 났다. 아무도 없는 스튜디오에 도착해 작업을 시작하면 내가 가장 열심히 하는, 최고라는 생각에 더더욱 힘이 났다. 이렇게만 열심히 하면 좋은 결과를

낼 수 있다는 기대감으로 일주일을 보냈다.

하지만 나의 어설픈 자신감과 기대감은 일주일 만에 무너졌다. 기대와 달리 성적의 큰 부분을 차지하는 마케팅 리포트 때문에 최고의 성적을 받지 못했고, 성적을 받고 선생님 앞에서 표정 관리가 안될 만큼 실망했다. 세인트 마틴 졸업 쇼는 모든 학생들이 쇼를 하는 인터내셔널 쇼 international show와 30퍼센트 정도의 학생만 뽑아서 프레스를 초청해서 학교 밖에서 하는 프레스 쇼 press show 두 가지가 있다. 모든 학생이 프레스 쇼에 뽑히기를 바라고, 거기에서 좋은 성적으로 상을 받기를 원한다. 성적이 모든 것을 이야기하지는 않지만, 어느 정도는 작업물의 척도가 되기 때문에 신경을 쓰지 않을 수 없다.

평소 성적에 집착하지 않는 학생 중 한 명이 바로 나였다. 성적이 어떻든지 간에 내가 최선을 다해 공부하고, 감사하는 마음으로 즐겁게 작업하는 것이 전부였다. 성적이 좋든 나쁘든, 그것이 나를 흔들지 못했다. 하지만 그런 나에게도 이번 졸업만큼은 큰 이슈였나 보다. 졸업 쇼의 테마는 하나님의 은혜였고, 지금까지 내가 하나님께 받은 아름다운 것들을 표현하는 것에만 초점을 맞추고 즐겁게 작업하고 있었는데, 좋은 평가를 듣게 되면서 나도 모르게 마음이 변했었나 보다. 성적을 받고 반응하는 내 모습을 보니 나를 움직이게 만들었던 원동력이 더 이상 처음의 영감이 아닌, 사람들에게 인정받고 싶은 마음이란 걸 알았다.

    성적을 받고 나서는 아침에 일어나는 것조차 고역이었다. 매일 7시에 일어나 힘차게 학교에 가던 내 모습은 어디로 가고 눈을 뜨면 '아, 하기 싫다'며 억지로 몸을 일으켰다. 학교에 여전히 일등으로 도착하지만 한 시간 한 시간이 힘들었다. 쥐도 새도 모르게 내 머리에 들어온 이미 망했다는, 최고가 될 수는 없다는 생각이 나를 지배하기 시작했다. 일등이 아니라면 할 이유가 없어진 것처럼 느껴졌다. 지금 와서 생각하니 부끄럽고 어이없지만 말이다. 내 작업을 통해 나의 주제가 잘 표현되고 전달되는 것에 집중해 작업했지만 어느샌가 내 목표는 일등이 되어 있었고, 내가 사람들에게 인정받는 것이 되어 있었다.

    하루하루 힘들게 1주가 지나자 최고는 아니어도, 내가 처음에 가졌던 그 주제를 표현하겠다는 생각으로 돌아와 있었다. 신기한 것이 욕심이 사라지고 나니 매일매일이 다시 즐거웠다. 가끔씩 지치기도 하고, 다른 친구들이 폭탄처럼 멋진 작품을 쏟아낼 때는 흔들리기도 했지만, 이미 확신이 있었기 때문에 크게 휘둘리지 않았다.

내 힘의 원동력은 내가 뛰어나다는 자신감도 아니고, 남이 해주는 칭찬도 아니고, 일등으로 도착해서 내가 가장 열심히 한다는 안심도 아니었다. 이제는 조금 더 일찍 6시 반에 일어나 기도하고 즐거운 마음으로 학교에 갔다. 매일이 새로운 날처럼 지하철역에서 내려 학교로 걸어가는 길이 가슴 뛰고 설렜다. '이제 이 길도 몇 달 안 남았구나.' 아쉬운 마음과 동시에 지금 이곳을 걸어가고 있다는 것이 가슴 터지게 설렜다.

시간이 흐르고 어제 이번 학기의 마지막 날, 지금까지 만든 여섯 벌의 옷을 선생님께 검사 받는 라인업이 있었다. 내가 첫 번째로 하겠다고 해서 아침에 처음으로 라인업을 했다. 나는 누구보다 열심히 작업했고, 총 일곱 벌을 만들었다. 열심히 했기 때문에 칭찬도 많이 들었고, 선생님들이 좋은 시선으로 나를 평가해줬다. 그렇게 라인업을 끝내고 학교를 나오는데 또다시 가슴 찡하게 감사했다. 칭찬을 받아서도 아니고 내가 일등을 할 거라는 기대감도 아니었다. 누구보다 즐겁게 6주 동안 작업할 수 있었다는 것에 대한 감동이었다.

마지막 학년을 보내는 많은 학생이 같은 시각에, 같은 공간에서 같은 일을 한다. 그 결과 누군가는 일등이겠고, 다른 누군가는 프레스 쇼에 들어가보지도 못하고 졸업할 수도 있다. 하지만 미래가 아닌, 지금 이 순간이 즐겁다. 학교 스튜디오에서 작업하는 수많은 친구들 사이에서 나는 미래에 대한 불안감이나 내가 최고라는 자만에 묶여 있지 않고, 현재를 기쁨으로 살아간다. 이런 삶이 큰 축복이라는 것을 오늘 또다시 느낀다.

    나는 이번 졸업 쇼에 대한 큰 기대와 설렘이 있다. 결코 일등에 대한 욕심 때문이 아니다. 내가 추구하는 패션이 아름답게 표현되어지기를 진심으로 바란다. 그리고 이런 나의 마음이 내가 만든 옷을 통해 사람들에게 전해지기를 희망한다. 결과에 연연하지 않겠다. 지금 이 순간을 즐기고 싶다. 나는 멋진 패션 디자이너가 되고 싶다. 오늘 마지막 날, 내 가슴은 뜨겁게 뛰고 있다. 결과와 관계없이 나의 현재와 미래는 모두 기쁨으로 채워질 것이다.

패션 다이어리

2012년 8월 10일 초판 1쇄 인쇄
2012년 8월 20일 초판 1쇄 발행

지은이 | 권순수
발행인 | 전재국
본부장 | 이광자

임프린트 대표 | 이동은
책임편집 | 박햇님
마케팅실장 | 정유한
책임마케팅 | 노경석 · 윤주환 · 조안나 · 이철주
제작 | 정웅래 · 박순이

발행처 | 미호
출판등록 2011년 1월 27일(제321-2011-000023호)

주소 | 서울특별시 서초구 사임당로 82
전화 | 편집(02)3487-1141 · 영업(02)2046-2800
팩스 | 편집(02)3487-1161 · 영업(02)588-0835

ISBN 978-89-527-6662-5 03810

본서의 내용을 무단 복제하는 것은 저작권법에 의해 금지되어 있습니다.
파본이나 잘못된 책은 구입하신 서점에서 교환해 드립니다.

미호는 아름답고 기분 좋은 책을 만드는
(주)시공사의 임프린트입니다.